## Praise for *False Positive*

"A fast-moving thriller . . . Readers who like defects in their heroes will love this guy, who knows he's not as good as he'd like to be. The final twist comes just as all finally seems well with the world. A dark, enjoyable novel. One of Grant's better works."
—*Kirkus Reviews*

"Smashing."
—*Booklist*

"Engrossing . . . Action-driven, the book's pace never stops until the startling conclusion, which will chill to the core."
—*Romantic Times Book Reviews* (Top Pick!)

## Praise for *RUN*

"Breathtakingly fast-paced."
—HARLAN COBEN, #1 *New York Times* bestselling author of *Tell No One*

"Smart, fast, and blazing with nonstop surprises, *RUN* owned me from the first page and, man, those pages kept turning! A perfect thriller."
—ROBERT CRAIS, internationally bestselling author of *Hostage*

"Reads with the velocity of data over a high speed line. Smart, intricate, dizzying, nothing is quite what it seems in this deftly written, twisty tale."
—ANDREW GROSS, #1 *New York Times* bestselling author of *No Way Back*

"*RUN* is a tightly written, expertly plotted, whiz bang of a novel with just the right dose of smart-ass."
—CHELSEA CAIN, *New York Times*
bestselling author of *Let Me Go*

"*RUN* is a fast-paced, sleek thrill ride. Andrew Grant knows how to keep you turning the pages."
—JEFF ABBOTT, *New York Times*
bestselling author of *Inside Man*

"*RUN* is an adrenaline-fueled thrill ride that will have your head spinning and your heart pounding."
—JOSEPH FINDER, *New York Times*
bestselling author of *Paranoia* and *Suspicion*

"High stakes, high tension, and nonstop action. Grant nails the world of sinister corporate scheming and big-money treachery—but don't even try to predict where this taut thriller is headed. Just hang on and enjoy this smart, original and fast-paced adventure."
—HANK PHILLIPPI RYAN,
bestselling author of *The Other Woman*

"Andrew Grant always delivers the goods, and *RUN* is his most intense thriller yet. Relentless, twisty, and blistering-fast, it's a book you don't dare start at bedtime."
—SEAN CHERCOVER,
award-winning author of *The Trinity Game*

"Fast-moving . . . high on adrenaline."
—*Publishers Weekly*

"Twists and surprises abound, the pace never slows, and the writing satisfies. So go ahead, read and enjoy this one."
—*Kirkus Reviews*

# *False Positive*

# False Positive

*A Novel*

# Andrew Grant

*Ballantine Books*
*New York*

2016 Ballantine Books Mass Market Edition

Copyright © 2015 by Andrew Grant
Excerpt from *False Friend* by Andrew Grant copyright © 2016 by Andrew Grant

Published in the United States by Ballantine Books, an imprint of Random House, a division of Penguin Random House LLC, New York.

BALLANTINE and the HOUSE colophon are registered trademarks of Penguin Random House LLC.

Originally published in hardcover in the United States by Ballantine Books, an imprint of Random House, a division of Penguin Random House LLC, in 2015.

This book contains an excerpt from the forthcoming book *False Friend* by Andrew Grant. This excerpt has been set for this edition only and may not reflect the final content of the forthcoming edition.

ISBN 978-0-345-54076-8
ebook ISBN 978-0-345-54077-5

Cover design: Scott Biel
Cover image: © Joana Kruse/Arcangel Images

Printed in the United States of America

randomhousebooks.com

9 8 7 6 5 4 3 2 1

Ballantine Books mass market edition: July 2016

For my parents:
Audrey and John Grant

. . . within the core of each of us is the child we once were. This child constitutes the foundation of what we have become, who we are, and what we will be.

—Dr. Rhawn Joseph,
*The Right Brain and the Unconscious:*
*Discovering the Stranger Within*

# *False Positive*

## Chapter One

*Friday. Late Afternoon.*

"I LIED." THE WOMAN LEANED AGAINST THE MINIVAN AND felt the warmth of the afternoon sun radiate into her back from the shiny white metal. She took a moment to imagine the impact her words were having at the other end of the line. Then she went back to watching the handful of cars and SUVs that were scattered throughout the lengthening shadows of Caffee Junction's horseshoe-shaped parking lot. There were more of them than she'd have liked. More than there'd been the previous two Fridays. But that was a minor detail, she told herself. An irritation. No reason to pull the plug.

"I see." Lieutenant Hale's grip on the dull-gray plastic handset grew tighter, and she wrestled the urge to smash it to pieces on her paper-strewn desk. She'd been moments away from leaving her office when the phone rang. Now there'd be no chance of beating the afternoon rush. A fitting end to an already dire week, she thought, flipping her little robot-shaped clock facedown on a stack of files. She didn't need to see the jagged second hand relentlessly taunting her as it swept around the dial. "You lied. Mind telling me why?"

"Simple. Money. I was paid to say what I said."

"Who paid you?"

"I don't know."

"How much did you get?"

"Fifteen grand."

"In one go?"

"No. Five grand before I made the call. Five after. And five when the guy's suspension was confirmed."

"That's a lot of money for one phone call."

"I guess."

"Why are you changing your story now?"

"I've got the money now. A chance to start over. I'm driving to my sister's, in San Diego. And I wanted to set the record straight before I get there."

"OK. Then this is what I need you to do. Come to the precinct. Write down what you just told me. Sign it. And stick around a couple of days, while we get this straightened out."

"Can't. Already left town."

"Then come back. Just for a couple days."

"No way. It's too dangerous. If whoever paid me finds out I'm talking to you . . ."

"They won't. We can help you. Get you somewhere safe to stay. A hotel."

"A hotel? Are you kidding me? I want a fresh start. A hotel's the worst place for someone like me. I'm not coming back to Birmingham. Ever. I'm hanging up now and—"

"Wait. You want to start over, you need a clear conscience. If you don't sign a statement, nothing will change. The detective will stay on suspension. There'll be an investigation. His career will be ruined. And that'll be on you."

"Why? That doesn't make sense. I'm telling the truth this time."

"How do I know that? Maybe you were telling the truth the first time, and you're lying now."

"What does it matter *when* I was lying? Point is, I'm a liar. My word's not worth shit, either way."

"How do I know you're even who you say you are?

Do you know how many crank calls I've had since the story hit the papers?"

"You know who I am. I used those code words you gave me when I called before."

"Conversations can be overheard. Code words can be bought. Or given away. Or stolen. They're a good start, but they're not conclusive. I need more."

"You've got my caller ID. You can see I'm using the same phone. And you record all your calls, right? You can compare the tapes."

"I will. Count on it. But I still need more."

"OK. I can give you more. When I called, Tuesday, I had this all planned out. I figured the story would leak. So I added something on top of what I'd been told to say. As insurance. I told you the detective had bitten me. Somewhere private. Remember? You wanted pictures. Doctors' reports."

Lieutenant Hale didn't reply. When she'd first spoken to this woman, her head had told her to reach for the rule book. As squad commander, she'd done what she was required to do. But as an ex–street cop, every nerve in her body had screamed. She'd felt like she was back in uniform, tiptoeing into an alley at night. And now, with this second call, it was as if an invisible hand was shoving her deeper into the darkness.

"And I was right." The woman walked to the front of the van, taking care not to snag her heels in the cracks in the sun-bleached pavement. "You were loyal to your guy. You kept that part out of the papers. No one else but me could know about it."

"That's not—"

"Goodbye, Lieutenant."

"Wait!"

"I can't. I'm going now. I've got a lot of ground to cover. You're the police. I'm trusting you. Do the right thing."

The woman ended the call. She broke the old-style flip-phone in half. Dropped the pieces on the ground. Climbed into the van. Scowled at the shiny, goalpostshaped H in the center of the steering wheel. Fired up the engine. Looped around the squat redbrick building, keeping her speed low as the van bounced clumsily across the pitted blacktop. Kept her distance from a blue Ford station wagon that was looking for a space in the shade. Then she left the parking lot. Followed the road back toward the interstate. And took the first on-ramp she reached.

The one that led northeast.

Back to the Magic City.

## Chapter Two

*Saturday. Early Morning.*

I'M IN THE CLOSET. IN THE HALLWAY. TWO BOARDS ARE LOOSE. IN *the floor. I pull them up. Wriggle into the space below. Slide one back in place, above me. Hook my arm through the gap. Grab Daddy's spare boots. Put them on the board, so it'll look like it hasn't been moved. Slide the other board back. Then settle down in the dark, to wait.*

*Just me and the bugs and the spiders.*

*Why's Daddy so late? I want him to come home. I want him to find me, so I can come out. I'm hungry. And I need the bathroom. Real bad.*

*The front door opens, but the creaks don't sound the way they're supposed to. The door doesn't close all the way. Daddy doesn't step into the hall. He doesn't kick off his boots. He doesn't start looking for me. He doesn't begin our game, the way he always does.*

*Someone shouts: "This is the police."*

*But it can't be the police, because Daddy's the police and it isn't Daddy's voice. It's another man's. A stranger's. Coming to hurt me?*

*"Police! Show yourself. Whoever's in the house, show yourself. Right now."*

*I know the rules. Never come out. Wait for Daddy to*

*find me. Whatever anyone says. It's the only way to stay safe. I hold my breath. Lie extra still.*

*"Come on." Another voice that isn't Daddy's. "The kid's got to be here, somewhere. We've got to find him . . ."*

Cooper Devereaux's subconscious took the sound of the blows raining down on his cabin door and merged them into his dream. They became footsteps. Invading his house. Heading down the hallway. Reaching the closet. He was seconds away from being discovered . . .

But the noise kept on getting louder. It didn't stop. Ten seconds thundered by. Twenty. And that wasn't right. That wasn't how it was supposed to go. Something stirred, deep inside Devereaux's brain. It dragged him back to wakefulness, chasing away the unwelcome echoes from the past, leaving him blinking and disoriented on his moldering leather couch.

"Hello?" Devereaux reached down, picked his gun up from the floor, and pulled it back beneath his empty, stained, patchwork comforter cover. "Who is it?"

## Chapter *Three*

*Saturday. Early Morning.*

JAN LOFLIN TOOK THE OUTFIT OFF THE HANGER AND HELD IT against her slender body.

She closed her eyes and tried not to retch as a wave of vulgar perfume and spilled beer and someone else's sweat washed over her. She recalled how it felt to pull the flimsy strips of shiny material over her head. How the neckline plunged obscenely toward her midriff. How the skirt barely reached the tops of her thighs. How it made her small, thin frame look a decade younger than her twenty-four years. How it made the men—*those* men—stare at her. Leer at her. Paw at her . . .

For a month after her meltdown she hadn't been able to open the closet door. For another two weeks she hadn't been able to touch the dress, or any of the other half-dozen similar ones that hung next to it. Or any of the wigs, lined up over their stands like hunting trophies on the shelf above. Now she was up to handling these things, but she still couldn't bear to put any of the slut-rags on.

Would she ever be able to?

*Maybe she wouldn't ever have to, if she did this next job right.*

Loflin replaced the dress. Lifted up a box of sparkly,

five-inch-heeled pumps from the closet floor. Pulled out the folder she'd stored there since it arrived unexpectedly in the mail the previous week. And moved back to the bed. She had ten minutes before she needed to leave. Fifteen probably, given that it was so early in the morning. And it was a Saturday. The I-65 should be slightly less insane than it was on a weekday.

Fifteen minutes. Enough time for her to check the facts for the thousandth time, before coming face-to-face with the next monster she was going to have to slay.

## Chapter Four

*Saturday. Early Morning.*

"POLICE. THIS IS OFFICER JACKSON. IS ANYONE INSIDE?"

"Jackson?" Devereaux hauled himself into a sitting position. "Come on in. It's not locked."

The ancient hinges screeched, then a man in a Birmingham PD uniform stepped inside and looked around the small, rectangular room. The only permanent fixture was a hulking iron furnace to his left. It completely dominated the space, and the way its giant metal chimney extended up into the pitched roof put him in mind of an organ in a crude, rural church. A camping stove was set up on the rough wooden floor, next to the furnace. Four empty baked bean cans lay on one side of it, and another ten fresh ones were lined up on the other. There were a dozen bottles of water. A stack of six-packs of Devereaux's favorite beer—Avondale Battlefield IPA. And three large glass flasks full of some kind of clear liquid that, given his profession, Jackson decided not to ask any questions about.

"What?" Devereaux caught the expression on the officer's face as he took in the decrepit state of the walls and the ceiling. Jackson risked another cautious step forward. The shaft of light from the door joined a line of cracks and gaps in the floor and the officer was hit by a sudden vision of a laser beam cutting the building in two. Although, given the condition the place was in, he figured a flashlight beam could probably do the job. The metallic blue Porsche gleaming in the sunshine outside the half-derelict cabin was the only external sign that Jackson had found his way to the right place. It left him thinking that Devereaux must have a very strange set of priorities.

"Officer?" Devereaux slid his legs out from under the comforter and slipped his bare feet into his scuffed brown boots. He was careful to make sure the gun remained concealed. "What's on your mind?"

"It's Lieutenant Hale. She wants you in her office. Immediately. If not sooner. Those were her exact words, Detective."

Devereaux followed Jackson's squad car at a distance, nursing his Porsche over the bumps and exposed tree roots in the rough forest track until he reached the start of the paved road. He knew from experience that a cell signal usually became available at around that point, but he allowed himself a couple of fast miles before easing off the gas and reaching for his phone.

"Devereaux." Lieutenant Hale picked up on the first ring. "Where are you?"

"On my way in, as ordered." Devereaux changed lanes and left a chrome-encrusted RV dawdling in his wake. "What am I being blamed for this time? Global warming?"

Hale was one of the few people who knew anything about Devereaux's past. She knew he had skeletons. She knew that being a detective helped him keep them buried. And beyond that, she understood that the police department was more than just a job to him. It had taken the place of his family, with all the sensitivities and raw nerves that came with the package. If she'd been dealing with any of the other detectives in her squad, her approach would have been different. More robust, given the urgency of the situation. But with Devereaux, she figured she needed to show a little patience. She couldn't afford for him to walk away, back to the only other "family" he'd known since he was a kid.

"You're not being blamed for anything, Cooper." Hale kept her voice deliberately calm and level. "In fact, it's the opposite. The accusation that was made against you? It's been dropped. Your suspension's been lifted."

Devereaux didn't respond.

"Cooper? Did you hear me? Everything's been taken care of. You're back on rotation."

"The accusation was dropped." Devereaux blasted the Porsche through a tight curve, enjoying the way the firm leather pressed against his back. "Why?"

"The woman who started all this? She called again. Last night. Admitted she'd been lying. Claimed she'd been paid to smear you, and wanted to clear her conscience before starting a new life in California."

"Did you believe her?"

"Maybe. Maybe not. We triangulated on the place where she made the call. It was a roadside bar, thirty miles outside of the city. The right direction for someone heading out west. We found the phone she used. It was in the parking lot. Broken. Snapped in two. There were no prints. But there was a witness. He gave us a description. Too generic to be much help on its own, but he thought the woman was driving a minivan. There's a lot of road between here and the coast, Cooper. We'll find her. Make sure her story adds up."

"I told you." Devereaux wove his way through a pack of gray-bearded bikers on rumbling, antique Harleys. "I did nothing wrong. This was down to someone I sent to jail, carrying a grudge. Or a relative of someone I locked up, out for revenge."

"You did tell me. I haven't forgotten."

"Leave it to me." Devereaux glanced in his rearview mirror, checking that all the bikers were still on two wheels. "I'll come up with some names. Knock on a few doors."

"Good approach. But that can wait. Have you got a bathroom fixed up at your atrocity of a cabin yet?"

"No. Why?"

"When did you last wash? Change your clothes?"

"Tuesday. Fashion and hygiene aren't big priorities when you get wrongly put on suspension."

"OK. Then go home. Shower. Shave. Do whatever you need to do to make yourself presentable. And get to my office, like ten minutes ago."

"Where's the fire?"

"You have a new case, Cooper. I'll tell you everything when you get here."

"Tell me now."

"When you get here."

"You know, Lieutenant, I don't appreciate this. One minute you suspend me over some anonymous bullshit, and the next you want me jumping through hoops and won't even tell me why. So here's the thing. I may not be feeling too good. I may need to take some sick leave."

"You're not sick, Cooper."

"I may need some personal time, then. You know my atrocious cabin roof needs fixing. You've seen the state it's in."

"Someone else can fix the roof, Cooper. OK? You want the bottom line? We have a missing person. A kid."

Devereaux didn't reply.

"A little boy. He's seven years old."

Devereaux felt like he was being pulled back into his dream.

"An orphan."

## Chapter Five

THE WOMAN WOKE AT FIRST LIGHT AND CHECKED HER PHONE. There were no new messages.

So far, so good.

She had no interest in going back to sleep so she reached for her book—a lighthearted introduction to what regular folk can learn from psychopaths—and spent the next couple of hours quietly reading. Then she felt the buzz of an incoming text:

*Devereaux's been reinstated. He's en route to Hale's office. Apparently a kid's missing and she wants him on the case. Unbelievable!*

The woman smiled, pulled on a fresh pair of surgeons' gloves, and got out of bed. She took her case from its place next to the door. Carried it to the bathroom. Took out the Ziploc bag she'd prepared five hours earlier. Removed the empty hydrogen peroxide bottle. Dropped it in the trash. Sprinkled a few bleached hairs in on top of it. Set the bag down next to the basin, ready to be used again. Placed a bottle of Rich Mahogany hair dye next to it. Then went back to the bedroom. To rouse the small, newly blond figure curled up in the other twin bed.

## Chapter Six

*Saturday. Morning.*

THE CABIN HAD ORIGINALLY BELONGED TO DEVEREAUX'S great-grandfather.

Devereaux had traced it through old city records fifteen years previously, and bought it in an attempt to reconnect with his family heritage. He slept there at least once a week, but Devereaux's real home was an apartment in the City Federal building on Second Avenue, a stone's throw from the police department headquarters in the heart of downtown Birmingham. He liked being close to the raw heartbeat of the city. He liked the building's height. The way it dominated the skyline, turning up its neo-classical nose at its plain, modern neighbors. He liked its polished white terra-cotta cladding (which was no longer falling off) and its balanced, elegant proportions. The bold neon sign that once again blazed extravagantly on its roof at night. But most of all he liked the fact that it had started its life as an office building. It's still the same on the outside. But inside, it's completely different. It had started over. Remade, top to bottom.

Just like him.

When Devereaux graduated from the Academy he bought a small, discreet studio on the sixth floor of a converted warehouse at Sixth and Sixth. He got it for a song, which was good because he hadn't wanted to invite questions about how a rookie street cop with no inheritance and no record of any legitimate employment could afford to live in a higher-profile place. He stayed there, even after he made detective. But his eye had been caught when the renovations began at the City Federal. His mind was made up by the time the neon sign was re-lit. And finally, he treated himself. He moved to a three-bedroom unit on the twenty-fifth floor. He was the first resident to occupy the newly refurbished building, and he added stunning city views—all the way south to the giant cast-iron statue of Vulcan, god of the forge, standing proud on his column at the foot of the Red Mountain—to the list of things he liked about the place. But that was the best part of ten years ago, and two of the bedrooms remained empty.

Devereaux unlocked his door and hurried inside. He stepped over the work clothes that were scattered across the dark walnut floor where he'd flung them on Tuesday night when he'd stormed home after Hale broke the news about his suspension. He peeled off his jeans and his Clash *"I Fought the Law"* T-shirt—which had been torn in a fight years ago with a couple of old-timers who didn't appreciate the irony of him wearing it to a cop bar—and quickly hit the shower. He was tempted to skip his shave, but the quantity of gray staring back at him in the mirror changed his mind. Finally, he grabbed a blue button-down shirt and a pair of khaki pants from the freestanding rack he kept in his bedroom in place of a closet. Pulled them on. And was good to go inside ten minutes.

One advantage of living in an ex–office building is the plentiful supply of elevators at your disposal—a holdover from the days when they were needed to whisk the eager wage-slaves to their desks as quickly as possible. But that day it seemed to take an eternity for one to arrive. The bank of polished brass doors seemed to be frozen in time after Devereaux hit the Call button.

Eventually a pair slid open and Devereaux rode down alone in a car, willing the antique indicator needle to move faster and replaying Lieutenant Hale's parting words in his head. A little boy. Missing. Runaway? Alone and vulnerable? Or worse?

Devereaux stepped out into the marble-lined lobby. He skirted around a little knot of older residents who were spending their Saturday morning standing next to the building's twin stacks of mailboxes and complaining about the fares on the DART trolleys. He headed for the exit.

Then he stopped.

Something about one of the seniors had caught Devereaux's eye. An old man. Maybe in his early eighties. He was standing apart from the rest of the group, leaning—almost hunched over—against the round font-like table in the center of the lobby. His thin gray hair was uncombed. His lean face was grizzled with white stubble. And he was wearing a light-colored raincoat, which made no sense on such a sunny June day.

The rest of the seniors drifted into an elevator and the doors closed, leaving Devereaux and the old guy staring at each other, twenty feet apart, like weary gunslingers in an old Western. Then the guy pushed himself away from the table and took an unsteady step toward Devereaux. His coat sagged open, revealing the dried bloodstain on his shirt.

"Cooper?" He was swaying on his feet. "Cooper Devereaux?"

"Who's asking?"

"Son, be careful. She knows."

Then the old guy sank to his knees and pitched forward, face-first onto the hard, tiled floor.

## Chapter Seven

THE WOMAN PULLED UP ALONGSIDE THE BLACK M-CLASS Mercedes and killed her engine. She knew she was out of range of the security cameras so she checked that no one was watching from the other parked vehicles, then wiped everything she could have touched inside the Honda clean of prints. She got out. Unlocked the Mercedes. Helped the little boy and his tiny knitted monkey switch vehicles. Scooped up the cuddly rabbit he'd dropped on the back seat. Then moved her case and his backpack from one trunk to the other.

She opened her case. Took out a rectangular nylon bag. Flipped it over so that the word *Worn* was visible. Unzipped it. Took off her sunglasses, wig, and earrings. Placed them inside. Dropped the Honda key in with them. Zipped the bag up. Turned it over. Opened the side that said *Clean*. Took out a fresh wig. Brunette, this time. Another pair of sunglasses. Tortoiseshell, not black. New earrings. A chunky, turquoise necklace. A matching bracelet. Then she closed the trunk. Climbed in behind the wheel. Checked herself in the mirror. Flashed a reassuring smile at the kid, who still seemed a little groggy. And pulled back out of the diner's parking lot.

She had a new car. A new look. And a lot of ground to cover before her mission would be complete.

## Chapter Eight

*Saturday. Morning.*

TIME SLOWED TO A CRAWL AS DEVEREAUX KNELT ON THE marble floor in the lobby at the City Federal building, keeping an eye on the old man's vital signs and willing the paramedics to pick up the pace. After eight minutes— each one of which felt like an hour—an ambulance finally pulled up outside. Devereaux passed on what little he knew to the crew and asked which hospital the guy would be taken to. Then, too impatient to wait for the elevator again, he took the stairs down to the basement garage. He reluctantly ignored his Porsche and continued to the department-issue Dodge Charger he kept in the adjacent stall. He climbed inside, and seventy seconds later he was parking in a spot that had just opened up on the street at the side of the police headquarters's sloping metal entrance canopy on First Avenue.

The detectives' desks were all empty when Devereaux pushed through the double doors from the elevator lobby on the third floor, but he could see Lieutenant Hale—five feet eleven, with swimmer's shoulders and jet-black hair halfway down her back—standing in her office doorway and gesturing impatiently for him to hurry up. As he drew closer he realized someone else was there, sitting behind Hale. Another woman. She looked a good fifteen years younger. Her bobbed, blond hair was lacquered almost rigid. She had a plain, oval face. And she was skinny to the point of anorexia.

"Cooper, this is Detective Jan Loflin."

Devereaux appraised Loflin for a moment, then held out his hand. "Cooper. Never Coop. Never Coops. Shame we're not meeting under different circumstances."

Loflin stood, and as they shook Devereaux could feel the nervous energy running through her. It was as if there was too much for her small body to contain, leaving her muscles to burn off the excess like the flares at an oil refinery. Devereaux was a foot taller and seemingly three times as broad, and her rapid tiny movements made him feel clumsy and oversized.

"Jan's on loan to us from Vice." Hale retreated behind her desk and scooped up a cup of coffee that had been perching on a stack of overtime authorization forms. "She comes highly recommended. And given that Tommy's helping out Colton while Levi recovers from his rotator cuff, I'm pairing the two of you up. For now, at least. We can take another look at things once the kid's safely home with his parents."

"Foster parents." Devereaux took the seat nearer the door.

Hale watched as Loflin shifted her chair a few inches closer to the window before sitting down and pulling a dog-eared Moleskine notebook out of her purse. She looked anxious. Hale hoped that was just down to Loflin being freshly back from sick leave, but she couldn't quash the nagging doubt at the back of her mind. Not completely. Loflin came with a reputation. Picking her up, even on a temporary assignment, was a risk. But it had seemed like a risk worth taking, with the team left shorthanded. And Hale had dealt with odd fish before, she reminded herself. Successfully. Just look at Devereaux. Saving misfits' careers was becoming her specialty.

"OK." Hale extracted a color, eight-by-ten portrait

from the chaos on her desk and held it up. "This is our missing kid. His name's Ethan Crane. Take a good look, guys. This picture's only two weeks old."

Both detectives studied the image, praying that the next photo they saw of Ethan wouldn't have been taken at a crime scene. He was a cute kid. He had fluffy, chestnut-brown hair. A smattering of freckles around his nose and forehead. A cheeky smile. Straight, white teeth. And a wary distance in his eyes that Devereaux would recognize anywhere.

"Good." Hale traded the glossy picture for a sheaf of creased papers and flicked away a crumb of chocolate that she'd dropped on the top page. "Here's what we know about Ethan Crane. He's seven years old. Orphaned. No living relatives. Placed in two previous homes before he was fostered, and subsequently adopted, by Joseph and Mary Lynne Crane. We're tracing the previous families, but don't have any information as yet. Joseph Crane's a V.P. in charge of project management at the University of Alabama down in Tuscaloosa, so he leaves home early and gets back late. Mary Lynne's a nurse, here in Birmingham. There are no red flags from any neighbors or co-workers. None that the uniforms have canvassed so far, anyway. They have a nice house over the mountain. The kids go to a good school—"

"Kids?" Devereaux sounded surprised.

Loflin carried on scribbling in her notebook.

"Yes." Hale reached out and prodded one of the slats in the vertical blind at the window, trying to block an offending ray of sunlight that had started to shine in her eyes. "Not long after adopting Ethan, Mrs. Crane—who'd been told she couldn't—got pregnant. They have another little boy. A biological son, named Dillon."

"That cause any problems?" Devereaux frowned. "I bet they didn't want the adopted kid around, once they had one of their own."

"Couldn't say." Hale paused. "Find out. So anyway, this Dillon, he's four years old. He's in pre-K, at the same school as Ethan. Uniform's tracking down their teachers. As for the parents, last night Mr. and Mrs. Crane went to dinner at their neighbors, the Ketter-baughs. Apparently it's a semi-regular thing. Four couples go, every few months. As they usually do, the Cranes put their boys to bed before heading next door at around seven pm. They kept an ear open for the boys by using an app on Mrs. Crane's smartphone. And every forty-five minutes or so, Mr. Crane went back to check on them in person. He checked for a final time at about twelve-thirty, when the couple got home, and everything was fine. Both kids tucked up in their beds, snug as bugs. Then, this morning, Mrs. Crane—who always wakes at five-thirty, come what may—went into the boys' room."

"They share?" Devereaux's frown deepened.

"Yes. So Mrs. Crane went in—for no special reason, she just wanted to see her kids—and found Dillon, thumb in his mouth, fast asleep. But no sign of Ethan. His comforter was kind of bundled up, to make his bed look occupied from a distance, but he wasn't there. She searched the house for him, thinking it was a prank. Then she started to panic. She woke her husband. And at five fifty-eight, she called 911."

"Did the uniforms search the place again, when they got there?" Devereaux knew he was clutching at straws. That little boy was gone.

"They went through all the usual hiding places. The attic. The basement. The works." Hale took a swig of coffee. "No dice. Nothing stood out from the parents' initial statements, either, or from interviewing the neighbors. Uniforms are still out canvassing the area. All available K9 units have been deployed. And five of our own people have given up their days off to help check the kid's favorite haunts."

"How about Find-a-Child?"

Find-a-Child was a national agency Hale had used three times before when kids had gone missing on her watch. Based out of Miami, it used hundreds of specially trained volunteers to flood carefully targeted areas with phone calls, hoping to uncover snippets of information that could be passed on to the police and developed into leads. All three of those kids had been recovered safely—one had been snatched by his estranged father, who was trying to take him to Nicaragua; one had run away, and was hiding in an abandoned storage shed at the edge of a cotton field; and the most recent had been taken by a man who thought the boy was an alien newly arrived on earth to direct an extraterrestrial invasion.

"I authorized bringing them in, right before you got here."

"Anything from Forensics yet?" Devereaux tried to push the edge of a carpet tile back into place with his foot, but it refused to cooperate.

"No sign of forced entry." Hale took another sip of coffee. "No blood. Plenty of fingerprints in the house, but no hits from any database. Still waiting on the rest."

"Any background on the Cranes?"

"They were screened extensively before being allowed to foster Ethan, and nothing seems to have changed." Hale was nursing her cup, anxious to conserve the final few drops of coffee. "No records of anything out of the ordinary, debt-wise. They denied having any enemies, and swore they haven't been threatened by anyone. I've reached out to Vice and Narcotics, just in case there's anything the Cranes aren't telling us."

"Any reports of Joseph Crane getting into fights? Or Mary Lynne?"

"None."

"And they've not received any demands?"

"No."

"Did they say if anything else was missing?" Devereaux could feel the quicksand sucking at his ankles, dragging him back to the times when emergency calls had been made to report *him* missing. "Other than Ethan?"

Loflin underlined something, but still didn't speak.

"Yes." Hale flipped to a paper at the rear of the sheaf. "The backpack Ethan used for school. Underwear—at least three pairs. Several T-shirts. And one pair of pajamas."

"What about toys? Or books?"

"Mrs. Crane says *Brian* is missing. That's Ethan's favorite soft toy. A stuffed life-size rabbit. What do you make of that?"

Devereaux shrugged.

"OK, then." Hale drained her cup and plonked it down on a pile of phone message slips. "In that case, you know the question. Stick or twist?"

Devereaux knew what the lieutenant was really asking. Should they treat the kid as a runaway—or potential homicide victim—and continue to handle it themselves? Or was there anything to suggest a kidnapping, in which case jurisdiction would pass to the FBI.

"Put a gun to my head, I'd say runaway." Devereaux ran a hand through his hair. "Kidnappings serve a purpose. They're done to extort money. Enforce compliance with something. Take revenge. Or get exposure for some wacky cause. There's no hint of any of those things here. On the surface, at least. So, unless we're dealing with something really freaky, like the kid being snatched by a cult or a pervert—or someone looking to sell him to a pervert—the chances are he ran. Or the adopted parents killed him, and are covering it up. Either way, I should head over there and take a closer look at them."

Hale noticed Loflin tense up in her chair. "You and Jan should."

"Right." Devereaux looked at the door, anxious to be moving.

"Good. Then you two get over to the Crane house. I'll reach out to someone I know in the Birmingham field office, off the record, and see if the Bureau's had word on any pedophile rings that are active in the area. And cults, just to cover all the bases. The Bureau's shit-hot with that stuff. And, guys, remember—time." Hale turned her robot clock to face the two detectives. "You know the first twenty-four hours are key if we're going to find this kid alive."

Devereaux stood, then stepped back to allow Loflin to leave the office first.

"Cooper?" Hale stood, too, reached across her desk, and took hold of Devereaux's sleeve. "Move fast. But handle this with kid gloves, OK? We already have the media coming out of the wazoo. And people like these? Ruffle their feathers too much and we'll be in the middle of a shit storm, whether we get the boy back or not."

Funny, Devereaux thought. There hadn't been any media interest whenever he'd gone missing. He could remember plenty of shit storms, though. And they'd all been focused squarely on him.

**Cooper Devereaux. Extract from
Disciplinary Record (Suspensions):**

| Date | Complaint |
|------|-----------|
| 06-21-96 | Use of Excessive Force |
| 04-16-99 | Use of Prohibited Police Tactic |
| 12-01-03 | Unjustified Arrest |
| 06-30-07 | Unlawful Killing of a Minor. Reckless Discharge of a Firearm |
| 05-08-10 | Assault and Battery |
| 07-05-12 | Shots Fired into Vehicle Without Justification |

*None of these complaints were ever substantiated, but really? Think
about it, Jan!*
   *Smoke / fire?*
   *Leopard / spots . . . ?*

## Chapter Nine

*Saturday. Morning.*
*Ethan missing for eight and a half hours*

DEVEREAUX HAD BEEN *OVER THE MOUNTAIN* HUNDREDS OF times in his life. To the classy suburbs that had once been sheltered from Birmingham's choking clouds of pollution behind the thousand-foot crags and later, after the demise of the ironworks, had used them as a buffer against the city's creeping urban decay. He'd dated a woman from over there. Visited friends. Arrested criminals. Pursued suspects. Confiscated contraband. Even considered buying property. But when Loflin blipped her Charger's siren to scatter the small crowd of reporters that had gathered at the end of the Crane driveway, the sight of the palatial Mountain Brook home and its crisp white exterior triggered another familiar sensation. *Not belonging.*

It was the same rush of emotion that had overwhelmed him when he first glimpsed the house he'd been sent to when he was six. House? More like a shack. Run-down. And tiny. The Crane residence was a mansion in comparison. Devereaux figured it must be close on five thousand square feet. And beautifully maintained. A child would need a good reason to run away from that kind of place. But as Devereaux knew from bitter experience, there are plenty of good reasons to run.

The Crane yard was huge, too. A neatly manicured lawn separated the house from the street. There was no fence, though, which on that day seemed like a mistake. The reporters and camera crews were constantly creeping forward from the edge of the street, where the first officers on the scene had told them to stay. The Crane grass had been a healthy emerald green, unlike the sun-scorched scrub that satisfied some of their neighbors, but now the delicate surface was getting torn up by the uninvited, encroaching feet.

A line of evenly spaced dwarf conifers was the only visible border on the property, delineating the parking area where a late-model silver BMW was standing in front of a dented green RAV4. To the far side of the house a broad bed of shrubs gave way to saplings, and then to mature trees. It was practically a private forest. Plenty of ground for a curious boy to get lost in. Or buried in.

Devereaux would have wagered a month's salary there'd be a decent-size swimming pool round back, too, where a kid could easily drown. He was squinting up at the roof and wondering whether the pitch was sufficiently steep to contain an attic, or at least a crawl space big enough for a kid to hide in, when Loflin leaned over and touched his arm.

"Are you ready?" Loflin reached for her door handle, but waited for Devereaux to nod before she stepped out of the car.

Devereaux could feel the reporters' eyes on his back as he and Loflin approached the house's gabled porch. He could hear voices, too, when they reached its glossy white door. They were coming from inside. A man's, angry and accusatory. A woman's, defensive and shrill.

Another inevitable aspect of the case.

Another unwelcome echo from the past.

Devereaux knocked on the door. Hard. The kind of knock that does more than request admittance. The kind that tells whoever's inside to shut up and behave themselves. The yelling stopped abruptly. Footsteps approached. The door opened an eighth of the way. A man's long, manicured fingers curled around its edge at chest height and a hairy big toe appeared at its base.

"What do you want now?" The hidden voice sounded desperate. "Why can't you leave us alone? Get off our property!"

"Police." Devereaux thrust his badge into the gap.

The door opened the rest of the way.

"Sorry." The man was a shade over six feet tall, stocky, with thinning blond hair. He was wearing pale blue pants and a wrinkled white linen shirt, and a lingering hint of stale alcohol hung in the air around him. "I thought you were from the TV. Or the papers. They've been outside all morning, trying to film us and take pictures through the windows. Come on in. Quick, before they start snapping again."

Devereaux shook his head and followed Loflin as she stepped past a neat line of shoes and entered the hallway. It was a pleasant space. Light and airy, with a faint scent of lilac. The ceilings were high. The doorways and staircase were broad. The walls were finished in a soft off-white, with a half a dozen Impressionist-style paintings in pale wood frames dotted at intervals along their length. The floor was pale wood, too, but with a two-foot gash carved into it near the foot of the stairs. Devereaux wondered which of the boys was responsible, and how the parents had taken it.

"Have you found Ethan?" A woman in dark gray yoga pants and a matching top rushed toward the detectives from deeper inside the house. She was tall—maybe five-nine or -ten—and was clutching a plump, ginger-haired little boy to her chest. "Tell me he's all right!"

"Mrs. Crane?" Loflin stepped forward to intercept the woman. Devereaux moved to the side, scanning the mother's expression and gauging her body language.

"We have over a hundred people out looking for Ethan, right now." Loflin stretched out and touched the woman's arm. "They're doing everything they can. But there are some things we need to check with you, to help them bring Ethan home. Is there somewhere we could sit and talk?"

The detectives followed Mary Lynne and Joseph to the living room. Mary Lynne's pace slowed as she walked and her shoulders sagged a little more with every step. Devereaux could practically see the hope draining out of her. She ground to a halt in the center of the room with her husband by her side and gestured for the detectives to take one of the four cream-leather couches that were arranged around a brightly patterned Turkish rug. Picture windows dominated one wall—though the tapestry-style drapes were closed just then—and the other three sides were filled with bleached oak bookcases. There was no sign of a TV, Devereaux noted. Or any toys.

The Cranes hesitantly settled themselves across from the detectives. Mary Lynne perched at the edge of her couch, hunched protectively over Dillon, who was noisily sucking his thumb. Joseph leaned back and stretched his left arm along the top of the cushions, but the tendons standing out like cords in his neck gave the lie to his attempt at appearing calm.

Loflin handled the introductions, then took out her notebook and started to walk the couple through the bones of the story Lieutenant Hale had outlined in her office. Mary Lynne handled all the questions, nodding or mumbling brief affirmatives, and struggling to hold back her tears when asked about finding that Ethan had vanished. Dillon snuggled further into her lap, occasionally wriggling his head, but generally seeming content to soak up the attention. Devereaux wondered if Mary Lynne had ever hugged Ethan that way. Maybe when Ethan was the only child in the house, he thought. But after baby Dillon arrived? He doubted it.

"Can you add anything, Mr. Crane?" Devereaux leaned forward, trying to make a connection with him.

"It's important not to ignore the tiny details. They can make all the difference."

"No." Joseph Crane flinched as if someone had pinched him. "My wife's covered everything. What I want to know is, what are you guys actually doing to find my son? Why are you here, asking us questions we've already answered? Why aren't you out looking for Ethan?"

"You agree with everything your wife just said?"

"Of course! Why are you wasting time?"

"Everything she said?"

"Yes! Now why—"

"Because when we arrived, it sounded like you guys didn't agree about something. What were you arguing about?"

"We weren't arguing. This is a very stressful situation, is all, and—"

"I heard you yelling, Mr. Crane. You were yelling at your wife. Why would you do that?"

Joseph Crane glowered at Devereaux, but his lips tightened and he didn't reply.

"Was it about Ethan? Was there a problem with him? With his behavior?"

"No."

"At home? At school, maybe? Have there been complaints?"

"Of course not! Ethan's a bright kid. His teachers are delighted with him."

"How about from his friends?"

Joseph Crane shook his head.

"From his friends' parents?"

"No."

"What about his . . . brother?" Devereaux switched his attention to Dillon, hoping for a reaction. "Boys fight, right? All the time. Did they go at it a little more than usual yesterday? Ethan's older than Dillon. Bigger. And he's not your natural son . . ."

"The hell are you suggesting?"

"Mr. Crane?" Loflin closed her notebook. "Here's the

thing. We're not looking to jam you up. We're not here to judge. We're here to help find Ethan. And if we're going to do that, we need to know everything. Good and bad."

Joseph Crane shifted his gaze to the maze of patterns in the rug, but didn't answer.

"If it turns out not to be relevant, we'll forget we ever heard it." Loflin spread her hands out in front of her. "Whatever it is. And if you need to change one of your previous answers, we won't be mad at you. But saving your son is more important than saving face. You need to tell us *everything*."

"No." A scarlet rash appeared on Joseph Crane's neck and started to spread up toward his face. "You need to—"

"It was me." Mary Lynne Crane sat bolt upright, startling Dillon then pulling him tighter to her chest. "I know I should have told you sooner, but I was ashamed. When we got home last night, Joe went to check on the boys one last time. It was my job to lock the kitchen door behind us. That's the way we always do it—Joe checks the kids, I lock up. Except that I'd drunk a little more than usual. A little too much, if I'm honest. I fixed myself a glass of water instead of dealing with the stupid door right away. And then I forgot about it. I went upstairs. And fell asleep. I didn't even take my makeup off. When I found Ethan was missing, I couldn't understand it. But now I do. It was my fault. Whoever took him, they just walked right in."

"You're sure you left the door unlocked?" Devereaux softened his voice.

"Let's not jump to conclusions." Loflin turned to Mary Lynne. "Maybe the door was unlocked this morning because Ethan had gone out and left it that way?"

"No." Mary Lynne started to shake, causing Dillon to whimper until she let him slide down and curl up on her lap again.

"Our son did not run away." Joseph Crane got to his

feet, his hands balling into fists at his sides, his face growing red.

"But he has run away before." Devereaux stated it as a fact, not a question.

Joseph Crane stopped moving, but neither he nor his wife replied.

"How many times?" Devereaux kept his voice neutral. "Four? Five?"

"Only once." Mary Lynne's answer was barely audible. "Sort of. For, like, an hour. He was mad at us. But he came back, so it doesn't really count, right?"

"What did he take with him, that time?" Devereaux leaned forward.

"A little bag." Mary Lynne looked heartbroken. "A couple of toys. His pajamas. Some clothes."

"And this time?" Loflin's voice was gentle. "Isn't his school bag missing? His pajamas? And some clothes?"

"You're making us out to be monsters, driving him away!" Joseph Crane flopped back onto the sofa and took Dillon from his wife, lifting him onto his knee and absentmindedly straightening the little boy's scarlet Mickey Mouse sleep suit. "The bastard who took Ethan, he took those things to trick you. He wanted to throw you off the scent. And it's working. You're useless."

"What about his toy?" Loflin kept her focus on Mary Lynne. "Brian? His stuffed rabbit? Brian's missing, too, right?"

"Yes." Mary Lynne's eyes were filling with tears. "Ethan takes that rabbit everywhere. He can't get to sleep without it."

"What about the other time he ran?" Devereaux kept his voice soft. "Did he take Brian then, too?"

"Yes." Mary Lynne sounded confused. "No. Not exactly. He has another rabbit. Bert. It's exactly the same as Brian. Ethan says they're twins. Last time, he took Bert instead."

"How do you know which one he took, if they're exactly the same?"

"They started out exactly the same, but now Brian's

falling apart. He's been hugged half to death. Bert, Ethan hardly touches. Never takes him out of his room. No idea why. He still looks brand-new."

"Could I see Ethan's room?" Devereaux stood up.

"Why?" Joseph Crane pulled Dillon back against his chest. "Because of some stupid toy? The crime scene guys already went through it."

"Oh my God!" A single tear ran down Mary Lynne's cheek, carving a meandering trail through the smeared remnants of the previous night's makeup. "You've found something, haven't you? Something you think belongs to Ethan?"

## Chapter Ten

THE WOMAN PAUSED, MOMENTARILY BEWILDERED.

When she'd been planning this phase, she'd put all her effort into finding an Internet cafe in a convenient location. Not an easy task these days, now that the smartphone is king for the moronic majority that doesn't understand security. It hadn't occurred to her that once she was safely online, she'd be hit with so many options. She allowed herself a moment to curse. Herself, for a lack of foresight. Disney, for the complexity of its website. The kid, for not picking somewhere else for his treat. (She'd been secretly hoping for something music-related, up in Nashville, given their general locale.) Then she got back down to business.

She figured that as long as she avoided all the packages that involved princesses, any of the other ones on offer would do.

It wasn't as if value for money was her key consideration.

## Chapter Eleven

*Saturday. Morning.*
*Ethan missing for nine hours*

DEVEREAUX STOOD ON HIS OWN IN THE DOORWAY OF THE boys' bedroom and took a moment to get a sense of the space.

The room was bright and sunny, with cheerful sky-blue paintwork. There was one window set in the middle of the longer wall, diagonally opposite the door. It looked out over the backyard—which, as Devereaux had predicted, contained an extravagant pool. Dense swathes of blue ash trees extended beyond another wide stretch of grass, blocking any other houses or buildings from sight and framing the view as if they'd been grown specially for the purpose.

A twin bed stuck out on either side of the window, with pine wardrobes and matching toy chests next to them. Devereaux guessed the left-hand half of the room was Ethan's. There were fewer posters and pictures on the walls. Only one toy—a rabbit—sitting on the bed. The comforter was plain blue, unlike the other one, which was a sea of colorful cartoon characters. And there were large, ugly blotches of gray powder on the headboard as well as each piece of adjoining furniture, where the crime scene technicians had been at their most generous.

The bedroom floor was wooden. The boards were broader than the ones downstairs, and the gaps between them were wider, too. A night-light shaped like a frog jutted out of a power socket low down on the wall at the midpoint of the window, and centered beneath that was a gaudy rug. A matching runner lay stretched out at the side of each bed.

Dillon's bed was the nearer one to the door. So, if someone had crept in during the night and taken Ethan, they'd have had to walk past Dillon. Twice. First to reach Ethan. Then to get back out, by now potentially carrying a struggling child. Was it feasible to do that without waking a sleeping four-year-old?

Devereaux tiptoed across the room, listening for creaks or groans from the floorboards. They didn't so much as whisper, so he tried again, walking normally. Again, there was no sound.

Devereaux moved back to Ethan's bed and crouched down to take a closer look at an alien-themed plastic cup that was lying on its side on the runner. The fabric around it was dry, but a roughly oval patch large enough to account for a few ounces of spilled water felt crunchy to the touch, as if recently soaked.

Devereaux dialed the number for the police department lab and while he waited for the answer to the question he'd asked, he wedged the phone against his shoulder and leaned down to pick up Ethan's toy rabbit. It was lying on top of the comforter, with its head on the pillow. Devereaux figured it was Bert. Twin brother of Brian. The toy Ethan had taken the other time he'd run away, but not last night.

The rabbit was heavier than Devereaux had expected, so he turned it over in his hands and tried to distract himself from the infuriating holding-music by looking for an explanation for its weight. He squeezed its floppy ears. Poked its stubby legs. Probed its shaggy, fake fur. Then jerked his hand back. A drop of blood oozed from the tip of his finger. He wiped it away and looked more closely at the toy. Something shiny was concealed in the long seam that ran across its belly. He tugged at the seam and found a row of safety pins. There were twelve. But four of them weren't lined up neatly, like the rest. They were crooked, as if they'd been replaced in a hurry. And one wasn't fastened at all.

Devereaux pulled on a pair of latex gloves. Unfastened the crooked pins. Looked inside the toy. Then returned his attention to the phone when the crime scene tech finally came back on the line.

## Chapter Twelve

*Saturday. Morning.*
*Ethan missing for nine and a quarter hours*

MARY LYNNE AND JOSEPH WERE SITTING OPPOSITE EACH other in the living room when Devereaux came back downstairs. Loflin was standing a few feet behind the couch Joseph had taken. She was watching as he tried to use an Apple MacBook to search for a register of local sex offenders. Mary Lynne kept glancing anxiously at the door. There was no sign of Dillon.

After a moment a toilet flushed toward the back of the house. Light footsteps drew closer, and the boy appeared in the doorway. He was carrying a twelve-inch-high plastic T-Rex. Mary Lynne stood and went to scoop up her son but he ducked, scampered to the farthest couch from the door, scrambled up onto it, and settled into the shelter of its deeply padded arm. All his attention was focused on his dinosaur.

Mary Lynne turned toward Devereaux and her eye was drawn to the toy he was carrying.

"Ethan's other rabbit?" She looked puzzled. "What are you doing with that?"

"It had been left on Ethan's bed." Devereaux opened the seam so she could see inside the toy. There was a multi-colored rubber ball. Seven large pebbles, worn smooth and shiny. Two pinecones. Four clothespins. A handful of quarters. And four scratched, battered Civil War soldiers. All Rebels. "Ethan's treasure. This is where he kept it."

"It doesn't look like treasure to me." Mary Lynne wrinkled her nose as if she was expecting the contents to smell bad. "It's junk! Where would he have gotten it from?"

"Could he have brought it with him, when he first came here?"

"No." Mary Lynne shook her head. "He brought nothing at all. The poor little mite. Even the clothes he was wearing were donated by the hospital where he went after he was taken away from the last family that had him."

"I'm wondering why he left these things behind." Devereaux pointed to the concealed opening in the rabbit's stomach. "He went to some trouble to keep them safe."

"What does it matter?" Joseph closed the computer and dropped it on the rug. He stood, moved closer to Devereaux, and scowled. "Ethan's still missing. And instead of looking for him, you're standing here asking dumb-ass questions about a bunch of old garbage. Who cares what he took? Or what he left? You should be out there, trying to find him."

"We are trying to find him." Devereaux glanced at Dillon, who was still absorbed by his T-Rex. "But to do that, we need to figure out whether Ethan left of his own accord, or if he was taken. Whether he was acting on his own, or if someone else was there, holding a . . . Persuading him."

"We don't know." Mary Lynne turned to Joseph. "How could we? We weren't in his room all night."

"No, you weren't. But one person was . . ." Devereaux nodded toward the couch.

"Absolutely not!" Joseph lowered his voice to an angry hiss. "You're not interrogating my son. He's traumatized enough as it is. Look at him!"

"I just need to ask him one question. How can that hurt? I bet it would make him feel better, trying to help his brother."

"I said no."

"Maybe if we brought in a counselor?" Loflin kept her distance, feeling the tension growing among the other three.

"No shrink's getting his hooks into my son." Joseph crossed his arms. "This is bull. You should be *doing something*!"

"OK." Devereaux held up his free hand. "You're frustrated. I understand. So let's try something else. Let's try to figure out how long Ethan was here. If we can do that, we might pin down how far he could have gone. Mrs. Crane, can you tell me this—did Ethan take a cup of water to bed at night?"

"Yes." Desperate creases lined Mary Lynne's face. "His alien cup. I always bring it to him when I kiss him goodnight."

"You put it on the toy box, next to Ethan's bed?"

"Right." Mary Lynne nodded.

"It was like that when you left him last night?"

"Of course. It's probably still there."

"No." Devereaux shook his head. "It's not. It was knocked over, sometime during the night. It ended up on the floor. On the runner. Almost level with Ethan's pillow. Now, Mr. Crane, you checked on the boys for the last time at, what, half-past midnight?"

"Right." Joseph looked away. "I already told you that."

"Was the cup still on the toy box at that time?"

Joseph muttered something incomprehensible.

"What was that?" Devereaux stepped closer. "Mr. Crane?"

"I didn't notice, OK? It was dark."

"There's a night-light in the room. It would have shone right where the cup was lying, if it had already fallen off."

"Look, I was tired. I didn't examine every inch of the freaking floor."

"What about earlier?"

"Maybe it wasn't Ethan who knocked the cup over. Or whoever took him. Maybe one of the crime scene guys did it."

"No. The cup was on the floor when the crime scene guys arrived. They took photographs before they began. So, Mr. Crane. Think. About each of the times you checked."

"I'm trying." Joseph shook his head. "But I don't remember. Not specifically."

"Honey?" Mary Lynne tugged at Joseph's sleeve. "How can you not remember? You must have stood right by the bed when you checked on Ethan. If there was water spilled on the floor, your feet would have gotten wet."

"I don't know." Joseph shrugged. "I just didn't notice, I guess. Maybe I wasn't close enough."

"I don't understand." Mary Lynne massaged her temples with her fingertips. "If you weren't close enough to step in the water, or see the cup lying by the bed, how could you be close enough to see if Ethan was in the bed?"

"That's crazy." Joseph avoided meeting his wife's eye. "You don't have to go all the way in to see if he's there. I didn't, this morning."

"It was light this morning. And I'd already found out our son was missing!" A note of hysteria had crept into Mary Lynne's voice. "But last night—Joe? What are you saying? You didn't go all the way in? Did you check on our boys, or not?"

"Of course I checked!"

"But did you go in? Did you go all the way to their beds?"

Joseph didn't answer.

"Did you go in? Joe!"

"Yes, I went in. The first time. To Dillon's bed, anyway. You know how lightly Ethan sleeps. It was all right for you—you were still at the party, having fun. You just had to listen out for your phone. But what was *I* supposed to do? I was the one who had to keep coming home and missing everything. If Ethan had woken up, it would've been an hour before he was back down again. Maybe longer. So I looked in from the doorway. It's what I always do."

A loud *crack* rang out around the room. Joseph staggered back, surprised at his wife's strength, his cheek stinging from the sudden blow.

"You didn't check on our boys." Mary Lynne's eyes had glazed over. "You lied to me. *You* let Ethan get taken. And you let me take the blame. I thought it was all on me, because I didn't lock that stupid door . . ."

## Cooper Devereaux. Extract from BPD.
## Academy Appraisal, 1993.

Three instructors went on record on separate occasions to express the opinion that Cooper Devereaux was an unfit candidate for the Academy. In particular, they cited his failure to adapt to the collegial nature of the institution, and his poor response to discipline and authority.

*All three instructors later withdrew their testimony.*
*Why? What pressure was brought to bear? Were they threatened? Paid off?*
*And by whom? What kind of friends does Devereaux have?*
*None of the instructors are still around to answer these questions.*
*A coincidence, Jan . . . ?*

## Chapter Thirteen

*Saturday. Late Morning.*
*Ethan missing for nine and three-quarter hours*

"WE SHOULD CALL THE LIEUTENANT." LOFLIN BLIPPED HER siren to scatter the swarm of reporters. The horde had tripled in size while the detectives were inside the house, and was now breaching the midway point of the Cranes' driveway. "Tell her to intensify the search."

Loflin paused, her attention taken by a sound from above the car. The *chop chop chop* of a helicopter, losing height. Loflin guessed it belonged to a TV station. One of the reporters must have called in their arrival, and the crew couldn't resist swooping down in the hope of filling local screens with pictures of a cute little boy being reunited with his family. Or better still—from their perspective, at least—a pair of hysterical, heartbroken parents being led away to identify a small, limp body.

"I'm not so sure." Devereaux retrieved an eyeliner pencil from the foot well and jammed it into a cup holder in the center console, adding it to half a dozen others.

"Oh, come on." Loflin slipped the car into gear. "Ethan's clearly run away. He's done it before. He took the same kind of stuff as the last time. Add to that the fact his parents are mean. And what you get is the need for more feet on the street, looking for him."

"I'm not convinced." Devereaux leaned back against the Charger's mesh headrest and closed his eyes. He was trying to picture Ethan huddled in his bed in the semi-darkness, hurriedly fastening his rabbit's safety pins. Securing his most precious possessions. And then abandoning them. "Ethan didn't take the same stuff as last time. He left his special things behind. If he ran away, why would he do that?"

"Are those things really that special? Maybe he left them because he didn't want them anymore. I didn't hoard that kind of junk when I was a kid. No one I knew did."

"You weren't an orphan. I guess your friends weren't, either."

"So what?" Loflin kept her foot on the brake. "Ethan was how old when the Cranes took him in? Three? That's very young. And now he's been with that family more than half his life. Would he even remember living anywhere else?"

"He was young, you're right. But before the Cranes, he had his real home. Then his parents died. He was sent to one foster home. Then another. And the second one was so bad he ended up in the hospital. He didn't even have any clothes of his own. Let alone any stuff. So yes. He'll remember. Even if it's on some subconscious level. And it's bound to affect how he behaves."

"Maybe, I guess." Loflin started to fiddle with her hair, tucking it behind her ears, and for the first time Devereaux saw that her right earlobe was missing. "I don't have much experience with kids."

"You get hurt?" Devereaux raised his hand to his own ear. "Gunshot? Knife wound? Bite?"

"Nothing like that." Loflin straightened her hair, pressing it tight against the side of her face. "Nothing so dramatic. It's just an inherited thing. I hate it, actually. Got teased mercilessly when I was a kid."

"See what I mean?" Devereaux gathered up a wad of

Dunkin' Donuts napkins and slid them into the door pocket. "Things stay with you. Take their toll."

"I guess." Loflin shifted back into Park. "Maybe we can't be sure the boy ran away. Maybe something else happened to him. So what do you suggest?"

"Start with the victim. Assuming there is one. Ethan. We need to find out what he's really like. Not the sanitized version the Cranes are feeding us. We need to talk to his teachers, as soon as the uniforms have tracked them down. And his previous foster parents. Meantime, let's head next door. Talk to the neighbors. The Ketterbaughs. The ones who had the party last night."

"Sounds like a plan." Loflin shifted into Drive and started to edge the car forward. "Could maybe shine a light on Joseph and Mary Lynne, too. Who goes out drinking and leaves little kids home alone?"

As Loflin weaved her way around to the next driveway, Devereaux did place a call to Lieutenant Hale. Not because he'd changed his mind about bolstering the search. But because he figured she needed to know what they'd learned. The team had been working on the assumption that the earliest Ethan could have disappeared was around one am. Now they knew he could have gone missing up to six hours before that. Up to a quarter of the critical first twenty-four hours could have already expired.

The odds of finding the little boy alive had suddenly gotten a whole lot slimmer.

## Chapter Fourteen

*Saturday. Late Morning.*
*Ethan missing for ~~ten~~ sixteen hours*

THE KETTERBAUGH HOUSE LOOKED MORE TRADITIONAL than the Cranes' on the outside, but inside it had been completely remodeled. The ground floor had been turned into an open-plan space, except for a small powder room tucked under the staircase. The kitchen was still in back—all stainless steel and blond wood and granite—and it flowed into a dining space that was dominated by a giant, circular wooden table beneath an extravagant crystal chandelier. Next was a living area, with a Noguchi coffee table surrounded by Eames leather-and-chrome couches, and the bay window next to the front door had been set up as a kind of reading nook. There was art on the walls—large, colorful canvases in the style of Miró and Rothko—and a five-foot-tall bronze sculpture of an embracing couple stood at the foot of the staircase.

Helen Ketterbaugh was curled up in the corner of her favorite couch, skimming the morning paper on her iPad, when Devereaux knocked on the door. She was wearing a bright, clingy, floral sundress that made clear that, despite her forty-five years, there wasn't an ounce of fat on her body.

"I'll get it, honey." Ian Ketterbaugh, her husband, was halfway down the stairs. He was a year older, but the tight white tennis outfit he had on confirmed he was in equally good shape.

Ian joined his wife on the couch and invited the detectives to sit opposite them.

"First things first." Helen gestured toward the kitchen. "Does anyone need a drink? Iced tea? Water?"

"Thanks, but no." Devereaux shifted his position slightly on the shiny leather cushion. "We just need to ask you folks a few questions, and then we'll get out of your hair."

"We're happy to help, Detective." Ian leaned down to adjust his shoelace. "But I'm not sure what we can do. We already told the other officers everything about last night."

"I know. And that was very helpful." Devereaux nodded. "But what we need to do now is put a little more meat on the bones. See, if—and I'm not saying this is what happened, it's just one theory we need to rule in or out—if someone else was involved in young Ethan going missing, we need to understand what the Cranes look like from the outside. How they are as a family. Their routines. How they behave. What could have made them stand out as victims. See what I mean?"

"I guess." Ian leaned back and crossed his legs. "So go ahead. We'll give it our best shot. We feel just awful about what's happened to that poor little boy. Right, honey?"

Helen nodded.

"How long have you known the Cranes?" Devereaux kept his voice warm and friendly.

"Since the hurricane. We were living in Vestavia Hills at the time, and our house got hit pretty hard. Joe was one of the volunteers."

"The university set up the volunteering." Helen crossed her arms. "The one where he works."

"Right." Ian put his hand on his wife's leg. "So Joe gave up his free time to come out and help us clear up. There was a hell of a mess. And not just our things. You wouldn't believe the kind of stuff that landed up in our yard. Files from a lawyer's office in Tuscaloosa. Kids' clothes. Pieces of cars. A fish—"

"So you became friends, bonding over sweeping up all this junk?"

"Right." Ian smiled. "We hit it off from minute one. Same wavelength, you know? So when the inspectors came out and condemned our place, rather than rebuild we started looking in Mountain Brook. And guess what? This house hit the market that same week. Right next door to the Cranes. Talk about a stroke of luck."

Devereaux noticed Helen turn her head away and stare at her foot.

"And Mary Lynne?" Devereaux asked. "Are you guys as close with her?"

"Absolutely. We couldn't ask for better friends or neighbors."

"How are the Cranes as parents?"

"I'd say excellent." Ian nodded. "They just love those boys. They'd do anything for them. And they treat the two just the same, you know. It was ages before we found out Ethan was adopted."

Helen's foot started to tap.

"Do they bring the boys 'round here often?"

"No, not really." Ian paused for a second. "We don't have kids, so there wouldn't be much for them to do."

"What kind of kid is Ethan, would you say?"

"He's a good boy. We don't see him much, except at church, but I hear he's doing well in school. Doesn't like football much, apparently. Probably because of where his dad works. Wait a minute. Don't tell me you pull for The Tide as well?"

"Oh, no." Devereaux shook his head. "You're not dragging me down that street. Let's try this, instead. Have you ever heard of the Cranes getting into fights

with anyone? At work? With other neighbors? Or anyone ever threatening them?"

"Hell, no. They're just not the kind of people to get
into fights. And I certainly haven't heard about any
threats."

"Disputes with contractors?"

"Nope."

"Have they fired any housekeepers? Or nannies?"

"I don't think so. Do you know, honey?"

"They haven't." Helen shook her head.

"Detective, is there much else you need?" Ian looked
at his Rolex. "Only I'm running late for a match . . ."

"No, I think we've got enough. Just promise me you'll
call if anything comes to mind that could help us. And if
you're not sure if it would help us, call anyway. A little
boy's life could be at stake. OK?"


Devereaux and Loflin loitered outside the front door
making small talk with Helen Ketterbaugh until Ian had
disappeared behind the trees in his convertible Mercedes.

"You know, maybe we do have a few more questions." Devereaux turned back toward the house. "Mind
if we get your take on a couple things, Mrs. Ketterbaugh?"

"Like what?"

"Seemed to me you weren't quite as enthusiastic as
your husband back there, when he was talking about
the Cranes."

Helen shrugged.

"Ian and Joe hit it off real well, I guess." Devereaux
paused for a moment. "But maybe it's not the same for
you and Mary Lynne?"

"No, that's not it. I like Mary Lynne just fine."

"But . . . ?"

"Look, Ian works all the time. Joe works all the time.
Aside from church, they see each other once a month.

Maybe twice. They drink beer. They talk football. They eat 'cue. What do they know?"

"And you?"

"I'm around more. I see more."

"Such as?"

"Ethan, for one thing. I'm sure the poor kid had a tough time in whatever hellhole he was stuck in before Mary Lynne brought him home, and I feel sympathy for that, but he's sure not the little angel everyone's making him out to be now that he's missing."

"How so?"

"Well, for a start there are the fights. With other kids in the neighborhood. Every time a little one winds up with a cut or a bruise, Ethan's behind it. You can be sure."

"How do you know?"

"Their moms tell me. They're always complaining about him."

Loflin took out her notebook, turned to a blank page, and handed it to Helen. "Could you write down their details? These other moms? We'll need to talk to them. But we'll be discreet. Your name won't be mentioned, I promise."

Helen hesitated, then took the book and scrawled down a couple of names and numbers.

"Thanks." Devereaux took the book, glanced at the page, and handed it to Loflin. "But why don't the teachers do something about it?"

"I'm not talking about at school." A hint of annoyance had crept into Helen's voice. "I mean around here. Ethan's always out, wandering about. Sneaking into people's yards. Getting into trouble."

"Where's his mother when all this is happening?"

"At the hospital. She works crazy hours. She has a whole network of tutors and babysitters and music teachers and such like. For a seven-year-old! And a four-year-old! I don't know why she had those kids if she's not prepared to look after them."

"So Mary Lynne pays all these people to watch both kids, but Ethan skips out?"

"Right. And what are they going to do? Tell Mary Lynne? They might as well say *Hey, Mrs. Crane, please fire me, and trash my Yelp score at the same time so I can't get any other work.*"

"Good point. But why don't the other parents complain?"

"They try, but Mary Lynne refuses to listen. And Ethan has a ready-made alibi."

Back in the car Loflin paused with her hand on the ignition key and turned to Devereaux.

"Interesting, what Mrs. Ketterbaugh had to say."

"Very."

"Puts a different complexion on things."

"It does." Devereaux was picturing a vulnerable little boy wandering the neighborhood, craving his real home, getting taunted by the other kids for being an orphan, being forced to defend himself . . .

"Regularly sneaking out of the house. Trespassing. Getting in fights. You've got to admit, it makes Ethan sound like a proper little terror."

"Not to me. I was hearing *neglect*. Sounds like the parents have no clue where Ethan even is most of the time. I want to know more about them. 'Specially Mary Lynne, if she's Ethan's primary caregiver."

"Want to go back and talk to her some more?"

"No. Not yet. Who knows? Maybe Helen Ketterbaugh's full of shit. I want more data. Let's call the other parents she told us about. Get their side of the story."

Loflin checked her notebook then called the first number, making sure her phone was on speaker. The harsh ringtone reverberated through the car's interior, then the call tripped to voicemail. Loflin left a message asking for her call to be returned without delay, then tried the other numbers Helen had given them. And met with the same result.

"Damn the weekend." Devereaux pulled out his own phone and checked his email. "No word on Ethan's teachers, either. Or the previous foster parents. So let's do this: Head for the hospital. It won't matter that it's Saturday, there. Some of Mary Lynne's co-workers will be around. They'll have no choice but to talk to us."

**BPD Internal Affairs Division. Extract
from Investigation into the Homicide Death
of Alexander Parker.**

Alexander Parker came to the Division's attention when he contacted BPD with a proposal to provide evidence of the previous and ongoing involvement of an active BPD Detective in criminal acts, including larceny, extortion, and grand theft auto. The Detective named in these allegations was Cooper Devereaux.

The investigation was closed, unsolved, upon the homicide of the informant, Alexander Parker. He was shot from distance with a high-power rifle. No weapon was recovered. Detective Devereaux had no alibi for the time the homicide occurred, but no solid evidence could be found against him. No other viable suspects were developed.

*A guy threatening to rat on Devereaux gets his head blown off? Fool me once . . .*

*Devereaux had no alibi? No one else was ever in the frame? Fool me twice . . .*

*What's Devereaux like on the range? Pretty good, I hear, Jan . . . !*

## Chapter Fifteen

*Saturday. Late Morning.*
*Ethan missing for sixteen and a half hours*

TRAFFIC WAS BACKED UP ON THE RED MOUNTAIN EXPRESS-way, as locals like Loflin still called it, so she took an alternative, twisting back route via the Cahaba Valley.

A giant billboard at the side of the road a little before the crest of the final peak showed a sweet, smiling angel. Standing next to her was an over-enthusiastic, trident-wielding devil. And sandwiched between them, there was a "handwritten" checklist like the kind kids pass around in grade school:

*Where will you be spending the Afterlife?*
Heaven    ☐
Hell       ☐

A dented silver food truck with a flat tire was parked in the shade thrown by the billboard. It had a sign of its own. It showed a fat, happy chicken. Next to it was a skinny, miserable rooster. And between the cartoon poultry, another checklist:

*How will you be spending the Afternoon?*
*Happy*     ☐
*Hungry*   ☐

"You've got to love that guy." Loflin pointed to the truck. "What a nerve. And the food's great. He only serves one thing. Chicken with white barbeque sauce. People drive out here specially to get it."

Devereaux wasn't impressed. He was very particular about his barbeque, and on principle he couldn't get behind a place that didn't serve pork. Or at least brisket. He thought about setting Loflin straight, but before he could speak he was interrupted by his phone.

"Cooper?" It was Lieutenant Hale. "Where are you?"

"Heading to UAB Hospital. A follow-up from an interview with the Cranes' neighbors."

"Good. Perfect. Listen. Big news. Two things. First, Find-a-Child has come up with a lead. There was a mini-van parked on the Cranes' street Friday night. A white Honda Odyssey. Two of their neighbors reported it. The information was filtered out at first because the van was seen between ten and eleven pm. Until your conversation with the Cranes, we thought Ethan didn't go missing until after half-past midnight."

"Anything on the plates?"

"No. We're not that lucky. But listen to the second thing. The lab found a medicine bottle. It was wrapped in used coffee-filter papers and jammed into an empty dishwasher detergent box in the Cranes' trash. It had been rinsed out, and its label had been removed. But the technicians still recovered enough of its contents to run an analysis. They found traces of triazolam. Do you know what that is?"

"It's a tranquilizer. Relatively mild."

"Right. Perfect for subduing a seven-year-old."

"You're thinking someone could have drugged Ethan, to make him easier to control?" Devereaux switched the phone to his other ear and signaled for Loflin to speed up.

"Right."

"What about the other kid? Dillon? He seemed pretty dopey, back at the house, I thought."

"I put two and two together, and came up with the same thing. We need a sample of his blood. An ADA's applying for a warrant as we speak."

"Hold on. What about Mary Lynne Crane? She's a nurse. She could be the one who doped the kids. If they were doped."

"Why would a mother do something like that?"

"To keep them docile while she's out partying with her husband."

There was silence on the line for a good twenty seconds, and Devereaux watched the tips of the exotic trees from the Birmingham Botanical Gardens peek into view in the distance.

"You're playing with fire here, Cooper. An accusation like that . . . remember the media."

"Remember the missing kid."

"Did either of them say anything that could possibly give you cause to believe they'd drugged those kids?"

"No. Of course not. But they didn't say anything about leaving the door unlocked till I leaned on them. Or about not checking on the kids properly. If Mrs. Crane drugged the kids, and gave Ethan too much? We can't rule it out."

"Maybe not. But let's put it on the back burner, OK? Keep our focus on finding the kid *alive*."

"I disagree. If these people murdered Ethan—even if they killed him by accident—we need to know right away. What if they run? If someone gets in their way? What about Dillon? You couldn't just leave him with them. And what if they go on TV and give some teary-eyed heartbroken parent act, then it turns out they're guilty? No one will listen the next time a kid needs help. It's irresponsible, not following it up."

Hale was silent again, this time for half a minute.

"How about this?" Devereaux couldn't bear to wait any longer. "We're en route to the hospital. We're going to talk to Mary Lynne's co-workers anyway, to dig into what kind of mother she is. Why don't we do that, and also find out if she has access to triazolam?"

"OK. Check on her access. And focus on her state of mind. See if she's been depressed recently. I'll get back to the FBI. Feed in the drug angle. See if it unlocks any doors at their end."

## Chapter Sixteen

SHE WAS A WOMAN OF HER WORD.

Except, of course, when she was forced to use deception to further her cause. That was different. *Ruse de guerre* had been acceptable for centuries. The one thing she'd never do was break a promise. Although when she saw the zoo of people in the hotel foyer, for the first time in her life she was tempted . . .

There were no clear lines. No signs of organization. Rowdy children were running everywhere. She was glad she'd left the boy outside in the Mercedes. She'd done it because he was still drowsy, and she hadn't wanted to draw attention to him—though she immediately saw that was an unnecessary concern, given the bedlam she was facing. But either way, the place didn't set a good example for a kid.

Any kid.

And enduring it would certainly be no way for *this* little boy to begin his treat.

## Chapter Seventeen

*Saturday. Early Afternoon.*
*Ethan missing for seventeen hours*

A HELICOPTER WAS TOUCHING DOWN ON THE ROOF OF THE Children's Center as Loflin approached the hospital's main campus. Devereaux watched it land and wondered if his father would have pulled through if he'd been airlifted to the Emergency Room forty years earlier, rather than being left to bleed out on a filthy wooden floor.

Loflin dropped the Charger in a no-parking zone and the two detectives made their way past the fountain and the gently rippling reflecting pool, and hurried into the chessboard-fronted main building. Devereaux recognized the receptionist who was peering out from a forest of indoor ferns at the counter—she'd helped him a couple of times before, when he'd been visiting injured colleagues—and she directed them to the trauma and burn center, where Mary Lynne Crane worked.

The room the detectives requisitioned to hold their interviews had started life as a closet. Then it spent time as an office, though the only sign of that period was a line of framed photographs on one wall, showing old scenes of Birmingham—grimy workers lined up outside their foundry before the Tennessee Coal, Iron and Railroad Company closed its doors; Vulcan fresh from his cast in 1903, before his triumphant visit to St. Louis; the Heaviest Corner on Earth at 1st and 20th, right after the Trust and Savings building was completed in 1912. But these days the room was mostly used for storing the flowers that any friends or relatives who didn't know better tried to send patients in the closely controlled environment of the trauma center. The bouquets that ended up there were supposed to be distributed to lonely souls without any, elsewhere in the hospital, but more often than not they were left to rot in their vases. As a result, the room stank of decay. It didn't strike Devereaux as an auspicious place to search for clues that might save a little boy's life.

The five nurses on that day's early shift each took their turn on the least decrepit of the chairs Devereaux and Loflin had scrounged up to furnish the otherwise empty, windowless room. Some of the staff brimmed with confidence, looking the detectives in the eye and relishing the hint of adventure in this departure from their everyday routine. Others were more hesitant, focusing on the marks on the walls or the stains on the ragged carpet tiles rather than the people asking the questions. But regardless of their style, each of them told a variation on the same story: Mary Lynne wasn't the best nurse in the world. She wasn't the worst. She was good at interacting with patients—especially younger ones. She was bad at keeping records, occasionally dropping the ball toward the end of busy shifts. Good at staying on top of new clinical research. Bad at accommodating last-minute shift changes. And so on.

Two of Mary Lynne's co-workers embellished the picture with a few less-flattering details. She was a poor timekeeper who took more than her share of sick days, according to one woman, though Loflin soon led her to admit that her own recent attempt to adopt a child had been unsuccessful. Mary Lynne sucked up to management and stabbed her peers in the back, said a guy who

Loflin quickly pegged as a rival who'd lost out to her for a promotion.

The door clicked shut behind the last of the early-shift nurses, and without a specific task to focus on, Devereaux felt the familiar catch in his chest at being cooped up in a relatively small space. He turned to Loflin, who was studying the old photographs. Neither detective spoke. The seconds became a minute. The minute became two. All the while the silence seemed to grow in intensity, bearing down on Devereaux until he could feel his head starting to swim. He closed his eyes, forcing himself to focus, eager for a distraction to latch onto.

"Are you OK?" Loflin reached out and touched his arm.

"Me?" Devereaux's eyes snapped open. "I'm fine. Thanks. I just don't like waiting. Where's the next batch of nurses? We need to get this show back on the road."

"We do." Loflin drew back her arm. "But, Cooper, listen, while we've got a minute, can I ask you something?"

"Sure. Fire away."

"Goodness, this is awkward. OK. Here's the thing. I really want to make it work in your squad, so I was wondering, I mean, I'm worried . . ."

"Don't be. Spit it out. Whatever it is."

"Cooper, are there stories about me? Rumors? About why I'm not with Vice right now?"

"I heard something about you coming back from disability?"

"Right. Only, I didn't get hurt. Not physically, anyway."

"Oh. I see. Well, OK."

"You're not freaked out?"

"Should I be?"

"No. But a lot of people are. Psych problems are treated worse than leprosy, a lot of the time. Especially in the department."

"Not by me."

"Thanks for understanding. I'm glad to get this out in

the open. In case you do hear any rumors. Because, bottom line? The doctor doesn't think I'm ready to go back undercover. That doesn't mean I'm not ready to be a good detective again. And a damn good partner. If you'll let me."

"Received and understood. But what about longer term? You see yourself heading back to Vice, when you get the green light for the sneaky-beak stuff?"

"I don't know. Talk about stressful. You don't like the waiting in this job? Try undercover work. There's no waiting. You're always working. Working to get accepted. Working to make your mark interested in you. Working to make him *want* you around. There's no respite. It's like trying to breathe someplace where there's not enough oxygen. It's suffocating."

"It sure sounds like it." Devereaux checked his watch. "You know, Jan, I need to make a call, real quick. Give me a minute?"

Devereaux paused in the corridor and checked the directory in his phone before selecting a number. His call was picked up after one ring.

"Eddie England." England had partnered with Devereaux for a spell three years previously, before moving to Vice on the promise of a promotion. One that had yet to materialize.

"Eddie—it's Cooper. Listen, buddy, I don't have a lot of time so I'll come straight to the point. Quick question. Jan Loflin. What can you tell me about her?"

"Not much." There was a moment's silence. "I was only on the same squad as her for a few months. She seemed nice enough. Quiet. Didn't hang out at the usual cop bars too much. Kept herself to herself outside of the job."

"How about when she was working?"

"She was a mixed bag, I guess. In some ways, she was brilliant. Undercover? She was a chameleon. Seriously. Think Meryl Streep, only better."

"Sounds impressive."

"Right. But in other ways, she was a disaster. Like she had tunnel vision. If she didn't get something, or agree with it, or if it didn't fit with the way she wanted things to be, she'd just blank it. Act like it didn't exist. Live in denial till she got written up for procedure violations. Happened at least twice, to my knowledge. It was weird. Hey—why do you need to know all this?"

"She's landed in my squad for a while. She's working a case with me. And I need to be sure, bottom line—is she a flake? Or can I trust her?"

England took a few seconds to consider.

"You can trust her, Cooper. Just don't marry her."

"Thanks, Ed. I won't. I'm not the marrying type. You know that. Listen, thanks again. Got to go . . ."


The detectives added a little variety to the questions they put to the nurses from the late shift, but they drew the same kinds of answers. And again, Loflin's demeanor subtly adjusted with each new face that came through the door. Her body language altered to mirror her subject. The tone of her voice shifted, too. Sometimes she came across as sympathetic. Sometimes hard. Sometimes amused. But every time one of Mary Lynne's co-workers tried to hide an agenda, Loflin sniffed it out. She had an uncanny, intuitive ability to latch onto any false note in an anecdote or opinion and not let go until she heard the truth.

When the door shut behind the final nurse, Devereaux and Loflin had to admit they'd uncovered nothing conclusive. No one had noticed any worrying traits in Mary Lynne's behavior. No one could cast any credible doubt on her ability or commitment as a parent. It was unlikely she'd handle triazolam on a regular basis, due to the kind of patients she came into contact with and potential contraindications with the other types of drugs they used in the unit. But it wasn't impossible. There were a few situations where triazolam could be legitimately prescribed. And there was a fully stocked pharmacy onsite.

Devereaux's experience was that people have ways of getting hold of whatever they want, if they're motivated enough.

## Chapter Eighteen

*Saturday. Late Afternoon.*
*Ethan missing for twenty-one and a quarter hours*

THE SUN WAS HOVERING LAZILY OVER THE ROOFTOPS WHEN Devereaux and Loflin emerged from reception. Drops of water from the hospital's fountain were refracting its beams into tiny rainbows that hung briefly in the air before splashing down into the uniform blue of the pool. Devereaux watched them for a moment, then his focus switched to a man on the far side of the concourse. He was pacing to and fro, and talking rapidly into his phone.

"Look." Devereaux stopped moving. "What's that guy doing here?"

"He was outside the Crane house earlier, with that herd of reporters." Loflin's forehead wrinkled. "I nearly hit him with my car."

"Very nearly." Devereaux took hold of Loflin's shoulder. "Maybe you should have hit him. Ever read his blog? But never mind that now. Come on. Back inside. Fast."

The doors to the Pediatric ER were at the end of a long, brightly lit corridor on the first floor of the main Children's Center building. They were painted to resemble the air lock of a spaceship, and made the entrance look like a warm and welcoming alternative to the inhospitable terrain depicted all around it.

Devereaux badged the triage nurse and asked her if any unidentified seven-year-old boys had been brought in, either unconscious or DOA.

"Nope." The nurse stretched both arms above her head. "None. Been a quiet shift. Boring."

"OK. How about—" The doors slid open behind Devereaux and a man hurried inside. It was Joseph Crane. He was holding the plastic T-Rex that Dillon had been playing with at the house.

"Mr. Crane?" Devereaux stepped across to block Joseph's path. "What's going on?"

"Dillon's toy." Joseph Crane was breathing hard. "He left it in the car. Went to fetch it for him."

"Dillon's here? Why? Blood test?"

"What? No." Joseph screwed his eyes closed for a moment. "This is a day from hell. He fell off the couch. Hit his head on the bookcase. I need to get back to him . . ."

Devereaux moved aside, waited for Joseph Crane to disappear around the corner, then turned back to the triage nurse.

"Dillon Crane. What can you tell us? Accident?"

The nurse shrugged. "Not for me to say."

Devereaux turned to Loflin, and her expression told him she was thinking the same thing. *First one kid disappears . . .*

"Jan, I need you to talk to the Cranes. Take them for a cup of coffee. Both of them. Together. Find out what happened. And don't let them out of your sight till I join you."

Devereaux pulled the curtain open a couple of inches and poked the head of the stegosaurus he'd borrowed from the stash of toys in the waiting area through the gap. He heard a delighted squeal from the cubicle, then drew back the curtain a little farther and slipped inside. Dillon was sprawled out on a hospital cot that had tall guardrails attached to each side. He was still wearing his Mickey Mouse sleep suit. His T-Rex was clutched tightly to his chest. And a bandage had been taped to his forehead, above his right eye.

"Dillon?" Devereaux crouched down so that he was at the same level as the boy. "It's me again. Cooper. Remember me? I came to your house this morning."

Dillon nodded, hesitantly.

"Good." Devereaux smiled. "Now, I was wondering. Would it be OK if my dinosaur plays with your T-Rex? He's called Steggy. He got left behind by all his friends."

"Yay!" Dillon sat up and brandished his T-Rex. "Dino Wars! Come on!"

Dillon grabbed the stegosaurus and played out a furious battle, complete with ferocious cartoon sound effects. The T-Rex was soon victorious, and Dillon ended up on his back with the models collapsed at his side.

"Dillon?" Devereaux reached out and retrieved the stegosaurus. "Steggy really enjoyed that, but he doesn't want to fight anymore. He just wants to be friends. Would that be OK? That they're friends?"

"I guess." A confused expression covered Dillon's face, as if he'd never considered such a possibility before.

"In fact, Steggy was hoping he could come back to your house tonight. Maybe have a sleepover? What do you think?"

"Yay! Dino sleepover!" Dillon sat up and held out his hand. "Can he come? I WANT him to come!"

"Well, I'm not sure." Devereaux pulled a puzzled expression. "Would there be room at your house? Remind me what it's like."

"My bedroom's 'normous. I share it with my brother."

"Your brother Ethan?"

Dillon nodded.

"*Maybe* Steggy could come." Devereaux looked like

he was struggling with a very serious problem. "But I do need to be sure there's enough space. See this cot? Let's pretend it's your room. Yours and Ethan's. Where would your bed be?"

Dillon pointed vaguely to one edge.

"OK." Devereaux nodded. "But help me out a little. Make sure I understand. Pretend your T-Rex is you, and put him where you sleep."

Dillon pushed the T-Rex to the side of the mattress.

"Good job! Now put Steggy where Ethan sleeps."

A sad, confused expression spread across Dillon's face. "Ethan's gone."

"Oh." Devereaux frowned. "Well then, let's try this. Pretend it's last night. Ethan was there with you when you went to bed last night, right?"

Dillon nodded, but looked like he was on the verge of tears.

"Good. So can you put Steggy where Ethan went to sleep?"

Dillon took the stegosaurus and set it gently on the pillow.

"Great!" Devereaux nodded. "Now, who else do we need? Who else was in your room last night?"

"No one."

"I don't just mean when you guys went to sleep. I'm talking about the whole night."

Dillon shook his head.

"What about your daddy? Did he come in and see you and Ethan?"

"No."

"I see. Now, this is important, Dillon. I need to be really clear about this, before I can agree to Steggy sleeping in your room. There needs to be someone else with you, at least for a little while, to help you look after him. So you need to tell me. Who else was in your room last night?"

"Andrew!"

"Andrew was in your room? That's good. Who's Andrew?"

"My hippo. He's blue. He's supposed to snore when you hug him but the thing in his tummy's broken and Daddy says you can't fix it without hurting him."

"Andrew's a toy hippo?"

"Uh-huh."

"I want you to think real hard, Dillon. Who else was there last night, when you and Ethan and Andrew were in bed? It counts even if you heard someone, but didn't see them, OK? Anytime—even for a second—before your mom woke you up this morning."

"A bug came."

"What kind of bug?"

"A stinging bug."

"Did you see it?"

"No. Felt it sting. It hurt."

"OK. So apart from Andrew the hippo and a stinging bug, there was no one else in your room last night?"

Dillon nodded, and a tear formed in the corner of his eye.

"It's OK, Dillon." Devereaux got to his feet. "You did good. Real good, buddy. You can care for the dinosaurs on your own, after all. Steggy can come visit. For as long as you want."

**Extract from Motion to Exclude Evidence Presented at Jefferson County Courthouse, Alabama.**

Counsel for the Defense in the case of the State of Alabama vs. Flynn moves that the quantity of cocaine seized in Ridout's Forest Hill Cemetery should not be admitted as evidence as it was not obtained during a legal search. Rather, it fell from Mr. Flynn's coat in the course of a vicious assault he suffered at the hands of a police officer—Detective Cooper Devereaux—after he had voluntarily surrendered himself into custody.

*This is not the only account of Devereaux beating on suspects. I could give you a bunch of others.*

*Why was Devereaux alone with the suspect in a secluded cemetery?*

*How many other times did this kind of thing go unreported? For every victim who came forward, how many stayed silent? 10? 100? Who knows?*

*See the pattern in this man's behavior, Jan . . . ?*

## Chapter Nineteen

*Saturday. Late Afternoon.*
*Ethan missing for twenty-two and a half hours*

THERE WERE TWO PIZZA BOXES ON LIEUTENANT HALE'S DESK when Devereaux and Loflin walked into her office, just shy of 5:30 pm.

"I figured you guys wouldn't have taken the time to eat." Hale gestured for the detectives to sit.

They both remained standing, each waiting for the other to move first.

"Is there an atmosphere in here?" Hale got to her feet.

"No." Devereaux took a seat, and Loflin followed suit.

"Are you sure?" Hale's hands had moved to her hips.

"No atmosphere, Lieutenant." Loflin fidgeted on her chair. "Just a little frustration, I guess. Ethan's still out there, and we don't seem much closer to finding him."

"I understand." Hale lowered herself back into her chair. "But we've all been here before. We need to keep the faith. Keep the momentum going. And you guys need to eat. Cooper, I got you anchovy. Jan, I didn't know your favorite, so I went with margherita."

"Mine's perfect." Devereaux helped himself to a slice, noticing how grease had escaped from the box and soaked into a heap of half-completed staff appraisal forms. "Thanks, Lieutenant."

"Margherita's great." Loflin took her box and set it on the floor. "I appreciate the thought."

"Good." Hale picked up one of the four stained, chipped coffee mugs she'd accumulated on her desk over the course of the day. "Now, listen to me. I took a call from the ADA while you guys were heading back here. Dillon Crane's blood tested positive for triazolam."

"Damn." Loflin lowered her head into her hands. "I was afraid of that."

"At the hospital, Dillon said he'd been stung by an insect last night." Devereaux took another slice of pizza. "Insect? Needle? Maybe I'm stretching, but—"

"Wow!" Loflin straightened up and made a time-out signal. "*Dillon* said? *At the hospital*? You spoke to him?"

"Of course. Dillon's the only one who might have seen what happened in that bedroom."

"But you can't just talk to a kid without a parent's consent! And Mr. Crane specifically denied his consent. Have you got any idea how many rules you broke?"

Devereaux shrugged.

"Did you find anything else out?" Hale set her mug down.

"Nothing useful." Devereaux shook his head.

"Shame." Hale frowned. "But it's always a long shot, dealing with a four-year-old."

"Forget what kind of shot it was." Loflin's hands balled themselves into fists on her lap. "It was totally irresponsible. Anything you learned would have been tainted. We couldn't have used it, anyway."

"Not in court, maybe." Devereaux dropped a sliver of crust back into the box. "But this isn't Vice. We're not trying to build a case. We're trying to save a kid's life. It was a risk, sure. But it was my call, and I took it. So sue me."

"Did you think about me for even one second?" Loflin banged a fist on her thigh. "You didn't tell me what you were doing! You didn't want me to interview the parents. You just wanted me to distract them. You used me."

"No." Devereaux tried to keep the frustration out of his voice. "We needed to know if it was a coincidence, Dillon showing up in the ER the day after his brother disappeared. That's why I wanted you to talk to them."

"Jan?" Hale prompted. "You picked up on that, right? And . . . ?"

"Even money, I guess." Loflin was regretting her outburst. "Nothing concrete. Let's just say if I had a kid, I wouldn't let it sleep over at the Crane house too often."

"I still like the mother for the triazolam." Devereaux turned back to Hale. "She's a nurse. She has access to drugs. She's used to administering them. And an empty bottle was found at her house. We should bring her in. Turn up the heat."

"No, Cooper." Hale shook her head. "We don't have sufficient cause. She swore to the ADA that she didn't give any drugs to either kid. She's distraught about it. And your last visit to their house probably ended the Cranes' marriage. I want Ethan back, not a lawsuit."

"Then what do we do? We can't sit on our hands and hope the boy just shows up on the doorstep in the morning."

"We're not sitting on our hands, Cooper. We've got a ton of things going on. I'm talking to the FBI. Find-a-Child's working flat out. We're re-canvassing. Searching, physically. The lab's on board. We're getting cooperation from Tennessee. Mississippi. Georgia. Florida. We've got his picture all over social media. And no one's going to stop looking until we find him."

"I get that, Lieutenant. I'm just frustrated."

"We all are, Cooper. But listen. Even before I knew Dillon's blood test result, I figured that if anyone had used triazolam on the Crane kids—anyone other than Mary Lynne—they had to get it from somewhere. So I did some digging. I went back to a bunch of my old contacts. And one name kept coming up. Jake Rutherford."

"My old C.I.?"

"The same. So I was thinking. Rutherford still owes you, right? For saving his skin. You could hook up with him. Encourage him to give you an insight into his customer base."

Devereaux pulled out his phone and took a minute to compose a text.

"This'll bring him out of the woodwork." Devereaux hit Send, then set the phone on the edge of Hale's desk. "Or send him running for the hills. It's fifty-fifty, with that one."

No one spoke for a couple of minutes, then Hale slid out from behind her desk and left the room. Devereaux ate more of his pizza and stared impatiently at his phone. Loflin levered open the lid of her pizza box with her toe, then let it drop straight down again.

Hale reappeared carrying the quarter-full pot from the coffee machine. "What? No one else is going to need it. Any word from Rutherford?"

"Nothing."

There was an electronic *ting,* but it came from Hale's computer, not Devereaux's phone. The lieutenant glanced at her screen, then swapped the coffeepot for her mouse and clicked on something.

"Jan?" Hale helped herself to some coffee. "Your lieutenant left me a voicemail this morning, and now he's following up. He wanted—"

Devereaux's phone vibrated.

"It's Rutherford." Devereaux opened the message. "He's agreed to meet. At McCarthy's old place. In two hours."

"Great." Hale put her mug on the desk. "How do you want to play it?"

"Rutherford's a lunatic." Devereaux slid his phone back into his pocket. "He's completely paranoid. If anything spooks him, he'll split. I should go see him. Alone.

I'm not trying to shut you out, Jan. But we're more likely to get a result if I go on my own."

"Don't apologize." Loflin couldn't keep the disappointment out of her voice. "I can see what you're trying to do."

## Chapter Twenty

THE WOMAN TOOK A MOMENT TO REFLECT ON HER PROGRESS.
There was a lot happening at once. The schedule was out of her control, of course. She'd always intended for the handover to be done much later, when everything was thoroughly prepared. When each step had been taken in its own proper time. But all things considered, she felt cautiously optimistic. All the plates were still spinning. And now she had the opportunity to *show* what she'd been teaching was true. That was so much more powerful than simply *telling*. Maybe it was an omen. A sign that at last the pendulum was swinging back in her favor.

She couldn't get carried away, though. The opportunity was far from a slam dunk. She had almost no time to prepare. To reset the stage at McCarthy's so that her own players were in place, ready to hand the detective the rope he'd need to hang himself. But she'd acted the second she'd received the heads-up. And she had a lifetime of experience to call on.

A lifetime of doing things that other people couldn't even imagine.

## Chapter Twenty-one

*Saturday. Evening.*
*Ethan missing for twenty-five hours*

DEVEREAUX PARKED HIS CHARGER AT THE ENTRANCE TO THE turnoff for Irondale Junior High and walked the final quarter mile down 16th Street South to what remained of McCarthy's International Dubbing Studio.

He moved slowly through the irregular shadows thrown by the trees onto the scrubby, dried-out grass at the edge of the pavement, cut across the street, then paused. A lemon-yellow 1974 Pontiac Firebird had been left in the lee of the strange, circular, long-deserted medical center cradled within the curve of the Crestwood Boulevard on-ramp. Devereaux recognized it as Rutherford's car. But that didn't mean Rutherford was nearby. Or that he was alone. And even if he was nearby, and alone, a man as unstable as Rutherford was not to be treated lightly.

Devereaux continued past the on-ramp until he reached the abandoned parking lot in front of the wrecked McCarthy building. Reginald McCarthy had established the studio in 1934, and at the time it was the largest of its kind outside of Hollywood. People thought he was crazy to build it so far from the West Coast, but he took no notice. He didn't need to be near where films were made, he figured, because he wasn't making any. He'd found a niche. His studio took films other people had made—and paid for, and taken the risk on—and dubbed them into foreign languages, ready for world-wide distribution. His payday was guaranteed, regardless of box office performance. And by keeping his voice artists away from the rest of the industry, he found it easier to pay them less than the going rate.

The business passed from father to son, and over time new services were introduced. Transfers from flammable celluloid film to newer, more stable media was big business for a while. So was copying from film to VHS. And then to DVD. But despite these innovations, McCarthy's was hit hard by lower-cost competition from the East. By 1996 the founder's grandson was ready to quit, but selling the lame-duck company was not an easy proposition. Then fate played its hand. A fire broke out in a storeroom full of long-forgotten reels of celluloid, leaving a very relieved Reginald McCarthy III to retire on his generous insurance payout.

The burnt-out building was never redeveloped. It became a magnet for local kids. For the homeless. For fortune hunters, who'd swallowed the rumors about Norma Jeane Baker working there before her Hollywood transformation and leaving behind a trove of lost movies featuring her voice. But for Jake Rutherford, it offered something else.

A spot in the corner of a noisy, industrial city like Birmingham was never the best place for a recording studio, and things had only gotten louder after I-20 was built almost directly overhead, so McCarthy's had soundproofed the artists' booths extra thoroughly. That made them perfect for conducting Rutherford's brand of confidential business, away from the prying ears of his competitors. And of the police.

Or so he'd thought.

Backing Devereaux's hunch, Hale had called in a favor from a contact in the Birmingham Field Office and arranged for the FBI to run a trial of its next generation surveillance equipment. The trap was set, and Rutherford walked right into it. He was given a choice: Become an informant, or go to jail. He didn't agonize over the decision for very long. And for the next eighteen months he fed Devereaux a steady supply of high-quality leads. Devereaux made so many arrests on the back of them that any other detective would have been guaranteed a promotion. The arrangement continued to run flawlessly, until one day the wheels came off altogether. Devereaux was in the middle of grabbing up some low-level dope dealers at a vacant apartment in Southtown when the enforcer for the local syndicate showed up, suspecting a spy had infiltrated his camp. Devereaux promptly arrested that guy, too, and handed Rutherford a sufficiently authentic beating that his cover wasn't blown. But in the aftermath the Brass decided that Rutherford would no longer be much use to the police department, so Devereaux advised him to leave town. He fled the same day, and promised not to return. Now the guy was back, and Devereaux had to question his motive: Greed? Stupidity? Or something else?

The old studio looked like a virus had swept relentlessly through its innards, eating away every trace of wood and fabric and leaving only the metal and concrete skeleton behind. The only things to survive the fire and the thieves had then been ravished by time, and were now coated with layers of slimy, dark gray dust.

The roof over the non-soundproof sections was missing, so when Devereaux stepped inside what had been the reception area, the yellow light spilling down from the freeway illuminated a trail of footprints leading toward the entrance to the auditorium. Devereaux paused. The Rutherford he remembered would not have left such an obvious sign of his presence.

A brief lull in the nearby traffic allowed Devereaux to catch a sound from the next room. A succession of sharp, staccato hisses. He moved forward to investigate and through the open doorway he saw a man, about twenty feet away. He was spraying graffiti at the bottom of the space where the giant silver screen had once been. It wasn't Rutherford, or anyone else Devereaux had seen before. This guy was around five-ten, and was in his mid-forties. He was wearing pale jeans and an Italian bicycle-racing-team T-shirt. The picture he was painting looked unsophisticated in contrast with the other images that had been sprayed on that wall. It depicted a pair of stick men, and one was cutting the other's head off.

"You!" Devereaux was angry. The chances of Rutherford showing up now were next to zero because of this fool. "Michelangelo! Drop the paint, and get lost."

"I don't think so, *Detective*." The guy turned to face Devereaux, and kept hold of his spray can.

Devereaux heard another sound behind him, and a second guy appeared in the doorway. He was a similar age to the man Devereaux had yelled at, but was two inches shorter. He was a few pounds heavier. He wasn't wearing a jacket over his Public Enemy T-shirt. But he was holding an AK-47 assault rifle.

"What's your next move, genius?" Devereaux stepped across so that he was directly between the two guys. "Shoot me *and* your buddy?"

"No one needs to get shot." The guy with the paint moved nearer to Devereaux, and his shadow closed in from the other side. "We're here to deliver a message, is all. You ready? Here it is. Jacob Rutherford: Leave him alone."

"Where is Rutherford?"

"Do I need to finish my painting?" The guy gestured toward the wall. "In case you're not following, the one on his knees is you. Rutherford never wants to see you again. Are we clear?"

"How do I contact him?" Devereaux edged closer to the guy with the gun.

"One more stupid question, and this'll be pointing at you." The guy reached into his jacket pocket and pulled out a battered Zippo lighter. He flipped it open and struck a flame. Then he squirted his can across it, igniting the propellant and sending out a jet of fire fourteen inches long. He was looking Devereaux in the eye but aiming the spray to his right, showering little flecks of molten paint all over the twisted frames of the folding auditorium chairs.

"All right, then." Devereaux felt a wave of calmness and clarity wash over him, the way it always did at times like this. Times when a solution to a problem became inevitable. A violent solution. His right fist flashed sideways, catching the heavier guy on the temple, then his hand opened and Devereaux grabbed the AK's leather shoulder strap before the guy staggered and fell. "Let's start over . . ."


Loflin steadied herself against the wrecked door frame, took out her gun in case Devereaux spotted her, then held up her iPhone and hit its video capture button. Her new partner had once again manipulated events so that he could be alone with a pair of low-lifes. But there'd be no doubt about the outcome this time. No wiggle room. No ambiguity to cloud the conclusion that Internal Affairs would be forced to reach.

She would make sure of that.

## Chapter Twenty-two

*Saturday. Late Evening.*
*Ethan missing for twenty-six and a half hours*

DEVEREAUX ONLY CARRIED THE STANDARD-ISSUE SINGLE PAIR of handcuffs, so once he had subdued both guys—and after giving them a last chance to tell him where to find Rutherford—he had them sit cross-legged on their hands between the first two rows of chair frames while he called headquarters. He asked for two units, ASAP: A squad car, to transport the prisoners. And a surveillance team to keep watch over Rutherford's Firebird, in case he came back to collect it.

Rutherford must have moved up in the world since Devereaux had last been involved with him. Not only did he have people to do his dirty work for him now, but they weren't stupid. By the time Devereaux caught up with them at headquarters, they'd already asked for their lawyers. Rutherford's resources must have improved, too, because a lawyer showed up within twenty minutes, despite it being close to 10:00 o'clock at night. A lawyer from a respectable firm, not the kind of drug-syndicate shyster Devereaux would previously have expected.

Devereaux hadn't seen Loflin since the meeting in the lieutenant's office. Hale had gone home as well and Devereaux was left sitting behind his desk in the semi-darkness, at a loss about what to do next. It was late, but he wasn't ready to take his foot off the gas. Not without making some worthwhile progress. And he was frustrated after hitting another dead end. He needed a distraction.

He thought about the files he had stashed at his apartment. He wasn't supposed to keep records at home, but, like most detectives, he did. He kept them encrypted, so no one else would understand them. And he didn't keep them for every case. Just the ones his gut told him could lead to trouble down the road. Trouble, like someone trying to torpedo his career.

There was a chance of finding whoever had tried to smear him in those pages, but the prospect of searching through piles of paper wasn't appealing. Especially not after the adrenaline-rush of the confrontation at McCarthy's. Then his mind turned to the old guy who'd collapsed at his building. Talking to him might be a higher priority, anyway. He'd seemed in bad shape. The files would be around later. The old guy might not.

The geriatric special-care unit at UAB was housed in a shiny white corridor with five rooms spaced evenly down each side. The air tasted bitter due to its high oxygen content, and the constant low droning sound from the HVAC system made Devereaux imagine he was on board a spaceship. It was a very modern environment for such ancient inhabitants, he thought. A sign of optimism? Or desperation?

The old guy Devereaux was looking for was in the second room on the right. The sliding glass door sucked back into place on its own after Devereaux entered. He guessed it was designed to keep airborne germs out and, where necessary, the occupant in. There was no danger of this guy trying to go anywhere he shouldn't, though.

He was lying in the bed, still as a board. His eyes were closed. His face was as colorless as the pillow he was propped up against. For a moment Devereaux thought he'd arrived too late. Then a faint movement caught his eye. A weak green line, tracing the guy's pulse across a wall-mounted monitor at the head of the bed, above the more static readings for respiration and oxygen saturation.

Devereaux checked the ID bracelet on the guy's wrist—Bronson Segard, DOB 1-13-38—then took the one seat that was provided for visitors. He looked up and wondered how many more times the feeble EKG signal could limp from one side of the monitor screen to the other before it stopped moving for good. It reminded him of the way an old clockwork robot his father had given him would jerk and stagger when its spring had almost wound down, and he was struggling to push the maudlin image away when his phone buzzed in his pocket.

It was a text from Loflin: *Where are you?*

*News? Ethan?* Devereaux replied.

*No. But we need to talk anyway.*

Devereaux told her he was at the hospital, followed up with the location of Segard's room, then turned back to the monitor. Another eight minutes crept by. The colored lines on the screen began to weave themselves into images of lost, scared children's faces. First his own, from his distant past. Then Ethan's, from the present. Alone. In danger. Devereaux couldn't shake the visions and was ready to leave, hoping a change of scene would clear his head, when he saw the old man slowly open one eye.

"Mr. Segard?" Devereaux stood and leaned over the bed. "How are you feeling? Are you OK? Can you hear me? It's Cooper Devereaux."

"Listen to me." The old man's voice was scratchy and barely audible. "Cooper—she knows."

"Who's *she,* Mr. Segard? And what does she know?"

"She knows who she is. And she killed my partner."

"Your partner? Were you a cop, Mr. Segard? And who knows? Who is *she*?"

"If she finds—" The old man gasped for air. "If she finds out. About your father. There are files. My partner kept records—"

The door slid open and Loflin walked into the room.

"Is this the guy you were telling me about?" She sounded out of breath. "Is he OK? Should I call a doctor?"

For a split second Devereaux could have sworn the old man's eyes grew wider. Then he clamped them shut and refused to say another word. And he stayed that way for ten more minutes, until a nurse arrived and asked the detectives to leave.

Devereaux and Loflin made their way back through the hospital, moving quickly along the deserted corridors until they reached the elevators leading to the reception desk. It seemed to take hours for one to arrive despite Devereaux impatiently pounding on the Call button, so he changed tack and took out his phone to call headquarters. Then he remembered the time. No one senior would be available, and he didn't want his inquiry getting buried at the bottom of some clerk's to-do pile. Lieutenant Hale would be able to put some muscle behind it, but he didn't want to get drawn into discussing his motives. Sending a text would be a much better option:

*Need info. Urgent. Any 70 to 80 y/o male homicide victims reported in Bham in last 2 weeks?*

The night air felt warm on their skin when Devereaux and Loflin finally emerged from the main entrance. The concourse was deserted. No traffic passed by. The fountain had been switched off. The reflecting pool's surface glinted, mirror-smooth, capturing a giant image of the almost-full moon floating high above in the inky sky. Devereaux closed his eyes. He enjoyed the moment of unexpected peace, until it was shattered by an approaching siren. Then he took a step closer to Loflin. "Jan? What did you want to talk about?"

"It's— I don't know." Loflin turned away, trying to stop the confusion from showing in her face. Which was the real Devereaux? The man she'd watched at McCarthy's, who stood in front of her now? Or the one she'd read about a thousand times in the file she'd been sent? Honestly, she had no idea. "It's nothing. Sorry I bothered you. See you in the morning, Cooper."

## Chapter Twenty-three

*Sunday. Early Morning.*
*Ethan missing for thirty-six hours*

IN THE CLOSET. IN THE HALLWAY. JUST ME AND THE BUGS AND
the spiders. Why's Daddy so late?

The front door creaks open.

"This is the police."

It's not Daddy's voice. It's a stranger's. Coming to
hurt me?

"Show yourself. Right now."

I hold my breath. Lie extra still.

"Come on. The kid's got to be here, somewhere.
We've got to find him."

Footsteps come closer. The closet door opens. The
light switches on. Coats swish on the rail. One of Daddy's boots falls over. The thump's real loud. Right above
my head. I don't breathe at all. I squeeze my eyes shut.
Any second now the board will lift up . . .

The stranger's phone starts to ring. If he goes to answer it, he might not find me.

Go! Answer it! Go! Answer it!

The phone keeps ringing. The stranger stays where
he is.

The phone keeps ringing. It's playing Guns N' Roses.
The intro to "Sweet Child O' Mine." Over and over . . .

———

Wait. A phone? Playing Guns N' Roses? In 1976? Relieved, Devereaux slowly floated back to consciousness. Then he reached out a hand, groping around on the nightstand for his cell.

"Detective Devereaux?" The civilian aide from headquarters sounded agitated when Devereaux finally answered.

"Yes. What?"

"Lieutenant Hale wants you in the office. Fourth floor. Right now."

Hale was standing in the corridor, talking on her phone, when Devereaux emerged from the elevator. He nodded and started to squeeze between her and the line of gold-framed portraits of past chiefs of the Birmingham PD, which were screwed to the wall behind her, but she ended her call, grabbed his elbow, and led him away from the conference room door.

"Cooper—quick heads-up before we go in. We've got company this morning. The FBI's here. Two agents. Both trained in profiling. Are you comfortable with that?"

Two years earlier the Birmingham PD had been stumped by a series of murders. Someone had killed the wives of three prominent businessmen, apparently vanishing into thin air between each crime. The media was doing its best to whip the public up into a frenzy of outrage, going all-out to portray the authorities as lead-footed incompetents. More and more manpower was thrown at the case, and eventually a possible suspect emerged. A locksmith who'd worked at each of the victim's houses over the last ten months, and who'd allegedly clashed with the women over the exorbitant unexpected extras he'd tried to charge them for.

Everyone in the department was delighted with this

long-awaited, face-saving breakthrough. Everyone except Devereaux.

Devereaux had spent hours at the crime scenes, trying to put himself in the killer's shoes, and had come up with an alternative explanation for the murders. He'd noticed that the three victims looked very similar, and had developed a theory that they'd been targeted by a local doctor whose own wife—who also resembled the three dead women—had abruptly left him, the previous Christmas Eve.

No one would listen to Devereaux. No one wanted to burst the sudden bubble of optimism surrounding the investigation. His idea was dismissed as psychobabble. So while the rest of the detectives were out chasing the wrong man, Devereaux followed his instincts. He staked out the doctor's house, on his own time, and one night followed him to a mansion belonging to the owner of a chain of cell phone stores. The guy was away in Atlanta, negotiating the purchase of a rival operation. His wife—who could have passed for the doctor's ex's younger sister—was home alone. Devereaux broke into the premises and found her kicking and scratching, the doctor's hands still locked around her throat.

Following this success, Devereaux had been inspired to join the FBI. He'd aced the written exams. Passed the physical. Taken a couple of college courses, to plug some gaps in his résumé. Shone at the interviews. Been told on the phone he was in. Had set his heart on working his way into the legendary Behavioral Science Unit. But at the last moment the rug had been pulled from under him. No one had been able to explain what had happened. No one had even been willing to try. But regardless, Devereaux had found himself back in Birmingham with bridges to rebuild with the police department. And resentment to burn with the Bureau.

"So this means that Ethan was kidnapped?" The cogs were spinning in Devereaux's head. "What happened? What did they find?"

"More about that in a minute." Hale squeezed his

elbow. "Don't jump to conclusions. What I need to know is, can you handle being in this meeting? I only want cool heads in there. I can brief you later, if that would be more . . . productive."

"No. Of course not. I'm glad the Bureau's here."

"Good. In that case, there's just one other thing before we go in. The text you sent me last night? About geriatric homicide victims? I did as you asked. I checked. And there are no records of any. Not in the last month. So whatever that was about, forget it. Focus on getting Ethan back. Nothing else. Are we clear?"

## Chapter Twenty-four

*Sunday. Morning.*
*Ethan missing for thirty-seven hours*

DEVEREAUX HAD ALWAYS THOUGHT OF THE FOURTH FLOOR conference room as the place where enthusiasm went to die.

He visited it as infrequently as he could get away with—usually he just went there for mandatory briefings about departmental reorganizations, which invariably made his job harder—and whenever he did set foot inside he was half expecting to find a team of scientists under the table, searching for the black hole that sucked all the initiative and optimism out of the room's occupants.

That morning, Devereaux felt like he'd walked into a completely different room. Large sheets of lining paper had been taped to the walls from floor to ceiling, creating fifteen separate focus areas. Twelve already had headings, handwritten in thick black ink—*Ethan Crane, Mary Lynne & Joseph Crane, Crane Friends, Crane Family, School, UAB, UAB Hospital, Triazolam, Honda Odyssey, Pedophiles, Cults, Threats / Demands*—and three were blank, held in reserve for future breakthroughs.

Most of the items pinned up so far related to the missing boy, his parents, and their workplaces, but Devereaux knew the sheets would quickly fill up as the investigation continued to gain pace. All the information was processed electronically, too, but computer logic can't entirely replace detectives' intuition. Plus these physical displays gave the case a sense of tangible momentum. They linked all the investigators with everything that was happening and helped to ensure that no clue was ignored and that no connection—however tenuous—was missed.

Loflin was already in the room, sitting at the right-hand end of the beaten-up rectangular conference table. She'd changed into jeans and a white blouse since Devereaux had seen her at the hospital, but the beginnings of dark circles were showing beneath her eyes and she'd clearly taken less time arranging her hair than usual. Devereaux was about to head to the opposite end of the room but she discreetly gestured for him to join her. He paused for a moment, eyeing the two extra-large Styrofoam coffee cups on the table in front of her, then took the adjacent seat.

There were two other people in the room besides Lieutenant Hale, and neither matched Hollywood's typical portrayal of dyed-in-the-wool FBI agents. Neither looked much like a young, thrusting, climb-the-ladder-at-all-costs type, fresh from the assault course at Quantico. Instead, they were older guys, in their early fifties, and both had a calm, safe-pair-of-hands vibe about them. They were wearing chinos and polo shirts, rather than expensive suits. And they were locked in battle with the laptop computer that sat in front of them.

Loflin slid one of the coffee cups across to Devereaux, catching its base on a gap in the veneer and almost spilling it. The room should have been refurbished years ago, and there were competing rumors circulating to explain its continued run-down state. One said that the department's entire decorating budget had been spent on remodeling the commissioner's office. The other, that a meeting room in a different building had been fixed up by mistake. It was a classic example of *chaos or conspiracy*, but Devereaux didn't care which was true. He didn't even care if *either* was true.

Lieutenant Hale settled herself at the head of the table and got straight down to the introductions. The agent with the computer had a shaved head and an inch-long scar to the side of his left eye. His name was Derek Bruckner. The other one, Stephen Grandison, had a nose that looked like it had been broken more than once. Devereaux could have pictured him as a boxer in his younger days.

"OK." Hale cleared her throat. "Now that we know one another, let's start by bringing my detectives up to speed."

"All right." Grandison had a deep, gravelly voice. "Here's what we know. Two minutes after six this morning, a maid went to service a room at a hotel called the Roadside Rendezvous off I-65, near Cullman, Alabama. In the bathroom she found two things: A hydrogen peroxide bottle, which was empty, and a bunch of hairs. Some were bleached. The others were chestnut brown, like Ethan Crane's. And they were curly, also like Ethan's. The maid had heard that the boy was missing, and she'd seen his picture on the news, so she told her boss. He called 911. The evidence was collected, and we're running the hair against a DNA sample from the kid's house to be sure. But there's also this. A description of the car the woman who paid for the room was driving. A Honda Odyssey. White. Same as the one reported on Ethan's street Friday night."

"Anything on its license plate?" Hale asked.

"Nothing useful." Grandison shook his head. "We ran what the driver wrote down when she registered, but it shows as belonging to a silver Jaguar in New York. We called the owner, and he confirmed his car's still in his garage. We've put out an alert on the plates, in case she cloned them, but it's more likely she wrote something down at random rather than give us the license number she's really using."

"What about the desk clerk?" Devereaux put his coffee cup down. "Didn't he or she recognize the boy from when they checked in? Didn't the local police show them pictures?"

"There was no point." Grandison spread his hands, palms up. "They showed up in the early hours of Saturday morning. The night clerk was on duty, and he said that a woman checked into the room. On her own. Their security tapes confirm this, but the woman avoided her face being picked up on camera so we can't compare her image against Ethan's teachers, or any of the other adults in his life. We're sitting the clerk down with an artist, and we'll circulate the woman's image ASAP. Try and get a match that way."

"Did he give much of a description?"

Bruckner consulted the notes on his computer. "He said she was Caucasian. Slim. Five foot four to five-eight. Straight, shoulder-length red hair. When he was pressed he couldn't swear it wasn't a wig, which suggests a possible disguise. And he couldn't pin down her age."

"What about a name?"

"We have a name from the credit card she used. We're running it, but the odds are, it's phony. I'm not holding my breath."

"So where was Ethan at this point?" Devereaux rotated his cup as he thought out loud. "Outside in her car, I guess. On his own? He could have been, if she'd drugged him. Or there could have been a second adult with him. How many room keys did the woman ask for?"

Bruckner rattled his laptop's keys again. "One. But a woman, working alone? That's unusual. Especially if she's planning on killing the kid."

"One key doesn't necessarily equal one adult," Grandison reasoned.

"True," Bruckner conceded.

"And there were signs that both beds had been slept

in." Grandison picked up his thread again. "One by an adult. One by a child."

"When did they check out?" Devereaux spun the cup the opposite way.

"They didn't." Grandison shrugged. "But we figure they've left, because their car and all their stuff's gone."

"This hotel's where?" Hale stood up and started to close the blinds over the room's nine windows. "Near Huntsville? Have we got any idea why this woman would take Ethan in that direction?"

"Have you guys checked on his relatives?" Bruckner turned back to his computer. "Do we know where they are? And Ethan's adopted, right? What about his birth mother?"

"Both natural parents are dead." Devereaux didn't have to check any notes to answer that one. "He has no other relatives."

"What about a crazy woman?" Loflin suggested. "One whose own baby died? Maybe around the time Ethan was born?"

"That's possible." Bruckner nodded. "It's worth following up on."

"If we're lucky, something like that will shake out." Hale turned to Bruckner. "But we can't count on it. What else do you have for us?"

"We got very little of value from either scene, so we're focusing on victimology. That's our best bet right now. We got nothing back from VICAP in terms of known offenders with similar MOs. Our next move will be to revisit the profile we're building, taking out the possibility that the kid ran away, and factoring in the tranquilizer, the prominent role of the woman, and the potential manipulation of her appearance."

"How long will that take?" Concern creased Hale's forehead.

"Too long, probably." Bruckner laid his hands palms-down on the table and fanned out his fingers. "Three million kids run away every year. And sixty thousand get snatched by non-family members."

———

Bruckner closed his computer and the two agents left the room. Devereaux wanted to follow their example, but Hale insisted he stay. She had to head upstairs to brief the captain in five minutes, so remaining on the fourth floor was convenient for her.

"Thoughts?" She looked at Devereaux, then Loflin.

"In a way, this could be good news." Loflin sounded tentative. "If Ethan's been kidnapped, he's most likely still alive. For now, at least."

"I'm not convinced." Devereaux frowned. "There's not much real evidence here. Only the car, the hair, and the peroxide. Those things are suspicious, granted. Especially when this woman lied about the plates when she registered. But it's not conclusive. It pretty much rules out the chance that Ethan ran away, but we shouldn't stop looking at the parents. This hotel sighting's the best lead we've had so far, but for all we know the woman could have been Mary Lynne, planting evidence to persuade us Ethan's still alive. If only we had a better description. Of the woman, or the car. I need to go and look for myself. Poke around a little. Ask a few more questions."

"Agreed." Hale checked her watch. "Both of you go. And hurry. Leave now."

## Chapter Twenty-five

THE WOMAN DIDN'T KNOW WHICH WAS WORSE: THE SWARMS of screeching children. The endless lines. The inane rides. Or the guys stalking around in creepy character costumes. But all these things were minor irritants, next to the problem of the security cameras.

It had been impossible to find out in advance how many there were, though not for a lack of trying. So she came up with an estimate, based on other places she'd taken kids for their treats in the past. At first, she thought her calculations were reasonably accurate. But she soon realized that there were way more cameras than she'd bargained for. They were well concealed, but once she got the hang of where to look, she saw they were everywhere. That was another strike against the place. If someone could sit in a bunker and watch the entire park on TV screens, it took away the advantage of its size. And made it harder to disappear into the crowd, should that become necessary.

She decided that for the rest of their stay, she'd switch wigs and sunglasses four times a day. That might be overkill, but it never hurt to take precautions.

## Chapter Twenty-six

*Sunday. Morning.*
*Ethan missing for thirty-seven and a half hours*

DEVEREAUX WATCHED VULCAN'S BULKY SILHOUETTE SHRINK in his mirror as he accelerated up the first straight stretch of I-65 as it led out of the city to the north, then he slowed to skirt around an ambulance that was tending to the victims of a collision. The future looked bleak for one of them, Devereaux thought. That reminded him of how Vulcan's torch used to glow red on days when there'd been a traffic fatality, back when he was a kid. Although in those days his father had him convinced that the torch changed color every time he took down a particularly dangerous criminal. Smiling at the memory he turned to Loflin, but she had her phone pressed to her ear. She was holding for the manager of the Roadside Rendezvous, to arrange for the night clerk to be waiting for them when they arrived, along with the maid who'd made the original report.

Thirty-three minutes later the detectives parked in the kidney-shaped lot outside the sprawling, single-story hotel and made their way to the reception area, where a tall, miserable-looking man was watching out for them from the side of a bank of vending machines.

"My name's George O'Brien." The man held a skinny

hand out toward Devereaux, then Loflin. "We spoke on the phone. I'm really sorry about this, but Dave isn't back yet. I really thought he would be, but—"

"Dave's the night clerk?" Loflin folded her arms.

"Right. His name's David Day, ironically. He'll be here in a minute, I'm sure. He had to find someone to watch his kid, and— You don't need to know about his personal issues. Geraldine is here, though. She's the one who found the stuff in the room. It's probably meaningless, right? She just watches too much TV and got a little crazy. Would you like to start with her?"

"How long until Dave gets here?" Devereaux glanced at his watch. "No bull this time."

"Two minutes. Five at the outside."

"OK. Well, he's the one who actually saw the woman we need to identify, so I'd rather start with him."

"Geraldine said something about a family thing that— That can wait, right? You want Dave first. Good. Come this way. You can use my office."

O'Brien led them to an unmarked door at the side of the reception counter. He unlocked it, and stood aside for the detectives to enter before him. The room was more storeroom than office, Devereaux thought as he stepped inside. The air was stale, and every inch of wall space was covered with shelves holding boxes of candy bars for the vending machines and toiletries for the hotel store. Packs of soda cans were piled up in the center of the room. Four new commercial vacuum cleaners, still shrink-wrapped, were sitting in front of a tiny window with a view of the highway. The small desk tucked in the corner and its pair of flimsy visitors' chairs looked lost amongst all the clutter, as if they were the things that didn't really belong there.

"Can I get you a drink while you're waiting?" O'Brien's forehead was starting to bead with sweat. "Coffee? Water? Soda?"

"No thanks." Devereaux pointed to the computer that was perched on one corner of the desk. "But you can tell me—that thing. Can you access your CCTV on it?"

"Absolutely. I showed the officers who were here earlier."

"OK, then. Fire it up. I want to watch the footage of the woman checking in Friday night, while we wait for your guy Dave."

O'Brien located the correct section of the file right away and turned his monitor so that the detectives had a better view. The woman appeared almost immediately, and Devereaux felt a physical jolt to see the person who'd most likely taken Ethan—or killed him—transformed from an abstract idea in his head to a realistic image on the screen. She was in the shot for just under forty-five seconds, and not once did she allow her face to be caught on camera. Devereaux had O'Brien play the segment again at half speed, to be sure.

"Smoothly done. No sign of any rings or distinctive jewelry when she handed over her credit card or took her key. And she looks a little short to be Mary Lynne Crane." Devereaux turned to Loflin. "What do you think? I'd say it's someone else. Someone who's done this before."

Loflin didn't reply. Her face was blank, her eyes were locked on the monitor screen, and her teeth had clamped down around her lower lip.

"Jan? You OK?"

"Yes. Sorry." Loflin pulled herself together. "It was disconcerting, watching that. How the woman moved. Like she was gliding along? Then standing stock-still? Not displaying a single signature tick or gesture? It was freaky. Like watching an automaton."

O'Brien's phone rang, and he spoke for a couple of seconds.

"Good news. Dave's arrived. He's parking his car, and he'll be inside in a moment."

O'Brien's phone rang again before the detectives could respond, and this time his expression was less relaxed.

"That was the housekeepers' supervisor. We've got a

problem with Geraldine. She's insisting you talk to her right now, or let her go home to deal with this family situation, whatever it is."

"Of course we *could* make her wait." Loflin turned the monitor back toward O'Brien. "But would she be as cooperative then? You don't need me when you talk to the clerk, do you, Cooper? We should divide and conquer. I'll go see what I can get from Geraldine, then I'll come back here to debrief. Mr. O'Brien, would you ask her to meet me in the room where she found the things this morning?"

"I can do better than that, Detective. I'll take you to the room. She's already there."

Devereaux waited for Dave to knock, then moved around behind the desk after they shook hands. Dave sat on a stack of soda cans, preferring them to either of the visitors' chairs. He was a heavy, unshaven guy in his mid-twenties, and he had on a blue shirt with the hotel's logo embroidered on its chest, a pair of navy pants, and black lace-up work boots. The tip of a tattooed dragon's claw peeped out from his rolled-up sleeve. And he smelled like he hadn't seen the inside of a shower stall for two or three days.

"Sorry, Detective." Dave ran his hand through his sandy hair, which was already beginning to thin at the front. "Couldn't find anyone to watch my boy. Had to bring him back with me."

"Where is he?"

"Outside. In my truck."

"Want to bring him in?"

"No—he's good. He's got his toys with him. Some picture books, too."

"How old is he?"

"Eight."

"Nice age. OK. Let's get down to business. About Friday night. When the red-haired woman checked in to the hotel. Does anything stand out about that?"

"Not really." Dave glanced toward the window.

"David!" Devereaux's voice was suddenly harder. "A boy is missing. His life could be at stake. A cute little guy, not much younger than your kid. So I need you to raise your game, here. Think. Does anything stand out?"

"Like what?" Dave looked thoroughly miserable.

"Did the woman seem nervous? Impatient?"

"No. She just walked in, totally normal. Told me her name. Gave me her credit card. Filled in the form. Took her key. Job done."

"When she filled in the form, did she use her own pen? Or did you lend her one?"

Dave thought for a moment.

"She used her own."

"Are you sure?" Devereaux hadn't seen the woman rummage in her purse on the CCTV footage. "This could be important."

"I'm sure." Dave leaned forward. "See, at night, I move the pot of pens off the counter, 'cause people are always stealing them. So if someone wants a pen to sign or whatever, they have to ask me. And she didn't ask me. She took one out of her jacket pocket."

"What did she look like? Not her clothes. Her face."

"She had this amazing red hair. Maybe real. Maybe a wig. I don't know. And a necklace, like a silver chain with a big star on it. Not a Jewish one. Fancier than that. It sparkled, even though the lights were down pretty low."

"What about her features? Her eyes? Her teeth? Her skin?"

"I didn't really notice."

"Dave, come on. You're a guy. A woman walks into your hotel, and you don't notice what she looks like?"

"It's like I told the other officer. When you're on nights and someone shows up that late, you're just hoping they don't shoot you or puke on the carpet. What they look like isn't an issue."

"OK. What about other people? Did you see the woman with anyone else?"

"No. She was alone."

"All right. One last question, then you can get back to your kid. When you heard that the police had been called to the woman's room this morning, what did you think? Were you surprised?"

"Why should I be?" Dave shrugged. "My job's to take their money, check they sign the form, and give them their key. What they do outside of that's none of my business. I don't ask, and I don't care."

"Fair enough. But if anything comes back to you that doesn't ring. true, give me a call, OK?" Devereaux pushed a business card across the desk. "Remember, this is important. Now, can you point me toward the room the woman had?"

"She was in 113." Dave stood up. "It's a courtyard room. Easier if we walk out together, and I'll show you."

Dave led Devereaux across the reception area. He nodded to the girl who was now behind the counter, opened the side entrance—ignoring the sign that said it was alarmed—and stepped outside. A dusty black 1988 Chevy Silverado Crew Cab was parked in the first space they reached, next to one of the clumps of ornamental bamboo that were set in small, raised brick beds throughout the lot.

"This is my truck." Dave stopped and pointed along the side of the pale brick building. "Room 113's straight down on the left."

Devereaux thanked him but didn't move right away. He was curious to catch a glimpse of Dave's kid, given the parallel with Ethan having also been left alone in a vehicle in that lot. Dave pulled open the truck's rear door and Devereaux saw a little boy sprawled out across the seat. He was lying on an old blue sleeping bag. Six or seven pillows were scattered around. And enough toys littered the cab to last a lengthy road trip.

"Hold on." Devereaux took hold of Dave's arm. "You

said you'd *had to bring the boy back* with you, just now. He spent the night here, didn't he? In the truck."

"No." Dave tried to pull away, and Devereaux could see his pupils starting to dilate.

"Don't lie to me, Dave. That wouldn't be wise."

"Look, I didn't want to bring him! I didn't have any choice! I'm not supposed to be working this weekend, OK? My girlfriend's out of town, and Charlie went out sick, and Mr. O'Brien said he'd fire me if I didn't cover, and my cousin let me down, and—"

"Dave, slow down. I'm not looking to jam you up. Help me out, and no one need know about your kid's little camping adventure. Not social services. Not your girlfriend. Just promise me you won't leave him in the truck again."

"OK. Yes. I will. I mean, I won't. No problem. Whatever you need."

"Good. Now, was your truck parked in this same spot last night?"

"Yes. It's my regular spot. Closest to the door."

"So this is what I'm thinking. There's a great view of the whole parking lot from here. If your kid was paying attention, he might have seen the woman arrive. Mind if I ask him about that?"

"It won't work. He's totally shy. Let me ask him."

Dave leaned into the truck, beckoned the boy to come closer, and started a whispered conversation.

"He says he did." Dave turned back to Devereaux, his face flushed. "He saw the woman drive up in her van, park, and go inside. She came back out and carried a boy, who was asleep, into one of the rooms. Room 113, like I told you. Then she went back to the van and fetched their bags."

"Excellent." Devereaux felt a surge of excitement. "Ask him about the boy. Did he have black, spiky hair?"

Dave ducked back into the truck for a second.

"No." He looked worried this time. "He said it was brown. And curly, not spiky."

"That's OK." Devereaux's heart was beating faster.

"That's good. Now, the van she was driving. See what he remembers about that."

"Not much." It only took Dave a couple of seconds to return with the answer. "Only that it was white."

"What about the license plate? Ask if he remembers it."

Devereaux had hit the Speed Dial button before Dave had even hauled himself all the way into his cab.

"Lieutenant?" He turned away from the sound of the giant V8 roaring into life. "I'm at the Roadside Rendezvous. We have a possible witness. And how's this? We have a partial plate for the Honda."

## Chapter Twenty-seven

*Sunday. Morning.*
*Ethan missing for thirty-nine hours*

LOFLIN WAS PERCHED ON THE EDGE OF THE LEFT-HAND BED when Devereaux reached room 113. She was staring at her phone, almost in a trance, but snapped out of it the moment she heard the door swing open.

Devereaux brought her up to speed on what he'd learned, and asked how things had gone with the maid, Geraldine.

"It was the damnedest thing." Loflin got to her feet. "She was half deranged. A total *CSI* freak. She thinks we live on the set of a giant TV show. I bet she's cried wolf a dozen times about all kinds of wacky things, but this time she actually came up with some genuine evidence. She showed me the trash can where she found the hair and the bleach bottle, and I called the lab tech who's handling it. He confirmed they're taking it seriously."

"How much hair was there?"

"Not much, in the trash. But the techs also found traces in the toilet bowl and the sink trap. Impossible to say how much altogether. But theoretically enough for a major trim. Remember how bushy his hair was in the photo?"

"Did they find anything else?"

"No. Not a thing. Not even any prints. The woman must have wiped the place down incredibly thoroughly. You can still smell the Windex. And yet she left the bottle, and some hair. So she either cut and bleached Ethan's hair, or wants us to think she did."

"Is there anything to prove the hair was actually cut here?"

"No. But you said the woman was seen carrying a kid in here. If Mary Lynne had killed Ethan and was looking to divert suspicion, I doubt she'd be dragging her dead son's body around as a decoy. That's pretty extreme. She didn't seem together enough. My gut says Ethan's still alive, and that he was just here."

"I hope you're right. But I could use some proof."


Devereaux stood in the center of the room, tuned out the background hum from the traffic on the nearby highway, and took a moment to evaluate the place. It was a master class in cynical design. The carpet was an inoffensive, neutral color, but its coarse fabric was chosen more for its ability to stand up to suitcase wheels than to pamper a tired traveler's feet. The bold, abstract patterns on the bedcovers gave the impression of warmth and brightness, but their real purpose was to disguise the stains that would inevitably be left by careless guests. The cushions and pillows were under-stuffed for comfort, but sufficiently oversized to hide the fake wood of the headboard. And the low-wattage bulbs in the lights were there to reduce electric bills, not provide ambience.

Devereaux's eyes were drawn to the bathroom door. Ethan would have spent time alone in there, assuming he'd been brought to the hotel. In which case, he must have known he was in trouble. But would he have been resourceful enough to help himself? To leave a sign? And how could he have taken anything in without the woman spotting it? No. It would be the other way around, if at all. The bedroom. Ethan would have had time alone there while the woman was using the bathroom. So where, exactly? Somewhere concealed, but not too high. Devereaux estimated Ethan's reach if he'd stood on the room's one chair, and his eye settled on the shelf holding the TV. Next to it was a remote control. Devereaux picked it up, blew off the residual fingerprint powder, and pried off the battery compartment cover. Then he set the unit on the bed and pulled on a pair of disposable gloves. Lifted out a piece of paper. Unfolded it. And felt his doubts evaporate.

Hale answered her phone on the first ring.

"I was just dialing your number, Cooper. I have news."

"Me first. Listen to this. I found something the techs missed in the hotel room. A flier for the Casey Jones Railroad Museum in Jackson, Tennessee. It was hidden in the TV remote. Ethan must have put it there. That must be their destination."

"The hotel's on the right kind of route if you're driving from Mountain Brook to Jackson." Hale's computer keys rattled in the background. "And a railroad museum is the kind of place a seven-year-old boy would like to visit. But why snatch a kid and then take him to a museum? Where's the sense in that?"

"What if she's planning on selling him? She could be using the lure of the trains to keep him cooperative before she meets her contact for the handover. There'll be lots of adults with kids at a place like that. They wouldn't stand out, even if Ethan realized something was wrong and started to pitch a fit."

"The museum's not open on Sundays. Damn. Nine am tomorrow's the earliest they could get in. It's a pretty small place. We'll have agents and local PD crawling all over it. The moment the woman shows up with Ethan, we'll grab her. Meantime, I want you back in Birmingham, pronto. Because my news? We've got a hit on the partial plate. In a homicide. A couple of weeks old. Nick Randall's running with it. I want you to sit down with him. Pick his brain. See if you can figure out the connection."

"Will do, Lieutenant. But here's another thought. The railway museum. Could you get the FBI to check its security tapes for yesterday?"

"Sure. Why?"

"The woman never checked out of the hotel. We don't know when she left. She could have already been to the museum. We could be too late."

**Extract from Lieutenant Danielle Hale's Most Recent Annual Departmental Overview Report.**

Lieutenant Hale noted that for the seventh year running, Cooper Devereaux was the detective with the highest number of arrests resulting from information obtained from Confidential Informants. He was also the detective with the highest number of Confidential Informants registered to him in total, and the highest number of new Confidential Informants registered during the course of the year.

*Why is it that Devereaux has such an affinity for criminals, Jan? All these years after his so-called reformation, and he still has so many underworld contacts? How come? And how does this really work? Devereaux busts a crook based on what? Information from another crook? Leaving a vacuum? Who fills it?*

*And what does Devereaux get in return . . . ?*

## Chapter Twenty-eight

*Sunday. Early Afternoon.*
*Ethan missing for forty-one hours*

THE ANTHRACITE GRILLE OPENED ON HIGHLAND AVENUE IN the early '90s, when Five Points South was still a district you thought twice about visiting after dark. The neighborhood has moved on since then, but the Anthracite? Not so much. There's a reason people call it *the bar that time forgot*.

Devereaux first went there the week it opened, and even then the place looked ten years out-of-date. Nothing had changed since. Nick Randall—the detective Devereaux and Loflin were waiting for—had actually called the owner once on a Friday night just after the millennium celebrations, saying he was "the Eighties" and that he wanted his decor back. It hadn't made an impact. But it did make the Anthracite an appropriate place to meet, since Randall's defining feature—aside from his sense of humor—was his inability to show up anywhere on time.

The waitress brought Devereaux a second beer and refilled Loflin's iced tea without waiting to be asked. Devereaux slowed down, rationing his drink out a sip at a time. He was down to the final half inch when he finally saw Randall making his way through the meager lunchtime crowd. It could be a challenge to remain patient around the guy, but he was the longest-serving detective in the unit and he'd put his years to good use. Not much happened on the seedier side of Birmingham that Randall didn't know about.

"Ever seen the movie *Alien,* guys?" Randall slid into the booth alongside Devereaux, almost hitting his head on the display of crucibles and fake pig-iron ingots on the wall above them. He grinned, nodded to Loflin, and signaled to the waitress to bring him a drink.

"Ages ago." Devereaux was hesitant. "Why?"

"Do you know Carlos Camacho? The bastard's been playing tricks on me for years. He's retiring next week. And he thinks he can throw a farewell party without me finding out. Wrong! So, I was thinking: A waitress. She looks like she's six months pregnant. She goes up to him with a tray of drinks. And boom! Her stomach explodes. Some kind of critter—maybe a toy dragon?—shoots out at him. Covers him in raspberry jam. What do you think?"

"Maybe you should just make him a nice cake."

Randall had achieved legendary status back in the days of typed reports when he'd iced his weekly case summary onto a cake and handed it to his lieutenant as a protest against the department's growing bureaucracy.

"I could do both." Randall's drink arrived, and he took a long swig. "Now, enough about Camacho and his party. Nice to meet you, Detective Loflin. And what about you, Cooper? What do you need?"

"Information, Nick. We have a case that might overlap with one of yours. Ours is a missing kid. A seven-year-old boy. We think he was snatched by a woman who was driving a white Honda Odyssey. We have a partial plate, and it matches a vehicle connected to your homicide. We need to figure out the connection, if there is one."

"Interesting." Randall drummed his meaty fingers on the table for a moment. "The Honda in my case was seen driving away from the site where a body was dumped. The vic was dressed like a hooker. And found in Lawnswood. But we're getting nowhere. We don't even have an ID on the body. We've pulled in all the usual pimps and low-lifes, and spoken to a couple dozen of the local girls, but no one said they knew her."

"Anything from the postmortem?"

"Not much. It was pretty clean, so we figure she was new to the game as well as new to Birmingham." Randall took a swig of his beer. "What about the missing boy? Is he the hooker's kid? Could your perp have killed my vic and snatched him?"

"No. He was orphaned when he was three. Honestly, we have no idea what the deal is. We're clutching at straws. The kid's been gone since Friday night . . ."

"I hear you. I'll get back out there tonight. Mix things up a little. Let you know if anything shakes out."

"Thanks, Nick. I appreciate it."

"I'll also reach out to Vice. See what they can tell us about fresh meat coming in from out of town. Maybe whatever kind of trouble killed my vic followed her here."

"Jan has contacts in Vice." Devereaux gestured toward Loflin. "You could ask them, right? Go straight to the horse's mouth. We could save some time, that way."

"Sure." Loflin sounded a little distracted. "No problem at all."

"Good." Devereaux nodded. "Nick, let's stay in touch on this one. Let me know immediately if anything breaks?"

"You got it." Randall eased himself cautiously out of the booth. "Always good doing business with you, Cooper. Now, I've got to get my feet on the street. There's somewhere I need to be."

"One second." Devereaux raised his hand. "Before you go, let me throw a name at you. Bronson Segard. He's seventy-seven years old. He might have been a cop. Does that ring any bells?"

"No. Sorry. Should it?"

"It has no reason to. It's a little left field. This guy Segard showed up on my doorstep yesterday. Then he collapsed. I visited him in the hospital, and he started babbling about a woman killing his partner. The thing is, there's no record of any old retired cops being killed."

"Is it connected to the kid disappearing?"

"If it is, I can't see how. I just don't like loose ends."

"Me neither. There's only one way to deal with a loose end, Cooper. Pull on it. The problem is, once you start, you never know how much will come undone."

## Chapter Twenty-nine

*Sunday. Afternoon.*
*Ethan missing for forty-one and a half hours*

RANDALL LEFT THE ANTHRACITE TO ROUSE A NIGHTCLUB bouncer who was a possible witness in a fatal stabbing he was investigating, but Devereaux couldn't follow him because Loflin had succumbed to all the iced tea she'd been drinking and had gone in search of the ladies' room.

Devereaux was frustrated. He wanted to be moving. Making something happen that would bring them closer to finding Ethan. Not sitting and waiting for someone who was in line to challenge the world record for the longest-ever bathroom break. To make matters worse, the waitress kept hanging around his booth, making small talk and offering him more drinks. In the end, partly to back her off, and partly because Randall's words of wisdom about loose ends were ringing in his ears, he picked up his phone and dialed the number for the BPD Human Resources Department.

"This is Mollie Allen. How can I help?"

Devereaux had gotten to know Mollie when he was struggling to straighten out his arrangements in the aftermath of his failed move to the FBI. They'd talked a couple of times a day for a week and a half, and become good friends in the process, even though they'd never met face-to-face.

"Mollie, it's Devereaux. I need another favor . . ."

"Cooper? You never write. You never call. And now you need *another* favor? Give me one good reason."

"To help out an old, sick, ex-cop."

"An ex-cop? They finally threw your ass out?"

"Not me! I'm looking for someone. A guy who showed up at my home. His name's Bronson Segard. He was born in January '38. And now he's in the hospital, hanging on by his fingernails. I want to make sure he gets taken care of. If I can find out if he has family, I can see to it he has visitors."

"Cooper, I'm only messing with you. Of course I'll help. Are you sure this guy was a cop?"

"Not one hundred percent. But pretty sure. Could you check for me?"

"Hold on."

Devereaux swigged a little more beer, and saw that the waitress was scowling at him now.

"Cooper?" Mollie was back quickly. "I found him. He retired eighteen years ago. He has an address over in Indian Springs, but there's no next of kin listed."

"OK." Devereaux nodded, even though Mollie couldn't see him. "How about this—can you find out who his last partner was? Maybe he could come to the hospital and hang out. Keep his buddy company."

"Hold on. I have to switch systems. Here we go. Looks like Segard had a few partners over the years. As you'd expect. The last one, he was with for over twenty years. A guy called Hayden Tomcik."

"Say that name again?" Devereaux fought to keep his voice level.

"Hayden Tomcik. Do you need me to spell it?"

"No, it's OK. There is one thing, though. *Tomcik* is an unusual name, I know, but could you see if there were any other guys called Tomcik in the department at the same time as Bronson Segard?"

Devereaux heard computer keys rattling at the other end of the line.

"Only him." Mollie sounded confident. "No surprise there."

"OK. Just one last question, then." Devereaux was ashamed he didn't already know the answer. "Could you give me Tomcik's current address?"

## Chapter Thirty

*Sunday. Afternoon.*
*Ethan missing for forty-one and three-quarter hours*

"COOPER?" LOFLIN HAD RETURNED FROM THE BATHROOM TO find Devereaux slumped in the booth, staring vacantly at the phony industrial memorabilia on the far wall. "You OK? You're awful pale all of a sudden."

"Me?" Devereaux got to his feet and picked up his phone from the bench. "I'm fine. Come on. Let's get out of here."

"Hey!" Loflin moved to block his path. "If something's happened, tell me. Don't shut me out."

"Nothing's happened." Devereaux stepped around her and started for the exit. "Come on. Stop wasting time."

Devereaux had left his Charger at the side of Highland Avenue in a wide patch of shadow thrown by the porticoed façade of Temple Emanu-El. He climbed in, fired up the engine, and waited impatiently for Loflin to catch up. The car was rolling before she even had the chance to fasten her belt, and Devereaux made a fast right onto 20th. Then he accelerated hard and didn't lift off the gas for another mile, until they emerged from the concrete bridge that carried the broad swath of rail lines through the heart of the city.

Loflin had expected it would take them seven or eight minutes to reach headquarters, given the weight of traffic. She revised her estimate to six minutes in light of Devereaux's driving. Then five. Then she began to worry they'd end up in the Emergency Room, instead. She tried to find something to distract herself, but the interior of Devereaux's car was as clean as the day it was delivered. There was no dust on the trim. No fingerprints on the glass. No junk in the foot well. Not a thing out of place, anywhere. The relentless tidiness started to feel oppressive, combined with the excessive speed, so Loflin reached for her phone as the last line of defense.

"Was that Vice?" Devereaux pulled over outside headquarters just as Loflin ended her call. "Any luck?"

"Yes and no." Loflin was wary, not knowing what had triggered Devereaux's surge of impatience and not certain it had fully passed. "My old partner was tied up. I didn't speak with him. But he's here, in the building. He'll be free in ten minutes. I should be able to catch him then."

"Good. Let me know the second you finish with him."

"Why? Aren't you coming in?"

"No."

Devereaux had been wrestling with his conscience as he drove. He knew the angle with Vice could be critical in finding out who brought the hooker to Birmingham and then dumped her body out of the Honda that was used to kidnap Ethan. He was still absolutely committed to finding the little boy. But there was one person in the world who was even more important to him. "There's someone I have to check on. I won't be far away. Shout if you need me."

The layout of the streets became less orderly the farther Devereaux drove from the city center. The houses he passed grew smaller, too. They were set back farther from the road, their wooden sides darkened with age and their roof shingles twisted by the years of hot Alabama sun.

Tomcik's house was a similar age to Devereaux's father's. It was in a similar neighborhood, and looked to be the same size and layout. That didn't surprise Devereaux. His father and Tomcik had both been cops. They'd have had similar incomes. Probably similar values and priorities. It made sense that the two guys would pick the same kind of places to live.

Devereaux tried the front door. It opened easily, and he hesitantly crossed the threshold. Once he'd stepped inside, Devereaux was hit by the smell. It was like being in an alleyway behind a low-rent butcher's shop on a summer's day. He took a shallow breath and started to move through the house, taking it room by room. First up was the dining room. Then the living room. And on to the den. In each of them Tomcik's possessions were strewn everywhere in a tangled, chaotic mess of discarded clothes, broken crockery, and scattered books.

Devereaux found Tomcik's body in the kitchen. The old guy was naked. His corpse was slack and floppy, rigor having long since passed. He was tied to a wooden chair. With wire. It was hard to tell what kind, because his flesh was swollen and had started to absorb everything it touched. His skin was pale and mottled, like grains of rice had been forced beneath the surface. His stomach was bloated, and gray-green slime had oozed onto the floor below him. Ants and beetles were feasting on it. Flies were buzzing around him. Maggots were wriggling in his nose and mouth. His chest was covered with burns. And a blood-encrusted tooth lay discarded on the table.

Devereaux cursed the bitter symmetry of the occasion: It was death that had brought him to Tomcik's house now, just as it had brought Tomcik to Devereaux's years ago, when he was a kid. Because Tomcik was the first guy he'd heard in his father's house, when he was six years old.

The guy who'd found Devereaux hiding under the floor in the closet.

The guy who'd broken the news that his father was dead.

## Chapter Thirty-one

*Sunday. Afternoon.*
*Ethan missing for forty-two and a quarter hours*

DEVEREAUX TOOK OUT HIS PHONE. HE DIALED A NINE. AND A one. Then he hit Cancel.

Instead of making the call, he pulled out a chair and moved it around the table to the only clean patch on the floor. And despite the stench, he took a little time to sit in silence with the old guy.

Devereaux hadn't realized it at the time—he was young, and there were plenty of other, more obvious things on his plate—but Hayden Tomcik had kept a close eye on him as he'd passed through his succession of foster homes. The first one, when he was six. The one he'd been moved to, weak with malnutrition, aged nine. The one he'd escaped to at thirteen, after a string of vicious beatings. And the one he'd run away from for good at sixteen, when he'd grown sick of being treated like an unpaid servant.

Tomcik had watched Devereaux stumble through school. He'd seen him graduate, then get cast adrift with no money for college and little prospect of honest work. He'd worried, as Devereaux slid down an increasingly degenerate spiral of friends and acquaintances. And he'd despaired as Devereaux finally, inevitably, sank into a life of crime.

The thing Tomcik hadn't understood right away was that Devereaux's struggles in class didn't stem from laziness. Or a lack of interest. And certainly not from stupidity. Devereaux's problem was his attitude. His refusal to labor through the endless, tedious steps his teachers laid out when he could see a quicker path to the same result. Or, sometimes, a much better result. So in the years that followed school, when Devereaux found himself surrounded with burglars and muggers and car thieves and extortionists, he didn't adopt any of their methods. He came up with his own approach. A more efficient one. He let the other guys commit the crimes. And when they'd amassed enough to make it worth his while he came after them, knocking them out of the game by any means necessary and taking all their proceeds for himself.

One night the latest pack of thugs Devereaux was targeting had tried to stick up a gas station. It was an impromptu thing—none of them had planned it, and as virtual amateurs they hadn't known another gang was lined up to hit the same place at the same time. In the resulting chaos the gas station clerk was killed, and Devereaux was one of those who got rounded up by the police. It wasn't his first skirmish with the law, but this time things were different. The clerk had died in the commission of a crime, so, even though Devereaux hadn't killed him, he was looking at a homicide charge.

Tomcik had been angry. He'd been frustrated. He'd been tempted to wash his hands of Devereaux altogether. He believed each person was responsible for their own actions, and should take what was coming to them. But he also believed in second chances. Especially when there were such extreme mitigating circumstances. So knowing that this was Devereaux's last chance, Tomcik had thrown him a lifeline. He'd given him the chance to do something right. To testify against the guy who'd actually pulled the trigger during the robbery.

Tomcik hadn't been certain that Devereaux would come through. *Honor among thieves,* and all that bullshit. But the twenty-two-year-old Devereaux had stayed the course, and then some. He played his part in the trial. He made a clean break from the people who'd been dragging him down. And he asked Tomcik to help him stay on the straight and narrow.

Tomcik had a lot of connections. He wasn't afraid to use them, and was able to blur some boundaries and massage the problematic areas in Devereaux's record sufficiently to get him accepted into the Police Academy. The attitude back then was it didn't matter too much what lines the recruits had crossed before signing up, as long as they used the experience to make them better cops. But it was also made clear: If they crossed those lines again once they pulled on a uniform, their next stop would be the inside of a jail cell.

Devereaux was older than the other recruits in his class. The path he'd taken had involved a lot more twists and turns. And he was a lot better off, thanks to the heap of cash he'd accumulated in his past life. He felt no obligation to return it, since he'd taken it from criminals. Where he could identify the original victims, he made anonymous donations to offset as much of their suffering as possible. The balance he invested— mostly in property, in the soon-to-be-regenerated heart of the city—to reflect his newly respectable position in the community. And to compensate himself for the years he'd spent in foster care without a cent to his name.

Devereaux and Tomcik had kept in close touch during the years following his time in the Academy, but after that the contact between them became more sporadic. Devereaux earned a series of promotions and grew ever busier. Tomcik retired. The two never argued, or formally agreed to stop seeing each other. It was just the way things worked out. And now it was another entry on the long list of regrets in Devereaux's life.

After ten minutes of vigil, Devereaux stood up. He wondered if he could rely on Loflin to cover for him much longer at headquarters. Then he pulled on a pair of latex gloves and started to retrace his steps through the house. The extent of the damage saddened him. Glass from shattered picture frames was scattered across the threadbare carpets in the hallway and the living room. Books and photograph albums had been flung on the floor, some with their pages torn out or crumpled. Furniture was tipped over. Chair legs were broken and splintered. Cushions were ripped open, with white fluffy stuffing spilling out of the tears. Drapes were torn down and left in heaps, tangled around their broken poles.

It was obvious that the mess had been caused by someone who was searching for something. The scale of the destruction and the fact that Tomcik had been tortured so viciously suggested it was something well hidden. And valuable. The question was, had they found it? Or had the old guy held out until the end, forcing his killer—or killers—to leave empty-handed?

The only room not completely trashed was the bathroom. On his first pass through Devereaux had assumed this was because there was nothing to fling around in there. Tomcik didn't belong to a generation where a man would own a whole bunch of potions and toiletries. But in light of the torture, Devereaux reconsidered. Perhaps the rampaging had stopped because the attacker had found out where to look?

Devereaux examined every detail of the room. There were several cracks in the off-white subway tile that covered the walls, but he put that down to the age of the property. One of the metal legs that supported the basin had been knocked off true, but Devereaux didn't see any way it could have been used to conceal anything. Nothing was tucked away behind the toilet. But finally, at the narrow end of the bath where the horizontal surface had been extended to provide an area for someone to sit, Devereaux spotted a slight scuffing on the linoleum floor.

The bath panel looked like it was attached with screws, but when Devereaux poked its outer edge it pivoted open, dragging gently against the floor. There was a space behind it. In it was a wooden box, like the kind fruit used to be sold in. It was full of files. The marks in the coating of dust suggested that two or three had been disturbed. Devereaux took a photo with his phone, then removed one of the files himself.

It was a police case file. From 1972. It was written in plain English—unlike the ones Devereaux illicitly kept— and it documented how Tomcik and his partner had systematically dismantled a gang of car thieves who broke up the vehicles they stole and passed off the used parts as new to numerous backstreet mechanics.

Devereaux lifted out the crate and took pictures of the cover of each file in turn. He was hoping to identify a pattern, or to work out if anything was missing. In the meantime, he pulled files out at random, sat on the edge of the bath, and continued to read.

The records Tomcik had kept told a fascinating story of life—and crime—in the city over three decades. Some things had changed, such as the kind of items that were stolen, and the relative prosperity of different neighborhoods. Other things hadn't, such as the greed and desperation that bred so much of the misery. It struck Devereaux that he'd stumbled across a window into his father's world, and at that moment he'd have given anything to be sitting in a bar, swapping war stories, getting to know his old man and the era he'd inhabited before his murder.

Then his phone rang.

"Detective Devereaux?" The civilian aide sounded even more excited than she had that morning. "Lieutenant Hale wants you in the conference room, right now. She says there've been developments."

Reluctantly, Devereaux replaced the file and slid the crate back into its hiding place. He returned to the kitchen to say a final farewell to his old guardian angel. Then he made his way along the hallway toward the front door.

## Chapter Thirty-two

*Sunday. Afternoon.*
*Ethan missing for forty-two and three-quarter hours*

DEVEREAUX STOPPED DEAD AT THE BOTTOM OF THE STAIRS.

He thought he'd heard a noise. From the hallway closet. It was in almost exactly the same spot as the one in his father's house, where he'd hidden for the final time that fateful night when he was six. Devereaux realized the closet was the only place in Tomcik's house that he hadn't searched, as if he'd instinctively shied away from it. He shook his head, thinking he was going crazy. Then he heard the sound again. Floorboards creaking. He crept closer. Now he thought he could hear breathing. Worrying that he was losing his mind, he pulled open the closet door.

Two people sprang out at him.

Two women, both with blond hair and high cheek-bones. One was wearing a red leather dress, short, with a neckline that plunged almost to her navel. The other had a white crop-top attached to a miniscule pair of Daisy Dukes with elastic straps.

The women weren't big, but their combined weight was enough to send Devereaux staggering back into the hallway. The one in the dress ducked under his outstretched arm and ran toward the kitchen, tottering on her ludicrous heels. The other kept coming at him, shrieking and spitting and clawing at his eyes. Devereaux regained his balance, batted her hands aside, and shoved her in the chest, pushing her away from him.

"On the floor," Devereaux yelled. "Facedown. Hands where I can see them."

The woman launched herself forward again, trying to kick Devereaux in the crotch. He stepped to the side, blocked her foot with his left hand, and as her body drew level he punched her hard in the side of the head. She flopped down instantly, like a puppet with its strings cut, and slid sideways until she reached the wall.

Devereaux checked her pulse, rolled her onto her side, then ran to the kitchen. The second woman was still there, wrestling with the lock on the back door.

"Stop." Devereaux kept his voice lower this time. "Turn around. Then lie down on the ground with your hands behind your head."

The woman turned and took a step toward Devereaux. She was brandishing a carving knife. The blade was ten inches long. It looked like a sword in her tiny hand.

"You've seen Indiana Jones, right?" Devereaux took out his gun. "Put the knife down."

The woman took another step.

"Hold it right there." Devereaux took aim at her chest. "I'm a Birmingham PD detective. I can shoot you dead, and no one will look at me twice."

The woman stared at him.

"You are . . . detective?" She spoke with a thick, Eastern European accent. "Police?"

"Right. Police. Now put the knife down."

"You have . . . papers? Show me!"

Devereaux wasn't in the habit of taking instructions from people with knives, but there was something confused and frightened in the woman's behavior that struck him as genuine. Keeping the gun on her, he reached into his pocket, pulled out his wallet, and showed her his shield. She stared at it for five seconds. Looked him in the face for another five. Then she dropped the knife and flung her bony arms around his neck.

## Chapter Thirty-three

*Sunday. Afternoon.*
*Ethan missing for forty-three and a half hours*

LOFLIN SHOT DEVEREAUX AN ANXIOUS GLANCE WHEN HE walked into the conference room. She wanted to know where he'd been. Who he'd seen. What he'd done. And whether she'd been a fool to think that maybe—just maybe—she'd been wrong to mistrust him.

Agent Bruckner watched as Devereaux tried to balance on the uneven-legged chair, two spaces down from Loflin. Then he hit a button on his keyboard that chased the FBI seal screen-saver away from the room's large projection screen and replaced it with an aerial view of the Casey Jones Railroad Museum.

"We've reviewed the security tapes from yesterday." Bruckner glanced over his shoulder, not completely trusting the technology. "There was no sign of our targets. Tomorrow, we'll have the place locked down tighter than a drum. The arrangements are all made. But I wouldn't bet a dime they'll show up. Because of this."

The image on the screen dissolved and was replaced by a photograph of a white Honda Odyssey.

"This was taken thirty minutes ago in a parking lot

outside a diner in the outskirts of Nashville. And this was left inside . . ."

The picture dissolved again, making way for a shot of a child's T-shirt. It was from Cedar Point, white, with a silhouette of a roller coaster picked out in red and orange. There was a chocolate stain on the right sleeve, and it looked ridiculously small cradled in one of the Honda's swiveling rear seats.

"Mrs. Crane confirmed it's Ethan's. She said he got the chocolate on its sleeve the day his father bought it for him, but he loved it so much he insisted on keeping it."

"Near Nashville?" Hale narrowed her eyes. "Isn't that a little far north, if you're driving from Birmingham to Jackson, Tennessee?"

"It is." Bruckner nodded. "But perfect if you're switching vehicles, and want access to routes heading northwest. Or northeast. Or southeast."

"Have you had any thoughts on why she took the kid in the first place?" Devereaux stood up and moved to another chair. "If she hasn't killed him, sold him, or demanded a ransom for him, what does she want?"

"Good question." Bruckner crossed his arms. "We've been focusing on that, obviously. But we have nothing conclusive so far."

"Is there any security camera footage of the vehicle they switched to?" Devereaux slid his new chair closer to the table.

"No." Bruckner shook his head. "There was only one camera covering the lot, and it was out of service."

"So we have no idea what kind of vehicle the woman's driving now?" Hale couldn't keep the disappointment out of her voice.

"None." Bruckner frowned.

"Or where she's going?"

"No."

"Whether she's working alone?"

"Not a clue."

"Any prints?"

"None." Bruckner's voice was flat. "The minivan was wiped clean. Even the back of the rearview mirror, which is the place most people forget. But we do have this . . ."

He hit the button again, and a view of the front of the minivan came up on the screen. Complete with its license plate.

"And the best part?" Grandison banged his fist on the table. "It hasn't been reported stolen. So we have an address. Here, in Birmingham. We'll be raiding it in forty minutes' time. And we also have this . . ."

The picture of the van was replaced by a copy of a driver's license. Its owner was described as female, five feet four, one hundred and thirty pounds, with green eyes and brown hair.

"Meet Angela Wild, our new prime suspect. If we're lucky, she left the Honda where she did as cover for bringing Ethan back to Birmingham. But in case she didn't, her name, picture, description, and credit card information are being disseminated nationwide. That way, the second she buys anything, stays anywhere, boards a plane, or rents a car, we'll know. Either way, she can't stay invisible for long."

The agents scooped up their things and left to complete their preparations for the raid. Devereaux hardly noticed them go. He was too distracted by the competing emotions—grief, shock, guilt, regret, anger—that had been fighting for the upper hand since he'd discovered Tomcik's body.

"This raid they're coordinating. What do you think, Cooper?" Hale slapped the table to get his attention. "Cooper! Are you with us?"

"Sorry." Devereaux held up his hand. "It could be just the break we need. I'm praying they hit on something. I doubt they'll find anything at the house, but circulating the ID might help."

"I feel the same. But we have to be practical. We can't afford to lose momentum if their efforts don't pan out. So what else are you working on? How about the connection with Randall's case? Any luck with that?"

"We talked." Devereaux nodded. "One new lead came up. The Honda—and now that we've seen the full license plate we know it's the same one—was used to dump a body. A hooker's. The best anyone can figure, she was new to Birmingham. If she came into town on her own, she's a needle in a haystack. But if she was brought in as part of an organized operation, we might be able to trace her. Find her killer. And through them, find Ethan. Loflin's using her contacts in Vice to sniff around for likely candidates."

"Good." Hale turned to Loflin. "Any luck with that, Jan?"

"I've asked the questions. Now I'm waiting for answers. There are—" Loflin was interrupted by her phone. She answered it, gestured to indicate that the call was important, and left the room to talk.

"Now that it's just you and me, Cooper, I want some answers." Hale folded her arms across her chest. "You brought in two young women this afternoon, right? Why? What's the connection with Ethan?"

"I don't know yet, Lieutenant."

"So what were you doing at some dead guy's house?"

"Remember Bronson Segard? The guy who collapsed at my building yesterday? He told me his partner had been killed. I didn't know who his partner was, then. But today I found out. So I went and checked his house. I found a body, along with the girls."

"Who's the victim?"

"A retired cop."

"Do you have a name? An ID?"

"Hayden Tomcik. He's been dead a while. He was tortured. Then murdered."

"This is the seventy- to eighty-year-old you were asking about?"

"Yes." Devereaux began to pick at a loose piece of veneer on the tabletop.

"Wait." Hale rubbed her temples. "Hayden Tomcik. The name's familiar. Wasn't he . . . He was the one who found your father?"

Devereaux nodded.

"Why didn't you say that? Oh. Wait. You kept quiet in the hope I wouldn't recognize the name, and you'd land the case."

Devereaux didn't respond.

"Cooper, don't ask me for that. The answer's no. You're absolutely *not* investigating his death. It's completely off the table."

"Lieutenant, I—"

The door opened and Loflin came back into the room, her face flushed. "Good news, Lieutenant. That was one of my old partners. A team from Vice has been watching a guy called Sean Carver for the last few months. Carver has a seafood distribution business, with a warehouse out near the airport. Vice says it's a front for other things. Girls, mainly. Also drugs. They're smuggled into the States via Key West, then driven up to Birmingham using Carver's seafood trucks. My guy thinks it's most likely the dead hooker belonged to Carver's organization. Probably those girls Cooper brought in, too."

"Good work, Jan." Hale nodded. "So where is this Carver? We need to throw a net over him, pronto."

"My old partner said Carver's wicked slippery. He dropped out of sight a week ago. But the next shipment from the Keys is expected on Thursday. The team from Vice is going to be waiting for it. The FBI is on board. So's the DEA. My guy says that if Cooper and I want in, he can make that happen."

"Tell your guy yes. Big picture, that's a piece of action we need. But as for Ethan, the clock's ticking too fast. Thursday'll be too late for him. Cooper, Jan, I need you to get back out there. Find out if the dead hooker is definitely connected to Carver's organization. Try and get a lead on Carver himself, too. And do it quickly. Time's getting away from us. Do whatever you need to do."

**Extract from BPD Human Resources File:
Cooper Devereaux.**

Contacted by IRS investigator. Asked to confirm Detective
Devereaux's current salary, unsocial hours payments, etc.
Also whether he is authorized for supplementary employment,
which he is not.

Contact reported to Internal Affairs Division.


*A detective with a Porsche? A penthouse apartment? A cabin in the
woods?*
   *How does he afford all that, Jan?*
   *Where does his money come from?*
   *Fingers / Pies . . . ?*

## Chapter Thirty-four

*Sunday. Afternoon.*
*Ethan missing for forty-four and a quarter hours*

DEVEREAUX GUNNED HIS ENGINE WITH FRUSTRATION AS HE pulled out of the police headquarters parking lot. He slotted his Charger into a gap in the light Sunday afternoon traffic and headed northeast through the incongruous mix of parking garages and ornate office buildings on First Avenue, doing his best to ignore the loaded stares he was catching from Loflin.

He should be the one investigating Hayden Tomcik's murder. Not whoever happened to be next up for catching a case. Tomcik wasn't some random victim. He was a retired cop. A good man who'd done way more than the job demanded. He deserved someone who'd show the same commitment to bringing him some justice, now that he was dead.

Devereaux cursed Randall. If he'd done his job right instead of coasting toward retirement, they'd already know all about this hooker. He cursed whoever had killed her. He cursed the woman who'd taken Ethan. He cursed Segard for collapsing with warnings on his lips, but the explanations locked in his head. He cursed . . . himself, for losing concentration and missing the turn for 60th Street.

"Cooper?" Loflin's attention was drawn to the whiteness of his knuckles on the steering wheel. "Where are we going?"

Sixtieth Street would have led them directly to the spot where the hooker's body had been dumped. Even more annoyed now, Devereaux decided to continue underneath the highway, then turn left into Aviation Avenue. From there he could skirt the cemetery and work his way down Messer Highway to Georgia Road, and start their foray into Lawnwood all over again.

He and Loflin both knew the area well from their days in uniform. They knew the kind of people they needed access to wouldn't surface much before dark. The neighborhood would be relatively benign before then. But daylight would give them a better sense of the drop site, and allow them to spot anything that had changed physically since either of them had last passed through the place.

Devereaux made the turn onto Messer, and one of the industrial buildings on the opposite side of the road immediately caught his eye. It was a warehouse, tucked away between a car rental franchise and a tractor dealer. The signage said *Carver Crustaceans*.

"That place." Devereaux nudged Loflin and pointed to the warehouse. "Is it Carver, as in *Sean* Carver?"

"Could be. We are near the airport. Want me to check?"

"That's OK." Devereaux squeezed the Charger through a pair of bollards at the side of the street and onto a patch of rough, weed-strewn ground. "I'll just head on in. Buy a pound or two of lobster. Ask a couple questions."

"You can't, Cooper!" Loflin grabbed his arm. "Carver's in the wind, and if this *is* his place, we're raiding it on Thursday. If you go in now, you could screw everything up."

"Finding something that leads us to Ethan is way more important than some future raid." Devereaux pulled himself free. "You heard the lieutenant. *Do whatever's necessary.*"

"This is wrong." Loflin took hold of the armrest as if she was afraid that Devereaux would drag her out of the car. "I'm staying here. I want no part of it."

Devereaux walked back toward the building and saw it was formed from two matching units joined together at the center. They had brick walls that were twelve feet tall, and curving corrugated steel roofs that more than doubled their height. The bricks were in poor condition. Much of the mortar was loose, and large patches of the dull brown paint that covered the metalwork were peeling badly.

Devereaux followed the wall until he found a door with a tiny, faded sign, which read *Reception. Please Ring Bell.* Devereaux pressed the button, and while he was waiting for a response, his phone rang.

"Detective Devereaux?" The civilian aide sounded harried. "What do you want me to do? Two of Ethan Crane's teachers have called. The mother of one of his friends has, as well. They found the cards that the uniforms left for them. Do I schedule a time for them to come in? Or do you want to interview them at their homes?"

"Neither." Devereaux tried the handle to the door, but it was locked. "That ship's sailed. Just call them back and thank them for their time."

Devereaux shoved the phone back in his pocket and rang the bell again. Still no one answered. To the right, a security camera had been mounted on the wall. It was eight feet from the ground.

Only eight feet. That kind of sloppy setup was practically an invitation. Devereaux slipped off his jacket and hung it over the camera. Took out an expired credit card he carried specially for this kind of occasion. Used it to ease open the door. Retrieved his jacket. And stepped inside.

The reception area was square, around ten feet by ten. The right-hand side housed a table and an immense, battered wooden counter. The foot-square marble-effect vinyl tiles on the floor were pale from excessive scrubbing, and there was a tank against the left-hand wall. It was home to half a dozen frisky lobsters, each with bright blue elastic bands around its claws. Straight ahead two perforated metal shelves, like the kind people have in their garages, were set on either side of a doorway. The shelves held an array of bizarre seafood memorabilia—stuffed animals, fish-themed board games, lobster-shaped cookie jars, crab tea-light holders—and the doorway was hung with broad multi-colored plastic strips to keep flies from getting through. The place was filled with a powerful smell of fish, so Devereaux figured there must be at least some legitimate seafood business going on in there.

Devereaux picked up a cuddly lobster from the top shelf and pushed his way through the plastic strips, holding the bright red toy in front of him like he was looking for a clerk to help him make a purchase. The doorway led to a storage and sorting room. It felt several degrees colder than the reception area. Three walls were covered with modular industrial shelving, and a roll-up metal door was set into the fourth. It was closed. The floor space was big enough for a forklift truck to operate in, and Devereaux estimated that three-quarters of the shelves' capacity was taken up with cardboard boxes. They were all the same size. He took one down at random and opened it. Inside, along with an extra large cold pack, was a pair of groggy two-pound lobsters.

Devereaux worked his way along the shelves, looking out for any irregularities in the boxes. At the far end, the shelves on the right-hand wall stopped three feet shy of the corner of the room. As he moved closer, Devereaux saw that this was to allow space for another door. He tried the handle. It was locked, but with a little attention from the pick he routinely carried on his key ring, Devereaux had it open within twenty seconds.

The door led to a corridor that ran the whole length of the other half of the warehouse. There were three rooms on each side, with staggered entrances so that people rushing out of them wouldn't run into one another. Devereaux looked into the first one. It was a storeroom, crammed with folded-down cardboard boxes, stacks of glossy catalogs, and giant sacks full of unrefrigerated cold packs.

The next room was a kitchen. Its end wall was kitted out with basic cupboards and drawers in some kind of fake reddish wood, a length of battered melamine countertop, a scratched stainless steel sink, a small microwave oven, and a coffee machine, which was hissing and gurgling as it completed its brew.

But Devereaux hardly noticed any of those things.

Because there was a woman's body lying in the middle of the floor.

## Chapter Thirty-five

*Sunday. Afternoon.*
*Ethan missing for forty-four and a half hours*

THE WOMAN LOOKED YOUNG, MAYBE IN HER LATE TEENS.

She was extremely thin. Scantily clad. She had tall black pumps on her feet. And a plastic Walgreens carrier bag pulled tight over her head.

Devereaux could see that she wasn't breathing, but he dropped the toy lobster and checked for a carotid pulse, anyway. He didn't find one. He took a close-up with his phone, loosened the bag, and pulled it up gently over the dead woman's forehead. He'd expected to see the after-effects of suffocation—blue lips, extended tongue, bulging eyeballs—but the woman's face was flawless. Beautiful, even. It was as if she were just in a deep sleep.

The only unusual aspect was the way her head seemed to be tipped slightly back. Devereaux rolled her partly onto her side, and he saw why that was. The back of her skull had been caved in. She must have died somewhere else—maybe in Florida, or in a truck on the way to Birmingham—and been stored here awaiting disposal. That would explain the lack of blood. The bag must have been to contain any other trace evidence—hairs, splinters of bone, chunks of brain matter—and stop it from leaving a trail back to Carver.

Devereaux was already halfway to his feet when he heard the telltale *click* of a switchblade opening. He spun around and saw a figure standing in the corridor, looking in. A man. He was wearing a blue suit with a white shirt and striped tie. His black Oxford shoes were brightly polished, and there was a blob of mud on the left toe-cap. He had a diamond stud in his left ear. And a knife in his right hand, low down at his side.

The man stared at Devereaux for ten seconds, then raised his knife. He touched it against the pad of his left index finger and nodded as if he was satisfied with its sharpness.

"Sean Carver?" Calm clarity flooded through Devereaux's body and he adjusted his feet, ready to react if the man rushed him.

The man didn't respond.

"Please." Devereaux pointed down at the woman's body. "Tell me you did this."

The man continued to stare at Devereaux. Then in one fluid motion he spun the knife around so he was holding it by the blade and bent his elbow, ready for the throw. Devereaux braced himself, preparing to dive out of the way. The man's arm started to move, but then his body lurched to the side. Devereaux registered the sound of a gunshot. The man jerked twice more. There were two more bangs. Then the knife hit the floor and the man slumped over sideways, with only his feet still visible through the doorway.

Devereaux sprang forward, pressing himself against the wall and drawing his own gun. He held his breath, waiting for the shooter to appear.

Instead, he heard a voice.

"Cooper? Are you in there? Are you OK?"

The voice was Loflin's.

## Chapter Thirty-six

THE WOMAN LOVED THE *REALITY* OF THE PLACE. BUT SHE hated the *name*.

*Business Center.* Exactly how much *business* was being done in that airless basement room at the theme park hotel? Precisely none, was her guess. And there certainly shouldn't be any. Parents were on vacation with their kids. They should be paying attention to their kids. How important did these people think they were? Their companies and practices and partnerships couldn't survive a day or two without them? Over the weekend? If so, they hadn't set them up very well. And given the way most of the children she'd seen were behaving, a little more parental supervision wouldn't go amiss. A *lot* more supervision . . .

On the other hand, free access to a room full of computers? All with high-speed Internet? And no one to keep records of who was using what? It was perfect. The ideal conditions for checking on her webcams.

The boy would be going home, very soon, and she needed to check that everything was still the way it should be.

## Chapter Thirty-seven

*Sunday. Afternoon.*
*Ethan missing for forty-five and a half hours*

"Do you want me to call my delegate?"

On the surface, it was classic Devereaux. An early shot across the bows. A warning that any shit thrown in his direction would be returned, shovel for shovel. But on this occasion—forty-five minutes after leaving the seafood warehouse—he was just going through the motions. His mind was elsewhere. It had drifted away to his cabin. That's where he wanted to be. Not in his captain's office. Even if the guy *had* come in specially on a Sunday . . .

"You're a disgrace." Captain Emrich was a year younger than Devereaux, and from the opposite end of pretty much every spectrum possible. "An embarrassment. A massive operation, totally screwed. Two states. Multiple agencies. Months of manpower. Tens of thousands of dollars. And what's left to salvage? Squat. Have you got any idea how bad this makes us look?"

*Have you got any idea how little I care?* Devereaux thought.

"Detective Devereaux had a good reason to be surveilling those premises, sir." Hale had shuffled her molded plywood chair a few inches closer to the captain's steel-and-glass desk and was leaning a little to the side, as if she was trying to physically position herself between the two men. "We have the welfare of a missing seven-year-old child to consider."

"What about the welfare of the dozen women who were about to be herded here like cattle on Thursday?" Emrich balled up a piece of paper and flung it into the wire mesh trash can near the door. "And the methamphetamine that will now end up on the streets of Birmingham, instead of in the incinerator? How many lives do you suppose will be ruined by your little—"

"I don't know." Devereaux couldn't help himself this time. "How many?"

"It was a rhetorical question. But this isn't. Can you give me one good reason why I shouldn't reactivate your suspension?"

"Yes."

"What?"

"Yes, I can give you one good reason."

"The detective's unique insights have been critical in this case." Hale glared at Devereaux, willing him to be quiet. "By removing him from the equation, the odds of us recovering the missing boy—Ethan Crane—would be seriously reduced. With that at the forefront of my mind, sir, along with the difficulty of explaining such a change in personnel to the press in the event of an unsuccessful outcome, I respectfully request you don't go down that road."

Emrich picked up a tiny wooden rake and paused, holding it an inch above a miniature Japanese garden he kept at a forty-five-degree angle on the corner of his desk. He told people it had been presented to him by the chief of police in Hitachi after he'd been there on a six-month cultural exchange. Devereaux couldn't have cared less about its origin. He was too busy wrestling the temptation to suggest that the captain should repurpose it. As a suppository.

"All right, Lieutenant." Emrich put the rake down without it touching a grain of gravel. "On your own head be it. But one more screwup, and I'll be looking to fill two vacancies."

Hale thanked Emrich and dragged Devereaux out of the office before he could open his mouth again.

"Cooper, sometimes you're your own worst enemy." She led the way to the elevator lobby, and Devereaux noted how much plusher the carpet was on the fifth floor. How there were no scuffs or scrapes on the walls. "You know that, right?"

Devereaux shrugged. He'd seen the likes of Emrich come, and he'd seen them go. Usually to resurface nearby, seeking elected office of some kind. Devereaux thought of them as pre-politicians. Which was the only thing worse than actual politicians, in his book, because there were more of them.

## Chapter Thirty-eight

*Sunday. Late Afternoon.*
*Ethan missing for forty-six hours*

AFTER THE FIRST THREE HUNDRED FEET, THE ROUTE FROM PO-
lice headquarters to the FBI field office was a straight
shot up 18th Street. It was a hair over three-quarters of
a mile. Three minutes in afternoon traffic. Devereaux
would have preferred a fifteen-minute stroll in the fading sunshine to purge his system after the encounter
with Emrich, but Hale insisted on taking the car.

The field office reminded Devereaux of a Hampton
Inn, and as they were clearing security he caught himself
idly wondering if the FBI had used the same architect.
Bruckner was waiting for them at the base of a scruffy
palm in a giant pot at the center of the building's sunny,
circular atrium. He shook Hale's and Devereaux's
hands. Led the way to the elevators. And two floors up,
ushered them into a meeting room. Its air-conditioning
was working overtime, and the place was freezing.
Grandison was already there, wearing a navy-blue FBI
windbreaker. He was waiting on his own at the far side
of a square wooden table that had chairs for twenty.

"Where's Detective Loflin?" Grandison stood as the
others walked in.

"She's not coming." Hale took the seat nearest the

door. "She's downtown. Buried in paper. She was trying to get an angle on Sean Carver ahead of the raid on his place, Thursday. There was a shooting. She's fine, but you know how it goes. There are procedures to follow. We'll have to do without her for a while."

"What happened with the Honda?" Devereaux sat next to Hale, keen to move the conversation along before it touched on the details of the debacle at the warehouse. He didn't need the agents adding their disdain to Captain Emrich's. "Did you find the owner?"

"No." Bruckner hit the space bar on his laptop, waking it up and causing a map of the United States to appear on the far wall. "It was a bust. The owners are in Hawaii, on vacation. Their van was stolen from an off-airport long-stay lot serving Shuttlesworth. But that's minor league—Pee Wee League—compared to what we've come up with now."

"You sound like a game show host." Hale drummed her fingers on the table. "Stop teasing. Just tell us."

"One second." Grandison walked to the door, flipped the lock, pulled down the blind, and returned to his seat. "OK. Now, before we get to the meat of things, we need to talk about profiling for a minute. We're not involved in some kind of black art like you see on TV. What we do is very methodical. We start with a known behavior—as evidenced by a crime scene—and then we extrapolate the kind of person who could have been responsible for it. The better the data, the better the profile we produce. But the problem we have with this case is that none of the crime scenes—the Crane house, the Roadside Rendezvous hotel room, and the Honda Odyssey—have yielded much material. So instead, we've had to go old school. We've been crunching numbers, looking for connections, factoring in experience and intuition. Fortunately both Bruckner and I have plenty of miles on the clock, because at first the task looked hopeless. Nearly three million kids go missing each year. But we weren't deterred. We soldiered on. And what we came up with is this."

Bruckner hit another key and ten red dots appeared on the map. One each in Alabama, New Mexico, California, Illinois, Minnesota, South Carolina, Arizona, and Massachusetts. And two, side by side, in Missouri.

"These are the cases I want to focus on." Grandison nodded to Bruckner. A little girl's smiling face filled the screen for a moment, her thick brown hair pulled back behind an Alice band, which was attached to a large pair of furry Pluto ears. Then the image receded into a frame with an arrow pointing to the dot on the map in New Mexico. "First, chronologically, was Albuquerque. Sixteen years ago, this girl—Miranda Gonzalez—disappeared. She was seven years old. She was last seen climbing into a green station wagon outside her school."

"There was a witness?" Hale was frowning at the girl's photograph.

"Three witnesses. All were under the age of ten. Their stories were wildly inconsistent. The only thing they agreed on was the color of the car."

A second picture flashed up on the screen. It showed a little boy this time, with wild blond hair and traces of ice cream smeared across his plump cheeks.

"The next kid disappeared fourteen years ago, when he was four. His mom had taken him shopping at a mall in the San Fernando Valley, outside Los Angeles. One minute he was by her side while she picked out polish for her toes at a nail salon. The next minute, he was gone. No one saw what happened. No witnesses. And nothing was picked up by the security cameras."

A third picture appeared. A skinny kid with dark, frightened eyes and a tiny head, which was swamped by his crisp, new Cubs cap.

"This little boy was also four. His family lived in the Chicago suburbs, and on spring break thirteen years ago his aunt took him for a day out in the city. They were rounding things off with a walk through the zoo when the kid said he needed the bathroom. The aunt let him go in alone. No one ever saw him come back out."

The fourth picture was of another boy. He was smiling cheekily, with his mouth open and his eyes half shut. He was wearing a baseball cap, too, though his was turned backward, hiding the team logo.

"This little guy—he was five. In Minneapolis. A decade ago. His nanny was walking him to a play date when she was attacked from behind. Hit in the head with something blunt. She woke up in the hospital. The weapon was never recovered, and there'd been no sign of the kid when the paramedics scooped the nanny up. When the parents realized their son hadn't made it to his buddy's they raised the alarm. The local PD traced the motorist who'd called 911 when he spotted the nanny lying at the side of the street. He said he couldn't be certain, but he didn't think the boy was there when he drove past."

The fifth picture was of a little girl. She was looking down at the ground and trying to tug strands of her curly red hair in front of her face.

"This girl's parents took her to Myrtle Beach to celebrate her seventh birthday. That was nine years ago. It was a sunny, summer day and while the kid paddled at the water's edge, her mother and father both fell asleep. When they woke up, there was no sign of the child."

The next kid to appear on the screen had wire-rimmed glasses and was wearing a Cub Scout uniform.

"Is eight too young to go hiking in the Grand Canyon? This kid's Cub Scout leader didn't think so. He took a party of twelve there, seven years ago. Only eleven came back, despite one of the largest manhunts the state has ever seen."

The seventh picture was of a little girl. Her face was dotted with freckles and she was using both hands to stop an adult-sized pair of Aviator sunglasses from slipping down her nose.

"This little angel apparently flew away from her home in Boston, four and a half years ago. She was six, and her parents believed she was a runaway until a sighting of her was reported in DC, heading into the Smithsonian. The witness couldn't recall seeing an adult with her, and the security tapes were no help. Again."

The next picture showed a pair of boys, grappling, arms around each other's necks, off balance and moments from hitting the ground.

"The story's a little different with these guys. They lived in St. Louis. As you can see, they were identical twins. Age twelve. Last year, their family's house caught fire just after one o'clock in the morning. It was the Fourth of July. The busiest night of the year for the fire department. The place burned to the ground. Fire department investigators confirmed it was arson. A heavy-duty accelerant had been used, meaning there was never a chance of pulling anyone out alive. But when the flames were finally put out, only the parents' bodies were found. There was no trace of the boys'. And the police could never uncover any motive for an attack on the family."

The final picture needed no introduction.

It was of Ethan Crane.

"Nine other kids." Hale's voice was hollow. "With Ethan, that's ten. How many of the others were found alive?"

"None." Grandison looked down at the floor. "None of the others were found at all."

## Chapter Thirty-nine

*Sunday. Late Afternoon.*
*Ethan missing for forty-six and a quarter hours*

DEVEREAUX'S EYES WERE LOCKED ON THE SCREEN.

Ethan's picture hadn't shrunk down like the others. It wasn't tied to the red dot over Birmingham by a Power-Point arrow. It was floating in the center of the map. The little boy's fate might still be up for grabs, and Devereaux felt the burden of pulling him back into the room settle on his shoulders. He knew he couldn't allow yet another child to drift helplessly into the shadowy realm of *never found,* and he couldn't shake the macabre procession of lost little faces from his mind.

"What was the common thread?" Hale forced a business-as-usual tone back into her voice. "How did you pull these particular cases out of such a large pool?"

"We factored in as many similarities with Ethan as we could put our fingers on." Grandison seemed relieved to get back onto practical ground. "Ethan's not a runaway, which reduces the numbers by an order of magnitude. He's not a confirmed homicide victim. He couldn't have been kidnapped by a family member, since he doesn't have any. No demands have been made by whoever took him. These things all helped. But the key that un-locked the puzzle was something Bruckner hit on. These kids? They were all orphans. And they'd all been taken in by foster families."

Devereaux felt his chest tighten.

"That could be huge, right?" Hale was looking for the positive. "It has to narrow the field of suspects enormously. Whoever took them, maybe he or she was fostered themselves, as a kid. Or they could have had a kid when they were young, who was taken into foster care. Or they could have applied to foster a kid, and been turned down. Or—"

"All those suggestions are possible." Grandison cut her off. "But they're not the most significant thing. Look at the map. What do you see?"

"The dots are spread around." Hale was reaching. "The abductions took place all around the country."

"Right. Which raises more problems. How did the person know where to find fostered kids? Why did he or she snatch them in so many states and jurisdictions? And let's think about the methods employed. In one case, the offender demonstrated meticulous planning. In the next, he or she appeared opportunistic. In another, organized. Then chaotic. Perhaps persuasive. And finally, extremely violent."

"Couldn't that be a sign of a psychological progression?" Hale asked. "Or a regression?"

"No." Grandison shook his head decisively. "These characteristics—if genuine—are generally considered to be mutually exclusive."

"If genuine?" Hale echoed.

"I'm coming to that, Lieutenant. First, we have to add the timing to the mix. Usually when a person commits a series of similar crimes, the interval between the occurrences diminishes, but is recognizable and to some extent predictable. Here, we can identify absolutely no relationship between the crimes themselves, or anything external—holiday, anniversary, sporting event, etc."

"What if the crimes weren't committed by the same person?"

"If the victims were regular, random kids, I might buy

that. But nine orphans? That's too specific a target to be coincidental. And for them to be abducted by separate killers, each with the skill to ensure their victim's body was never found? No way. My money's on there being one offender."

"Is this connection definite?" Devereaux's throat was dry. "Or is it guesswork?"

"No guidance we produce is *definite*, Detective." Grandison shrugged. "You know that. There's always a margin of error. In this case, the margin's bigger than usual, because of the lack of material we're working with. But Bruckner and I have been doing this a long time. We know what we're talking about. And we've hit on something you absolutely need to take into account, going forward."

"OK. What?"

"Whoever took these other kids—and most likely Ethan—actually can't be profiled."

"What kind of offender can't be profiled?" Hale was growing impatient.

"There are two kinds. One is the hard-core addict, because long-term drug abuse makes their behavior too erratic."

"This doesn't feel like the work of an addict. The crimes are too complex. And they occur over too long a period."

"I agree. Which means we're looking for someone much more dangerous. Someone who's capable of controlling every aspect of their behavior. Who knows intimately which parameters we measure when we're building a profile. Who . . ."

Grandison saw the expression on Hale's face, and suddenly he was reluctant to finish his thought. Devereaux had no such scruples.

"Someone who works in law enforcement," he said.

## Chapter Forty

THE WOMAN'S TRIPS TO THE BUSINESS CENTER WERE BECOM-
ing an addiction.

A welcome distraction, anyway. A respite from the
less-than-encouraging reports she was receiving from
Birmingham. An escape from the Technicolor anarchy
of the theme park. And a reassuring window into the
ordered world she'd spent her life creating.

Webcams were one of her all-time favorite inventions.
She'd used them in her own properties since the first generation had been released. But that kind was bulky and
obtrusive compared to the newest ones. Ones so small
and discreet they can be used pretty much anywhere, as
long as you're not seen installing them. Something that's
not hard to achieve, given how stupid most people are.
How unaware they are of their own security. How they
fall into easily predictable routines, such as leaving their
houses at the same time, every day of the week . . .

The woman liked certainty. Thanks to her oldest set of
webcams, she knew things were still all straight at the
place she'd prepared for the boy. She figured she'd give
him one more day, then it would be time to head over
there.

And thanks to her newest set, she could be sure everything was also lined up and ready for the next lost soul
who needed her help.

## Chapter *Forty-one*

*Sunday. Evening.*
*Ethan missing for forty-eight hours*

DEVEREAUX HUNG UP RATHER THAN LEAVE ANOTHER MES-
sage on Loflin's voicemail, climbed out of his car, and
waved away the middle-aged parking valet who'd been
looking hopefully in his direction. Toward the city center he could see Vulcan, whose illuminated back and
shoulders were peeking through a gap in the distant cot-
tonwood trees. He smiled, remembering how as a kid
he'd snickered at the giant's lack of underwear. Then he
made his way up the path to the last in the line of crumbling nineteenth-century mansions that were still cling-
ing resolutely to the side of the hill.

There was a thick, leather-bound ledger on a table just
inside the entrance to the house, and an old Bakelite
telephone. But no answering machine. And no computer. Such modern devices would ruin the ambience of
the place. And they'd conflict with the owner's dislike of
electronic records.

Paper can't be hacked. And it's so much easier to
burn . . .

The maître d' made a show of paging through the ledger, then turned to Devereaux and shook his head.

"I'm sorry, sir. We have nothing available this evening."

All the principal rooms on the first floor had been combined to maximize the space in the restaurant's dining area. The plaster on the walls was deliberately rough—or rustic, according to the interior designer from Atlanta who'd handled the recent remodeling. It was painted the color of antique parchment and had been complemented by a series of framed watercolors of exotic birds. There were four tables up front, side by side, filling the width of the room. The four beyond them were set end-on, to allow for the bar with its prodigious supply of rare wine, which jutted out from the side wall. And at the far end, six more tables were laid out in a rough rectangle near the entrance to the kitchen.

Of the fourteen tables, only nine were taken.

Devereaux spun the ledger around, opened it, took out a pen, and crossed through the first name he saw.

"Seems you've had a cancelation." He returned the book to the maître d'. "You're lucky I dropped by. Table three? I'll seat myself. Have someone bring me a beer while I take a look at the menu."

Devereaux took a seat at the table in the far corner of the room, beneath the giant image of a toucan. He didn't look at the menu. And nobody brought him a beer. Instead he sat quietly, wondering how useful the little bronze sculpture at the center of the table could be as a weapon, and calculating how long it would be before anything happened. The owner would want him taken care of quickly, before the ripple of anxiety his entrance had provoked could lead any of the other diners to leave. And he'd certainly need to be dealt with before the people who'd reserved his table turned up and caused a scene. It would just depend on where the owner was that night. Whether he had any muscle already on the premises. Or if he'd have to send out to one of his other—more colorful—establishments.

Eleven minutes passed. The glances from neighboring tables grew less frequent, but Devereaux could sense the tension still simmering in the room. People were eating unusually slowly. The waitstaff were moving around as little as possible. Eventually one of them emerged from the kitchen carrying a wooden tray of bacon-wrapped beef tenderloins. He was taking them to a group of sharply dressed guys in their mid-twenties, at the table nearest the door. The aroma was intoxicating and Devereaux was tempted to grab a plate, just to up the ante. He resisted. But when another waiter went by with fresh silverware, Devereaux didn't pass up the opportunity. He reached out and helped himself to a steak knife. Just in case.

After another seven minutes a pair of stocky guys in dinner suits appeared. They emerged from the kitchen and walked straight up to Devereaux. One moved in close to his table. The other hung back, his hands low in front of him and an impassive expression on his face.

"Good evening, sir." The first guy leaned down toward Devereaux and lowered his voice. "It's time to leave, asshole. Get on your feet. Don't give me any trouble."

"Have your boss come out and tell me himself." Devereaux sat back and crossed his arms.

"That's not going to happen." The guy kept talking, quietly, through his fake smile.

"It is, if you really don't want any trouble." Devereaux smiled back. "He comes out and tells me himself. Or I don't leave."

"He's not here."

"Do you know who I am?"

"A cop."

"Not *what* I am. *Who* I am."

"We know your name, yes."

"Then your boss *is* here. Bring him out, and we can all be civilized."

The guy grabbed Devereaux's shirt, just below his collar. Devereaux felt the calm clarity flood through him. He looked the guy straight in the eye. Took hold of his hand. Rotated his wrist, breaking the guy's grip. Forced the wrist around farther and snapped it back, locking the joint. Pushed, until the guy's forearm was flat on the table. Then took the steak knife and drove it down through the guy's sleeve, its tip biting deep into the wood below.

"Let's think this through." Devereaux leaned back in his seat. "You're not going to kill me in here. You know what your boss would do to you for dragging his customers into a murder inquiry. And you don't have what it takes to make me leave. So, here are your choices: You can stay there, all twisted and hunched-up and ridiculous-looking. Or you can have your boss come out here and talk to me. I'd tell you to take your time deciding, but people are starting to stare . . ."

The kitchen door swung open once more, and another man appeared. He was tall, but painfully skinny with sparse, ginger hair and a haggard, pockmarked face. He wore a Zegna suit. An Armani shirt. Prada shoes. A TAG Heuer watch. But none of these trappings could disguise the wariness in his eyes that came from not having had enough to eat or anywhere dry to sleep too many times in his life.

Devereaux stood, and the two men faced each other. Every person in the room expected one—or both—to pull a knife or a gun. Absolute silence filled the restaurant. Five seconds ticked away. Then, at the same instant, Devereaux and the skinny guy sprang forward. Their chests slammed together. They grabbed hold of each other. Twisted around. Grappled. Pushed. Pounded each other on the back. Finally, they both let go.

And by then, they were both laughing hysterically.

## Chapter **Forty-two**

*Sunday. Evening.*
*Ethan missing for forty-eight and a quarter hours*

THE SKINNY GUY'S NAME WAS TOM VERNON.

He'd moved to Birmingham with his family just before turning thirteen, and had made Devereaux's acquaintance the moment he set foot in his new classroom. The two kicked lumps out of each other in the yard at their first recess together. And were inseparable for the rest of their time in school. Vernon had brought Devereaux food each time he'd run away from home, and once had even hidden him in his bedroom closet for three days to escape a winter storm. They'd been closer still during the unsavory years that followed graduation. Right up until the day Devereaux signed up for the Police Academy. After that, their paths didn't cross too often. And that was a situation both had been happy with for a very long time.

Vernon's euphoria lasted another twenty seconds, then his street sense kicked back in. He gestured for his thugs to bring Devereaux, and led the way into the kitchen.

"Twenty years?" Vernon leaned against a stainless steel counter.

"Twenty-four."

"Twenty-four years, and you suddenly want to talk? Now?" Vernon picked up a meat-tenderizing mallet and swung it casually between his fingers. "Tonight? Why?"

"I want to talk, but not here." Devereaux gestured to a trio of chefs, semi-concealed in the plumes of steam that the tiny kitchen's extractor fans were struggling to deal with. "Somewhere private. Just you and me."

"Why?"

"I have some news. You'll be interested. I guarantee it."

"You must have mixed me up with the memory of someone else you turned your back on, *Detective*. I'm not a moron."

Devereaux reached into his pocket, pulled out a gold signet ring, and set it down on the counter. Vernon lifted the ring, held it up to the light, then handed it back.

"You wearing a wire?"

"No." Devereaux put the ring away. "I didn't even bring my gun. Search me, if you like."

Vernon's office had started life as the house's master bedroom. It had a large window that overlooked the street at the front of the restaurant. That was better than security cameras, in Vernon's book. There was no chance of anything being recorded. Two battered leather armchairs were arranged near the window, facing out. A dusty, dark-red rug bridged the space between them. A scarred wooden steamer trunk served as a table. A pair of overflowing ashtrays filled the room with the stench of stale cigars. The only other furniture was a leather-topped desk pushed against the blank wall and a typist's chair tucked under it.

"That ring." Vernon flopped into one of the armchairs. He was happy to speak freely now that he'd established Devereaux wasn't wearing a recording device. "It looked like Sean Carver's."

"It was Sean Carver's." Devereaux took the other chair.

"How did you get it?"

"I took it off his corpse."

"Carver's dead?"

"As a doornail."

The expression on Vernon's face didn't change. "When did he die?"

"This afternoon. At his lobster warehouse."

"Why haven't I heard about this?"

"The Feds are keeping it quiet. Word won't come out till the morning."

"Are you sure? Did you see the body?"

"I'm certain. I shot him."

"Cooper—seriously. What the fuck?"

"The papers will say my partner pulled the trigger, but that's wrong. She's taking one for the team. I'm back from suspension thirty-six hours, and Internal Affairs crawling up my ass on another deadly force inquiry is the last thing I need right now."

"You're telling me you retired Carver. And now you're here. Should I be worried?"

"No. You should be pleased. Because Carver left a vacancy. I'm thinking you could be the guy to fill it."

"You were Carver's guy on the inside? I don't believe you."

"Take a look out of the window, Tom."

"So some police sniper can shoot me?"

"No. So you can see the Porsche parked out front. A brand-new 911. In sapphire blue. License plate DVRX. And then tell me: How many cops do you know who drive a car like that? Cops getting by on their regular salaries, anyway."

"I don't need to see your car, Cooper. After what we went through together I always kept an ear open for you. I heard things, over the years. A couple of guys going down, when maybe they shouldn't have. A half-dozen excessive-force beefs. I figured, maybe if you were a little light on the evidential side of things, you might hand out some justice yourself rather than roll the dice in court. I know how your mind works. But this thing with Carver? This is crazy. This blows me away. What the hell happened to you? Or were you playing us all, right from the start?"

"I wasn't playing anyone, Tom. Have you got anything to drink in here?"

Vernon rose and went to the desk. He pulled out a bottle of whiskey and two chipped, cloudy glasses. Poured a generous measure in each. Handed one to Devereaux. And sat back down.

"Remember when we were young?" Devereaux took a sip of his drink. "People got hurt from time to time. But they always deserved it. Until the thing with the gas station. That clerk? He shouldn't have taken a bullet. That wasn't right. It shook me up. Left me vulnerable. People pissed in my ear. They made me believe, if I had a badge, I could stop other innocent people getting hurt. And at first, that's what happened. But I was naïve, Tom. I was stupid. Gradually, my eyes opened. I saw what was happening. The police were hurting just as many innocent people as we used to. Maybe more. They just didn't get sent to jail."

"You could have come back to us."

"I nearly did. But then I thought: Why? If I stayed where I was, I could have the best of both worlds. Make more money. And not get arrested."

"Makes sense. For you. But me? I'm doing OK as I am. What if I come in with you, and end up like Carver?"

"Carver was stupid. He was greedy. He was impatient. And he didn't listen. I should never have brought him on board in the first place."

"What did he do?"

"Long story short, we needed a new guy down in the Keys to handle importation. Carver came up with a name. I ran some checks. I didn't like what I saw. And I said no. But this guy turned Carver's head with talk of huge extra profits. He thought I'd change my mind when I saw all the extra cash. Instead, the Feds got wind of what the guy was doing, with him being so reckless. He rolled on Carver. Gave up a big shipment we've got coming up from Florida, Thursday night. I found out the Feds are going to raid it. And that Carver's fixing to sell me out, to save his own skin."

"What an asshole. Seriously? You had no choice, Cooper. You had to clean house."

"I did. And now I need to replace Carver. I could find someone new, with all the potential to get bitten in the ass all over again. Or you could do it. What do you say?"

"I'm flattered. But I need to think."

"What's to think about? This is right up your alley. Come on, Tom. Yes or no?"

"Let's get together tomorrow. I'll give you my answer then."

"I need to know now. When word spreads about Carver, the blood'll be in the water. The sharks'll be swarming in no time. No. I can't miss a beat. The transition needs to be seamless."

"What kind of numbers of girls are we talking, here?"

"Nothing you can't handle. You're an experienced guy. You're sensible. I can trust you. The details, we can work out tomorrow. For now, I just need to know: Are you in? Or out?"

Vernon picked up his glass and returned to the desk. He took the bottle and poured himself another measure. A bigger one, this time. He held the glass up to the window and swirled the golden liquid around for a moment. Then he drank it in two large gulps.

"All right. I'm in."

"Good decision, Tom. Now, there's just one thing I need from you to seal the deal. One piece of information . . ."

## Chapter Forty-three

THROUGHOUT HER LIFE, HER CAREER—HER MISSION—THE woman had been a lightning rod for information. She drew it to her, attracting the little details that combined to build the foundations she based her life's work on. It wasn't just a passive process, though. She didn't sit back and wait for knowledge to find her. She sought it out. Dug for it. Cultivated it. Unearthed it from the most unlikely places. Eventually she was even able to harvest it from the electronic brains of the nation's most secret institutions.

The key point was, wherever the information came from, the flow was one way. From elsewhere, to her. It had always been that way. But now, for the first time, that polarity was going to be reversed. And she certainly hadn't been ready for that to happen.

The phone call had been a shock. Not the origin— she'd recognized the caller's number or she wouldn't have answered—but the subject. The demand that was made. The corner she'd been backed into. The information she was now committed to giving up.

Would she have agreed to the meeting, if she'd had more time to think? Probably. A problem had arisen, and it needed to be contained. There was no point hiding from it. That was a lesson life had reinforced, time after time. But she still felt an overbearing sense of dread as she climbed in behind the wheel of her Mercedes.

Dread, of losing control.

Of her life. Her work. And her destiny.

## Chapter Forty-four

*Sunday. Evening.*
*Ethan missing for forty-nine and a quarter hours*

"WAS HE CERTAIN?" HALE PUT HER WHISKEY GLASS DOWN ON Devereaux's coffee table and started to pace.

"No." Devereaux wished she'd stop. The constant pointless movement was annoying him and her shoes were squeaking on his polished wood floor. "How could he be?"

"Do you trust him?" Hale stopped just short of the chrome-plated warship captain's binoculars that Devereaux kept on a stand by the window.

"You know the story of the frog and the scorpion, right? So, no. Of course I don't trust him. But he wasn't lying, either. And he wasn't making it up. The real question is, how reliable are his sources? Better than anything else we've got, is my guess."

"He didn't balk too much when you told him to ask?" Hale returned to the cream suede couch, kicked off her shoes, and tucked her feet up beneath her.

"He took a little convincing."

Devereaux had told Vernon that the price for replacing Carver in his "organization" was information about the dead hooker. It was a long shot. One Hale had been reluctant to ask Devereaux to take, given the people it would bring him in contact with. But she figured if the FBI was right about Ethan Crane's abductor being connected to law enforcement, she had little choice. Not if she wanted the Cranes to see their son alive again.

"Vernon didn't question why you couldn't go through police channels?"

"That was the first thing he questioned." Devereaux took a sip of his own whiskey. "I told him I could do that. But it wouldn't make me look too peachy when the person I was asking about woke up dead the next morning."

"His information was pretty vague. He wasn't trying to put you off the scent?"

"I don't think so. I listened to his calls on the extension phone. He talked to four people. They all said the same thing. No one knew anything about a hooker being killed that night."

"But one talked about the body being dumped?"

"Right. Only one. Vernon ran him through it, back and forth. His story held up. He said a white Honda Odyssey pulled up at the side of the street, right where the body was found the next morning. He saw its side door slide open, and a body-size bundle roll out."

"Did he see who was in the van?"

"It was too dark for a positive ID, but he was sure there was only one person. A woman. Short. Petite. Blond hair."

## Chapter Forty-five

*Monday. Early Morning.*
*Ethan missing for sixty hours*

IN THE CLOSET. IN THE HALLWAY. WHY'S DADDY SO LATE?

*Footsteps come closer. The door creaks open. The light switches on. Coats swish on the rail. Daddy's boot falls over. Right above my head. I don't breathe at all. I squeeze my eyes shut. It gets brighter, even with my eyes closed. The first board's been moved. The second board moves. The stranger's found me! He's going to hurt me. Kill me . . .*

*I try to wriggle away, deeper into the space. The bugs and spiders scatter and run. I can't move. A hand grabs me. A man's. He pulls me. Grabs me with his other hand. He drags me out. Lifts me up. His arms are crushing me. His coat is scratching my face.*

*The man carries me to the kitchen. He puts me on a chair. Pats my head. Crouches down next to me, so his face is level with mine.*

*It's Detective Tomcik. He's younger. He's not dead.*

*"Cooper? Listen to me, son. I have some news. It's important. I'm sorry to tell you this, but your daddy? He's been hurt. Real bad."*

*I don't answer. I can't think . . .*

*"Son? Do you understand me? Your daddy? He's dead."*

Devereaux opened his eyes. He was sitting up. Shivering. Everything around him was black and white, like it had been in his dream. Except the space was bigger. And the objects were different. He could see a white wall, ten feet away. A picture of his cabin. A rack of clothes. Gray drapes, covering a window. Sheets and blankets, soaked with sweat. A silver alarm clock on a nightstand. A cell phone.

A little color began to bleed into his vision, and Devereaux realized he was in bed. In his apartment. Not in his father's house. And then he knew what had happened. His dream had run its course this time. Nothing had interrupted it. He'd reached the moment when he'd found out he was an orphan.

The moment that had haunted him since he was six years old.

Whether he was dreaming, or wide awake.

Crowded from three directions by a jumble of grim, functional parking structures, the Jefferson County morgue looked like a multi-story garage itself, only with its sides blocked in. It was easily the most unattractive concrete building in a city that even the locals agreed had its share of unattractive concrete buildings. Devereaux thought that was appropriate, for a place no one ever wanted to visit.

He was there on Hale's orders, and he was on his own. Loflin was still on restricted duty following the shooting at Carver's warehouse, but Devereaux suspected she hadn't argued very hard against being kept at her desk. She hadn't even shown up there by the time Devereaux had left headquarters, a few minutes previously. He'd tried again to reach her on the phone, and was sick of hearing her voicemail greeting. She'd been incommunicado since before he'd been dragged into Captain Emrich's office the previous afternoon. Devereaux couldn't understand that kind of attitude. With Ethan now missing for close on two-and-a-half days, the only thing that could have kept him away from the investigation would have involved him being on a mortuary slab, himself.

Devereaux parked in the half-empty lot and made his way to the staff entrance. The pavement all around it was cracked and littered with cigarette butts. Devereaux had smoked when he was a kid. It had lost its appeal once he was old enough for it to be legal. And now he smiled at the irony—stepping over things that kill you on your way to the place you go when you're dead.

Devereaux buzzed the intercom and after a couple of minutes Dr. Liam Barratt appeared in the doorway, dressed in faded blue clinical scrubs. Barratt was Birmingham's longest-serving medical examiner. Everything about him was round—his body, his face, his glasses—and he was growing rounder with every passing year. His path had crossed with Devereaux's many times, and Devereaux was amazed at how cheerful the guy always seemed, given what he did for a living.

"Cooper!" Barratt was grinning. "Good to see you, buddy! Come on in."

"Thanks, Liam." Devereaux stepped inside, trying not to breathe the chemicals in the air and hoping he wouldn't be there for too long.

"Tell me what you need." Barratt turned and started past the paintings of sailboats that lined the corridor, his rubber work boots slapping against the rough carpet as he walked. "But talk as we walk. I have a group of medical students on their way in from UAB. We're introducing them to their cadavers today, and I always like to line up a few surprises for them."

"Liam?" Devereaux hadn't moved. "Any chance we could do this in your office?"

Postmortems were to Devereaux what photographs were to aborigines. The first time he'd sat in on one he'd sworn he could see the victim's soul being hosed away down the drain at the end of the procedure along with the blood and chunks of tissue that had been left over when the body was sewn back together. The image had stuck with him through the years and now the slightest glimpse—or whiff—of a mortuary room made him reaffirm his private oath that when his own time came, he'd die alone in the woods where his body could decompose unmolested.

"For you, my old friend, we can." Barratt checked his watch. "I remember how you feel about these things. But if I miss the chance to hide one of my TAs in the cooling locker, ready to jump out on an unsuspecting med student, I won't forgive you."

Barratt's office was small and spotlessly clean. Every inch of three of its walls was crammed with paintings of mountains from all around the world. The fourth was reserved for Barratt's impressive collection of certificates and letters of commendation. Below the most colorful of his diplomas there was an orange Nespresso machine on a small wooden cabinet. Barratt fired it up and cranked out two espressos. He handed one to Devereaux, then slid onto the chair behind his desk, smiling all the while.

"You should come by more often, Detective." Barratt downed his coffee in a single gulp. "I never use the machine when I'm on my own."

"Or we could meet at Starbucks." Devereaux took a sip. "I prefer my hot beverages without the hint of formaldehyde."

"I guess I'm used to it." Barratt chuckled. "But if you didn't come for my hospitality, what do you want?"

"I need to pick your brain." Devereaux set his cup down. "Do you remember a Jane Doe, a prostitute, brought in a couple of weeks ago? She was found on waste ground near 60th Street."

"I half remember the case." Barratt reached for his computer keyboard. "Let me refresh my memory. OK.

Here we go. What about her, Cooper? I already sent a full report to Detective Randall."

"I know. I've seen the report. But I need you to go beyond that. Forget the normal things you look for. For example, was there anything unusual about this girl? Even if it was just a feeling you had? Something you couldn't measure, or quantify?"

"Cooper? What's this about?" Barratt's smile had faded.

"I'm probably clutching at straws here, Liam, but it's important. There's a link to a case I'm working. A missing kid. He's been gone since Friday night, and time's running out for him. We think he was taken by a woman who was driving a white Honda. We think the Jane Doe's body was dumped out of the same car. If we can find out more about the connection, it might lead us to the boy."

Barratt stared at Devereaux for a moment, then nodded. "OK. I'm with you." He consulted his computer again. "Let's see. You've read the report, so you know the facts. Her throat was cut. She suffered a single fatal incision. Probably with a four-inch blade. It left no distinctive marks, so there's nothing to help you there. But if you're looking for my interpretation, I'd say this was a utility killing. There were no hesitation wounds. No defensive wounds. Most likely it was a means to an end. Done for convenience, not in anger or for a thrill. I'd also say there's a high probability the killer has done this before, and treated it as a somewhat routine act. The only other noteworthy aspect you already know—the girl died somewhere else, and her body was moved postmortem."

"That's good, Liam. But is there anything about the victim herself? Where she was from? Her background?"

"I'm pretty sure she's Eastern European. Probably Hungarian. Her dental work is quite distinctive. I couldn't get a match on her records, so she quite likely came here illegally."

"Nick Randall said you thought she was new to hooking?"

"Right. Her clothes spoke for themselves, but she was well fed. There was no indication of drug use. And no recent sexual activity."

"Anything else?"

"Nothing I can think of."

"Please, Liam. Wrack your brains. Go for a walk. Meditate. Pray, if you have to. Just give me something. A little boy's life is on the line."

Barratt took a moment, then shook his head. For the first time Devereaux could remember, a frown spread across his face.

"OK." Devereaux swallowed his disappointment. "Thanks, Liam. Now I need you to do two more things. They might sound paranoid, but trust me, they're vital. First, if you do think of anything, call me on my cell. Right away. Only me. Only on my cell. And second: If anyone asks, I wasn't here today."

## Chapter Forty-six

PHYSICALLY, THE WOMAN WAS EXHAUSTED. BUT EMOTIONally and mentally, she was on top of the world.

She'd stayed up far too late, drugging the little boy, leaving him at the hotel, and driving out to the meeting at an anonymous diner off Route Four. Looking back, she couldn't believe she'd been so nervous! How could she have thought it was too soon to present the information? Yes, it was sooner than she'd have liked. Sooner than she'd planned. But circumstances had overtaken her, and left her no choice. She'd had to lay it all out: The past, the present, and the future. Place her life's work in another person's hands. Close her eyes. And pray.

She needn't have worried. In fact, she should have done it earlier. Of course her message had gotten through! She was a good teacher. Her preparations had been thorough. Her genes were on her side. And so, of course, was the truth . . .

## Chapter Forty-seven

*Monday. Morning.*
*Ethan missing for sixty-two hours*

THREE DOORS HAD BANGED SHUT IN CLOSE SUCCESSION.

Barratt's office. The exit from the morgue. And Devereaux's car. One after another. Each one louder than the one before. Taken together, a perfect summary of the case, Devereaux thought. Every time it felt like he had something to go after, a door slammed in his face. Closing him off. Keeping him from getting closer to Ethan Crane. Wasting a little more time.

Time the little boy might no longer have.

The route from the morgue to police headquarters was a cinch. A straight shot up 14th Street South, past Regions Field and Railroad Park, under the Amtrak lines, and right into First Avenue. It was less than a mile. Three minutes in the morning traffic. Not far enough to be sure. But long enough for Devereaux's attention to latch onto a silver BMW X5. It had left the morgue parking lot right after he did, and then maintained a steady two or three car interval the rest of the way.

Devereaux could have turned into the headquarters parking lot and given the BMW no option other than to drive past. He could have called for backup, and had the driver pulled over. But that wouldn't have suited Devereaux's temperament. He preferred to take a more hands-on approach to anything he perceived as a threat.

He kept going straight on First, then swung left into 26th Street where it ran below the Stephens Expressway for a stretch. There were few other cars on the closed-in lower level, so Devereaux accelerated hard between the thick, exhaust-stained concrete pillars, forcing the BMW to speed up and close the gap between them. There was no doubt now that he was being followed, so when 26th emerged into the fresh air, Devereaux took another left onto Seventh Avenue. He passed the side of Marconi Park and on toward the pale art-deco façade of the courthouse that squatted beyond the intersection, straight ahead. He slowed down for the rough section of pavement where the recent construction hadn't been finished properly, and went left again onto 22nd Street before he reached the library. Then he passed the side of the Cathedral of St. Paul and turned right onto Second Avenue, emerging just a block away from his building.

Devereaux let the Charger coast down the ramp leading to his basement garage, pressed the clicker he kept clipped to his visor, and waited for the roll-up barrier to rise out of the way. He scanned the interior to make sure it was deserted. Satisfied, he pulled a hard right and nosed into the first visitor's space in the row by the wall. The BMW raced past him then stopped dead, its tires squealing harshly in the enclosed space. The barrier began to roll back down. Devereaux slammed the Charger into Reverse and pulled straight back, blocking the base of the ramp. Then he opened his door and stepped out, one hand on his Glock.

It was time to ask some questions.

The BMW's front doors opened simultaneously and two men climbed out. They were both in their mid-thirties, with neat haircuts and smart gray suits. And they were both holding square, black, Sig Sauer pistols.

"Drop your weapon and lie facedown on the ground." The guy who'd been driving had a low, calm voice. "Put your hands behind your head. Federal agents. You're under arrest."

## Chapter Forty-eight

*Monday. Morning.*
*Ethan missing for sixty-two and a half hours*

DEVEREAUX RAISED HIS GUN AND FIRED ABOVE THE AGENTS' heads. The shot was deafening in the enclosed space, but the discomfort was worthwhile. Devereaux had hit his target. A rusty wire cage attached to the whitewashed ceiling. The lightbulb inside it shattered, causing the circuit breaker to trip and plunging the garage into darkness. Devereaux moved to his right, agonizingly slowly to avoid making any sound, and he reached the shelter of a dusty Ford Taurus just as the emergency lights kicked in.

"This is your final warning." The first agent's arms were stretched out and he was snapping his gun from side to side as he scanned the indistinct shadows thrown by the dimly lit rows of cars. "Surrender yourself. Right now."

Devereaux slid his hand into his pocket. His fingers worked their way through its contents until they found the keys to his Porsche. His thumb located the recessed panic button on the rear of the fob. And pressed.

In its stall at the far side of the garage the Porsche's lights began to flash manically fast, staining the fume-ridden air a dirty orange, and its alarm howled like a scalded banshee. Devereaux heard the agents start toward it. He scuttled forward, dodging between the parked cars and the rough concrete wall until he reached the double doors that led to the stairs. He eased the doors open, slipped through the gap, and closed them silently behind him.

Devereaux was about to start up the perforated mesh steps when he spotted a plastic container of rat bait fixed to the floor in the corner, beneath a pair of horizontal, four-inch pipes. He doubled back. Checked the trap's depth. Wrenched it free. Jammed it through the doors' D-shaped handles. Turned back to the stairs. And reached for his phone.

Lieutenant Hale answered on the first ring. "Cooper, where are you?"

"I just left the garage, under my building. Two agents followed me here. They tried to arrest me. What the hell's going on?"

"Damn. Emrich pulled me in and told me, like, one second ago."

"Told you what? That they think I'm the one who took Ethan? This is crazy!"

"No, Cooper. That's not it at all."

"Look, I get that I fit their profile, but check my record! I was here in Birmingham when the other kids disappeared. I've never even been to half those states."

"Cooper! They don't think you took the kid. They were on you for another reason."

"What other reason? What have *I* done?"

"The Feds were watching Vernon last night. They saw you go into the restaurant. They had parabolic mikes trained on the upstairs window."

"But that's bullshit! I told you I went to Vernon's!"

"I know. I explained it to Emrich. He's handling liaison on this personally, with the special agent in charge of the Birmingham Field Office. A guy called Larry McMahan."

"What happens next?"

"You said you got away?"

"Damn right."

"Are either of the agents hurt?"

"No. They're fine."

"Good. Emrich wants you to surrender. Go back. Find them. Emrich's coming down there himself with McMahan, to straighten everything out."

Emrich was coming in person, instead of letting Hale handle it? That couldn't be good. Next stop, Internal Affairs, was Devereaux's guess. And another long spell out of the field.

"Cooper?" The anxiety was plain in Hale's voice. "Did you hear me?"

"I heard you, Lieutenant. No problem."

"Good. Now don't do anything stupid."

## Chapter Forty-nine

*Monday. Morning.*
*Ethan missing for sixty-two and three-quarter hours*

DEVEREAUX WAS PINNED IN BY AGENTS FROM BOTH DIRECTIONS.

He could see a pair of them in a blue Lincoln sedan parked beneath the flag flying from the Longshore Building on Second Avenue, twenty yards from the City Federal's south entrance. He spotted another pair in a black Suburban in the corner of the open lot on Arrington Boulevard opposite the other, east entrance. Devereaux toyed with the idea of creating a diversion. He could call 911 and say someone was trying to drag a kid into a minivan. The chaos that would be caused when the squad cars arrived would give him plenty of opportunities to escape. But he rejected that option right away. It was in bad taste, given that Ethan was still missing. It could hurt the investigation. And it would take too long. The agents he'd trapped in the garage would have the door open any minute. Or they could leave it jammed, use the clicker in Devereaux's Charger to open the barrier, and run up the vehicle ramp.

Arrington Boulevard was his preferred direction so Devereaux made his decision. He stepped out onto the sidewalk. Turned left in front of the City Federal's line of solid, Ionic columns. Glanced across the street as he passed the entrance to the First Commercial drive-through ATM, to make sure the agents had seen him. Made another left into Third Avenue, following the brick and terra-cotta perimeter of the Massey Building, and then ducked between the spiral-fluted pillars and through its fake-gold entrance doors.

Devereaux badged the doorman then stepped past him, heading down a broad, brightly lit corridor with a pale purple carpet that led deeper into the building. He ignored the sober brass plaques identifying the half-dozen law firms that rented suites in the building and followed the carpet all the way to the rear exit, emerging into a scrubby square of grass and rubble where three of the attorneys parked their Cadillacs. Keeping low, he used the cars for cover until he reached the narrow, roughly paved alley that runs between Arrington and 20th. Then he turned right. Sprinted another hundred yards along the uneven surface. And unlocked the entrance to a small garage that was tucked away behind a tattoo parlor.

There were only five stalls in the garage, and Devereaux had rented all of them since before he moved into the City Federal building. He paid cash, a year at a time, money up front, and had never met the landlord in person. He only used one of the spaces. He kept a dull green 2003 Jeep Grand Cherokee there. It had false plates. Smoked glass. A full tank of gas. And a hook-up to a trickle charger to make sure it was always ready to go.

Devereaux fired up the Jeep and drove directly to Shuttlesworth Airport—passing not far from the spot on 60th Street where the hooker's body had been dumped—and pulled into the short-term garage. He parked the Jeep in a grubby two-space alcove next to the entrance to the elevator lobby on level two. He made his way to arrivals. Then took a cab straight back into the city.

———

Devereaux had the cab drop him outside Tom Vernon's restaurant, and he made no attempt to hide as he approached the entrance. The maître d' scowled at him as he stepped inside, but this time Devereaux didn't worry about finding a table. He just told the guy to fetch his boss.

Three minutes later Devereaux was back in one of the leather armchairs in the second-floor office, sitting next to his childhood friend. He held a finger to his lips, then mimed the action of writing on his palm. Vernon nodded and fetched a pen and a pad of paper from the desk.

*FBI listening,* Devereaux wrote.

Devereaux passed the note to Vernon. He read it and nodded. Then he pulled out an antique gold lighter, set the note on fire, and dropped the flaming remains into an ashtray.

*Need to put agreement on ice. Too risky right now. Need to ride out investigation. Find leak. Then talk. OK?*

Vernon read that note, too, burned it, then motioned for Devereaux to hand the pad to him.

*How long will that take?*

Devereaux shrugged.

*How long have Feds been snooping?*

Devereaux shrugged again.

*How got on to me? What they want? Watching my other places?*

Devereaux shrugged for a third time.

*OK.* Vernon wrote quickly. *Contact when time right. You did stand-up thing, warning me. Will remember it.*

Devereaux motioned for the pad.

*Welcome! But need 1 favor. Limo / SUV nearby? Black windows? + driver?*

Vernon nodded.

*Take me to airport? Need to disappear . . .*

Devereaux climbed into Vernon's black Escalade when it pulled up outside the restaurant, fifteen minutes later.

He couldn't see any agents watching from the mansion across the street, but he knew they were there. And as if for confirmation, a silver Ford Taurus had tucked in behind them before they reached the first intersection. Devereaux told the driver not to take any special precautions, so the Taurus had no trouble staying on their tail all the way to Shuttlesworth.

As they approached the airport Devereaux directed the driver to the short-term garage. The Taurus followed, keeping close through the sprawling maze of curving access roads. The Escalade rolled up to the nearest entry machine and the driver reached out and took a ticket. The barrier rose. The Escalade pulled through. Then Devereaux told the driver to stop. Back up. And slam into the barrier hard enough to disable its mechanism, but not to snap its red-and-white-striped arm right off.

A Toyota minivan had pulled up behind the Taurus, penning the agents in. It took them four minutes to extricate their car and negotiate the next entry barrier in line. Four minutes was plenty of time for the Escalade to ascend one level and stop near the elevator lobby, blocking the view of any passersby as Devereaux switched vehicles. And then pull away, with no one else in the world knowing that Devereaux was no longer on board.

## Chapter Fifty

THE WOMAN HAD EXPECTED THE BOY TO BE BOUNCING off the walls when she got back from her lunchtime visit to the Business Center. Especially after the late start they'd made that morning.

A placatory promise of ice cream was already on her lips as she unlocked the door. But when she pushed it open, she was greeted only by silence. For a moment she panicked. Could he have wandered off, despite the warnings she'd drummed into him? Cried for help, and been taken away by another guest? Or a hotel employee? Found where she'd hidden the phone, figured out how to plug it back in, and called the front desk? Or the police?

The woman ventured farther into the room to investigate and heard slow, heavy breathing coming from the bed by the window. It was OK. The boy was propped up on a mound of pillows in front of the TV. *Blue's Clues* was playing, but the sound was off. He was fast asleep.

She leaned against the wall, letting her heart rate return to normal. Then the woman took a step toward the bed, ready to wake the boy and suggest they return to the park. But before she could reach out and touch him, she changed her mind. A little time quietly reading in the air-conditioned room would be much more pleasant than diving straight back into the screeching mayhem outside in the blazing sun.

The woman pulled a novel out of her suitcase and settled into the armchair near the window. She read half a page. Then she put the book back, swapping it for a stack of four worn manila folders that had been buried beneath her clothes. She fanned the folders out on the carpet at her feet and read the faded, handwritten titles:

*Raymond Kerr.*
*Cooper Devereaux.*
*Mitchell Burke.*
*Madison Nesbitt.*

She picked up the last file, opened it, and studied the black-and-white photograph that was stapled inside the front cover. It was of a little girl. She was five years old, with wide, innocent eyes. Fine, pale hair. Crooked teeth. And a beaming smile. The woman hardly recognized her younger self.

She closed the file and ran her fingers across the title, feeling the letters as if they were Braille.

*Madison Nesbitt.*

That was a name she hadn't used for many, many years.

## Chapter Fifty-one

*Monday. Early Afternoon.*
*Ethan missing for sixty-five and a quarter hours*

DEVEREAUX DROVE ALL THE WAY TO THE END OF THE TRACK.

It was a route he used infrequently. He'd stumbled across it by accident years ago when he'd spent one of his suspensions searching for long-nosed armadillos, and he regularly checked that it wasn't shown on any current maps. He tucked the Jeep into the shade of a dense stand of Virginia pines. Checked it would be hidden from the air. And left to cover the final mile to his cabin on foot.

There were two things he was very clear about. He wasn't running. And he wasn't hiding. He'd done enough of both in his past. Now he just needed a place where he wouldn't be disturbed. And he needed time to think.

Lieutenant Hale was the only person in authority who knew about the cabin, and he trusted her completely. She wouldn't betray him. The rest of the machine was still in motion—the Find-a-Child telecanvassers, the legions of officers with descriptions of the boy and the woman, the news segments on TV asking people to be vigilant, the social media outreach, the FBI delving into the law enforcement angle—but Devereaux sensed that something was eluding them. He couldn't shake the images of the missing kids' faces looking down at him from the screen at the FBI field office. They were flashing in his memory like the illustrations in a magic lantern, jumping and jerking from one snapshot to the next. He thought that if only he could slow the pictures down, he'd be able to see what connected them.

Devereaux reached the cabin and went inside. He scooped up a can of beer—part of his supply from the previous week—and lay down on the couch. He needed to broaden his focus. Empty his mind. Allow the individual images to float free, then coalesce into a pattern he could make sense of.

Devereaux breathed deeply, closed his eyes, and thought about the dead woman. The Crane house, with its unlocked back door. Ethan's secret treasures, hidden inside his toy rabbit. The woman waiting outside, in her stolen Honda minivan. The hair dye, left behind in the hotel . . .

His trance was broken by the growl of a car engine and the crunch of tires rolling over dried mud. Devereaux jumped up and moved to the door. A police Charger was fifty yards away, bumping its way up the track. There was still time for him to make a break for the woods. No one knew the area like he did. He could get to his Jeep with minimal risk. Get back to the road. And find somewhere else to hole up until he figured out his next step.

Devereaux didn't move. There was only one car coming, after all. And running blind had never appealed to him. He always liked to know who or what he was up against. So he drew his Glock and watched. The Charger drew closer. It was moving slowly, pitching and rolling over the cratered surface. Then it stopped abruptly, twenty yards away. The driver's door opened. And a woman climbed out.

"Cooper?" Loflin took a tentative step toward the cabin. "Hey, Devereaux? Are you here? It's Jan. We really need to talk . . ."

## Chapter Fifty-two

*Monday. Early Afternoon.*
*Ethan missing for sixty-five and three-quarter hours*

LOFLIN WALKED GINGERLY TO THE CENTER OF THE CABIN'S only room, stood for a moment, then turned three hundred and sixty degrees. Devereaux watched her move, and figured she was searching for something to say that wouldn't sound insulting.

"So." He slid his gun into its holster while her back was turned, then sat down on the couch. "What are you doing here? Why aren't you behind your desk?"

"I told the lieutenant I was out getting counseling."

"But you're not."

"No. Because I want to talk."

"To me? About what?"

Loflin shrugged, then crossed to the wall and poked gently as if she thought her finger might sink into the wood.

"How did you know I'd be here?"

"I didn't. I guessed."

"How did you find the place?"

"I heard the lieutenant giving a uniform guy directions, Saturday, before he came to fetch you. I have a good memory."

"Evidently. So what do you want to talk about?"

Loflin shrugged again, but stayed silent.

Sixty seconds crept past before Devereaux ran out of patience.

"OK, enough." Devereaux stood, took hold of Loflin's arm, and started to steer her toward the door. "You're wasting my time. I need to think. A child's life's on the line, and you're not helping. Go back to headquarters. Go to a bar. To a therapist. Anywhere. Just find someone else to annoy."

"No." Loflin wriggled free and moved back to the center of the room. "Look, I'm not *trying* to be a pain in your ass. It's just—this is important, but it's so hard for me . . ."

"What is?"

"Cooper, I'm exhausted. I was up all last night. My eyes didn't close till dawn. And I'm so conflicted. Working undercover nearly killed me, but at least I knew who I could trust. *No one.* But now . . . Do you know how long it is since I've had a regular partner? And then I get *you.*"

"What's that supposed to mean?"

"Nothing." Her whole body suddenly sagged. "Forget it. This is ridiculous. I should go."

"Not so fast." Devereaux blocked her path to the door. "What did you mean by that? You got *me*?"

"Nothing." Her hands balled into fists. "It's just . . . I really want this to work out. Being in your squad. I want to fit in. To be accepted here. But people talk. I've been hearing things, and, Cooper—I'm worried. About teaming up with you. You're so . . . secretive."

Devereaux's first impulse was to throw her out of the cabin and tell her not to come back. But then he thought back to the phone call he'd made to his old partner, Eddie England. At least Loflin had raised her concerns to his face. She deserved some credit for that. And she looked so thoroughly miserable, standing there in front of him like a heartbroken child. Pools of tears were forming at the bridge of her nose and magnifying the dark circles beneath her eyes. Devereaux could practically feel the anguish and isolation radiating from her.

"OK." Devereaux checked his watch, then gestured to the stack of six-packs. "I'd hit a wall, anyway. A break might help. Grab a beer. You've got as long as it takes you to drink it. Ask me anything you want."

"I don't think so. I should go."

"You should stay. You obviously have questions. And you look like you need a drink."

Loflin hesitated.

"Well, maybe one won't hurt." She went to the pile, separated a beer can from its plastic yoke, and came over to the couch. "There's nowhere else to sit. Can I join you?"

"Why not?"

She turned to lower herself down and her heel knocked into the can Devereaux had started before she arrived. It fell, and a stream of beer started soaking into the wooden floor.

"Shit!" Loflin grabbed the can and set it upright. "I'm such a klutz! I can't believe I did that."

"Don't worry about it. You're not the first person to spill a drink in this place."

Loflin pulled a wad of Kleenex from her purse and started to dab at the dwindling puddle. "Let me at least clean it up."

"Leave it." Devereaux waved his hand. "You're making a clean spot. It makes the rest of the floor look dirty."

"It is dirty. It's filthy! So's this whole place. How can you keep it so nasty when your car's like an OR?"

"That's your first question? That's really what you want to know about me?"

"No. I want to know . . ." Loflin held up the beer can as if trying to gauge how much time the liquid inside would buy her. "Let's try this. Between leaving school and joining the department. What did you do?"

"I got by. Doesn't matter how. Ask me something else."

"OK. You're a detective. How come you can afford a Porsche and a penthouse?"

"Because of my hard work and dedication. Ask me something else."

"How many times have you been suspended?"

"A few. Comes with the territory. Happens to everyone with enough years under their belt. Including you, *Detective*."

"What about marriage? Ever been down that road?"

"No."

"Are you seeing anyone?"

"No. I'm single. And I'm staying that way."

"Oh, you had a nasty breakup. I get it. Recently?"

"No. Years ago."

"How many?"

"Eight."

"Wow." Loflin sipped her beer. "You sure take your heartbreak seriously. What happened?"

"Couldn't tell you." Devereaux shrugged. "One day: Boom. It was over. Bitch cut me out of her life. Refused to even sit down with me and talk about it."

"She was another cop?"

"No. A lawyer."

"Was it a lawyer-cop thing? There's bound to be friction."

"Could have been, I guess. Or maybe I just got on her nerves. I was home a lot, around the time it ended. I figured she liked me better when she saw me less."

"Were you out on disability?"

"No. Suspension."

"Over what?"

"A total crock. I shot a kid, and everyone got in a wad about it."

"Holy shit, Cooper." Loflin's purse slid onto the floor. "A kid? Why?"

"He was going to shoot my partner. In the back. From six feet away. There was no chance he'd have missed. And there was no time to shout a warning. So I stopped him. Then I ran in to secure his weapon. That's when I saw he was fourteen years old. He died in the ambulance on the way to the ER."

"Cooper, that's awful. I'm sorry."

"Don't worry about it. No one forced the kid to pull a gun on a cop. He got what he deserved. I just wish they hadn't suspended me. It sent me stir-crazy. Then when I came back they made me work in the archives for a week, which was even worse."

"That's too bad. Being on suspension does suck. And now you have the Feds coming after you, from what I heard this morning."

"I'm not worried about them. Emrich could have stopped the whole thing before it got started if he didn't have such a huge hard-on for me. No, what we need is to turn the spotlight back on the Feds. See how far they've gotten with finding the one of their own who took the orphans."

"You think this woman is a Fed?"

"She has to be. She couldn't be a cop."

"Why not?" Loflin finished her beer and set the can on the floor. "A cop could have moved to each of the states where a kid disappeared. There was enough time between cases."

"I guess." Devereaux stood and fetched another beer for each of them. "But the whole thing's weird. Why snatch only orphans? And why those particular kids?"

"Opportunity. She took a kid in each city she was posted to."

"Maybe. But how did she single out the orphans? You'd think orphanages would be easier targets. Foster records are hard to get your hands on. And why did only one kid disappear from each state?"

"Maybe more disappeared, but we don't know about them yet?" Loflin put her drink down, unopened.

"Aside from Ethan, these aren't new offenses. One slipping through the net, I could believe. In one place. But at least one in eight other states? I can't see the Feds missing that many."

"We're assuming these kids are dead." Loflin got up

and started to pace. "What if they're not? They could have been kept alive. Taken somewhere else. That would explain the lack of bodies."

"But what made them targets in the first place? They were different ages. Different genders. They had different economic backgrounds. And they were from different locations. There must have been other kids in foster care in those cities. Why pick those specific kids?"

"Interesting angle." Loflin came to a stop, halfway between Devereaux and the door. "We should look at Ethan again. Start digging."

"Not *we*." Devereaux glanced down at the floor where the beer had spilled, then met Loflin's eye. "*You*. There's someone I need to talk to."

## Chapter Fifty-three

THE WOMAN WAS BEING A LITTLE SELF-INDULGENT, SHE REAL-
ized.

She'd come to the Business Center to attend to some
practical matters, but before she got around to them she
allowed herself the luxury of an extra few minutes with
her webcams.

The little girl was being home-schooled, just as the
woman had been herself for a time. She didn't know
why. And she didn't really care. The kid seemed happy
enough. The mother treated her well, from what she
could see. Right now, for example, it was lunchtime. The
girl was out in the yard, playing with her dolls, acting
out make-believe scenarios the way seven-year-olds do.

The woman congratulated herself. She'd done well,
given how little time she'd had to prepare for this addi-
tional case. That was the benefit of experience. These
things became second nature. She'd thought about passing this job to her successor, but in the end decided to
handle it herself. One more go-around, before she
handed over the reins. Because there were two unique
aspects to this scenario that fascinated her: Where the
girl was living, and who she was living with.

The woman had never had to save two unrelated kids
in the same city before.

Or rescue a kid from its own natural mother.

## Chapter Fifty-four

*Monday. Early Afternoon.*
*Ethan missing for sixty-six and a quarter hours*

DEVEREAUX'S CELL NETWORK JUST ABOUT STRETCHED TO THE outer fringes of the woods where his cabin was located, but he didn't want to stop the Jeep where it could attract attention. He didn't want to go anywhere he'd be recognized, either, so he continued to the last Cracker Barrel you pass before entering Birmingham's city limits. It was a place he'd seen often as a kid, but never visited. He didn't get to eat out much, back then. But he did learn to read early, and remembered thinking that anywhere with a barrel might be a good place to hide.

He pulled into the parking lot and took the farthest space from the line of cutesy wooden rocking chairs on the restaurant's veranda. He wondered for a second whether they were real, and if so, who would want to spend time sitting there bathed in the fumes and the noise from the highway. Then he popped the Jeep's glove box and took out a disposable phone. One of five he kept in there. It wasn't that he'd suddenly lost faith in Lieutenant Hale. He just didn't believe in taking unnecessary risks.

"Cooper?" Hale sounded surprised. "Why are you calling me from this number? Wait. Don't answer that.

Just tell me you haven't left the country, or done anything stupid."

"No. I'm still in town. And I have a sane reason to call. I need to know who you put on the Tomcik homicide."

"No. You don't. You need to get your ass in my office, pronto. I've spent most of the morning assuring Captain Emrich and the pair of storm troopers he brought in from Infernal Affairs that you had a good reason for what you did. You did have a good reason, didn't you, Cooper?"

"Yes."

"Well?"

"Keeping away from Emrich and Infernal Affairs."

"That's not a good enough reason!"

"It is from where I'm standing. I figure I have work to do, if we're going to find Ethan. I can't do that from inside an interview room."

"You can't do that if they put you back on suspension, either."

"Am I back on suspension?"

"No. Not yet, anyway. But not for lack of trying on Emrich's part. Luckily for you, the agents' boss, McMahan, is an old friend of mine. I told him you'd been acting under my orders when you visited Vernon at the restaurant. We should have checked they didn't have an ongoing action there, but that oversight was on me."

Devereaux was momentarily distracted by the screeching of tires and blaring of a horn as two SUVs nearly collided, their drivers confused by the vague sun-bleached markings on the pavement.

"Thanks, Lieutenant. But I still need to talk to whoever you put on the Tomcik case."

"No, you don't. I don't want you anywhere near that investigation."

"But—"

"Listen, Cooper, I don't want you talking to anyone. I don't want you sniffing around this case. I want clear blue water between you and anything to do with Hayden Tomcik. Understand?"

"No. I don't. Look, this isn't personal. It's not about Tomcik and my father. It's about finding Ethan. Another piece of the puzzle, at least."

"What piece?"

"The hooker whose body was dumped out of the Honda? I think she was killed at Tomcik's house."

"Why?"

"Other hookers were there. They were also Eastern European. Tomcik was murdered, so a killer was there. And I remember seeing a patch on the floor of the kitchen that was much cleaner than the rest. Something had been mopped up. It could have been blood. A lot of blood."

"I'll have it checked out."

"What's to check? The forensics report will tell us in two seconds. If there wasn't blood, then I'm barking up the wrong tree. Just tell me who's running with the case and I'll ask them."

"I'll have it checked out. But you're to have no contact with the Tomcik case, Cooper. This is important."

"What's this about, Lieutenant? What aren't you telling me?"

"Think about it for a minute. The girls from Tomcik's house? They're prostitutes. Illegal immigrants. Vice is working on the link between them and Sean Carver's racket, which the Feds and the DEA are crawling all over. I won't lie to you. Things aren't looking good for Tomcik. And the last thing you need, given your history together, is to get any of his stink on you now."

## Chapter Fifty-five

LUNCH BREAK WAS OVER.

The little girl ran back inside the house, ready for whatever lesson her mother had lined up for her next. The woman watched until the child had disappeared from the screen, then closed the browser window. She opened three more. Logged on to three of her web mail portals. And made the final checks on her deliveries.

It was tedious work, but it paid to be thorough. She made a mental note to stress the point with her successor. The kind of things they needed couldn't be picked up at a local store. And they couldn't be rustled up at the last moment. Not without drawing undue attention. Timing and coordination were everything.

And that was made extra difficult when you couldn't risk using the same supplier for more than one product. You couldn't use the same one for subsequent jobs. You couldn't schedule multiple deliveries on the same day. You had to use different names. Pay with different credit cards. You couldn't call, to sort any wrinkles out over the phone.

And you certainly could never meet anyone face-to-face.

## Chapter Fifty-six

*Monday. Afternoon.*
*Ethan missing for sixty-eight and a half hours*

DEVEREAUX STOOD ON THE STONE PATH A HUNDRED FEET from the steps that led to Vulcan's column and nervously checked his watch.

Waiting in that place took him back to his childhood. The column had been clad in marble in those days, concealing the original rough limestone that was now visible again, but the sensation of doubt and worry he felt remained the same. As a kid, he'd gone there whenever he was on the run from a foster home, wondering if Tom Vernon or another one of his school friends would come through with their promises of food and shelter. That day he'd gone to meet Mike Freeman, a cop he'd known since the Academy. They'd been through plenty together, over the years. But Devereaux still couldn't be sure that Freeman hadn't reported his questions to Lieutenant Hale. Or even Internal Affairs.

Five minutes later—ten minutes after Freeman should have arrived—Devereaux caught sight of him skirting around a gaggle of young kids who'd been rolling down the grassy slope where the water cascade used to be. Freeman was a little younger than Devereaux, but the years hadn't been kind to him. His fondness for cold beer and fried food hadn't helped, either, and as he drew close Devereaux could see the sheen of sweat covering his old friend's ample cheeks and forehead.

"Hey, Cooper." Freeman was breathing heavily. "Mind if we find somewhere to sit?"

The two men walked together in silence until they reached a wooden bench. It was in the shade of a pink dogwood, and out of earshot of the kids and parents and old folks who were scattered around, enjoying the afternoon sun.

"Thanks for coming, Mike. I appreciate it." Devereaux shifted a little closer. "What I need to know doesn't sound like much, but it's important, believe me. It's about the forensics report for the Tomcik homicide. Was—"

"You need to drop this, Cooper." Freeman held up his hands. "Right now. Anything that connects you to Tomcik—bury it. Then forget you ever knew him. Tomcik was toxic."

"I don't believe that. The man saved my life."

"Maybe he did. But I won't beat around the bush, Cooper. There are other things, and they don't look good."

"Like what?"

"I can't get into it."

"Mike, come on! Don't hold out on me."

"I'm not. But where do I even start?" Freeman shrugged. "Tomcik's whole life's a hornets' nest. Internal Affairs had been sniffing around him for years. They never got a result, but things were different back then. Cops closed ranks, no matter what. The climate's different these days. And now that he's dead, it's open season. Forensic accountants are being brought in to run down some kind of money trail. And don't forget the girls you found. Whether Carver smuggled them in or whether someone else did, they're here illegally. They were being pimped out. And they were at Tomcik's house."

"We don't know anything about those girls."

"We do. Vice has sat them down with translators. A

picture's starting to emerge. There's talk of connections with Mexico, maybe also Canada. And Tomcik's neighbors have reported seeing other girls coming and going at strange times. For all we know, Tomcik was behind the whole thing himself. He could have been dirty his entire career. So for your own good, Cooper, stay out of this."

"OK." Devereaux raised his hands as if in surrender. "I get the picture. I'll back off. If you just tell me this one thing: Was there any trace of a second victim's blood in Tomcik's house? In his kitchen? Enough to suggest a second homicide?"

Freeman didn't answer. He sat in silence for a moment, then made to stand up.

"Mike?" Devereaux reached out and grabbed his sleeve. "I'll find out. One way or another. A little boy's life is at stake. So if you really want me to stay out of trouble, tell me. Right now."

"I should never have come here." Freeman flopped back onto the bench and crossed his arms over his protruding gut. "OK. Yes. Large traces of blood were found. Consistent with a victim bleeding out. Someone had tried to clean it up with bleach. Same with the smaller trace near the back door."

"There were two victims, aside from Tomcik?"

"Isn't that what I just said?"

Devereaux took a breath. "Any DNA?"

"The samples are at the lab. It's too early for any results."

## Chapter Fifty-seven

*Monday. Afternoon.*
*Ethan missing for sixty-nine and a half hours*

LIEUTENANT HALE WAS A BALL OF IMPATIENCE, BOUNCING back and forth behind Devereaux's and Loflin's chairs as she waited for Bruckner and Grandison to arrive at the fourth-floor conference room. She contained herself until they'd taken their seats. Then she turned and gestured to the wall displays with both arms spread wide.

"Look a little different, don't they?" She scooped up a handwritten note from the floor and pinned it back on the *Crane Friends* section. "Because we've explored all the usual avenues. We've searched, and re-searched, and searched again. But we still don't have Ethan. We've gone well beyond the sixty-hour mark, and you don't need me to tell you how serious that is. What I will say is that me going to Mary Lynne and Joseph and telling them their little boy's not coming home? Not an option. The Birmingham PD and the FBI getting skewered in the press for failing to save him? Not an option. And what I'll tell you is this: I know you've all been giving a hundred percent. But we need more. We need to do whatever it takes to find Ethan. We need to look at whoever needs to be looked at. Does everyone follow?"

There was a murmur of assent around the room.

"Good. Now, remember—this is about finding Ethan, and nothing else. I don't want any tribalism or defensiveness here. OK—let's get the ball rolling. As you all know, yesterday afternoon Detective Devereaux rescued two girls from the house of a guy called Hayden Tomcik. A homicide victim."

"Tomcik?" Bruckner had fired up his laptop and was taking notes. "That name rings a bell. He was a retired cop?"

"Yes, he was." Hale nodded. "Now, since yesterday, Vice has been working with the girls, and they've pieced together the bulk of their story. It's not an unusual one, sadly. They're from Hungary. They wanted to come to America to make their fortunes. They got hooked up with a bunch of low-lifes who smuggled them here with a couple dozen other girls, all crammed into some kind of modified cargo container. They had no money, so the deal was they'd pay for their passage when they arrived. Working in the *hospitality* business. Only their understanding of hospitality didn't match what the assholes who'd brought them here had in mind."

"The assholes being Sean Carver's crew?" Bruckner stopped typing for a second.

"Correct." Hale frowned. "These girls told Vice they were transported in the same group as the girl Devereaux found dead at Carver's warehouse. And they each separately identified a picture of the girl who was found with her throat cut on 60th, a couple of weeks back. The one whose body was dumped out of the white Honda that was used to abduct Ethan Crane."

"And this guy, Tomcik?" Bruckner was shaky with the pronunciation. "Why were the girls at his house? What was his involvement? Was he tied into Carver's crew?"

"We're still working to clarify Tomcik's precise role." Hale shot a hard stare at Devereaux, who stayed silent. "The girls say they were trying to escape, which is consistent with their behavior. But listen. Any dotted lines will be firmed up in due course. They're not the priority right now. Ethan is. And here's where we stand: You predicted a law enforcement link to Ethan's kidnapper. Carver is the common factor in all the evidence we have relating to Ethan—a prostitute Carver smuggled into the country was killed, and her body was dumped from the vehicle that was used to abduct Ethan. Therefore, the current law enforcement link is to the Carver investigation. Who knows what other cases may have been involved in the past. But it means we need to cross-reference all personnel from the Carver investigation against their status and location when the other orphans went missing. We need that for the Bureau. For anyone who transferred into the Birmingham Police Department. And for the DEA. We know that whoever we're looking for is smart. And apparently above suspicion. They've been doing this for sixteen years, minimum, and getting away with it."

"Lieutenant, do you know what you're asking for?" Bruckner had closed his computer and was looking distinctly pale. "A needle in a haystack. A giant haystack."

"I do know. And I'm asking for it yesterday."

## Chapter Fifty-eight

THE WOMAN HOPED THAT THE LITTLE BOY HADN'T FALLEN asleep again. At least not unless he'd finished the task she'd set for him.

She hurried back from the Business Center, let herself into their room, and straightaway saw she needn't have worried. The boy was sitting on the bed, cross-legged, still working his way through the stack of problems she'd left him with. There were 144 of them, altogether. He had to pick between two possible answers for each one. Then put a candy in the green bowl for option A. Or in the blue bowl for option B.

The woman had told him that when he'd answered all of the questions, she'd count the candies in both bowls. She'd told him there'd be a prize if there were the right number in each one. But she hadn't told him that if he answered the way she expected him to, all the candies would be in the blue bowl. And that she'd also check how many of the spare ones he'd eaten without permission . . .

This was an exercise she'd developed herself. The questions were carefully designed to test a subject's attitude to a set of moral conundrums. They were posed from different angles and used contrasting language to ensure rogue responses were not disproportionately weighted. And the stolen candy aspect gave it an interesting, alternate dimension.

The result wasn't the only criterion she used, obviously. There was the painstaking research, before rescuing each kid. The detailed observation of his or her behavior, during their treat and in the hotel. The subtle word association games she sneaked into their conversations. But it was the final assessment. The way to be sure that the next step was absolutely necessary.

She'd never known a kid able to escape its genes.

But she felt it was only right to check.

## Chapter Fifty-nine

*Monday. Late Afternoon.*
*Ethan missing for seventy hours*

THIS GUY, TOMCIK? WHAT WAS HIS INVOLVEMENT?

Agent Bruckner had asked the question, and Devereaux knew it would make no practical difference who answered it. The past couldn't be changed. A man's actions couldn't be undone. But somehow, given everything that Tomcik had done to help him, Devereaux felt an obligation to be the one who uncovered the truth. However ugly it might turn out to be.

Why did he need to uncover it? Why did he not already have the answer? Devereaux felt a wave of regret wash over him. He should have stayed in better touch with the old guy. He should have helped him. Protected him, the way Tomcik had protected Devereaux after his father was killed. Kept him on the straight and narrow. Unless the temptation would have proved too great, leading Devereaux to stray from the path as well? Maybe that's why Tomcik had reached out to him. Pulled strings to get him into the police department. Eased him into place, like a sleeper agent, in case he was ever needed.

Devereaux felt like the ground beneath his feet was suddenly a little less secure.

Tomcik's front door had been locked, but Devereaux took care of that in seconds with his expired credit card. Inside, the house felt different, too. That's always the way after a forensic team's been to work and there's no owner left to straighten up. Things get dumped in the wrong locations, altering the ambience of a place. The stink of chemicals never gets properly dispersed. And the presence of so many people carrying out their morbid tasks—technicians, photographers, paramedics, detectives—leaves some intangible, psychic residue. Devereaux remembered that from his father's house. The atmosphere was never the same after the police tore it apart. Strangely, though, that was still the only place he ever really thought of as home.

Devereaux made straight for Tomcik's bathroom. He paused at the side of the tub and held his breath. The investigation had been focused on the kitchen, but if the crime scene techs had been über-efficient . . . Devereaux forced himself to stop borrowing trouble. He prodded the edge of the bath panel. It gave an inch. He swung it open wider, peered inside—and felt his intestines turn to lead.

The box was gone.

The files would be in the evidence locker by now. Secured. Cataloged. Photographed. How could Devereaux get his hands on them, without anyone finding out? He'd come up with a dozen different ways—and rejected every one—when another thought hit him. He'd read nearly every one of the files, yesterday, before being summoned back to headquarters. The contents were interesting, but hardly earth-shattering. Not worth committing murder for. There were only three or four files he hadn't touched. What were the odds of those ones being radically different? And yet, what was it Segard had said, from his hospital bed? *My partner kept records . . .*

Tomcik's bedroom was the farthest room from the entrance, so Devereaux started there. The old man's broken possessions hadn't so much been processed as stirred around and heaped up in piles, like some kind of abstract art installation. Devereaux wondered who'd clean them up. And what would happen to the property? Who would want to live there now? That was another problem with his father's house. It had stood empty for ages after the old man was killed. Devereaux had liked to sneak away from his foster home and hang out there on his own. It used to drive his foster parents crazy. They'd go out of their minds with fury. Lock him in their basement for a whole day without food each time he was caught there. But he still kept going back.

No one could compete with the memory of a cop killed in the line of duty, Devereaux figured. Maybe it would have been better if he'd been fostered by another cop. Someone who understood what the job meant. Suddenly Devereaux was conscious of a void in his life, and for a crazy moment he wondered if he should apply to foster a kid, himself. Then he stepped back onto the landing, and closed his mind to the past.

He worked his way slowly and systematically, room by room, throughout the whole house. He shifted every piece of furniture. Looked in every drawer and closet. Checked for hidden compartments and false panels. Looked behind every picture. Tested every inch of floor and wall for hollow areas.

And found nothing.

The tech crew had been particularly thorough in the kitchen. The floor, walls, countertops, table, chairs— even the ceiling—had all been thoroughly sprayed and scraped, but strangely that made the room seem shabbier. Every last dent and scratch and scuff was laid bare, shorn of its protective layer of everyday dirt. It seemed impersonal, too, as if all humanizing residue had been dissolved away with the grime, leaving only the inanimate structure behind.

Devereaux trudged back along the corridor, feeling dejected, until his gaze settled on the door to the closet.

He realized it was the one place he hadn't checked. He hadn't deliberately ignored it. His subconscious must have guided him away, once again. He still wasn't keen to look inside. But it would be crazy to walk away and leave this one stone unturned.

There was nothing hanging from the rail in the closet, and the shelf—the twin of the one where Devereaux's father had kept his hats and gloves—was empty. The walls seemed solid. But Devereaux noticed a series of parallel scratches on the floor. He used his phone as a flashlight to get a clearer view, and saw the damage was recent. He was suddenly terrified that someone had beaten him to the jackpot. Then he remembered the women who'd hidden in there, the day before. They'd been wearing ridiculously tall shoes. They'd probably shuffled around nervously, causing the damage with the tips of their heels.

Devereaux was almost certain he'd hit on the explanation, but he still couldn't turn away. Without consciously deciding to, he crouched down. His fingers moved on muscle memory, scrabbling for the join between the boards. The first one he tried was stuck solid. The second one moved. Only a fraction of an inch, but enough to tell him it wasn't nailed down. He kept prying at it, and didn't give up until it came loose. He lifted it. Shone his flashlight into the gap. And saw the side of a black metal box.

The next two boards came away more easily, and as more light flooded the space Devereaux could see a small footprint in the dust to the side of the box. A cleaner strip of wood, an eighth of an inch wide, was also visible around two of its sides. Someone had stepped into the crawl space, recently. They'd removed the box. Then put it back in a slightly different position.

## Chapter Sixty

*Monday. Late Afternoon.*
*Ethan missing for seventy and three-quarter hours*

DEVEREAUX LIFTED THE METAL BOX OUT OF THE CRAWL SPACE and carried it to the living room. He sat down on the couch and set the box next to him. It had a lock, but that had already been forced. The lid swung open easily. Inside, Devereaux counted twenty-two files, with room for another four or five. He pulled one out at random and saw it was divided into two sections. The first followed a standard format, much as the files in the other batch had done. It had copies of police department forms along with supplementary notes typed on official paper and signed by the case officers. The second part was Tomcik's personal contribution. It was all hand-written, and some passages were bordering on illegible.

The case involved a local pimp called Kelsey Pike. Tomcik had arrested him multiple times over an eighteen-month period, and if his reports were true, Pike was a very nasty piece of work indeed. He was accused of rape. Vicious beatings. Drug dealing. Extortion. But on every occasion he'd escaped without conviction. The cops suspected witness intimidation and bribery, but nothing had been proved.

Tomcik arrested Pike for the final time in September

1971. Pike had believed one of his girls had been holding out on him, trying to scrape a little extra cash together to buy clothes for her infant son. She'd wound up in the hospital. Pike had made bail. And then disappeared. Tomcik and his partner had gone through the motions of looking for him. They didn't find him. But Pike's body did show up, six months later. It was discovered by some workmen in the basement of a building that was being prepared for demolition. The corpse's legs had both been broken, and several of its teeth were smashed.

No assailant was ever identified.

The next file Devereaux looked at told of a rapist who'd been active in the poorer suburbs of Birmingham in 1973. He was suspected of a string of attacks, but was only arrested twice. The first time he walked, after the victim withdrew her complaint and refused to testify. The second time, he attacked a sixty-two-year-old grandmother. Tomcik was called to the scene. The rapist tried to run. He was hit by a passing car, and died later that day in the hospital.

The driver was never identified.

The next dozen files told similar stories. Tomcik was apparently adept at finding ways to ensure that when the justice system left cracks, the city's vilest evildoers didn't slip through them. Not too many times, anyway. What he'd done wasn't strictly legal. In truth, many of his actions were downright criminal. Could these have been the things that Internal Affairs had caught wind of? Devereaux had never advocated vigilantism, but he could understand why Tomcik had acted the way he had. He'd been wrong, but he hadn't been *wrong*. Devereaux was beginning to feel guilty for doubting his old mentor. Assuming that these kinds of things were all that he'd done . . .

Devereaux reached for another file, and right away he saw that the format was different from the others. There was no official opening section. Only Tomcik's handwritten entries, which were laid out in the style of a ledger. At the top of each page was the title UGR, followed by a series of names. The first was "*Flossie,*" in quotation marks. Then "*Bella,*" "*Trixie,*" "*Ginger,*" and more, all in the same vein. Then came dates. Then a value in dollars, ranging from $100 to $700. And in the last column, a country. Mexico. Or Canada.

*Mexico or Canada.*

The countries he'd heard Freeman mention that afternoon, in relation to human trafficking . . .

## Chapter Sixty-one

THE WOMAN STOPPED TALKING AND TURNED HER BACK.

Dealing with naughty kids was nothing new to her. Even the most placid ones were bound to have at least one insolent episode in the course of an expedition. This little boy had been remarkably low maintenance ever since leaving Birmingham three days ago. He hadn't acted up at all, right up until he realized it was his last night at the park. He wanted to stay longer, which the woman took as a kind of compliment. But she certainly wasn't going to stand for his refusal to go to bed while she went to work on removing all traces of their presence from the room.

Her training had taught her how to handle even the most willful of children. The key was to make them desperate for your attention, not the other way round. Her experience over the years had shown her lots of ways to achieve this, but she found turning her back was the simplest method. Kids instinctively know you won't give in to their demands if you're not even listening to them.

She always had to work a little harder with kids she was rescuing, of course. It had been much easier with her own daughter.

But then, look at the genes . . .

## Chapter Sixty-two

*Monday. Evening.*
*Ethan missing for seventy-one and a quarter hours*

THE FIRST PAGES IN TOMCIK'S UGR FILE DATED BACK TO THE 1970s, but the entries kept coming long after Tomcik had retired from the department.

Devereaux was slumped on the couch, robotically flicking through one sheet after another. His eyes were half registering details from the '80s and '90s and 2000s. His brain was struggling to come to terms with what he was seeing. His imagination was linking the handwritten names with the frightened faces of the girls he'd found in Tomcik's closet. And with the lifeless faces of the girls from Carver's warehouse and the dump site on 60th Street.

By the time he reached the 2010s, Devereaux was feeling utterly dejected. He was about to admit defeat when he noticed a loose piece of paper lying facedown at the bottom of the metal box. Assuming it had fallen from one of the files, he fished it out and turned it over. And saw that, instead, it was an index sheet for the whole set. It listed twenty-six titles.

The first one read: *UNDERGROUND RAILROAD.*

It took a moment to sink in. Under Ground Railroad. UGR! He'd gotten it wrong. Hale had gotten it wrong.

Internal Affairs had gotten it wrong. Tomcik hadn't been smuggling girls into the country. He'd been spiriting them out. Getting them over the border, north or south. And then probably back to their home countries. But wherever they went when they left the United States, it didn't matter to Devereaux. What counted was that even though Tomcik may not have been playing by the rules, he'd by no means been in the wrong. He hadn't been *toxic,* as Freeman had called him. He'd been rescuing the weak. The vulnerable. He'd been a hero.

Devereaux leapt off the couch and started spinning around the room, punching the air while his feet unintentionally stirred up the smattering of broken ornaments and books and cushion stuffing that covered the floor. He gave himself a minute to celebrate. Then he bent down to recover the index sheet, which had floated off the couch in all the excitement. He grabbed it, and his eye fell on one of the titles farther down the list. He blinked and looked again, to check he wasn't seeing things. He sat back down. Steadied himself. Cross-referenced the remainder of the entries against the subjects of the files he'd just worked through. Highlighted three more names. Then pulled out his phone and called Hale.

## Chapter Sixty-three

*Monday. Evening.*
*Ethan missing for seventy-two and a quarter hours*

LIEUTENANT HALE WAS WAITING FOR DEVEREAUX IN THE lobby of his building when he arrived. She greeted him with a cold stare, and they rode up in the elevator together in silence.

"Your mind works in strange ways, Cooper." Hale waited for him to open the locks on the door to his apartment. "Who hears their boss order them not to investigate a homicide—under any circumstances—and then goes to the victim's house regardless and pokes around under his floorboards? Give me one reason not to put you right back on suspension."

"I'll give you two." Devereaux walked through the open-plan living space to the corner kitchen and took a couple of beers out of the refrigerator. "It's a good thing I didn't listen to you. I cleared Tomcik's name by poking around under those boards. And I found the key to getting Ethan back."

"You're talking about the missing files?" Hale hesitated, then took the bottle Devereaux offered her.

"Right." Devereaux crossed the room, stopped in front of the giant window, and raised his bottle to the distant figure of Vulcan. "They concerned four people.

Me. Raymond Kerr—the guy who killed my father, may he burn in Hell. And two names I didn't recognize. Mitchell Burke. And Madison Nesbitt."

"Mitchell Burke?" Hale moved and stood next to Devereaux. "That name rings a bell."

"I Googled him in the car on the way back here. He was a murderer. Strangled a dozen people in Birmingham in the late sixties and early seventies. His last victim was Madison Nesbitt's father. Tomcik was the one who brought him down."

"What happened to him?" Fine lines traced their way across Hale's forehead. "Is he still in jail? I don't remember reading about a trial."

"There wasn't one." Devereaux took a mouthful of beer. "It was suicide by cop. Madison Nesbitt's mother was already dead, so she was left an orphan. She ended up in foster care, like I did. I figure Tomcik kept an eye on her, the same as he did for me. Hence the files."

"You think this Nesbitt took them?"

"Well, I didn't. Kerr and Burke are dead. Who else could it have been? A random stranger? I think she found out, or figured out, that Tomcik had a file on her and the asshole who killed her father." Devereaux turned his back to the window. "She went to Tomcik's house and tortured him into giving up the files. Then fate threw a curveball. I'm guessing that a hooker—the one who wound up getting dumped on 60th—showed up looking for Tomcik's help at exactly the wrong time. So Nesbitt killed her to keep her quiet. A utility killing, like Dr. Barratt said. Bronson Segard—Tomcik's longtime partner—must have been with the girl. He was wounded, but got away. I bet the second blood trace in Tomcik's kitchen is his."

"Nesbitt could have used the Honda to dump the girl's body." Hale drummed her fingers on the bridge of Devereaux's binoculars, leaving a line of overlapping smudges on its shiny surface. "But why would she bother moving it?"

"If she understands law enforcement like the FBI

thinks she does, she'd definitely have left the body where we found it. We might not have busted our asses looking for a missing whore—sad, but true—but one of Carver's pimps certainly would. They wouldn't allow a valuable asset to just disappear. And if her body was found at Tomcik's house, next to his, that would spark off the hunt for a cop killer. Nesbitt wouldn't have wanted that kind of attention if she was preparing to abduct a kid. She was probably staking out the Crane house the whole time she was in town."

"OK." Hale took hold of Devereaux's elbow. "I've heard enough for now. I'll talk to the Bureau. See what they know about Nesbitt. In the meantime, try to work up some leads of your own. Then get some sleep. And pray that by the morning I've forgotten about the crap you pulled today."

## Chapter Sixty-four

*Monday. Late Evening.*
*Ethan missing for seventy-five hours*

BEING TOLD TO GO TO SLEEP IS ONE THING. GOING TO SLEEP IS
another thing altogether.

Devereaux's first foster mother used to shriek at him
to go to sleep, every night. He always wanted to play. Or
read. Or explore. To do anything but close his eyes and
be transported back into the crawl space under the
closet with the spiders, where Tomcik found him. His
foster mother never knew that, though. He never told
her. He just closed his eyes and waited for the yelling to
stop. Then he got out of bed. Slipped his clothes on over
his pajamas. Climbed out of his bedroom window. And
ran back to his father's house. No one new lived there
yet. He had the whole place to himself. He could do as
he pleased. Just like when his daddy was at work. All he
had to do was steer clear of that closet.

Devereaux's second foster home was too far from his
father's house to make nocturnal visits feasible, and he
was out of the habit by the time he was moved to the
third. But for some reason that night, lying cocooned in
soft Egyptian cotton and with the drapes wide open so
he felt like he was floating above the city, all he could
think about was that old house. He knew sleep wasn't

coming any time soon. So he got out of bed. Changed into clean clothes. And grabbed the keys to his Porsche.

He had to find the way to his childhood neighborhood more by instinct than memory, because so many of the landmarks had changed. The trees he remembered had grown bigger—or were missing entirely. The stores where he'd bought candy on the rare occasions he had money were both closed. The street corners he'd fought for, shoulder to shoulder with his friends, had mostly been remodeled.

Devereaux paused at the last intersection before his father's street and closed his eyes so that he could picture the place as it had been. He opened them. Turned. Coasted around the final, shallow curve. And found himself facing an empty space.

The space wasn't completely empty, Devereaux realized. There was a rusty chain-link fence slung between cracked concrete posts. Giant weeds. Overgrown bushes and trees. Broken glass. Wooden packing crates. Garbage and abandoned household appliances of every kind. Just not a house.

Devereaux pulled out his phone and checked the GPS. It confirmed he was in the right place. But what the hell had happened there? He got out of the car and pushed through a hole in the fence. He moved forward cautiously, using his phone as a flashlight and trying to weave around the worst of the thorny foliage that was tearing at his face and clothes. Chunks of half-buried rubble caught his feet, tripping him or throwing him off balance by shifting when he stepped on them. He slowed, approaching the looming shadows where his father's house had been, and heard a sharp, snapping noise to his right. An animal? It was close. He spun toward it, ready to defend himself. Then he relaxed.

"Hi." Devereaux took a step back, conscious now of the stench from the skinny, half-naked, gray-haired guy who was trying to scuttle further beneath a tangle of branches. "Who are you?"

"Are you from the government?" For a second the old guy looked quite fierce.

"No. I'm from here."

"What do you mean? Don't talk in riddles, man."

"I'm not. I was born here. In the house that used to be right in this yard."

"There hasn't been a house here for years."

"It was years ago when I lived here. In my father's house. Right on this spot. Did it burn down, or something? Do you know what happened to it?"

"It didn't burn down." The old man shuffled forward as if he wanted to leave the shelter of the branches, then thought better of it and reversed. "They knocked it down. They had to."

"They knocked it down?" Devereaux felt a surge of anger flood through him. "Who did? When?"

"In 1980."

"Don't be ridiculous. How would you know that?"

"I know my dates—1776, 1865, 1918, 1945, 1969, 2001—"

"Who was President when they knocked it down?"

"The peanut guy."

Devereaux wasn't expecting that. "Who won the World Series?"

"The Phillies."

"Who won the Super Bowl?"

"Who the hell cares?"

"OK. In 1980, the house was demolished. Why?"

"Easy. No one would buy it. The place was cursed. The whole lot still is. That's why no one bothers me when I sleep here. Till you showed up, anyway. Stay, and you might see the Devil himself. He used to live here. When I saw you coming I was pretty sure you were him."

## Chapter Sixty-five

*Tuesday. Early Morning.*

THE MAN DRAGS ME OUT. HE LIFTS ME UP. HOLDS ME AGAINST *his chest. His coat is scratching my face.*

*He carries me to the kitchen. Puts me on a chair. Crouches down, so his face is level with mine.*

*It's Detective Tomcik. He's old now. His skin is gray. Slimy bugs are crawling out of his nose.*

*"Cooper? Listen to me, son. Your daddy? He's dead."*

*Where is Daddy? Why isn't he here?*

*I'm outside the house now. I can see in. I can see me in the kitchen. With the detective. He's still old. Other men are there. They have big hammers. They're breaking down the walls. Smashing the doors. Making holes in the floor. A machine is next to me. It has huge jaws. It's reaching up and tearing off the roof. Everything's broken. Everything's falling down. Falling on me . . .*

## Chapter Sixty-six

THE WOMAN WAS PLEASED WITH THE BOY'S BEHAVIOR THAT morning.

Her stern treatment the night before had paid off. The boy had soon quieted down. He'd gone to bed. Slept well. And not complained at all when she'd woken him, despite the earliness of the hour. He'd showered and gotten dressed nice and quickly. Stood patiently by the door while she gave the room one last check. Then walked peacefully by her side as they'd made their way to the Mercedes. That was important. There weren't many people up and about yet. Not much of a crowd to get lost in. The woman didn't want anything to happen that would draw attention to them.

She made sure the boy was settled in the back seat, strapped in safely with his little monkey to cuddle—Brian the rabbit had fallen from favor during the drive south— then checked that their luggage was stowed correctly. And finally, although it wasn't really necessary because she was certain she'd packed all the essentials before setting off on the trip, she did a quick inventory of her emergency kit: First aid supplies; wigs; glasses; sedative; Mace spray; knife; gun; and a couple of special items she liked to have on hand in case of extreme circumstances.

Some would say the woman was paranoid.

She preferred to say *thorough*.

## Chapter Sixty-seven

*Tuesday. Early Morning.*
*Ethan missing for eighty-three and three-quarter hours*

DEVEREAUX COULDN'T MOVE.

"Sweet Child O' Mine" was riffing away on his night-stand, but there was nothing he could do about it. His arms were pinned down. He couldn't reach the phone. He couldn't answer it. He couldn't ask whoever was calling for help. His father's house was being demolished all around him. Debris was falling on him, and . . . Wait. Why was the house being knocked down? What had it done to offend anybody?

Devereaux opened one eye the tiniest crack, convinced that grit and dust would blow in and blind him. None came. He opened his eye the rest of the way. He saw the picture of his cabin. His crisp white walls. His steel-gray drapes. His clothes, lined up on their rack. And felt the relief flood through him. He was in his apartment. And he was safe.

His phone was still ringing, so he grabbed it.

"Cooper, where were you?" Hale sounded annoyed. "It took you an age to pick up."

"Sorry. A house was falling on me."

"What the hell are you talking about?"

"Nothing. Just a dream I was having. I'm awake now. What do you need?"

"Are you alone?"

"What kind of question is that?"

"An important one. Is anyone with you?"

"No."

"If anyone is with you, and you can't say directly for any reason, I want you to tell me the routine maintenance on your vehicle is up-to-date, and the records guy can go to hell. OK?"

"Lieutenant, why all this cryptic bullshit? There's no one here."

"OK. That's good. Sorry if I yelled before. I'm not having the best of mornings."

"Why? What's up?"

"It's not even seven am and I've already had my ear chewed off by the Bureau because of you. Twice!"

"What did I do?"

"First thing? The operation at the Casey Jones Railroad Museum you pushed for? It was a complete waste of time and effort. And second? Your theory about Nesbitt? It's not a flier."

"No? Why not?"

"The guy who strangled all those folks in Birmingham? Mitchell Burke? Were you driving when you Googled him? Or did the website use very small letters?"

"I don't follow."

"Burke didn't kill Nesbitt's father. Burke *was* Nesbitt's father. It took the Bureau about three nanoseconds to shoot me down."

"Seriously? But—"

"It doesn't matter, Cooper. Because Madison Nesbitt is dead, too. She died in 1975, when she was sixteen years old. She was killed in a fire. At the foster home she'd been sent to. The whole place burned to the ground."

"I'm sorry, Lieutenant. I had no idea. I hope—"

"Don't worry about it. I'm not calling to give you a

hard time. Wait till you hear the next thing. The real news is, we don't need Nesbitt. We have another suspect. The FBI received an anonymous tip, an hour ago. They followed up on it right away. They raided a home. And recovered a T-shirt, which Mrs. Crane has confirmed belongs to Ethan. They also found a vial containing traces of triazolam."

"Was the homeowner there?"

"No."

"Do we at least have a name?"

"We do. Jan Loflin."

"*Detective* Loflin?"

"The same."

"No way." Devereaux switched the phone to his other ear. "Someone's made a mistake. Or they're framing her. This is crazy. It's bullshit. Loflin's not old enough. The first little girl disappeared sixteen years ago."

"I don't know about the other kids, Cooper. Maybe the Bureau's wrong about them. But it's definitely Loflin who took Ethan Crane. The FBI got hold of the clerk at that hotel where the hair dye was found. David Day. They emailed a picture of Loflin to him. He positively ID'd her as the woman he'd checked in. Her hair was different and so on, but her missing earlobe? That was the key. That jogged his memory."

## Chapter Sixty-eight

*Tuesday. Early Morning.*
*Ethan missing for eighty-four hours*

DEVEREAUX HAD CLIMBED OUT OF BED AND STARTED TO PULL on clothes while he was still on the phone.

His first impulse was to get out on the street and help hunt Loflin down. Hale appreciated the sentiment—she felt as betrayed as Devereaux did, if not more so—but she told him to stay at home and stand by. His apartment was centrally located. She wanted her people evenly distributed and ready to respond to any sightings at a moment's notice. Not scattered all over the city and having to race back from whatever far-flung shadow they'd found themselves chasing. Loflin might have been on loan from Vice, but in the Bureau's eyes the new chief suspect was one of Hale's detectives. That was embarrassing enough. It would be worse still if the police department couldn't bring her in, and she ended up being tracked down by an agent.

Devereaux hung up the phone and lay down on the bed, but he couldn't get back to sleep. He couldn't get Loflin's lies out of his head. How had he not seen through her? He started to run through the time line of events in his head. She must have snatched Ethan Friday night and taken him to the motel, then rushed back to headquarters on Saturday morning when the balloon went up. Looking back, she had been a little jumpy at the briefing in Hale's office. But then so cool at the Crane house. Sitting in on the meetings with the FBI. Driving to the Roadside Rendezvous. Interviewing the nurses with him. Talking about her time in Vice. Vice, which was the division that had contact with Sean Carver's organization. And had been about to blow that organization wide open, until Loflin had shot Carver and stopped the raid in its tracks . . .

The thought of Loflin's account of working undercover triggered another memory:

*You're always working. Working to get accepted. Working to make your mark interested in you. Working to make him want you around.*

The ice-cold bitch had been taunting him. She'd described exactly what she'd been doing. She *had* made him want her in his life. He'd even asked her to stay for a beer at his cabin when she'd seemed so upset. But the real question was, what had she done with Ethan? Where had she hidden him while she was worming her way into their investigation? And where was the boy now?

Devereaux wanted to ask her, in person. He was willing his phone to ring. But then another thought hit him. A few variables had changed, but their working theory was that whoever had taken Ethan had also dumped the hooker's body. That person was a small woman with blond hair, according to Tom Vernon's contact. And that person killed Hayden Tomcik.

Devereaux stood up and moved to his bedroom window. He looked at the city stretched out below him, distant and gray without the warmth of the sun's first rays. Loflin may be the one who'd murdered Tomcik. Tortured and murdered him. He was going to find out. He would make absolutely sure. And if she had, Devereaux was going to follow his old guardian angel's lead.

He was going to begin a second set of files.

And Loflin's would be the first entry.

## Chapter Sixty-nine

*Tuesday. Early Morning.*
*Ethan missing for eighty-four and a quarter hours*

DEVEREAUX STAYED AT HIS BEDROOM WINDOW UNTIL THE sun began to stain the eastern face of the Wells Fargo Tower with pink. Then he wandered to the kitchen and started to make coffee. He gave up before it was ready to brew. He opened the fridge. There was nothing he wanted to eat. He went and sat on the couch. He looked for something to watch on TV. Nothing appealed to him. He searched his bookshelves. Pulled out a new paperback he'd been dying to read. And couldn't get through the first paragraph.

His sense of calm had disappeared and now something disconcerting was scrambling his brain, stopping him from settling to any task. At first he thought it was Loflin's treachery that was throwing him off balance. Then he wondered if it was because his theory about Mitchell Burke and Madison Nesbitt had been so far off the mark. He wasn't used to being that badly wrong. Or it could be his concern for Ethan Crane, now that the lifeline he hoped they'd found had turned to dust in their hands.

Devereaux turned each possibility over in his mind.

He dismissed them, one by one. And was left with a different conclusion altogether. He was being bothered by his dream. It went back to a seed that had been planted the night before, when he'd discovered that his father's house had been demolished. Why had that been necessary? Why would no one buy it? His father had been a police officer. A hero. And it wasn't like he'd been killed on the premises. There were no bloodstains or bullet holes for prospective buyers to get in a wad about.

Computers weren't really Devereaux's thing, but he did keep an old white MacBook on a shelf under his coffee table, ready for ordering late-night pizza and Chinese food. He went back to the couch and pulled it out. He fired it up. Started its browser. Typed his father's name and the date he was killed into Google. He sat with his finger poised over the keyboard for thirty long seconds. And finally hit Return.

The search engine came up with surprisingly few hits. Far fewer than it would have done if a cop had been shot by a serial killer thirty-nine hours ago, rather than thirty-nine years. It only took Devereaux ten minutes to read the main articles that came up on the screen. The most detailed account was in a blog post written by an ex–Birmingham detective. He'd been trying to get a campaign for a new memorial for fallen officers off the ground, and had apparently known Devereaux's father personally. Next came an article from the only one of the local newspapers to have digitized its back issues from so long ago. After that there was a passing mention in a piece written by a local amateur historian. The rest was dross, too vague and insubstantial to be any help at all.

Devereaux closed the computer and shoved it back on its shelf. He was frustrated. Each account of his father's death was basically the same. They all said that Kerr had shot him—the newspaper adding the speculation that his murder was in retaliation for the slaying of

Kerr's disciple—before being killed himself in a shoot-out with other officers.

This didn't tell him anything he didn't already know.

And it did nothing to ease the mental itch that was driving him crazy.

## Chapter Seventy

*Tuesday. Morning.*
*Ethan missing for eighty-five and a half hours*

DEVEREAUX CALLED HALE'S NUMBER FROM THE CAR.

He left her a message that he'd be at the police archive if she needed him. He knew she'd wanted him to stay home, but the archive wasn't far from his building and he couldn't risk not telling her where he was going. The older, pre-computer-era paper records are kept 160 feet underground in what used to be a nuclear bomb shelter, and there's absolutely no hope of cell service there. The only way to contact someone who doesn't have their own switchboard extension is to call the operator and have them paged.

Devereaux couldn't believe he was re-entering that place of his own free will. As he descended in the express elevator, the strange sensation that stems from being so far beneath the surface came rushing back to him. There were physical aspects—the lack of any natural light, the slight increase in pressure, and the bitter, metallic tinge to the artificially recirculated air. But for Devereaux, the psychological component of being buried so deep was the real problem. He tried not to think about the millions of tons of earth above him. Or what he'd do if there was a fire, and he had to reach the surface in a hurry. He had bad enough dreams already. And his mental state wasn't helped by the memory of something an archivist had once told him. The little mole-like guy had gleefully pointed out that the level where they worked was twenty-five times lower than the bodies of the victims whose records they kept.

Devereaux didn't recognize the officer manning the reception desk, which helped to keep small talk to a minimum as he went through the rigmarole of signing in. He explained that he was looking for the files relating to officer-involved shootings from 1976, and even though he already knew where they should be, from his brief posting in the archives, he listened patiently to the directions he was given.

Devereaux had wanted to read Tomcik's report on his father's death when he'd last been there, but the file that contained it had been missing. He was confident it would have been found by now so he hurried to the correct section of tall, green shelves. They were crammed with plain cardboard boxes, coded designations scrawled on their fronts with permanent marker. Except in one spot. The place where Devereaux's father's information should have been. It was still empty. Devereaux reached up and ran his finger along the chipped surface of the shelf, stirring up a thick layer of dust.

Undeterred, Devereaux tried a different angle. He searched for records of officers killed in the line of duty. Again, he drew a blank. Next, he tried looking for information on Raymond Kerr. This time Devereaux did find a file, but all it contained was a list cross-referencing Kerr's previous victims.

There was absolutely nothing relating to his father.

Devereaux was frustrated. With his previous experience of the archives he'd thought pulling one file would have been quick and easy. He was conscious of the search for Loflin taking place aboveground, and he didn't want to let Lieutenant Hale—or Ethan Crane— down if there were urgent developments. But at the same time, the need to find out more about his father's death and the events that followed it had taken hold of him like a fever.

Swallowing his pride, Devereaux returned to the desk and asked for help. The officer rattled his keyboard, and a minute later turned back with a discouraging expression on his face.

"There's good news. And there's bad news. The records you want are definitely here. But they've been ten-seventeened. I'm sorry, bud. There's no way I can let you have them."

Devereaux knew what a 10-17 was. A file designation beginning with a 10 was an executive order restricting access to its contents. A 17 meant the information was only available to the rank of captain and above. If they'd been dealing with a 10-16—where a lieutenant could request access—Hale might have been persuaded to help Devereaux out. But Captain Emrich? Devereaux might as well ask to sleep with his daughter.

"No problem." Devereaux fought to keep the disappointment out of his voice. "It's not your fault. My lieutenant didn't know, either, or she wouldn't have sent me down here. There are two more things she wants me to pick up, then—" Devereaux looked at his watch. "Shoot! I'm already late. I wasted so much time looking for that other information. My ass is in a sling, here, big-time. Is there any way you could help me? I could run and grab one set of files she wants, and you could get the other one? I'd really appreciate it."

"I guess." The officer didn't sound too enthusiastic. "What do you need?"

"Motor vehicles. Moving violations. Mountain Brook. Second half of July 1967."

"Really? That section's miles away. What else does she want?"

"Grand larceny. Fine art. Specifically, Italian old master oil paintings. Everything from 1972."

"Oh. That's even farther away. OK. I'll handle the motor vehicles. You take the fancy stuff."

"Thanks. You're a lifesaver."

Devereaux waited until the officer had disappeared into the valley between two great mountains of shelves, then darted around the desk. He opened the top left drawer. Lifted a plastic tray full of cheap ballpoint pens and paper clips and thumbtacks. Retrieved a small, shiny key from underneath the detritus. Used it to unlock the top right desk drawer. Pried the lid off an ancient Folger's coffee can. Tipped out a much sturdier key. Took it. And sprinted down the last aisle on the left, all the way to the far wall, where the dull gray cabinets that held the restricted files were housed.

## Chapter Seventy-one

*Tuesday. Morning.*
*Ethan missing for eighty-six hours*

DEVEREAUX WAS BACK ON THE RIGHT SIDE OF THE DESK WHEN the other officer reappeared.

"Mountain Brook?" The guy was a little out of breath. "July '67? Are you sure?"

"That's what my lieutenant told me." Devereaux pulled a puzzled expression. "Why? Wasn't anything there?"

"Nope. Nada. Meaning I trailed across the length of a football field and back for no reason."

"This is weird." Devereaux shook his head. "There were no records of stolen paintings in 1972, either. This whole trip was a wash."

"Is your lieutenant pissed with you?" The officer pushed past Devereaux and flopped back down in his chair. "Or does she have a mean sense of humor?"

"She's not. Yet. And she doesn't, as far as I know." Devereaux turned and started for the exit. "But I'm sure going to find out. Thanks for your help. And sorry for wasting your time."

Devereaux waited until he was hidden behind his Charger before loosening his shirt and producing the file he'd tucked hurriedly into his pants. He figured he could worry about how to return it later. Right then, his priority was finding out what it contained. He was tempted to snap the brittle, red seal immediately, but he knew that sitting in the archive parking lot reading a bunch of stolen official documents wouldn't be his smartest move.

By the time he'd driven back to his building, parked, and ridden up to his apartment, Devereaux's mood had changed entirely. He didn't even want to touch the file anymore, let alone look at its contents. Even after almost forty years, the memory of Tomcik breaking the news of his father's death still haunted him. The intangible thought of it was bad enough. He didn't know if he could face reading about it, blow by blow, right there in black and white.

Devereaux dropped the file on his coffee table and turned his back on it. Then he sat on the couch and stared at its impersonal, typewritten label for ten long minutes. His mind was flipping one way, then the other. *Read it. Smuggle it back, unopened. Read it. Smuggle it back . . .*

In the end, he decided to read it.

The file was slim. Inside the coarse manila cover there were only five pages:

- Tomcik's report.
- Detective Jenner's report. Jenner had been Tomcik's partner, until he was killed trying to stop a convenience store robbery while off duty, three months later.
- A forensic report, signed by the officer who'd examined the crime scene.
- The medical examiner's report, detailing the injuries to Devereaux's father and Raymond Kerr.
- A statement from the officer-involved-shooting inquiry board, confirming that Tomcik's and Jenner's use of fatal force had been fully justified.

Devereaux started with Tomcik's report. The style was terse and direct, as it had been in the files that

Devereaux had read at his house. The narrative recounted how, acting on information received from a confidential informant, Tomcik and Jenner had gone to Detective Devereaux's house because they believed his life to be in danger. Finding the front door open, they entered the premises. They encountered Raymond Kerr standing near Detective Devereaux's prostrate body. They called out to Kerr, identifying themselves as police officers and ordering him to drop his weapon and get down on the floor. Kerr failed to comply, and instead turned and raised his weapon in a threatening manner. Acting solely in self-defense, Tomcik and Jenner opened fire. Paramedics were called, but arrived on the scene too late to save either Detective Devereaux or Raymond Kerr.

Jenner's report said essentially the same thing—it was obvious to Devereaux that they'd concocted them together—and their statements were backed up by the forensics report and the medical examiner's conclusion. As far as the paperwork was concerned, there was no room for misunderstanding. It was a slam dunk. Devereaux was not surprised in the least that the firearms board had ruled the way it did.

But he did have one other question.

How could every single person involved in the case have been lying?

## Chapter Seventy-two

THE WOMAN HAD STAYED AHEAD OF THE GAME FOR SO LONG for a reason.

Actually, for several reasons. She was smart. She was subtle. She was patient. She was organized. She was disciplined. And these were all traits that had enabled her to develop a set of rules, and to stick to them. It didn't matter if she was tired. If she was hungry. If there was something else she'd rather be doing. If circumstances called for a particular response, she answered. Always. And without question.

Until that morning.

She knew there was a chance her vehicle had been spotted at the meeting she'd attended on Sunday night. She'd been the first to enter the diner. The other person could have been in the parking lot, waiting for her to arrive. Watching. Noting the details of her Mercedes. Gathering information. That's what she'd have done, if the roles had been reversed. So according to her rules, she should switch to another vehicle. A clean one. Which would be easy to do, because she had one standing by, not far from the route she was on. A standard move in her rigorously prepared game plan.

But nothing was standard anymore.

She had a unique rendezvous coming up, and she could see that allowing someone else a hint of something familiar—even if it was just a car they recognized—could actually help her.

She wasn't breaking her rule, she reassured herself. She was flexing it.

Giving herself an even greater chance of success.

## Chapter Seventy-three

*Tuesday. Morning.*
*Ethan missing for eighty-six and three-quarter hours*

BRONSON SEGARD WAS LYING COMPLETELY STILL WHEN Devereaux stepped into his room in the hospital, thirty minutes later.

Devereaux had given no thought to what he'd do if Segard had fallen into a coma or died. It was as if his brain had defaulted to a primitive, instant response mode, and was only capable of looking one step ahead at a time. When he saw the old man's pallid, almost transparent skin it struck Devereaux that he might have made an error of judgment. But given he was there—and in the absence of other options—he figured he may as well soldier on.

"Mr. Segard? It's Cooper Devereaux. Do you remember me? I need to talk to you. Urgently. I need your help."

The old man didn't respond.

"It's about my father." Devereaux leaned in closer. "You knew him. He was your friend."

The old man showed no reaction.

"Mr. Segard? Can you hear me?"

There was still no answer. Devereaux was about to turn and head for the door, bereft of further ideas, when his eye settled on the monitor above Segard's bed. The little dot had suddenly picked up the pace on its journey across the screen.

"Mr. Segard, give it up. I can see your pulse rate increasing. I know you're awake."

Segard opened his eyes.

"Busted." His voice was like a soft breeze blowing through dry grass. "Now knock off that needing-me bullshit. Accept it. You're wasting your time. Look at me. I'm wasting away. How can I help you?"

"I need your brain, not your body." Devereaux perched on the edge of the bed. "I'm looking for information. About my father. To do with the night he was killed. I've seen the file. I read Tomcik's report. And Jenner's. And I need to know why what they said was wrong."

"I wasn't Tomcik's partner, back when your father bought the farm. And I never worked with Jenner. I don't know what they wrote in those reports."

"Jenner was killed only a few weeks after my father. And it was the Kerr case, for Pete's sake. It was huge. It made Tomcik into a rock star. You guys must have talked about it."

"Not really."

"I know you did. You came to my building. You gave me a warning. You said, *If she finds out about your father*. I figure the *she* is Loflin. But you know more. You know something, anyway. And whatever it is, I need you to tell me."

"What did Tomcik's report say?"

Devereaux told him, keeping as close to Tomcik's words as he could remember.

"That sounds like what happened." Segard clasped his hands, making the tendons in his wrists stand out like wires.

"No! Not you, too." Devereaux felt like he was going crazy. "That *is not* what happened. The reports all said my father was killed at home. But he wasn't. *I* was the one at home. And I was *alone*. Tomcik came and found me there, afterward. That's when he told me my father had been killed. I remember it like it was yesterday. I still dream about it. And Jenner was with him when he pulled me out of the place I was hiding. So why would he lie in the report? Why would they both lie?"

"Son, we need to step this back a little." Segard started to wheeze. "First question. Have you found out about Madison Nesbitt?"

"Yes, I have. But she's dead. She was killed in a fire in 1975."

Segard shook his head, which made his snow-white hair rustle softly against the stiff pillowcase.

"She—" Segard's wheezing grew stronger, obscuring his words.

"Was the daughter of a murderer," Devereaux suggested, trying to pick up the thread.

"That, too—" Segard broke off again, wracked by a fit of coughing. "Her father was a scumbag called Burke."

"Mitchell Burke." Devereaux nodded, willing the old man to continue breathing long enough to finish the story. "He strangled a bunch of people."

"He did. Till Tomcik took him down. In '68, I think. Madison was nine years old. She went into the system, and ended up in foster care. Tomcik made sure she went to a good family. Kind people. Had heaps of money, too, which was a bonus. They adopted her when she was ten. That's when they changed her name to theirs. Nesbitt."

"She was born Madison Burke?"

Segard nodded.

"She had to go through life knowing her father was a serial killer?" Devereaux was horrified.

"Yes." Sadness spread across Segard's face. "She was a difficult child. Trouble was never far behind her. She could never escape her genes, I guess. I wasn't honestly too surprised when the fire happened. All those deaths. What a tragedy . . . Anyway, Tomcik learned. He had to break the cycle. So with you, he did things different."

"Because I *was* different." Devereaux pushed himself

away from the bed, sending an avalanche of fishing magazines sliding to the floor. "My father was a cop, like him. Like you."

"Your father was *not* a cop. He just wanted to be one. He bought an old Javelin squad car when the department was done with it. Lived in a cop neighborhood. Took a job as a security guard, so he could wear some kind of uniform. And he had to tell you something. He was always going out all night. You were a kid. You believed it. So Tomcik made it true. He fudged the paperwork. You could do that kind of thing, back then. He changed your last name, right away. Or more like, he gave you a last name. Your father had never enrolled you in school, so you'd never had much use for one. Tomcik made it look like you'd been a Devereaux all along. Part of a good Alabama family. Ties right back to the Bonapartists. Never a Kerr. He made you the son of a detective, Cooper. Of a hero. Not of a monster."

## Chapter Seventy-four

*Tuesday. Morning.*
*Ethan missing for eighty-seven and a quarter hours*

DEVEREAUX HAD ALWAYS MADE A POINT OF ONLY HURTING
people who deserved to be hurt.

That had been his way even before he joined the police. Whether he'd been dealing with thieves. Bullies.
Drug dealers. Muggers. Extortionists. Arsonists. Fraud-
sters. Rapists. Sadists. Killers. They'd all been bad people. They'd all had their punishments coming to them.

But the truth was, Devereaux hadn't ever been motivated solely by an urge to make a living. Or defend soci-
ety. Even when he was in uniform. There was a part of
him—if he was completely honest—that had always enjoyed the violence. He'd kept that fact in the shadows.
Disguised it. Given it other names. But there was no hiding from it now. Segard had exposed everything.
Devereaux didn't have a cop's blood in his veins. He had
a murderer's blood.

Segard had been wrong about only one thing. Tomcik
may have had the best of intentions. But the cycle of
destruction hadn't been broken.

Not yet, anyway.

Devereaux didn't know how to form a noose, so he
tied a Honda knot—the kind cowboys used to make las-

sos with in the Old West—then slung the rope over the beam in the center of his great-grandfather's cabin.

Except that it wasn't *his* great-grandfather's cabin anymore. It was *somebody else's* great-grandfather's cabin. To him, now, it was just *a* cabin. He had no business being there. He had no family ties to the place. The decaying wooden structure couldn't magically connect him with any previous generations. And that was just as well, given what lurked in his DNA. He'd thought he was a good man. Or that he at least had the potential to be good. Because his father was good. But thanks to Tomcik's meddling, Devereaux's assumption was wrong. His logic was faulty. It was a false positive. His relatives were poisonous. Therefore *he* was poisonous. He could see that now. It wasn't his foster families' fault he'd gone off the rails in his younger years. His schools weren't to blame, either. For his poor grades. His bad disciplinary record. The kind of people he hung out with. It was unavoidable.

It was written in his genes.

Looking back, the FBI had been right to reject him. They were the only ones who'd ever taken a proper look. They'd done the psychological tests. Picked up on his deficiencies. And seen what everyone else had missed.

He was cursed. He contaminated everything he touched.

The sooner the world was rid of him, the better off it would be.

## Chapter Seventy-five

IF EVERYTHING WAS STILL ON TRACK, THIS WOULD BE THE LAST stop she'd have to make.

It had involved a slight detour to reach another Internet cafe, but the woman wanted to check on her webcams one last time. To be certain that everything was ready for their arrival, less than a hundred miles up the road. They were tantalizingly close. But she'd invested so much time and effort over the last few months it would be crazy not to take a few more minutes and make sure every detail was still perfectly on track.

The woman was desperate for things to run smoothly, since she'd have company with her for the first time. She wanted the torch to be passed without a hitch. And she didn't want to get bogged down in any avoidable snafus that could make her late getting to the girl's house for the start of the next phase. The more time the girl spent with her mother, the more opportunities there'd be for the plan to be knocked off track.

Normally the woman wouldn't be too anxious about a thing like that. If something unexpected happened, she'd just wait. Retrench. Bide her time until the circumstances were to her liking. But now, time to wait was something she didn't have.

They'd been on the road since before dawn, so as soon as she was done with the computer the woman let the boy stretch his legs and use the restroom. She changed her wig and her cardigan, one last time. Made the boy change his shirt. Checked the car. Retrieved a discarded sweatshirt and his cuddly rabbit from the foot well and threw them in the trunk with the other things she'd need to dispose of.

But she let him keep his little monkey.

She was thorough. Not heartless.

## Chapter Seventy-six

*Tuesday. Late Morning.*
*Ethan missing for eighty-eight hours*

DEVEREAUX NEVER GOT AS FAR AS PUTTING HIS HEAD
through the loop in the rope.

Would he have done it if the beam hadn't collapsed
when he tried to test its strength? He was adamant that
he wouldn't have. That the whole thing was symbolic.
That it was just a way to help him get over the shock of
learning about his heritage.

A shaft of sunshine blazed into the room from a new
hole that had been torn in the roof when the beam gave
way. Devereaux lay on his back, pinned in place by
pieces of the wooden framework and dislodged shingles, and stared up through the gap. He could see the
blue sky, way above the cabin. Closer to him specks of
dust and tiny fragments of wood floated aimlessly,
trapped in the bright confines of the light. He stayed
still, watching them drift. They were displaced and un-
wanted, just like him. But unlike him, they didn't have a
choice.

He moved one leg, freeing it from the debris. He
pulled the other one clear. Then he heard a car approaching. He threw off the rest of the clutter and a

second later he was on his feet and heading for the door.

He figured it would most likely be Lieutenant Hale. The officer at the archive must have realized he'd been played and raised the alarm. His lieutenant would have called Hale, out of professional courtesy. And she would have wanted to contain the damage. The worst case would be that she'd sent a pair of uniforms to bring him in, again. If so, he could get to the woods long before them. Retrieve his car. Head back to the archive. Return the file. And then, when he was ready, he'd face the music on his own terms.

The engine note grew louder, but when the car appeared Devereaux could see it wasn't Hale's. Or a squad car. It was a Subaru station wagon. In dark green. It was moving fast. The driver was confident. Or reckless. A kid had probably stolen the car, and now was out to drive around until he wrecked it or got it stuck in a ditch. He'd probably pass right by—why would he be interested in a broken-down old cabin when he had someone else's vehicle to play with?—but Devereaux reached for his Glock anyway, just in case. He held it ready, down at his side. Then he caught his first proper glimpse of the person behind the wheel.

It was Loflin.

Loflin, who'd killed Tomcik.

Tomcik, who'd given Devereaux his name.

Discovering the true identity of the man Tomcik had killed had thrown Devereaux for a loop, at first. But the reality had sunk in now. And he could see that nothing had really changed. Tomcik had stopped a serial killer. That was the bottom line. He was a cop. It was his job. Devereaux would have done the same thing, in his shoes. A murderer is a murderer, whoever his offspring may be.

Devereaux felt the familiar calm clarity descend upon him. He understood what it was now. Where it came from. But he didn't reject it. Or fight it. Even though he knew it was a murderer's legacy. He saw that he could use it. He stepped back behind the cabin door and waited for Loflin to come closer. She had a debt to pay for what she'd done to Tomcik.

But she also had Ethan.

First things first.

## Chapter Seventy-seven

*Tuesday. Late Morning.*
*Ethan missing for eighty-eight and a quarter hours*

LOFLIN JUMPED OUT OF THE CAR, LEAVING THE DOOR OPEN and the engine running.

"Cooper? Are you here? It's Jan. I need your help. Right now! I'm in a whole heap of trouble."

"I'm inside." Devereaux kept an eye on her through a crack in the door.

Loflin raced across the open ground toward the cabin. Devereaux waited for her to cross the threshold, then grabbed her by the hair. He pulled her forward and flung her against the wall. She slammed sideways into the wood and slid down to the floor. Devereaux picked her up. He hauled her to the couch. Pushed her face-first into the cracked leather surface. Put his knee between her shoulder blades to hold her in place. And jammed his gun against the base of her neck.

"You kidnapped an innocent child, Jan." He leaned down so that his mouth was near her ear, close enough that he could smell the lacquer in her hair. "You killed a retired cop. That's two lines you can't uncross. I could beat you to death and drag your body into town behind my car, and they'd still give me a medal. You know it's true. But I'm a fair-minded guy. I'm going to give you a chance to avoid that happening. All you have to do is tell me where Ethan is."

Loflin started to mumble into the cushions so Devereaux let her raise her head a couple of inches.

"I don't have him." She gasped for breath. "I didn't take him. You've got it all wrong."

"There was an eyewitness." Devereaux pressed harder with the gun, breaking the skin and drawing a little blood. "At the hotel. The clerk I spoke to. David Day. The one you carefully avoided seeing on Sunday. He ID'd you from your photo. And Ethan's clothing was found at your house. You can't talk your way out of this, Jan. The time for bullshitting is over. Tell me where the boy is. If Ethan doesn't walk away from this mess, neither do you."

"I can explain." Loflin was almost shrieking. "This witness? Dave the clerk? I didn't deliberately avoid him. And he didn't identify *me*. He made a mistake. You need to listen. Because I know where Ethan is. Or where he's going to be. Very soon. That's why I'm here. Why I came to find you."

"Quit lying."

"I'm not lying! You want to know who kidnapped Ethan? It was my mother! She looks just like me. The clerk obviously mixed us up."

"What's your mother's name?"

"Rebecca Loflin."

"What was her maiden name?"

"Rebecca Nesbitt. But she was born Madison Burke."

Devereaux let Loflin go. She flopped forward and sprawled on the couch for a moment. Then she rolled over, hauled herself upright, and turned to face him.

"Why don't you believe me?" Tears of frustration were starting to form in her eyes. "I'm not lying. I swear to you."

"Madison Burke's dead, Jan." Devereaux kept his voice calm and level. "She was killed in a fire. At the Nesbitt house. A few years after they'd adopted her."

"No." Loflin was adamant. "She didn't die. She survived the fire. She was the only one who did."

"The FBI says she died."

"What would they know? They weren't there. The Nesbitts lived in the middle of nowhere. They had no neighbors. No family. No friends. The kids were home-schooled, so there were no teachers. My mother was practically the same age as her foster sister, Rebecca. She had no driver's license. No photo ID was on file anywhere. Neither of them had ever been to a dentist's office in their lives. So when the fire department finally showed up, she pretended to be Rebecca. No one ever knew the difference."

"Why would she do that?"

"You know who her father was, right? She wanted to get out of his shadow. She saw the opportunity. And she took it. Wouldn't you have done the same?"

Devereaux took a moment to think about it. Could things have been bad enough for her to steal another kid's identity? He wasn't convinced. But he didn't doubt it strongly enough to dismiss her story out of hand.

"Let's talk about the present." Devereaux took a bottle of water from his pile and wiped away a layer of dust that had fallen from the roof. "You're saying your mom has taken Ethan?"

Loflin nodded.

"Did she take all those other kids, as well?"

"There were some others." Loflin nodded again. "I'm not sure if it's as many as the FBI think."

"What did she do to them? Did she kill them?"

"I don't know. I guess so. I'm still piecing things together."

"Is Ethan still alive?"

"Yes."

"Are you sure?"

"Positive. But I know she has something planned for him. I think it's something bad. We have to stop her. You have to help me, Cooper. I can't do it on my own."

"Hold your horses. You knew your mom had kidnapped Ethan the whole time we were searching for him. You were stringing us along. Not to mention that poor kid's parents. Why should I trust you now?"

"No." Loflin shook her head violently. "Listen. I didn't know what she was doing. Not all along. I was in denial. Looking back, all those years ago, there were clues, I guess. I can see that now. But it only became fully clear two nights ago. My mom's sick. She's terminal. All my life she talked about me following in her footsteps. Carrying on her work. It's only since her cancer brought us closer that I realized what she meant. I humored her for a few months. Who can say no to a dying mother, right? At first it was easy. She talked me into sweeping up a couple of drug dealers and a gang enforcer who'd got off on technicalities. She had me use my contacts at the department to find new evidence. They were people with bad genes, she said. And after them, it was you. She sent me a whole file making you out to be the new Al Capone. Then, Sunday, at the Roadside Rendezvous, I saw her on the CCTV. She'd hidden her face, and she was in disguise, but it wasn't enough to fool me. That's why I left the manager's office when I did. Not to avoid the clerk. So I could call my mom. We fixed to meet, that night. And she laid it all out. Ethan. The other kids. All of it. The FBI found a couple of things of Ethan's that she'd given me as proof, at my house. And some of the tranquilizer she'd used on him. They put two and two together, and skipped a generation. I should have told someone—you, Hale, Bruckner, Grandison—I get that. But I didn't know what to do. I panicked. We're talking about my *mom*, Cooper."

## Chapter Seventy-eight

*Tuesday. Late Morning.*
*Ethan missing for eighty-eight and a half hours*

DEVEREAUX HAD BEEN WATCHING LOFLIN THE WHOLE TIME she was talking.

The years he'd spent with the police department had honed his instinct for sensing lies, and he wasn't picking up anything that worried him. But he was also aware that Loflin was light-years away from the people he normally pulled off the streets. She was no drug dealer, claiming not to know how a dead rival's blood came to be on a baseball bat in the trunk of her car. Or a factory worker, denying she'd found out a co-worker was sleeping with her husband the night before the slut mysteriously disappeared. Loflin was an undercover detective whose life depended on her ability to deceive.

"You told me your mom was a psychologist." Devereaux took a sip of water, still unsure whether to believe her. "It's quite a leap, from counseling to kidnapping. How did it happen?"

"It was a gradual thing." Loflin straightened her blouse. "She'd always been obsessed with genetic inheritance, since she was a little girl. Because of her father, I guess. She was always reading theories about destiny and such. She studied it at graduate school."

"How could a kid in her shoes afford graduate school? Did someone give her a scholarship?"

"She didn't need one. Everyone thought she was Rebecca, so after the fire she inherited the Nesbitts' money. A ton of it. College, graduate school, starting her own practice, funding her research, none of it even scratched the surface. And whether it was her destiny, I don't know, but she went on to get hired by the FBI. As a contractor, not an agent. Her specialty was helping people deal with trauma. Kids, in particular. Including, one day, the daughter of a serial killer in New Mexico who'd been shot by the police."

"So how did it work? Your mom had suffered when she was a kid, so she wanted to pay it forward?"

"No!" Loflin's eyes blazed. "She's crazy, but she's not evil. She thinks she's rescuing them from their fate. She thinks that without her, the kids would be doomed to follow in their parents' footsteps."

"So why take Ethan?"

"You don't know?" Loflin stepped forward and touched Devereaux's shoulder. "Cooper, all the kids she took? The orphans? Their fathers were *all* serial killers. That's the link. From mom's father, to her, to them."

*And from my father to me.* Devereaux was stunned.

"Ethan's father killed his mother." Loflin took her hand back and swept her hair out of her face. "She was his seventh victim. He cut her throat when she found out about victim number six. An au pair they'd hired illegally from Venezuela. The neighbors heard screaming. The police were called. The father was shot. And Ethan was taken into care."

"Did Ethan know about his father?"

"I'm not sure. He was pretty young. He may not have."

"Your mom was his caseworker?" Devereaux forced himself to change tack. "Why wasn't this flagged up? Bruckner or Grandison should have done a full background check on her when they came up with the law enforcement angle."

"Bruckner and Grandison wouldn't have known about her. These days, all the records are centralized. My mom's senior enough that she can get printouts of the entire database. A kid doesn't have to be her patient for her to find out about him."

"Then how did she find out about me? *I* didn't even know about my father."

"Because of the cancer, indirectly. She was cleaning house, ready for when the end came. The old guy Tomcik was the one who'd gotten her placed with her foster family. She knew he'd been keeping tabs on her, up till the fire. She suspected he'd kept a file. She didn't want any records left behind, so she went to get it. And found yours at the same time. You're another child of a serial killer, and she believes it's her mission to save you."

"She's crazy."

"You think?"

"Crazy, but smart, too. It was she who lied to the lieutenant to get me put on ice then brought back in time to catch this case, I bet."

"Right. But I didn't know at first. She just told me to report on what you were doing. I thought it was just for background, not to confirm her plan was working."

"She wanted me close, but not too close. So she had you jerk me around like a puppet, swallowing her misdirections like I was fresh out of uniform."

"No. I didn't know about any of that until Sunday night, when she told me about Ethan."

"How did you leave things with her, Sunday? Does she believe you're doing what she wants? Going to meet with her?"

"Yes. What else could I do? If she stopped trusting me, she'd cut me off. We'd lose touch. I figured our only chance of saving Ethan was for me to play along. And it was working. I know where she's taking him. We still have time to get there ahead of her."

Devereaux had heard enough. He'd made his decision.

"Come on." He checked that he had his keys and

headed for the door. "We need a cell signal. Then we need to contact Lieutenant Hale. Get her to put a hostage rescue team—"

"I already tried, Cooper." Loflin hadn't moved. "She didn't believe me. And you can't blame her. The *evidence* against me looks pretty compelling."

"That's crap. I'll talk to her. She'll believe me."

"What if she doesn't? Didn't you already tell her my mother was the kidnapper? You didn't know she was my mother then, and you used her old name, but might the lieutenant not think you're flogging a dead horse, here? Trying to save face? And if she doesn't believe you—which she probably won't—she'll order you to arrest me. What would you do then?"

Devereaux was running through rescue scenarios in his head, weighing the odds of needing reinforcements.

"I'm not worried for myself." Loflin shrugged. "I'm innocent, and I can prove it. It would just take time. But if I don't show up when my mother's expecting me, she'll think I've betrayed her. It'll be the kiss of death for Ethan."

There were ways in which involving Lieutenant Hale made sense. But in one respect, her presence would be a major disadvantage.

"She's not going to buy it, Cooper. Believe me. I spoke to her right before I drove over here. Her mind's made up. Look, this isn't about me saving my own ass. I've done nothing wrong. Except break procedure, and I'll take whatever's coming my way on that. I'll turn myself in. I'll resign. I'll go to jail, if I have to. But first, we've got to save that kid. I couldn't live with my conscience, otherwise. It's down to you and me, Cooper. Whether he lives or dies. At this point, we're Ethan's best hope. Actually, we're his only hope."

Devereaux was confident he wouldn't need help to save Ethan from a cancerous old woman. But that wasn't the clincher. Another factor was weighing on his mind. The likelihood that Loflin's mother was the one who'd killed Tomcik. And the drawback of facing her in front of an unnecessary witness.

## Chapter Seventy-nine

*Tuesday. Late Morning.*
*Ethan missing for eighty-eight and three-quarter hours*

ONCE THEY WERE IN THE CAR, LOFLIN WASN'T INTERESTED IN any more talking.

Several times Devereaux tried to spark up a conversation—to apologize for the way he'd treated her back at the cabin, to ask about her experiences growing up, to explore the common ground that must have given them—but on each occasion she shut him down with a grunt or a wave of her hand. All her concentration was devoted to guiding the old Subaru away from the cabin, and then getting away from Birmingham itself as quickly as possible.

They'd been on the road for seventy minutes when Loflin made a sharp right into the mouth of a tiny track. She kept going for another mile. The car was pitching and bouncing like a boat in a storm but still she refused to lift her foot off the gas.

The expanse of cotton plants on the right-hand side of the track abruptly gave way to a patch of scrubby woodland. Soon an old wall became visible through the trees. After another half mile the undergrowth parted, giving access to a gate. It was made of wrought iron, ten feet tall and twelve wide with fancy Doric motifs set into the rail at the top. A length of chain with a heavy-duty pad-lock was dangling near the center. The pillars on either side were stone—stained and crumbling—with polished granite spheres perched on top. The one on the left was leaning inward, threatening to collapse at any moment.

Devereaux wrestled the gates open just wide enough for the Subaru to fit through. The ground on the far side was softer. It was lined with tire tracks. He counted four sets. Three were starting to fade, but one was definitely fresh. Loflin saw them, too, and shot Devereaux a worried frown as he climbed back into the car alongside her.

The track followed a gentle arc through what Devereaux guessed had been formal gardens before the forest started to reassert itself, and led to the front of a huge plantation-style mansion. Six Doric columns held up a portico with a peeling Greek-key frieze above two rows of classically proportioned windows. The roof was steeply pitched, and a cupola—the largest Devereaux had ever seen—extended the whole length of its peak. Steps ran up to the porch between the central pair of pillars, leading to an ornately paneled double-width front door that had definitely seen better days.

One side of the door was standing open. And parked near the bottom of the steps was a black M-Class Mercedes.

"Shit." Loflin pointed to the SUV. "That's Mom's car. She made good time. And she could be anywhere. This place looks massive."

Loflin was in favor of charging straight in and getting the confrontation over with, but Devereaux took a more measured approach. He insisted that they walk around the perimeter of the house first to get an idea of its layout and possible alternative entry points. They moved slowly, trying to lessen the sound their feet made as they crunched through the sun-dried grass, and by the time they'd completed the circuit Devereaux had counted thirty ground-floor windows. They were all the same size. All their shutters were closed. And all were covered with sturdy, inch-and-a-quarter-diameter steel bars. The bars definitely weren't part of the original design. But they were the only things in a decent state of repair.

The only other potential entry point—or escape route, if things went badly—was an angled trapdoor three-quarters of the way along the left side of the building. It was situated next to a cluster of standpipes like the kind used to fill heating tanks with oil. The hinges showed signs of having recently been opened, but when Devereaux drew closer he saw the trapdoor was held shut by another industrial-strength padlock.

Their only option was to go straight through the front door, as Loflin had originally suggested. Devereaux went first, and found himself in a wide hallway with a broad, curving staircase in front of him. All around, the paint was peeling from the walls, revealing patches of plaster and brick. Niches on both sides of the staircase stood empty. Two gilded picture frames were still hanging away to the left, but their contents had long since been removed. A white alabaster statue of a Greek god lay smashed on the floor in the corner. The space was illuminated by a weird greenish light and Devereaux was immediately hit by the smell of chemicals mixed with damp, like at a swimming pool.

Loflin followed, and after the echo of her footsteps died away they stood still for thirty seconds, listening. The house was completely silent. There was no clue which way to go.

"Where did your mom tell you to meet her?" Devereaux kept his voice to a whisper.

"She wasn't specific." Loflin shrugged. "She just gave me directions to the house."

"Try calling her."

Loflin yelled, "Mom, you here?"

There was no reply.

"Try calling her on the phone."

Loflin pulled out her cell, feeling embarrassed, and hit a speed dial key. They could hear the muffled ringtone coming from her handset, but no answering melody from her mother's end. The house remained obstinately and unhelpfully silent.

"Shall we go up?" Loflin put the phone away. "Down? Or search the ground floor, since we're already here?"

It took them less than three minutes to establish that Loflin's mother wasn't in any of the eight large, empty, moldering rooms on the ground floor. Devereaux's instinct was to go down, so next they checked the basement. The front section was empty, save for leaves and other detritus that had blown in through the holes that time had worn in the stacks of ventilation bricks beneath the porch. The rear section, which could have been reached from the trapdoor they'd seen on the outside, was separated by a rough brick wall with a rickety wooden door near one end. It opened easily. But they couldn't go through. Because behind it was another door.

It was made of shiny steel.

And it was locked.

## Chapter Eighty

*Tuesday. Early Afternoon.*
*Ethan missing for ninety hours*

THE LOCK WAS A SOLID ONE.

Solid, but not impregnable. It took Devereaux just over a minute to get it open. He mimed a countdown from three. Pushed the door. Stepped forward, his gun and flashlight held steady in front of him. And immediately regretted not choosing to go upstairs.

The space was effectively a room inside a room, and it was kitted out like a private mortuary. There was a stainless steel dissection table, with a porcelain headrest that made the hairs on Devereaux's neck dance like they were blowing in the wind. There was a bench full of cutting tools. A small autoclave. A shelf, with a dozen or so empty glass jars lined up, large to small, left to right. A thing like a glass coffin, set on a gurney trolley. Three shiny cylinders, six feet tall by two feet in diameter, plumbed in against the wall. But no sign of Ethan. And nothing to persuade Devereaux to stay.

"What the hell was that?" Devereaux couldn't get up the stairs fast enough.

Loflin shrugged. "Are you OK? Do you need some air?"

"No." Devereaux got hold of himself. "Let's keep going. We should try the second floor."

The grand staircase opened onto a landing with ten doors leading off it. Devereaux waited for Loflin to catch up, then pointed to the first one on the left. He pushed the door open and crept inside. The room was set up as a kid's bedroom. A girl's. It smelled of lilac. The floor was covered with soft, pale pink carpet. The walls were papered with jungle scenes, showing dozens of exotic animals in their natural habitats. Hampers overflowing with cuddly animals covered the floor. And in the bed—in animal pajamas, under an animal comforter—was a creepy-looking, little-girl-size doll.

Loflin turned and sprinted for the door. Devereaux heard her feet clattering down the landing, and then the sound of vomiting. For a moment he was puzzled. Then the truth hit him, and he felt his own stomach start to rebel. The figure in the bed. He recognized the face. It was Miranda Gonzalez. The actual girl. Her own body, preserved. Not a doll. The one who'd disappeared in New Mexico, sixteen years ago. Loflin's mother's first victim.

Devereaux went to check on Loflin. She was sitting on the top step, her head between her knees, breathing heavily, pale as a ghost. Then he moved on to the next room. He paused outside, dreading what he might find, but spurred on by the fading hope that he could still save Ethan.

Devereaux pushed open the door. This room smelled of leather. It was set up like a baseball stadium. The Twins. There was a diamond marked out on the floor, complete with ochre sand. A pitcher's mound in the center. Seats painted on the walls, with false perspective carefully employed to extend right up to the bleachers. And at the plate—in the angle of the walls at the far corner—was a little boy. A little boy's body, anyway. It was propped up, somehow. Dressed in pinstripes. Bat raised, ready to receive a pitch. Its face was obscured by the peak of its cap, so Devereaux had to get uncomfortably close to be certain, but it wasn't Ethan.

Devereaux was about to leave when he spotted something that made his skin crawl even more. A webcam. It was mounted on the wall, tucked in amongst the painted cameras of the press corps. It made him wonder how many others there'd been in the house. Downstairs. In the basement. The awful mortuary room. Miranda's bedroom. And then a worse thought hit him: Was Loflin's mother watching him, right now?

Pushing thoughts of Big Brother aside, Devereaux moved on to the next room. Here the theme was space. The ceiling and three of the walls were painted a bluey purple and speckled with stars. On the fourth wall there was a magnificent mural of the earth rising above the moon. Beneath it was a mock-up of the inside of a Saturn V command module, but with only one seat. And strapped into it, wearing a tiny astronaut costume complete with NASA mission patches, sat a perfectly preserved six-year-old girl.

The next door opened onto a replica of Andy's bedroom from *Toy Story*. All the main characters were there: Woody. Jessie. Bullseye. Mr. and Mrs. Potato Head. Slinky Dog. Etch. Wheezy. Stinky Pete. And on the bed, Buzz Lightyear.

Buzz was much bigger than the other toys. He was the size of a seven-year-old child. For a moment Devereaux's heart refused to beat. Then he rushed across the room. Pulled back the visor. And saw the face he'd last seen staring imploringly down at him from the FBI's projection screen.

There was no doubt this time. The search was over. He'd found Ethan Crane.

## Chapter Eighty-one

*Tuesday. Early Afternoon.*

LOFLIN APPEARED AT THE DOOR THIRTY SECONDS AFTER Devereaux called her.

She was pale, and she clearly did not want to come inside. But when she saw Ethan's body lying frozen on the bed she pushed her fear aside and took her place next to Devereaux.

"Did you check for a pulse?"

"Yes. There is one. It's faint as hell, but he's hanging in there. And look . . ."

Devereaux pointed to a clear tube that emerged from Ethan's left sleeve and snaked up to a bag of fluid tucked away behind Bo Peep and her sheep on a narrow shelf above the head of the bed.

"Angel of mercy killers usually sedate their victims before they finish them. They believe they're saving them, so they want to avoid causing pain. If your mother hasn't gone beyond that stage yet, Ethan's still got a chance. You stay here. Watch over him. And call 911. I'll keep looking for her."

"Wait." Loflin looked like she was on the verge of panic. "I don't have a gun. I had to surrender it, until the verdict comes back on the Carver shooting."

"No problem." Devereaux took out his gun and offered it to her. "Here. Take mine. I have a spare."

The room next to Ethan's—the last one on the same side of the corridor—was a bathroom. So was the room opposite it. The next one, working back toward the stairs, was another bedroom. The walls were plastered, but not decorated in any way. A pink carpet lay rolled up on the floor. The mattress and the frame of the bed were bare. In the center of the room several boxes of Barbie dolls were stacked up next to some cans of paint and a pile of books with pictures of the world's most famous dollhouses. But there was no kid. And no sign of Loflin's mother.

Devereaux opened the next door and was faced with an expanse of crisp white paintwork. The drapes at the window were steel gray. A chrome-finish twin-bell mechanical alarm clock sat on the nightstand. There was a single picture on the wall. Of a cabin. *His* cabin. Below it there was a clothes rail on a wheeled stand. Devereaux moved closer to examine the garments hanging on it. There were blue button-down shirts. Khaki pants. Black T-shirts. And at the end, a Clash "I Fought the Law" shirt. Devereaux took it off its hanger and checked the back. There was a hole. It was in the right place, but it was freshly made. And cut with nail scissors, rather than ripped during a brawl.

"Cooper! It's so good to see you."

Devereaux spun around, still holding the shirt. A woman had appeared in the doorway. She was five-feet-four tall with fine, shoulder-length blond hair. In every way a gaunt, older version of Loflin, right down to the absence of her right earlobe. She was holding a stainless steel tray in her hand with a can of beer and a glass balanced on it.

"Would you like a drink?" She held the tray out. "I got you Avondale Battlefield. Your favorite."

"Thank you." Devereaux threw the T-shirt on the

bed, then took the tray and set it down more gently. "What should I call you? Madison? Rebecca? Mrs. Loflin?"

"Call me whatever you like. Now drink your beer. I got it for you specially."

Every muscle in Devereaux's body was straining to grab the woman and shake the truth out of her about what kind of drugs she'd given Ethan. But over the years he'd learned the hard way. With some people, you have to vary your approach.

"Thank you." Devereaux sat on the bed, bringing his head down to the woman's level, and poured himself some beer. The can was already opened. The "glass" was made of puny plastic, and Devereaux nearly crushed it when he picked it up. He readjusted his grip and lifted it to his lips. But he didn't take a sip. He just wanted to sniff the liquid, to try to get a sense of what kind of sedative the woman was using.

Whatever it was, it had no discernible odor.

"Do you like your room?" The woman was staying well out of his reach. "I want you to feel at home."

"I do like it." Devereaux sniffed the beer again. "The other rooms are good, too. Very imaginative. Great attention to detail. Do you have a favorite?"

"No. The rooms aren't for me. It's what the children think that counts."

"I'm hardly a child, Madison."

"We're all our parents' children. We're defined by the genes they pass on to us. It's about biology, Cooper. Not chronology. The fact you're a little older is neither here nor there. It's just a result of it taking me longer to find out about you."

"To find out what about me?"

"About your father. Who he was. What he was."

"John Devereaux? A Birmingham PD detective?"

"Are you in denial, Cooper? Or are you trying to play me? We both know the truth about the stock you come from. And why you're here."

"OK. You're right about me. But what about Ethan

Crane? You know there was a screwup with the records?"

"There was no screwup."

"There was. You wouldn't know, because it didn't come to light until we started investigating his disappearance. It's not your fault. It's Child Services'. They got the paperwork switched around when Ethan was put into the system. His real father was a welder. He was burned alive in an accident at a construction site. He wasn't shot by the police. The kid in the Buzz Lightyear suit? He doesn't belong here. His genes are normal. So let's do this. Let's get him out of here, so you can save the right little boy. The one who needs your help. Just confirm one thing for me—you've only given Ethan the sedative, right? Whatever comes after that—the thing that finally puts him to sleep—he hasn't had it?"

"He hadn't, when you were poking and prodding him a few minutes ago." The woman checked her watch. "But it's OK. He's getting it right now. My daughter's taking care of everything. It's her first time, and I'm truly proud."

## Chapter Eighty-two

*Tuesday. Afternoon.*

THE TWO WOMEN WERE WORKING TOGETHER?

Of course they were! Loflin herself had told him she was being groomed to take over from her mother. Then she'd shown up at his cabin with her whole "pity me" spiel, which ended up with her bringing him out here. On his own. With no backup. Even Lieutenant Hale had no idea where they were. No one did.

Devereaux couldn't believe he'd been so stupid as to leave Loflin alone with Ethan. If the boy died, it would be his fault. His only hope was that Loflin was dragging her feet, if this really was her first time. Devereaux stood up. He had to get back to Ethan's room . . .

"Stop!" The woman had produced an orange Taser gun from behind her back. "You know what one of these can do, don't you? You've probably used one yourself. So sit back down. And drink your damn beer."

Devereaux sank back onto the bed. He moved the tray to his lap, then raised the glass. His hand was shaking. He lifted the drink almost to his lips. And spilled it. Beer ran down his chin and onto his chest. He cursed and grabbed the Clash T-shirt with his spare hand. He wadded it up. Made as if to use it to mop his face. Then he flung the glass at the woman. He gripped the tray through the T-shirt. Held it in front of him like a shield. And charged forward.

The Taser darts deflected off the tray and buried themselves in the wall, away to Devereaux's right. He kept moving. Dropped the tray. Grabbed the woman by the arm. Spun her around. Pulled his handcuffs off his belt and snapped one around her wrist. He reached for her other arm. And felt something cold and hard pressing against the back of his skull.

"Let my mother go."

Devereaux spun around, aiming to grab the gun, but Loflin had been expecting the move. She sprang back, out of his reach, and kept the weapon trained on his head.

"Stop!" Loflin's voice was loud and shrill, but far from panicky. "Now sit down. Near the wall. Cross your legs. Put your hands on your head. And keep them there."

Devereaux took a moment to assess the situation. Loflin was clearly serious, so he slowly positioned himself on the smooth wood floor. The woman stepped toward her daughter, beaming with maternal pride.

"Darling, your timing's beautiful." She held up her wrist with Devereaux's handcuffs dangling from it. "Have you got a key for this thing?"

"Mother, you sit down, too. This isn't what either of you think."

## Chapter Eighty-three

*Tuesday. Afternoon.*

THE WOMAN ALMOST FELL INTO DEVEREAUX'S LAP.

She lowered herself to the ground and the loose hand-cuff banged into his knee. Her hand fluttered like a butterfly against his ankle, bringing home to him just how frail she was. It seemed incongruous to him that someone so tiny could be the cause of so much trouble, and like when her daughter shook his hand in Lieutenant Hale's office, three days ago, it made him feel clumsy.

"Jan?" Devereaux kept his eye on the gun. Loflin was holding it steady and aiming at a neutral point on the freshly painted wall, midway between his head and the woman's. "Let's remember why we came here. We need to think about Ethan. To make sure he's safe. That's the best way to help your mother."

Loflin didn't respond.

"How is Ethan?" Devereaux was trying to make eye contact. "Did you give him anything to . . . put him to sleep?"

"Of course I didn't." Loflin didn't move the gun. "He's fine. I disconnected the sedative and replaced it with saline. He'll be awake pretty soon."

"That's fantastic, Jan. But we need to be sure. We need to call the paramedics, and—"

"I already called them. An ambulance is on its way. And two squad cars."

"So why are we still here?"

"Because I'm looking to end this properly. I'm happy to take whatever consequences come my way. But I need a promise from each of you first."

"Don't know if I can do that, Jan. You know how this works."

"Hear me out, at least. Then decide. I need you to understand something about my mom."

"What about her?"

"She's crazy. Literally insane."

"You think?"

"Hey!" Loflin's mother stiffened.

"Mother, be quiet." Loflin's voice was calm and controlled. "Let me help you. Cooper, what I need you to understand is that however awful the things my mom did were, she honestly believed she was helping. She was wrong, but she believed she was right. And she doesn't have much time left. I don't want her to spend what little she has in jails and courthouses. I don't want her story splashed across the tabloids. I don't want her to die as some kind of sideshow freak."

"I'm not turning a blind eye, Jan. I'm not letting her walk away."

"I'm not asking you to. But when you're writing up what happened, I want you to remember what I said. Be balanced with the facts. Don't go for the jugular. Take the middle road. Can you do that?"

Devereaux took a moment to weigh her words.

"I'll do my best to see she gets what's fair."

"Good enough. Thank you. Now, Mom. You heard what Detective Devereaux just said. He was reasonable, right? And all the things you told me about him? All the things you said he'd done in that dossier, which were supposed to prove how he was just like his father? To convince me to bring him here? They're not true. I've talked to him. Watched him in person. Worked with him. Is he perfect? No. Does he have flaws? Yes. Make mistakes? Sure. But his heart's in the right place. Look how he busted his ass to save little Ethan—which is the same thing you thought you were doing."

"What's your point?"

"I want you to drop this whole Devil-in-the-blood thing. It stops here. No one else needs to die. I want your word on that."

"OK." The woman raised herself up onto her knees. "I give you my word. Detective?"

The woman reached out toward Devereaux as if to shake on it, then dropped her hand to his leg. She pulled the backup weapon from his ankle holster and threw herself sideways, toward the door. Loflin fired at her. A bullet smashed into the wall, to the side of Devereaux's elbow. The woman loosed off three shots in rapid succession, still scrabbling for a way out. Loflin fired again, and the woman shrieked with pain. Blood blossomed from her upper arm. She was knocked off balance. She righted herself. And loosed off two more shots.

Devereaux grabbed the woman's feet. He spun her onto her back, dived on top of her, and knocked the gun out of her hand. Eight feet away Loflin dropped her gun, too. Then she crashed to the ground. She was clutching her side. Blood was oozing out between her fingers. Devereaux scrambled forward. He picked up the Clash T-shirt from where he'd dropped it earlier and pressed it against her, trying to stem the bleeding.

"Stop her." Loflin's voice was weak, and she struggled to raise a hand to point at the door.

The woman had disappeared.

"Keep up the pressure on that wound." Devereaux jumped to his feet. "I'll be right back."

The corridor was empty. Devereaux had no way of knowing which way the woman had gone. Down the stairs, to fight another day? Or to Ethan's room, to finish the job Loflin had interrupted?

Devereaux wasn't in the mood to take chances. He

headed to Ethan's room. The boy was on his own, still in his Buzz Lightyear costume. He was starting to stir, and the line had become detached from his sleeve. Outside, Devereaux heard a car engine roar into life. He shook his head. Picked Ethan up. And went back to check on Loflin. Clearly she was crazy, too, but at least she'd done the right thing with the boy.

The blood was still flowing, mixing a sharp metallic tang that caught in Devereaux's throat with the harsh residue of cordite in the air. Devereaux checked Ethan's breathing then set him down on the bed, took a fresh T-shirt from the rail, and used it to add more pressure to Loflin's side.

"Where's my mom?" Her voice was barely audible.

"She got away. But don't worry. The uniforms will pick her up. And if they don't, we've got plenty of time. We'll find her. She can't get up to too much harm, right? She's hurt. She's sick. And there can't be too many kids like Ethan out there for her to *save*."

Loflin tried to struggle into a sitting position, but Devereaux gently eased her back onto the floor.

"We've got to stop her." Loflin's fingernails dug into Devereaux's forearm. "Right now."

"Why? What's the rush?"

"I know where she's going."

"Great. Tell me."

"Not great, Cooper. Terrible. She's going after your daughter."

## Chapter Eighty-four

*Tuesday. Afternoon.*

"WHAT ARE YOU TALKING ABOUT? I DON'T HAVE A DAUGH-ter. I don't have any kids at all." Devereaux tried to get Loflin to lie down so that he could increase the pressure on her wound.

"But you do!" Loflin fought against him. "My mom found out about her when she was building her file on you."

"No way. This is bullshit, Jan. Just some other line your mother spun to make me look bad. There's no way on earth I'd abandon a kid, if I had one."

"I know you wouldn't, Cooper. Her mother kept it from you, I guess."

"Who's her mother supposed to be?"

"I don't know her name. My mom didn't tell me, and I didn't think to ask. An old girlfriend?"

"I haven't had a girlfriend in years. How old is this kid supposed to be?"

"Seven."

"I wasn't with anyone seven years ago."

"And the year before, Cooper? Babies take time to grow."

"I'd have been with Alexandra Cunningham."

"The girl you told me about? The lawyer?"

"Right. We broke up right after Thanksgiving that year."

Loflin waited for Devereaux to do the math.

"You think she was pregnant *when* we broke up?"

"I think you guys broke up *because* she was pregnant. You said she cut you off? No explanation? And she wouldn't even see you? I think she didn't want you to know, because she didn't want you in the baby's life."

Devereaux let the blood-soaked T-shirt fall to the floor. His head was suddenly swimming. His whole life—ever since he was six years old—he'd dreamed of having his father back. He'd have done anything to be reunited with him. His absence had been the driving force behind everything he'd done, good and bad. It had cast a shadow over every chapter of his life. And now, to think that he had a daughter who'd been deprived of her father, not by a murderer's bullet—or a cop's bullet, as it now appeared—but by her mother's whim? Her judgment that Devereaux would be an unsuitable parent? Her decision to cut him off, as if he were dead? Devereaux was struggling to comprehend.

"Why didn't you tell me?" Devereaux forced himself to focus. He got up, fetched a clean T-shirt, and pressed it into place. "When we were talking. At the cabin."

"I didn't know if I could trust you, back then." Loflin winced. "My mother had convinced me you were some kind of monster. It was natural to believe the girl's mother wouldn't want you in her kid's life. And I was focused on saving Ethan. Would you have still helped me, if you'd known your daughter was at risk, too?"

"Of course I would. By stopping your mother."

"Stopping her how?"

Devereaux didn't answer.

"Exactly. I couldn't hand my mother to you on a platter. And I didn't get the danger your daughter was in. I'd never been here, then, remember. I didn't know what my mother was doing to the kids. Not exactly."

"You didn't know what she was doing? What did you think? She was throwing tea parties for them?"

"Maybe I didn't want to know. How did you feel, when you found out your father was a murderer? Did you welcome it? Did you rejoice? Relive all the terrible things he'd done, in your head? At least my mom thought she was helping the kids."

Devereaux was silent for a moment. The truth was, he actually had felt a morbid compulsion to learn about Raymond Kerr's crimes. And that was long before he'd known they were father and son.

"Did your mother say where my kid lives?" He eased the pressure on Loflin's side.

"No." Loflin looked down to assess the bleeding. "In Birmingham somewhere, I guess. She never mentioned a specific address."

Devereaux took another shirt from the rack and tossed it to Loflin.

"The blood loss is slowing, but you need to keep the pressure on. I'm heading back to the city. I'll call Hale on the way. And I'll tell her to send more paramedics. Can you watch Ethan till they get here?"

"Sure."

"Good. And Jan—do you even know my kid's name?"

Loflin shook her head. "I'm so sorry, Cooper. I hope you find her before my mom does."

## Chapter Eighty-five

THE WOMAN DIDN'T HAVE TIME TO CHANGE VEHICLES.

She only had one more car available, and it was too far away. Not that she was guilty of poor planning. The location she'd chosen to hide it was entirely logical, in view of her overall scheme. The problem was that she'd positioned it before snatching Ethan. Before her daughter had turned traitor. Before she'd been seduced by that devil, Devereaux.

The woman could no longer trust her daughter to keep quiet. She knew about Devereaux's progeny. There was too high a likelihood she'd tell him. Devereaux himself was temporarily marooned but he had a phone, no doubt. He'd seen the Mercedes. He would undoubtedly call his people and put them on alert. They'd be looking for her. Trying to head her off before she could reach the girl. But the woman wasn't worried. Because there were two things she knew that the police didn't.

There were four spare sets of license plates in her trunk, each from a different state.

And she knew exactly where the girl was.

## Chapter Eighty-six

*Tuesday. Afternoon.*

DEVEREAUX RAN ALONG THE LANDING AND DOWN THE
stairs, then stopped dead when he reached the porch.

All four of the Subaru's tires were flat. Devereaux
hadn't heard any bangs, so Loflin's mother must have
fixed the valves before she fled in the Mercedes. And
done that despite carrying a gunshot wound. The professional in Devereaux saluted her thoroughness. The
newfound father in him cursed her with every bad word
he knew. Then he pulled out his phone and called Lieutenant Hale.

"Don't yell until you hear what I have to say."

"You have three seconds." Hale didn't sound like she
was expecting to be placated.

"First, I've found Ethan. He's safe and well. He was
anesthetized, and I have paramedics en route to check
him out."

"Really? Cooper—that's fantastic. Seriously. All is
forgiven. Where are you?"

"I'll get to that in a second. Right now, I need you to
get every unit we have out looking for a black M-Class
Mercedes, Alabama license plate A68 0508, probably
inbound to Birmingham from the southeast."

"Can you tell me why?"

"The woman who took Ethan—she's driving that Mercedes. I think she has another target in the city. A seven-year-old girl this time. She knows her cover's blown, and she's on her way to snatch the kid right now."

"What's the address for this little girl?"

"I don't know."

"What's her name?"

"Her surname's probably Cunningham. Her mother's name is Alexandra Cunningham. Or was. She may have gotten married, I guess. That's all I have right now."

"OK. Hang on."

Hale put Devereaux on hold while she made the necessary calls, and was back on the line after sixty seconds.

"It's all in hand. So, who is this woman who took Ethan?"

"She *was* Madison Nesbitt. She didn't die in that house fire, after all. Long story short, she switched identities with one of the DOAs and is now known as Rebecca Loflin."

"Another Loflin?"

"Detective Loflin's mother. She's a psychologist. She contracts for the Bureau. That's the law enforcement connection."

"Is Detective Loflin involved in this?"

"She played a part, yes. A smallish one. But she was manipulated by her mother. In the end, she's the one who saved Ethan. She shot her mother, and took a bullet herself."

"What about you? Are you hurt? Where are you?"

"I'm fine." Devereaux gave her the location as precisely as he could, along with an outline of the horrors he'd found in the other bedrooms.

"More help's on its way. And Loflin's mother—she's wounded, too?"

"Yes. Gunshot wound to the upper left arm."

"Good. I'll alert the local hospitals. Hold the line—I have another call coming in."

Hale was reconnected after two minutes.

"OK. If that Mercedes shows itself within city limits, we'll find it. And there's progress on the girl. We've nailed down a possible address for her. A unit's on its way there now. We haven't found a school registration for her yet, so we're putting units on all the grade schools in her district."

"Thanks, Lieutenant. I'll get back as soon as I can. The vehicle I was using is out of commission, so I'll have to grab a ride back to the city in a squad car when one arrives."

"One more question, Cooper. The name Alexandra Cunningham sounds familiar to me. Weren't you seeing someone with a similar name, a few years ago?"

"Yes. I was. With the same name. It's the same person."

"So why would Loflin's mother be going after your ex-girlfriend's kid?"

"Because . . ." It was still weird for Devereaux to say out loud. "Because, she's also my kid. And no, I didn't know about her. Not until a few minutes ago when I found out this monster was stalking her."

Devereaux hung up and went back inside, intending to check on Ethan and Loflin while he waited for the squad cars to arrive. But when he reached the landing, he walked past the room they were in. He continued to the next one, and went inside it instead. The one that was being made over. Prepared, he now realized, for his daughter.

An image formed in Devereaux's head of a small figure lying on the bed, inert, as Ethan had been. A little girl. But he couldn't picture her face. He didn't know what his own daughter looked like. Or what she was called. He poked at the boxes of Barbies with his foot. Were they his daughter's favorite toys? Or a random selection, based on a gender stereotype?

He had no idea.

Just like he had no idea how to save her.

## Chapter Eighty-seven

THE WOMAN WAS TAKING A CHANCE, EXPOSING HER REAL hair in public. But she needed to look convincing, and wigs don't look right when they're wet.

The bullet her daughter had fired at her had only nicked the fleshy part of her upper arm, and the woman had been able to stop the bleeding on her own without too much trouble. Now she changed into a tank top so the bandage would be visible. Splashed water on her head. Mopped up the excess with her discarded blouse. Slipped the blouse into her bag. Concealed herself in the cubicle nearest to the entrance. And waited.

Devereaux's daughter was the only girl in the afternoon swim class and there was no one else in the women's locker room when the kid wandered in, dripping and pleasantly exhausted, at the end of the session. The woman discreetly watched her get changed—agonizingly slowly—then emerged from the cubicle. She made a play of trying to swing her bag over her shoulder, wincing at the apparent pain, and clutching at the bandage on her arm.

"Are you OK, miss?" The girl kept a wary distance, but she was too inquisitive to ignore the woman's plight altogether.

"I will be! Thank you, young lady. I'm having a bit of trouble with my arm. I had a little surgery on it, and I hink I came back too early. I thought swimming would help it get better quickly, but I guess I was wrong."

"What's the matter with your arm? Why did you need the surgery? Did you get hurt?"

"Kind of. I'm a police detective, and I got in a shoot-out with two very bad people. It worked out OK, though, because they're in prison now—they'll be there for a very long time—and my arm will be better soon."

"Does it hurt?"

"Sometimes it does. Like right now. It's killing me. Say, you wouldn't be an angel and carry my bag for me, would you? I'm having a real hard time dealing with it."

"Carry it where?"

"Just out to the foyer. My husband's meeting me there. How about you? Is your mom here to take you home? Or your dad?"

"My mom is. She's waiting for me in the pool cafe."

"Great! That's right through the foyer. What do you say? Will you help me out?"

The girl took the bag. She held the heavy door open, and followed the woman out of the locker room. But when they reached the open expanse of the foyer the woman stopped, sagged over, and put one hand on the girl's shoulder.

"Oh my goodness, I'm not feeling good at all. Help me look for my husband, would you? Is he here? He's short. And fat. He has gray hair and little round glasses. Can you see him?"

"No." The girl scanned the area around the reception counter, the notice board advertising forthcoming events, the entrance to the cafe, the door to the men's locker room, and the two exits to the parking lot. "Don't think so."

"I need to sit down." The woman staggered over to a wooden bench beneath a large framed photograph of Jennifer Chandler, Olympic gold medal in hand. "Are you sure my husband's not here?"

"Don't think he is. Can't see any old fat guys."

"He's such an airhead. Maybe he forgot what we arranged. Maybe he's still in the car. Could you go to the window and look out? See if there's a black Mercedes SUV parked nearby? Do you know what SUVs look like?"

The girl nodded, scampered to the floor-to-ceiling window, then came straight back.

"It's there. Right outside."

"Great!" The woman tried to stand up, but couldn't straighten her legs. "Oh no. This is terrible. I don't know what's wrong with me. I can't make it. Could you help me up?"

The girl tried to pull on the woman's good arm, but didn't have the strength to get her on her feet.

"This is terrible." The woman was on the verge of tears. "This has never happened to me before. I need my husband to help me. I don't want to be stuck here for the rest of my life!"

"Would you like me to go get him?" The girl's face lit up at the idea. "He's right outside. It'll only take me a second."

## Chapter Eighty-eight

*Tuesday. Afternoon.*

DEVEREAUX WAS ON I-65, HARING DOWN THE BIRMINGHAM side of New Hope Mountain, when his phone rang.

"Cooper, I have news." Lieutenant Hale's voice was tight with tension. "Alexandra Cunningham? She called 911 half an hour ago. Reported her daughter missing. Nicole. She disappeared from Underwood Swimming Pool on South 26th. *Your* daughter, I should say. I'm so sorry."

So his daughter's name was Nicole? What a way to find out.

"She disappeared from a swimming pool?" Devereaux gestured to the officer who was driving him to pull around an open-top Lexus that had merged from the Montgomery Highway. "How? Why was she there in the first place? Why wasn't she at school?"

"It turns out she's home-schooled. Her mother takes her to the pool for swim lessons every Tuesday. She has done for the last semester and a half. Today was no different, until Nicole went to get changed after the lesson and didn't reappear from the locker room. She must have come out, obviously, but no one saw what happened to her."

Devereaux was stunned. A vision of Loflin's mother

drugging his little girl filled his head. Dragging her to an SUV. Driving her somewhere. Freezing her in time in a freaky facsimile of her bedroom . . .

"What's happening now?" Devereaux fought to push the images away.

"An Amber Alert has already gone out. Nicole's description has been circulated. Along with Loflin's mother's and details of the Mercedes. Alexandra Cunningham's phones are being intercepted. And a female officer is with her, in case of developments."

"Where is Alexandra? Is she still at the pool?"

"No. She's at her home. She had to be smuggled out of the pool. The press got wind that another kid was missing and started hovering like flies round a you-know-what."

"Give me the address. I'm going over there."

"I'm not sure that's a good idea, Cooper."

"I'm going, Lieutenant. This kid's my daughter, too. So it's up to you. You can give me Alexandra's address, or I can get it myself."

"OK." Papers rustled on Hale's end of the line. "Give me a minute. Let me find where I wrote it down. But you're not going on your own. I'll meet you there."

## Chapter Eighty-nine

*Tuesday. Afternoon.*
*Nicole missing for one and a quarter hours*

THE HOUSE ALEXANDRA CUNNINGHAM HAD MOVED TO WAS smaller than the one she'd lived in when Devereaux had been seeing her. And it was in a less prosperous neighborhood—the southern edge of Homewood, rather than the center of Vestavia Hills. He'd assumed she'd relocated to get away from the memory of the time they'd spent together, and had expected her to have chosen something similar to what she'd had before. Or better. But her motivation had actually been quite different.

Alexandra Cunningham had been taught at home by her mother, and had sworn she'd do the same for any kids she ever had. Nicole was unexpected—and Alexandra was bringing her up alone—but she saw no reason to break her promise. She was a successful woman. Independent. She'd made good money as a lawyer, for a good number of years. She had plenty stashed away. Admittedly, an adjustment to her lifestyle had been necessary. A change in the standard of her accommodation. And a shift to shorter hours, doing consulting work for other law firms. But taken together, those measures gave her the flexibility she needed to educate her daughter the way she chose.

If Devereaux had called by twenty-four hours earlier, he'd have sworn Alexandra Cunningham hadn't aged a day in the eight years since he'd last seen her. But the woman who opened the door when she saw Devereaux and Hale hurrying up her front path looked eighty years older. She was stooped. Her eyes were red from crying. Mascara streaked her cheeks. Her red hair was tangled, where she'd been frantically twisting it while she waited for news.

"Cooper?" Her voice was hoarse. "What are you doing here? Have you found Nicole?"

Devereaux shook his head.

"Then you can't be here. You can't be involved. You—"

"Alex, I know."

"You . . . Oh. How?"

"I found out. This afternoon. Someone told me."

"Who did?"

"That doesn't matter."

"You need to go."

"No. We need to talk."

"We don't. I can't. Not while—"

"All right. Knock it off." Hale was looking over her shoulder, anxious that someone would spot them and bring down a horde of reporters and TV people. "We can do this inside. The last thing any of us needs right now is a public scene. Plus, Detective Devereaux has been working a related case. He might have some useful insights, which could help us bring Nicole home. And if she is his daughter, I think he has the right to know what's going on with her."

## Chapter Ninety

*Tuesday. Afternoon.*
*Nicole missing for one and three-quarter hours*

THE HALLWAY IN CUNNINGHAM'S HOUSE WAS SHAPED LIKE AN upside-down T.

Straight ahead, Devereaux caught a glimpse of a kitchen. It didn't look like Cunningham's taste had changed too much over the last eight years. There were plain white cabinets. A white marble countertop. Stainless steel appliances. A pair of black leather stools next to a high breakfast bar. Only a pair, Devereaux noted, with a touch of relief.

Devereaux's impression of continuity was reinforced when Cunningham led the way to the right, into her living room. A couch and a love seat were arranged in the far corner, forming a ninety-degree angle. A modest-size TV was fixed to the wall, along with a couple of prints, which Devereaux recognized from her old house: *Nighthawks,* by Hopper, and *Starry Night,* by Van Gogh. The other walls were taken up with tall wooden bookcases, and a carefully distressed antique writing desk was tucked under the window. Devereaux could just detect the faint scent of sickly sweet potpourri. Cunningham's favorite kind.

"Please." Cunningham gestured to the couch. "Sit."

Devereaux took a corner spot and glanced at the nearest bookshelf. He recognized pretty much all the titles. They were all in alphabetical order by author, the way Cunningham had always been fanatical about. Her DVDs were the same, too, except for a small selection of children's movies. So much about the room was familiar that for a moment Devereaux could see himself living there. He tried to picture what things would have been like if Cunningham hadn't broken up with him. Could he have handled it? Her home was so low down and boxed in compared to his apartment. And so cluttered. But when he scanned her possessions, he realized there wasn't too much that was new. She'd clearly used the intervening years to shed things from her life. The things she must have not wanted around. Like him. And once his mind started to dwell on what wasn't around, it jumped inevitably to Nicole.

"So, Alex. I guess we have a daughter."

Cunningham nodded, hesitantly.

"I'm going to grab a glass of water." Hale headed for the door. "I'll give you two a minute."

"She's called Nicole?" The name still felt strange on Devereaux's lips. "Good choice. After your mother?"

"Yes. Thanks. Mom passed right before Nicole was born, so it seemed appropriate."

"Can you tell me about her? What she's like?"

"No, Cooper. I'm sorry. I can't. Not while she's missing. It's too much. I can't talk about her. Her being gone—it's eating me up inside."

"At least tell me what happened. Eight years ago."

"Not right now. Maybe later. I'm not used to this kind of thing. This is your world, Cooper, not mine. My child is kidnapped, I freak out. I don't go into interrogation mode."

"I'm not in interrogation mode. I just want you to tell me about my daughter, like you should have done before she was born. Why didn't you tell me, Alex?"

"You know why. You remember how things were, back then. You? A father? Please."

Devereaux walked to the window. He stared out into the yard, then his eyes shifted their focus to the reflection of the room. It made him feel like he was on the other side of the glass, looking in at another possible life he'd been denied by his past.

"What did you tell her?"

"Nicole?"

"Yes."

"About what?"

"Me. Her father. Why she doesn't have one."

"You selfish bastard, Cooper. You're making this about you? Nicole is missing. That's all that matters."

"This is about Nicole. Don't you remember what losing my father did to me? Have you got any idea of the number of deals I tried to make with God, if He'd just let my daddy come back home? The bad choices I made when he didn't? In my case, it was fate calling the shots. But you chose that same path for our daughter. You *chose* it, Alex."

"How could you try to make deals like that? What were you thinking? You knew your father was dead."

"Because that's what grieving kids do. I told myself, the detective who broke the news? Maybe he was wrong. People make mistakes, don't they? Or maybe my daddy had just been hurt. He could be in the hospital, in a coma. Or he could have lost his memory. But when he woke up, or remembered who he was, he'd come find me. Or he could be a spy, off on a mission so secret everyone had to think he was dead. But when he was successful, he'd come back and find me. For years, every foster home I was in, every time there was a knock on the door or footstep on the path, I'd pray it was him coming to find me."

"Nicole's not in a foster home, Cooper. She lives here, with me."

"I know. But this still matters, Alex. What did you tell her?"

"You've got to understand, I had no idea you had

those crazy ideas. I thought it was for the best. I'm sorry, Cooper. I told her you were dead."

Devereaux didn't say anything. He wanted to go. Get in his car. Drive far, far away from that house. But at the same time, he couldn't leave. Unsatisfactory as it was, being there was the closest he'd ever been to his daughter. The closest he might ever be.

"I didn't do anything deliberately to hurt her, Cooper." Cunningham came and stood next to Devereaux. "What I did I thought was for the best. Better than letting her think you didn't love her enough to stick around, anyway."

"Better than letting her know you kept her a secret from me?"

Cunningham didn't answer.

"I wish you would have told me about her, Alex."

"I know." Cunningham looked down at her bare feet sinking into the deep pile of her rich blue carpet. "But back then, when she was on the way, I couldn't handle it. I couldn't handle *you*. Not after what happened with that boy. The one who . . . died. So I did the only thing I thought I could."

"I did nothing wrong, Alex. I saved my partner's life. You don't have to be a certain age to pull a trigger. And that was work. You could have given me a chance at home. You didn't have to write me out of her life without letting me *try* to be a father."

Cunningham didn't reply.

"Have you got a picture of her?" Devereaux turned to face her. "I don't even know what Nicole looks like."

"A picture?" Cunningham wiped a tear from her eye. "Are you joking? I've got thousands."

## Chapter Ninety-one

*Tuesday. Afternoon.*
*Nicole missing for two hours*

DEVEREAUX HAD BEEN SHOWN DOZENS OF PHOTOGRAPHS BY
the parents of missing kids over the years.

First it had been paper prints. Loose, or in frames, or
mounted on the wall. Later, digital images took over. On
camera screens and computers and phones and tablets.
But whatever the format, the pain he'd seen etched into
the parents' faces was the same. And on every occasion
he'd tried to imagine how it must feel to be left with just
a picture where once you had your own flesh and blood.

When Cunningham passed him the iPad she'd retrieved from her desk, he knew what those other parents
had experienced. He scrolled through the images, from
babe in arms to precocious, curly-haired toddler to viva-
cious blue-eyed little girl, and he'd never felt such agony
or emptiness or loss. The primeval urge to defend his
child swept over him, and if he'd known where Loflin's
mother was at that instant there was no force on earth
strong enough to stop him from going after her.

"I'm so sorry, Nicole." Devereaux touched the most
recent picture with his finger. The girl had Alexandra's
eyes, but maybe his nose? Then for a horrible moment

Devereaux wondered what else the child might have inherited from him. "I'm sorry I couldn't protect you."

"Don't, Cooper." Cunningham gently took the iPad from him. "How could you have protected her? You didn't know about her. And even if you had, what difference would it have made? You can't wrap kids in cotton wool. You can't watch them twenty-four-seven."

"Maybe not. But you don't have to leave them in swimming pool bathrooms on their own at any time. Where were you? Why weren't you with her?"

"I was right there, in the cafe. She knew I was waiting for her. We did the same thing every week. She was supposed to get changed and come meet me. But she never showed up. I asked around but no one had seen her, so I called 911, and the police said something about a woman who might have done this kind of thing before? Cooper, I'm just so scared—"

"You were in the cafe? Why didn't you go to the locker room with her? Help her change?"

"She can get changed on her own, Cooper. She's seven years old, not seven months. And besides, I had work to do. It's not easy keeping everything running on my own."

"Being on your own is your choice, Alex. You could have stayed—"

"Oh no. We're not going there. I'm perfectly capable of standing on my own two feet. I'm supporting my daughter just fine."

"*Our* daughter." Devereaux dropped his voice a couple of decibels.

"OK." Cunningham breathed a long sigh. "Our daughter. That'll take a little getting used to."

"For you and me both. And I didn't mean you're not capable. Hell, you always earned four times what I did. It's just—if I'd known about Nicole, I wouldn't have let the woman go. I'd have stopped her before she got to the pool."

"Stopped which woman? What are you talking about?"

"It doesn't matter. This is so messed up."

"Wait." Cunningham turned and grabbed Devereaux's sleeve. "You know something about the woman who took Nicole? What aren't you telling me?"

"We're going to stop her. We're going to get Nicole back. I swear."

"But who is this woman? Why's she doing this?"

"She's a psychologist. A civilian who works for the FBI. She abducted another kid in Birmingham on Friday night. I caught the case. And I got the kid back, safe and sound. But in the process, the woman was injured. So was another detective. My partner. The way things panned out, I had to make a choice: Stop the woman right away, or make sure the boy and my partner were OK. I didn't know about Nicole at that point, so I focused on the others. I figured we'd have time to scoop the woman up before she did any more harm."

"So this was revenge? For the kid you saved? How did she even know about Nicole?"

Devereaux was silent for a moment. He didn't want the woman's entire thought process to come to light at this point. Cunningham had already decided he was unfit to be around her kid because of his job. Her learning that his father had been a serial killer was unlikely to help his cause.

"I'm right, aren't I?" Cunningham got to her feet. "This is your fault. You put our daughter in danger. You brought this witch to our door. You—"

"Ms. Cunningham, please." Lieutenant Hale had reappeared in the doorway. "Detective Devereaux certainly isn't to blame for this woman's criminal activities. He's done more than anyone to bring her to justice. What we need to focus on is what we do together, going forward, to bring Nicole home safe."

"You're right." Cunningham sat back down, but she left a wider gap between herself and Devereaux than there'd been before. "I overreacted. I apologize. But what can we do? Waiting around to hear something is killing me. How long until this bitch will get in touch with her demands?"

Neither Devereaux nor Hale replied.

"What?" Cunningham looked confused. "Isn't that what kidnappers do?"

"Based on how she behaved in the previous case, I don't think she will get in touch." Hale took a step closer. "We won't be able to talk to her. But we can talk to the next best thing."

"Her daughter." Devereaux got to his feet. "She's in the hospital. Let's go."

Devereaux paused when they reached the front door and turned back to Cunningham.

"Alex, what's Nicole's favorite toy?"

"This is no time to play Disneyland Dad, Cooper." Cunningham scowled.

"I'm not. This is serious. I need to know."

"Why?"

"I'll tell you when Nicole's home and safe."

"OK. It's an easy one. Barbie. She's totally obsessed. You should see her room."

## Chapter Ninety-two

OF ALL THE PLACES THE GIRL COULD HAVE ASKED TO GO FOR her treat, she chose a water park.

The woman was appalled. It was going to be worse than Disneyland. And harder to deal with disguises, too. She'd have to get multiple swimsuits for them to change into. And swim hats, in place of wigs. If only she'd had more time to prepare. Or to convince the kid to reconsider. But it had been hard enough to persuade her to come up with an idea in the first place.

Getting the kid into the Mercedes was straightforward enough—the woman had surprise on her side—but once they were under way, the kid turned into a ferocious dervish. It was like she was possessed, writhing and twisting and screaming and trying to kick and bite. It took every trick in the book to calm her down—which was quite a feat, while driving—and after that all suggestions for alternative trips were met with a return of the histrionics.

An hour later, and the chance to negotiate was gone. The woman had been forced to use the last of her triazolam to keep the kid quiet while she figured out a route and called ahead to book them a hotel. A treat—even a ghastly one—deserved to last at least a full day.

The woman would never have thought it, but she was glad this was going to be her last outing.

The challenge would be getting her daughter back in the fold before it was time for the next one.

## Chapter Ninety-three

*Tuesday. Late Afternoon.*
*Nicole missing for two and three-quarter hours*

LOFLIN WAS PROPPED UP IN BED IN A ROOM JUST LIKE SE-gard's when Hale and Devereaux reached the hospital. She was sore from the surgery and sluggish from the anesthetic, but the bullet itself had caused no lasting damage.

"Cooper. Lieutenant." Loflin smiled when she saw the pair approach, but then a worried frown spread across her face. "Your daughter? Did you save her? Is she OK?"

"No." Devereaux shook his head. "Your mom beat me to her."

"Shit." Loflin pushed herself up from her pillow and tried to swing her legs out of the bed. "That's what I was afraid of."

"Jan, lie back down. It's not your fault. You're not your mother. But we do need your help. We have to understand what happens when your mom thinks she's saving a kid. I need you to explain real clearly, step by step."

"You saw what she does." Loflin flopped back and pulled the baggy hospital pajamas tighter around her tiny frame. "When we were at the house. In the bedrooms. Who can understand that? My mother's bat-shit crazy. That's all there is to it."

"I know, Jan." Devereaux moved closer. "But will she risk going back to the house, knowing that we'll be watching the place? Will she hide? Will she run? Or will she panic, knowing we're looking for her? See what I mean? I need to know how she thinks."

"Well, she must have another house, right?" Loflin shifted her position slightly. "Or somewhere like it. Not all the missing kids were at the one we found."

"Where would it be?" Devereaux felt a surge of dread inside him.

"I have no idea. She never mentioned it. She didn't even tell me about the one we were at until a couple of days ago."

"Think, Jan. Please. I need to know where she's taking my daughter. I don't have much time."

"You've got a couple of days, I guess, depending on what she picks."

"On what who picks? Picks for what?"

"For her treat. The first thing Mom always does, she told me, is take the kid on a treat."

"She does? That's great! We can pick Nicole up there. Where does your mom take them?"

"There's not one set place." Loflin clutched her side and grimaced. "It depends on the kid. She lets each one pick. It could be Disney. A museum. The Grand Canyon. Anywhere. As long as it's within the United States. She wouldn't try to go overseas. Not even Hawaii."

"Wait a minute." Hale closed in from the other side of the bed. "Your mother abducts these kids, then takes them on vacation? You sure you're not selling us a line here, Jan? Buying your mom some time?"

"No." Loflin's voice was drying out. "You've got to understand. She truly believes she's saving the kids. She wants to do something nice for them, before . . . you know. It's actually very thoughtful, in a completely twisted way. And it gives her the opportunity for something else. The test."

"What test?" Devereaux glanced nervously at Hale.

"She's convinced what she's doing is necessary, because the kids have inherited defective genes. Genes that make them dangerous." Loflin reached over to the nightstand and took a sip of water. "But before she does anything, she tests them using some special procedure she developed. Just in case they're not tainted."

Devereaux's stomach turned over at the thought of his daughter being *tested* by this woman.

"You sound sold on all this." Hale was having a hard time concealing her frustration.

"I heard my mom raving about genetics for years. I know her theories by heart. It doesn't mean I believe them."

"But this is good news, right?" Devereaux knew he was clutching at straws. "My daughter could pass the test? She might not be in danger after all?"

"I wouldn't count on it." Loflin sank back against her pillows. "You saw how the test worked out for those other kids."

"Your mother does know she's a total hypocrite?" Devereaux glared down at his partner. "Has *she* passed her test? Have you? Is she planning a murder/suicide pact when she's done with my daughter?"

"Certainly not suicide, although she is sick." Loflin paused, her strength fading. "Don't you see? In her mind, what she's doing proves she *has* escaped her genes. Because she's saving people. She thought I'd escaped, too, but now she's sure to have doubts because I helped you and Ethan."

"Wait." Hale had recovered some of her composure. "Back up, Jan. You said your mom lets the kids choose where they go? Are you sure about that?"

"Absolutely." Loflin nodded weakly. "She always lets them pick their favorite place."

"OK. Cooper, can I speak with you for a moment? Outside?"

Hale ushered Devereaux into the corridor and waited for the heavy glass door to slide shut behind them.

"Listen. This is our break. All we have to do is contact Alexandra and find out what Nicole would choose to do. That'll tell us exactly where Loflin's mother is going to be. Cooper—this will turn out OK. Ethan's safely back with Mary Lynne and Joseph. Soon, your daughter will be with you. I can feel it."

## Chapter Ninety-four

THE WOMAN WAS BEGINNING TO THINK THE PROBLEM WASN'T only with the preparation.

She'd have been more comfortable with extra time to research the water park, for example. What exactly was an Acapulco Drop? Or a Neptune's Plunge? And how assiduously would she need to avoid being swept into them?

It would have been less suspicious if she'd had time to spread the purchase of extravagant quantities of swimsuits and hats across a wider variety of outlets—physical and online—rather than relying on what could be found at Target or Meijer in a couple of hours the next morning.

A greater supply of sedative would certainly have been advantageous.

But the real issue lay with the child herself. She wasn't like the others. Controlling her was beyond a challenge. Because there was a flaw in the woman's concept.

This child wasn't an orphan.

Posing as her real mom, returned to reclaim her and bring her home—it simply didn't hold water.

## Chapter Ninety-five

*Wednesday. Early Morning.*
*Nicole missing for sixteen and a half hours*

THE HOUSE IS SILENT. SHE DOESN'T ANSWER WHEN I CALL. BUT
she must be here, somewhere.

I open the closet door. In the hallway. Check behind
the coats hanging on the rail. I find no one. But there's a
pair of boots on the floor. They're tall. Industrial-
looking. One falls over. It makes a strange sound when
it hits the floor. A hollow sound. There must be a space
underneath. A space where a kid could hide . . .

I push the boots aside and run my fingers around the
edges of the board. Find a place to grip, hidden in the
shadows. Start to pull. The board moves easily. Light
spills through the gap. Spiders and bugs scatter in all
directions. And I see the girl.

She tries to wriggle away, farther into the space. But
she's trapped. She can't get away. I remove the second
board. Reach down. Grab her shirt. Lift her out. Hug
her to my chest. Carry her to the kitchen.

I set her down on a chair. Start to bend down, so my
face will be at the same level. Then I catch sight of my
reflection in the window. I'm short, now. My hair is
blond. It reaches my shoulders.

There's something wrong with my ear . . .

———

Devereaux made sure not to look in the mirror when he used the small, harshly lit bathroom in his hotel room, the next morning. He didn't have long until the joint FBI/police briefing, and he didn't want to reawaken the memory of his dream. He already felt tired and off his game. He'd been late to bed after helping to call all the hotels within a fifty-mile radius of the U.S. Space and Rocket Center in Huntsville, which Alexandra Cunningham had unhesitatingly named as the place Nicole most wanted to visit.

They'd been searching for a record of Loflin's mother. They had to check registrations under her real name. All of her former names. Plus the alias she'd used at the Roadside Rendezvous motel near the Casey Jones Railroad Museum. Their efforts had all been in vain. And then he'd hardly slept, haunted by the hideous vision of his own face morphing into hers.

The FBI had used the hours of darkness to set up a mobile command post in the Space Center's parking lot. It consisted of two huge trucks, set up to look like TV outside-broadcast vehicles to disguise their purpose and account for the array of satellite dishes and other communications equipment that covered their roofs. They were hiding in plain sight, right by the entrance to the Davidson visitor center, and in the shadow of the center's giant Saturn V rocket.

One whole end wall inside the nearer truck was filled with computer monitors, showing images piped in from the park's security cameras. Larry McMahan—the agent in charge of the Birmingham field office—was standing and watching them when Devereaux arrived at eight-thirty, half an hour before the center was due to open to the public. Bruckner and Grandison were already in place around a folding metal conference table and a minute later Lieutenant Hale entered the truck and joined them.

McMahan turned away from the screens, eager to get

down to business. Now that Loflin's mother was linked to the Bureau, he was anxious to take care of the dirty laundry quickly, before it got aired in public. He'd pulled plenty of strings, and brought a lot of resources into play in a short length of time. The fact that the woman had shot a cop—and taken another cop's kid hostage— had only strengthened his hand.

"Danielle, good to see you." McMahan nodded to Hale and took his place at the head of the table. "Gentlemen. This briefing shouldn't take long. Everything is in place, exactly as agreed last night. We have agents at all entrances to the center. In the security control room. At each of the key attractions, with double teams at the Rocket Park and the Shuttle Park. There are four pairs roving within the grounds. We have people at the ice-cream concession. The cafe. The souvenir store. We have two agents monitoring the entrance to the parking lot, and two more checking any cars that arrived early, posing as annual-subscription sellers."

McMahan's briefing continued for another five minutes, with the in-depth information about the wider investigation provided by Lieutenant Hale. The longer it continued, the more Devereaux felt an intangible sense of competence and determination fill the room. He was still on edge—and knew he would be until Nicole was in his arms, safe and well—but he was satisfied with the Bureau's response, even if it was somewhat driven by self-interest. By the time McMahan took the floor again to wrap things up, Devereaux only had one question.

"What's my role in all this? Where do you want me to be?"

McMahan gestured to the bank of monitors behind him.

"Watching these. The subject is known to be adept with disguise, and you're the only one here who's actually seen her recently. You're best placed to spot her, if she's attempting to alter her appearance. Conversely, she knows what you look like. We can't risk putting you in

:he open because if she sees you, we lose the element of
:urprise."

Devereaux was disappointed—he desperately wanted
to be outside, hunting the woman down, saving his
daughter—but he knew McMahan was right. He wished
the others luck, then took one of the hard plastic chairs
and positioned himself in front of the screens.

After his dream, Devereaux had been anxious to avoid
the woman's image. Now he was desperate for her face
to appear. The screens remained static, as if frozen in
time, for the next eight minutes. Then a flood of people
washed through the gates and spread out between the
attractions. Men. Women. Young and old. Single and in
couples or larger groups. With and without children.
Some marching purposefully, with a definite destination
in mind. Others loitering, checking maps and studying
their smartphone apps. But there was no one who
looked anything like Loflin's mother, or the pictures
Alex had shown him of Nicole.

Devereaux settled back in his chair and tried not to
deliberately focus on one screen, or search for one like-
ness. It was a technique he'd learned years ago, when
he'd taken a surveillance course at the Police Academy.
The idea was to let your eyes rove freely across the
whole area, and leave it to your subconscious to intui-
tively pick out the relevant image.

Devereaux stayed that way, barely moving, hardly
even blinking, for another thirty minutes. He was practically in a trance when Loflin's words about her mother
from the previous afternoon floated back into his head.
*She truly believes she's saving the kids. She wants to do
something nice for them* . . . That sounded wonderful,
especially when he measured it against some of the foster parents he'd had as a kid. But how could he explain
the insane paradox? In the woman's mind, *saving*
equaled *killing*. Devereaux just couldn't fathom that
kind of logic.

The thought brought into focus another area where the woman had an advantage over him. He didn't have a clue how her mind worked. But she clearly understood him. She knew him well enough to lay a trail of bread crumbs he couldn't help but follow. She'd left Ethan's treasure where he was bound to find it. And the trimmed hair, at the Roadside Rendezvous. And the railroad museum flier. She'd even known things about him he hadn't known himself. Fundamental things. Like who his father really was. And that he had a daughter.

Devereaux pulled out his phone, called Bruckner, and asked him to come and take over watching the monitors. He'd realized he wasn't going to find the woman by looking inside the park. He was going to have to look inside her head.

## Chapter Ninety-six

*Wednesday. Morning.*
*Nicole missing for nineteen hours*

IT'S A FRACTION OVER NINETY-EIGHT MILES FROM THE SPACE and Rocket Center to the UAB Hospital parking lot.

Devereaux covered the ground in sixty-nine minutes, dumped his car in a space reserved for emergency vehicles, and practically ran the rest of the way to Loflin's room.

"Did you find her?" Loflin was sitting up in bed and looking as though the night's sleep had done her a world of good.

"Not yet." Devereaux moved the visitor's chair nearer to the bed. "We went to the place Alex thought Nicole would pick for her treat. We took enough Feds to invade a small country. And so far, zip."

"That's awful. Maybe Alex was wrong?"

"Maybe. But I doubt it. I think I was wrong. Because of how I pictured your mom. I saw her as a criminal. I tried to anticipate what a criminal would do. But she's not just a criminal, is she, Jan? You said so yourself. She believes she's saving these kids. She's on a mission. That's a different kind of motivation altogether. I need to understand her better if I'm going to stop her from harming Nicole. And to do that, I need your help."

"OK." Loflin sat up straighter in the bed. "I'll try. What do you need?"

"This is the $64,000 question, Jan. And before you answer, remember I'm not looking to hurt your mom. Or get even with her. I just want my daughter back."

"I get that, Cooper. And, hey, I held a gun on her. I shot her. So I'm totally on board with stopping her from hurting another kid. Especially yours. Just tell me what I can do."

"I need to know how to contact her."

"I'm sorry, Cooper." Loflin sagged back against her pillow. "I can't help you with that."

"Please. It's vital. For Nicole's sake."

"I'm not saying I won't. I'm saying I can't. I don't know how."

"You're her daughter. You must have a way. Even if it's just for emergencies."

"I don't, Cooper." Loflin leaned forward and lowered her voice. "I'll be honest. I know this could make me look bad, but I tried to get in touch with her myself. Today. To find out what her state of mind's like. I've been driving myself nuts with worry in case she comes here to punish me for turning on her. But it was no good. She wouldn't pick up."

"You have a number? Can I try it?"

"Feel free. It won't help. The number's out of service. This used to happen all the time. She was always getting new phones. She said she kept losing them. Looking back, I guess she ditched them whenever she thought they were too hot to use."

"Let me give it a shot. Just in case."

Devereaux dialed the number Loflin gave him, but had no more luck than she'd had.

"When your mom would get a new phone, how did you find out the number?" Devereaux pushed the chair back so that he could straighten his legs.

"I had to wait for her to call me."

"How about texting?"

"I'd text her all the time. She never replied, though.

She said she didn't like doing it. And there's no point trying now. She's not blanking us. That number's history. The phone's either in pieces, or at the bottom of a lake."

"OK. What else is there? Email?"

"No. She didn't use it. She said she was techno-illiterate."

"Really?"

"It's true. She hated computers. I never saw her go near one."

"Thanks, Jan. You're a genius." Devereaux stood up, shoved the chair against the wall, and left the room on the double.

## Chapter Ninety-seven

*Wednesday. Morning.*
*Nicole missing for twenty and a quarter hours*

THE IT TECHNICIANS HAD MOVED TWELVE MONTHS PREVI-
ously to a spacious glass and steel addition at the back
of the Support Services Bureau on Fourth Avenue. This
had caused a lot of bad feeling—why should the geeks
get a new "clubhouse" while other police department
buildings were closing all over the city?—but the people
who worked there didn't care. They felt they deserved it,
after years of plying their trade in a dingy, airless basement. And no one complained to their faces, anyway.
Not unless they wanted their work to end up at the bottom of the pile.

Spencer Page was unusual in that he'd started his police department career in the field. He'd moved into
technical support five years later, after recovering from a
serious leg break he'd suffered in a fall while chasing a
burglar down a fifteen-story fire escape. Some detectives
didn't like working with him after that, as if he were a
bad luck charm. Or lacking in character, for choosing
not to get right back on the horse. But whenever he had
the option, Devereaux always picked Page. He thought
it was smart, the way he'd come back to a role that better suited his talents. And the experience he'd had on the

street made him a little more accommodating than some of the career techies. He understood how important it can be to get information fast, regardless of overtime restrictions. How sometimes the material you're asked for doesn't have to be genuine, as long as it looks real— like a well-photoshopped picture or a fake phone bill—if that's what it takes to loosen a stubborn criminal's tongue. And that sometimes it's better not to ask why the request is being made in the first place.

Page was tall and skinny, and he was wearing his trademark plain black T-shirt and skinny jeans with his ID clipped to a studded leather belt. He met Devereaux in the IT department's small refreshment area, which was known as The Custard Bowl because of its luminous yellow walls. The two men shook hands, Devereaux declined Page's offer of a drink, then they perched opposite each other on high stools at a round metal table in the corner of the room.

"Spencer, I need your help." Devereaux flicked away a curled-up remnant of lettuce that had fallen out of someone's sandwich.

"Name it, buddy." Page grinned. "If it's legal, it's yours. And if it isn't legal, it's yours, anyway. Just don't tell anyone."

"Thanks. I appreciate it. Now here's the thing. I need to find someone, like yesterday. She's snatched a kid, and now she's in the wind. She's got eleven dead bodies in her wake already, and I want to stop her making it twelve. The problem is, we've got nothing on her. Nothing at all. We've tried all the normal ways, and come up with zip. The only angle I can think of is something that's up your alley."

"OK. Shoot."

"This woman, she painted a picture of herself as being techno-illiterate. However, I know for a fact she was using a bunch of webcams, and must have been dialing into them from all over creation. Which doesn't sound so illiterate to me. And knowing how everything she does is deliberate, and designed to mislead and misdirect, I'm thinking this means she doesn't want people to know about how up-to-date she is with how these webcams work. There must be something about it she wants to hide. Which means I want to find it. And I'm praying it's something that'll help me figure out where she is."

"I'll be straight with you, Cooper." Page ran his fingers through his straggly, straw-colored hair. "That's longer than a long shot. Unless I catch her actually trying to access the cameras, there's almost no chance. And even then there are all kinds of tricks she could play to disguise where she truly is."

"Does she have to be able to access the cameras? Because she can't get to them. They aren't online anymore. They're in the evidence locker."

"Then, honestly, a snowball has a better chance of raising a family on Beelzebub's front porch than we do of tracing where she is."

Devereaux slammed the palm of his hand on the table in frustration.

"Hey, buddy." Page looked around, hoping Devereaux hadn't drawn too much attention to them. "Listen. Don't despair. These webcams. What were they hooked up to? Was any other equipment recovered along with them?"

"There could have been. Maybe. I don't know. All I saw were the cameras."

"Well, you never know till you try, right? Give me the case number. I'll dig those suckers out, and if there's anything to be found that'll help, I'll find it. You have my personal guarantee."

## Chapter Ninety-eight

*Wednesday. Morning.*
*Nicole missing for twenty and a half hours*

DEVEREAUX STAYED AT THE TABLE AFTER PAGE RETURNED TO his desk.

Another bright hope had dimmed, and seemed certain to fizzle out altogether. Devereaux felt trapped, as if each blind alley he'd run down had combined into an impenetrable warren he couldn't find his way out of. He closed his eyes, pushing back against the darkness, searching for another option, when he felt his phone begin to buzz in his pocket.

"Devereaux, where are you?" It was Agent Bruckner.

"At the Support Services Bureau. Back in Birmingham."

"In Birmingham? Excellent. Hold the line. I'm patching in Grandison."

There were a couple of electronic squawks in his ear, then Devereaux heard Grandison call out his name.

"OK." Bruckner was exuberant. "We have a breakthrough. And Devereaux, you're about to be one proud dad. Listen to this. Alexandra Cunningham just got a call. From Nicole. She'd found Loflin's mother's phone, sneaked away with it while the woman was taking some kind of medicine, and raised the alarm."

"Where are they?" Cooper jumped down from the stool and started toward the exit.

"Nicole didn't know, exactly. Only that they were in a hotel. It sounds like the woman doped her while she checked in, like she did with Ethan, so Nicole didn't see any signage. They did go out to get a bunch of swimsuits and stuff this morning, but they came back in through a side entrance, so it was the same problem."

"They went shopping for swimsuits?"

"Right. Nicole said they were on their way to a water park, which is what she picked for her treat. Your ex was a little off the money on that one. Anyway, the officer who was with Alexandra told Nicole to hang up the phone and keep it with her as long as she could, so we could trace it via GPS."

"I guess." Devereaux would have preferred an old school solution. "Why didn't they tell her to run screaming to the lobby?"

"Too dangerous for Nicole, and any other civilians who might be nearby. The woman's armed, dangerous, and unstable. Correct procedure is to locate her, secure the premises, and send in Hostage Rescue."

Devereaux didn't reply.

"Are you still there, Devereaux?"

"I am. Give me the address of the hotel."

"Wait. I'm being told that the phone's on the move. It's on I-20, heading south. That's consistent with the direction to the water park. Devereaux, listen. Birmingham PD has units en route to intercept. They also have an eye in the sky. They have it covered. And to be sure, we're coming, too."

"That's good." Devereaux had just made the turn onto 18th Street, running hard as he zigzagged his way to the City Federal building. "But I'm closer. I'm heading down there myself. Just do me one favor. Have someone call Traffic. Tell them to expect me. I'll be in a blue Porsche."

"Roger that."

"Devereaux, wait. This is Grandison. Don't do that.

Stay where you are. In a situation like this, where the subject is driven by ideology, the last thing you want to do is make her feel cornered. If that happens, and she feels there's no way out, she *will* kill her hostage. That's not speculation. That's a one hundred percent certainty."

## Chapter Ninety-nine

THE WOMAN PULLED OUT ONTO THE HIGHWAY AND STRAIGHT-away checked her speed.

She didn't want to draw attention to herself. She'd switched the license plates again, but even so a zealous traffic cop might note the color and model of the car she was driving and decide to take a closer look. The level of risk was higher than she was happy with, but there was no alternative open to her.

At least the girl was behaving better now. She'd still been a little feisty that morning, when they went out to buy the swimming supplies. Making sure she didn't bolt down one of the long, cluttered aisles in the three stores they visited had been exhausting. And the girl hadn't been happy about returning to the hotel, either, when the woman needed to change the bandage on her arm for a waterproof one and take her second batch of meds. But since then, the girl had been an angel. A miracle transformation had occurred. It was wonderful.

The only other frustration was having lost her phone.

The woman had switched to that one before they reached the hotel, and it was the last of her disposables.

If only she'd known what was going to happen, she could have bought another at the store.

*Wednesday. Late Morning.*
*Nicole missing for twenty and three-quarter hours*

DEVEREAUX WAS BURNING THROUGH THE MILES THAT SEPA-
rated him from his daughter.

He was halfway to the turnoff for the water park,
thinking ahead, planning how he'd handle every con-
ceivable trick the woman could throw at him, when his
phone rang.

"Devereaux?" Bruckner sounded concerned. "I have
new information. The phone is still moving. The woman
didn't leave the highway at the water park. She's con-
tinuing southbound."

"Roger that. I'll keep on the highway myself. What
about her vehicle? Is she still in the black Mercedes? I
don't want to accidentally pass her."

"Let me check. I'll get right back to you."

Devereaux hung up and eased back slightly on the
gas, and right away his phone rang again.

"Hey, buddy." It was a male voice, slightly distorted,
and it took Devereaux a second to place it as Page's.

"Hey. What have you got for me?"

"I just finished with your girl's webcams—and the
server they were hooked up to—and the news is, we
were both right. Like I thought, there's no way to figure

out where she could be right now. I could tell you where she was the last ten times she accessed them, though, if that would help."

"It might. Can you email me the details? I'm driving right now."

"Can do. No problem. And that leads me to the part *you* were right about. There's no way this lady is a Luddite. I'll give you an example. I traced the location of the last place she accessed the cameras from. Then I looked at what other activity there was from the same IP address at the same time. And guess what I found? She logged on to seven email accounts, each from a different provider. And on top of those, two other sets of webcams."

"Spencer, this could be the mother lode. What do the emails say?"

"I couldn't possibly hack her accounts without a warrant. That would be illegal."

"So what do they say?"

"They're mainly to do with deliveries. A weird combination of things. For example, chemicals. Kids' toys. Decorating supplies. That's all I've found so far."

"What was the delivery address?"

"There were a couple. One is right here in Alabama, a little way outside Birmingham. The other is in Missouri. St. Louis, actually."

"Has anything been delivered to the St. Louis address recently?"

"Not in the last couple of weeks. But plenty in the last year. I haven't checked all the emails yet, though."

"OK. Can you send me those addresses as well?"

"Sure. No problem."

"What about the other sets of webcams? Can you tell where they are?"

"That would be beyond the power of a regular mortal. So, yes. One set's here in Birmingham."

Page read out an address, and Devereaux's foot instinctively pressed harder on the gas. The cameras were at Alexandra Cunningham's house.

"And the others?"

"In St. Louis. At the same place the deliveries were being sent to."

"This is great information, Spencer. It could make all the difference. Thank you."

"You're welcome. I hope it helps you catch this asshole. In the meantime, I'll keep digging and—"

"Spencer, thanks again." Devereaux's call waiting was beeping. "Got to go . . ."

Agent Bruckner was back on the other line.

"Devereaux, you need to slow down. The helicopter can see you. You're only a quarter of a mile behind the woman. She's ditched the Mercedes, and she's driving a silver Nissan Armada now. There are four unmarked units ahead of her, and two behind. The ones in front are going to start slowing the traffic. There are people up ahead preparing a fake census point. So hang back, but be ready to move. We don't know if Nicole will be under any kind of sedation. And remember what Grandison said. If the woman feels her situation is hopeless . . ."

Devereaux didn't need Bruckner to finish the thought. He was well aware of the difficulty of extracting a hostage from a vehicle. Especially a child who might be drugged. He just had to hope the guys posing as census-takers were good at their jobs. His daughter was four hundred yards away from him. She was in mortal danger. And all he could do was ease off the gas and trust in a bunch of strangers to save her life.

*Wednesday. Late Morning.*
*Nicole missing for twenty-one hours*

THE TRAFFIC SLOWED DRAMATICALLY.

It continued to dawdle for another five miles. Then the highway straightened, and they reached a section where the shoulder was wider than usual following the construction of a new section of road. Devereaux passed a temporary sign saying *Traffic Census. Pull Over If Directed. Federal Mandate.* He sped up, weaving his way past the other vehicles, watching closely for the Armada.

Devereaux spotted the silver leviathan a hundred yards ahead. It was approaching a pair of officers who were standing at the side of the carriageway, in high-visibility vests. They were holding orange-and-white-striped batons and as Devereaux watched, one of the men stepped forward and directed a car, seemingly picked at random, into one of four pens that had been laid out on the shoulder, using tall fluorescent traffic cones.

The officer selected another car and waved it across to the shoulder, then stepped toward the Armada. He gestured with his baton. The Armada's turning-light came on. And its brake lights. It started to move to the right. Devereaux's foot was poised above his gas pedal, waiting for the woman to swing back onto the highway and surge forward. But she didn't. She rolled into the rear, right-hand pen. Her way forward was blocked by the first car that had been pulled over. Devereaux stopped behind her, cutting off her only other escape route.

Devereaux jumped out of the Porsche as one of the officers pulled open the Armada driver's door. The officer dragged a blond woman in jeans and a jade green tank top out from behind the wheel. He shoved her down on the ground. Started to cuff her. But it wasn't Loflin's mother. On the far side of the SUV, the other officer was grappling with a broad, shaven-headed man he'd pulled from the passenger seat. Devereaux registered surprise as he ran forward. He wrenched open the rear door. And saw a small figure curled up on the back seat, hugging a stuffed toy dog.

It was a little girl.

But not Nicole.

THE WOMAN HAD TO GAUGE THE DISTANCE VERY CAREFULLY.
She had to stop the car close enough to the pay phone so that she could grab the girl if she twigged something had gone wrong with her scheme and tried to run. But the car also had to be far enough away so that the girl wouldn't overhear the conversation. Then she'd *know* her scheme had failed. And given her previous behavior, that would be asking for trouble. It was a delicate balance.

The woman smiled as she waited for her call to be answered. This was one situation where age was on her side. She was old enough to remember life before everyone was dependent on cell phones.

Losing her last one certainly had its disadvantages.

But overall it was worth the inconvenience, to have gotten the police off her back. And she was grateful to the girl for that, if nothing else.

*Wednesday. Late Morning.*
*Nicole missing for twenty-one and a quarter hours*

DEVEREAUX LEFT THE CENSUS OFFICIALS TO STRAIGHTEN OUT the mess with the family from the Armada and pulled back onto the highway.

He had no definite destination in mind but figured that if the woman had sent her phone south for them to follow like obedient puppies, he'd be better off heading north. The next exit was three miles farther on, and with every yard he traveled in the wrong direction Devereaux beat himself up a little more for having let the woman slip through his fingers at the mansion. The negative thoughts were still gnawing at him as he raced down the off-ramp, ready to loop under the highway and rejoin on the opposite side, so he was glad of the distraction when his phone rang again.

"I know, Cooper. It was a debacle." It was Lieutenant Hale's voice this time. "Loflin's mom won that round. But I don't want to hear about it. Because it doesn't matter. We've finally caught a break. An eyewitness reported seeing the woman at a hotel, and the location matches with the phone call Nicole made. She said she saw two incidents in the parking lot. First, the woman was hovering around the trunk of a silver Nissan SUV. The witness thought she was trying to steal something, but think about it, Cooper. Where was the woman's cell phone found? Where exactly?"

"In the Armada's trunk."

"Right. And the second thing. A few minutes later, the woman got into a screaming row with a kid. A girl, aged around seven or eight. The kid wanted to go to some water park, but the woman was insisting they go with their original plan, and head to an airplane museum."

"The Space and Rocket Museum?"

"No. Some place in Robins, Georgia, called the Museum of Aviation. It's a fair drive. Two-thirty, two-fifty-ish miles from Birmingham, depending which route you take."

"I've never heard of the place."

"Me neither. But airplane museums have never been my thing."

"What about Alex? Does she know if it was a place Nicole had ever wanted to visit?"

"I haven't asked her. There are a lot of other calls I need to make, Cooper."

"How come it took so long for us to hear about this?"

"The witness didn't call right away. She said the thing with the trunk she wasn't sure about, so she wouldn't have mentioned it on its own. It was the way the woman and the girl acted around each other that spooked her. There was nothing tangible. Just the way they were yelling. The distance between them. And at the end of the argument, the woman grabbed the girl and almost threw her into their car. A black Mercedes, by the way. There was nothing conclusive on its own, but enough to nag away until the witness found a pay phone and made the call."

"She didn't have a cell phone?"

"She was an older lady. She said she doesn't hold with cell phones. She doesn't own one."

"Did you speak to her yourself?"

"I did. Dispatch routed her through."

"What did your gut tell you, Lieutenant? Was she on the level?"

"I think so. It was noisy and the line was bad but I pressed her hard about the woman, and she gave me a decent description. Take away the hair color, and it tallies pretty close to what the clerk at the Roadside Rendezvous said. And when she got off the phone, I called the hotel she claimed these things happened at. The clerk there confirmed that someone sounding just like her description had checked in late last night. And had been driving a black M-Class Mercedes."

Devereaux took a moment to think through what Hale had told him.

"All right. So what's the plan? Converge on this Museum of Aviation?"

"You got it."

"OK, Lieutenant. See you there."

## Chapter **One Hundred and Four**

*Wednesday. Late Morning.*
*Nicole missing for twenty-one and a half hours*

DEVEREAUX ENTERED ROBINS, GEORGIA, INTO THE Porsche's GPS system but after a couple of seconds, when it came back with a choice of two possible routes, he pulled over to the side of the road.

He was suddenly overcome with the same feeling of discomfort that had hit him at the mansion when he'd spotted the webcam. He felt out of control, like an unwitting participant in an unknown game. The more he tried to shake it, the more he felt the presence of an invisible hand above him, jerking his strings.

Both of the bold red lines on the GPS screen were pointing more or less southeast from Birmingham. Which was the opposite direction from St. Louis. Where the woman's second set of webcams was located. And where she'd arranged for chemicals and other odd things to be delivered.

A coincidence? Or another attempt at sending the police and the FBI to the wrong place?

Devereaux didn't know.

*Wednesday. Afternoon.*
*Nicole missing for twenty-one and three-quarter hours*

DEVEREAUX HADN'T TRAVELED OUT OF STATE VERY OFTEN.

The few places he had visited, he'd liked. Such as Virginia, with its acres of trees and rolling green countryside. And Chicago, where the insanely cold winter had blown through his thickest coat like it was a vest. Or Arizona, where the crazy cacti that grew wild everywhere made him think he'd been dropped onto a surreal movie set.

He'd always wanted to see more of the country. A road trip was always near the top of his list of things to do—next year. But as he stared out of the Porsche's windshield—first as he powered north, past Huntsville again and onward to the outskirts of Nashville, then northwest through the rest of Tennessee, into Kentucky, and finally Missouri, robotically following the instructions barked out by the GPS—Devereaux observed next to nothing.

The journey took five hours forty-one minutes. He stopped twice for gas. The rest of the time he kept the needle high up on the speedometer. It was north of a hundred for considerable distances, and the portable beacon Devereaux had placed on the dashboard was the

only thing standing between him and the dozen traffi
cops he'd left floundering in his wake.

Devereaux was shell-shocked when he arrived at th
address Page had given him, reeling from the sustaine
assault the road noise and vibration had made on h
senses. And when he'd recovered enough to properl
take stock of his surroundings, he registered surprise, a
well. In the past, when he'd thought about St. Loui
he'd pictured Busch Stadium or the Gateway Arch. Bu
now he found himself in an ordinary residential neigh
borhood. The street was long and slightly curved witl
wide sidewalks and neat family house after neat famil
house. Each one was elegantly set back from its broad
landscaped front yard. Some had kids' bikes and scoot
ers propped up against fences or lying on the grass. The
area couldn't have been further removed from the gothic
wilderness where he'd found the woman's ruined mansion if it had been on another planet.

Devereaux called Page. He asked him to double-check
the address to make sure it matched the location of the
woman's webcams. As far as Page could tell, it did. Still
dubious, Devereaux hung up and saw he'd missed half a
dozen calls from Lieutenant Hale on the drive from Birmingham. He debated calling her back. She might have
an update about Nicole. It could be good news. Or bad.
But she'd also yell at him for not going to Georgia, as
he'd agreed to. He didn't have time for that, so he called
headquarters instead and spoke to Hale's civilian aide.
She told him Hale was still at the airplane museum, but
there was nothing else to report.

Devereaux decided to trust his instincts. He wasn't
being completely irresponsible. If the report of the exchange in the hotel parking lot was true, then Hale, the
FBI agents, and the Georgia police would be more than
equal to handling things on their end. But something
told him he was likely to be closer to the action where he
was.

It was tempting to find a place to stake the house out
and wait for the woman to show her cards. The problem

was, Devereaux didn't know for sure if she'd come. Or even if it was her house. She could have been using one of the tricks Page had mentioned to disguise the location of the webcams. Given the shortage of time, Devereaux decided he needed to force the issue. To find out if he was on the right path. Or if he'd talked himself into the longest wild-goose chase of his life.

And the most disastrous.

Particularly for the daughter he'd never even seen.

*Wednesday. Evening.*
*Nicole missing for twenty-seven and a half hours*

DEVEREAUX PARKED THE PORSCHE TWO STREETS AWAY, in the opposite direction from the route in from the highway, and walked back to the house.

No lights were on, and there was no sign of movement. The plot was open, so he walked around the side of the garage and inspected the rear of the property. From the patio he could see into the kitchen and the living room. Both were furnished, but with bland basic items that expressed no personality at all. The drapes were closed in the upstairs windows. There was no sound of voices or TVs or music to suggest that anyone was home.

A large red alarm klaxon was prominently mounted just below the roofline at the front of the house, and another was visible high up at the back. Devereaux looked through the kitchen window. There were alarm sensors on the window and door frames, but no sign of a PIR device. It was the same story in the living room. Devereaux returned to the front of the house and knocked on the door as a cover for checking the security. Again, he saw no PIRs. Only a generous smattering of perimeter sensors.

This setup made sense if the house really did belong to the woman. Passive Infra-Red sensors are invaluable when they're working properly, but they're notoriously unreliable. Over ninety percent of false alarm activations are down to PIR malfunctions. The woman would want her property to be secure, but she couldn't afford the risk of annoying her neighbors—or alerting the police.

Devereaux hurried back to the Porsche and squeezed into the tiny area that passed as a rear seat. He pulled out the razor-sharp switchblade he'd carried since his teens and plunged it through the carpet-covered hardboard parcel shelf. He hacked around in a rough circle. Then he tore out one of the enhanced-bass premium-audio speakers he'd paid an arm and a leg for when he'd ordered the car, four months earlier.

Back at the rear of the house, Devereaux held the speaker against the kitchen door so that its magnet was as close as possible to the sensor. He used the blade of his knife as a lever to enlarge the gap in the frame. Then he slammed into the wood with his shoulder, splitting the frame and opening the door without shattering the glass or triggering the alarm.

The first floor had the feel of a model home. All the walls were painted pale yellow. Several reed diffusers gave off a strong scent of jasmine. Each room had one piece of furniture too few: a living room with no coffee table, a dining room without chairs. Up close, the quality of the materials was nowhere near what it promised from a distance. Devereaux glanced into each one on his way to the staircase. He paused at the bottom, settled himself, then ran up two steps at a time.

At the top of the stairs the landing forked to the left and the right. Devereaux went to the right. Four doors were laid out ahead of him. The first led to a bathroom. The second, a bedroom. The scene inside came as less of a shock than when Devereaux had discovered Miranda Gonzalez, the day before, but his mind still rebelled against the reality of what he saw. The room was illumi-

nated by two giant chrome-plated floodlights on adjus
able metal tripods. The walls were covered with styliz
murals of 1920s cars and buildings in black and silv
In the center of the room was a raised podium, and lyin
on it was the body of a tiny boy kitted out in a miniatu
tuxedo, complete with silk scarf and bow tie. On th
floor a silver champagne bucket was filled with imit.
tion ice cubes and a real, unopened bottle of vintag
Cristal.

Devereaux came out of the room, took a breath, an
checked behind the third door from that half of th
landing. It led to another bathroom. The fourth door le
to another bedroom, but this one was empty.

Devereaux moved back along the landing and starte
down the other branch. The layout was the same: tw
bedrooms and two bathrooms. The first bedroom h
tried was empty. That meant something unpleasant wa:
most likely waiting for him behind the last door. He
paused. Steeled himself. And went inside.

This room was set up as a NASCAR circuit. One wall
was painted like a row of garages, with the crews brandishing their tools for a fuel stop and tire change. The
other walls made up the grandstands, teeming with ec-
static, cheering spectators. But the real action was
straight ahead: two cars—actually beds with elaborate
wooden bodywork bolted onto them, one blue, one
red—were neck and neck, the missing twins behind the
wheels, locked for eternity in fraternal rivalry.

Devereaux pulled out his phone, ready to call Hale,
but he hesitated before hitting the Call key. It was clear
that the woman had been at work here. But he had no
proof she was planning on coming back. She may have
some other property they were yet to discover, and he
didn't want to divert any resources that might be needed
to find Nicole by prematurely calling it a result. He went
back downstairs, intending to look for a door to a basement in case that contained any clues as to the woman's
intentions, but then it occurred to him that there was a
much more obvious place to try.

---

The inside door to the garage opened off the family room. Devereaux used the Porsche speaker's magnet to circumvent its alarm sensor, picked its lock, and stepped through into a space that would originally have been large enough to hold three cars until a wall had been built all the way across it, halving its depth. A giant washer and drier had been installed against it, and there was a door set into the center, secured with three hefty bolts.

Devereaux slid the bolts back and opened the door, revealing a kind of air lock between the other side of the wall and the main door to the driveway. He guessed it was to enable deliveries to be made safely while the woman was away. She could give the parcel guys a remote opener for the outer door, so they could leave their goods securely and out of sight, but without having access to the rest of the house.

Devereaux switched on the light and saw that a large cardboard box had been left there. He checked the paperwork stuck to the outside. It had been an express delivery, scheduled for earlier that day. He opened it. Scooped out a generous layer of Styrofoam peanuts. And froze when he saw the contents.

There were two dozen Barbie dolls. A pair of Barbie drapes. A Barbie light shade. And a Barbie comforter cover.

Everything you'd need to make a Barbie-loving girl feel right at home.

THE CLERK THOUGHT IT WAS STUPID, COMING TO AN INTER-net cafe and paying extra for a computer that couldn't go online.

The woman didn't care what the clerk thought. It was the only way to make sure the devious brat she was saddled with couldn't log onto email or IM or Twitter or whatever seven-year-olds used to send messages these days. And she obviously couldn't leave the girl unattended in the car. Not after what the kid had pulled at the hotel.

The extra cost—and the extra time she'd spent getting to the place—proved to be more than worthwhile, however. The woman took the opportunity to relieve one of the raucous teenagers who frequented the place of his iPhone. The computer she rented for herself did, of course, have Web access. And through it, she made one last check on her webcams. A check that had revealed a very nasty surprise waiting at her house.

Devereaux.

How he'd found the place, goodness only knew. Her daughter hadn't been aware of it, and there were no records tying her to the address. Not directly, anyway. And he wouldn't have been able to navigate through the ones that did exist. But that was of no matter. The key take-away was something that the woman had discovered at an early age. Something that had become the mantra she'd lived by ever since.

*Praemonitus, preamunitus.*

Forewarned is forearmed.

*Wednesday. Evening.*
*Nicole missing for twenty-eight hours*

THERE WAS NO LONGER A DOUBT IN DEVEREAUX'S MIND.

He pulled out his phone, ready to call Hale and have her send in the cavalry. Then something he'd said to Loflin at the hospital the previous night resurfaced in his mind. The woman wasn't an ordinary criminal. Her behavior was beyond Hale's expertise. It was beyond Bruckner's and Grandison's, too. Beyond everyone's.

Except, perhaps, his.

Devereaux canceled Hale's number and called Loflin instead. He asked her for a simple favor. Next he called Page, and asked him for something a little more complicated. Then he put his phone away. He moved to the living room. Sat down on the couch's uncomfortable synthetic-tweed cushions to wait. And welcomed the calm clarity as he felt it start to blossom in his chest.

Devereaux didn't recognize the number that showed up on the screen twenty minutes later, but he answered his phone, anyway.

"Cooper?" The woman sounded confident. "What are you doing in my house?"

"I'm here to collect my daughter." Devereaux kept his voice soft and even. "It turns out she doesn't like water parks. Or airplane museums. Or psychopaths."

"Then she'd better be kept away from you, Cooper dear, as you and I are cut from the same cloth."

"Are we?"

"You know we are."

"You'll need to remember that, in a little while."

"Why?"

"Because we need to talk about what we're going to do. How we can fix things so that my daughter comes home with me, and no one else gets hurt."

"That's a lofty goal, Cooper. I'm sorry to be the one to disappoint you."

"Bring my daughter to your house. Unharmed. Let her come home with me. And in return, I'll let you walk away. That's as good an offer as you're going to get to-night."

"You know that can never happen, Cooper. Because even if I believed what you say, you know I can't let *you* walk away. Not with what's in your bloodstream. It wouldn't be responsible."

"Then how about a trade? Me for my daughter."

"You see? We are alike. That's what I was about to suggest."

"OK, then. How do we make it happen?"

"You found the way to the garage?"

"I did."

"Good. Go there. Roll up the outer door. No more than six inches. Slide your gun underneath. And any other weapons you have. Then sit on the ground, cross your legs, and put your hands under your butt. Understand?"

"When?"

"Now."

"Now? That won't work. I need—" Devereaux's phone vibrated and he risked quickly removing it from his ear to check the incoming message. "Actually, scratch that. Of course now will work. I'm on my way. Give me thirty seconds."

*Wednesday. Evening.*
*Nicole missing for twenty-eight and a quarter hours*

DEVEREAUX EJECTED THE BULLETS FROM HIS GUN AND dropped them into a Cardinals mug he took from a cupboard on the wall in the kitchen. He moved his switchblade to his back pocket. Then he went to the garage. Found the door opener. Cranked it up two inches. Shoved his gun out. And remained on his feet.

Ten seconds later Devereaux heard a car door slam. Then footsteps, and the scrape of metal on asphalt as someone picked up his gun. After another twenty seconds there was a second slam. Then the garage door started to roll up the rest of the way. Devereaux instinctively moved to the side and ducked down to see what was happening outside.

The Mercedes was parked sideways on the driveway, blocking the view of anyone passing by on the street. The woman was standing next to its passenger door. Nicole was with her, wrapped in a bulky, brightly colored beach towel. The woman's hands were gripping Nicole's shoulders while tears poured down the little girl's face.

"What's wrong, sweetheart?" Devereaux took a step forward, then stopped dead. The woman had pulled away the towel, letting it fall to the ground. He could see that Nicole was clutching a well-loved cuddly rabbit under one arm. She was wearing a blue pinafore dress. And over it, an old-fashioned life preserver. It was made of tan leather, laced up in front, with a series of vertical cylindrical pockets, which would originally have held the flotation aids. Only now the pockets were linked together with a sheaf of red, white, and blue wires. The red wire extended to the side and connected to a switch that the woman held in her left hand.

"It seems that neither of us was specific enough with our terms, Cooper. I didn't stipulate that the bullets should still be in your gun. And you didn't stipulate that your daughter should still be in one piece."

"You're right." Devereaux focused on the woman's left hand. "We were both remiss. Maybe we should start the negotiation over. How about this: my daughter, alive and unharmed, in exchange for your daughter in the same condition."

"Nice try. But my daughter isn't here. And she isn't in danger."

"She's not far from here. And she's in mortal danger."

"She's in the hospital. In Birmingham, Alabama. And she's completely safe."

"She was. Until I signed her out on my way up here."

"You didn't sign her out. She's still in the hospital, tucked up in bed, fast asleep."

"I need to show you something now. Jan would want you to see it. It's on my phone. I'm going to reach into my pocket and take it out, so don't get twitchy with that panic button, OK?"

Devereaux retrieved his phone, pulled up a photograph, then handed it to the woman.

"Oh my God! What have you done?"

"As you can see, your daughter's buried up to her neck in sand. The mask she's wearing is a professional diver's model, which guarantees an absolutely airtight seal around the face. It's connected to an oxygen tank with, let's see . . ." Devereaux made a show of looking at his watch. ". . . thirty-four minutes' supply. That's a little less than planned, because you took longer to get here than I'd expected."

"Where is she?"

"That's the interesting part. She's thirty minutes' drive from here. That means if you got going right away you'd have a little less than four minutes left to remove the mask before she suffocates. If you knew where to go. Which you don't. I'm the only one who does. But I'll be happy to tell you. Just as soon as you put down that switch and let my daughter go."

"You wouldn't leave Jan to suffocate! That's inhumane. You're bluffing."

Devereaux stepped forward until he was directly in front of the woman.

"Who's my father, Madison?" He stared her straight in the eye. "If you were right about all those kids—if it was necessary to *save* them the way you did—then I'll absolutely leave your daughter to suffocate. I'll do it in a heartbeat. And you know I will."

The woman stepped away. Her back pressed against the Mercedes. But she didn't release the switch.

"Think about it." Devereaux spread his arms out wide. "You know all about me. You know all about my father. Can you see any scenario where you kill my daughter and I let yours live?"

The woman dropped the switch. Devereaux took Nicole's hand and started to slowly lead her toward the garage. They'd backed three feet away. Six. Then the woman flung herself forward, trying to retrieve the dangling red wire. Devereaux picked the girl up and spun her to the side. He kicked the woman as he turned, catching her in the shoulder and knocking her down. The woman stood straight back up and sprang at Devereaux, scratching and clawing at his face. He tried to fend her off with one hand but she was too wild. He had to put the girl down. The woman jumped on his back as he leaned forward. He straightened, spinning and slamming her into the side of the Mercedes. Her head cracked against its side window, starring the glass, and she slid to the ground, finally still, blood flowing freely from the back of her scalp.

Devereaux turned, his eyes searching for his daughter. She was ten feet away. Her fingers were tugging at the laces securing the bomb vest. She almost had them undone. The vest was starting to slip from one shoulder.

"No!" Devereaux threw himself at the girl, desperate to stop her.

He was too late.

He landed at her feet, right as the vest hit the ground.

*Wednesday. Evening.*

Nothing happened.

Devereaux struggled to his knees and gingerly picked up the vest. Something was wrong. The wires were real. So was the switch. But the material in the pockets? It wasn't any kind of explosive Devereaux had come across before. He sniffed it, and realized what it was.

Play-Doh. The vest was a fake. It wasn't dangerous at all.

Devereaux hugged his daughter. Thoughts and emotions were flooding over him in an irresistible tide, but out of the deluge one name kept screaming to him. *Brian. Brian! BRIAN!*

Who the hell was Brian?

No. *What* the hell was Brian?

There, on the floor, six feet away, lay the cuddly rabbit Nicole had been carrying. Devereaux raced across to it. He picked it up. Ran out of the garage. Flung it high over the roof of the Mercedes. And was knocked flat on his back when the C-4 packed inside it detonated.

## Chapter *One Hundred and Eleven*

*Thursday. Late Morning.*

EVERYTHING'S BROKEN. EVERYTHING'S FALLING DOWN. FALLING
*on me . . .*

*The man lifts the boards. He finds me. Reaches down.
Grabs me. He's going for my neck. He's going to stran-
gle me with something.*

*Another man comes. He has a long, narrow
board. He puts it down, next to me. They roll me
on my side. Slide the board under me. Tie me to it.
Fix a mask over my face. Lift me up. Hold me
high between them. The mask is scratching my
face.*

*They carry me to a truck. Put me inside. Close me in.
I start to fight. I must get out. But I can't move. I can't
breathe. I can't see . . .*

"Daddy?"
It was a girl's voice. She was nearby.
"Daddy?"
What did she want? Who was she talking to?
"Nicole? Listen to me, sweetheart."

It was a woman's voice now. Alexandra Cunningham's.

"Your daddy? He's OK. He's not awake enough
talk to you right now. But he will be. Very soon. The
you can come back and visit with him whenever yo
like."

# Chapter *One Hundred and Twelve*

*One Week Later*

THE SIGN ON THE BILLBOARD BY THE SIDE OF THE ROAD HAD been changed while Devereaux was cooped up in the hospital. There were no more angels on it when he came out. Or devils. Or pictures of any kind. The sponsors had changed their approach. Now they were just using giant blocks of text:

*LIFE IS SHORT. ETERNITY IS NOT.*

The owner of the food truck had followed suit. He'd dispensed with his illustrations, too, and had responded with a few words of his own:

*LUNCH BREAK IS SHORT. OUR CHICKEN IS HOT.*

Loflin had arrived at the pull-off before Devereaux. She was standing next to the hood of her Subaru when he got there, at exactly the time they'd agreed to meet. Two portions of the truck's signature chicken were set out in front of her, ready for them to eat.

"This place is OK, I guess." Devereaux took a tentative bite, still not fully forgiving the lack of pork or beef. "But I do like the idea of solving the serious issues in life by eating 'cue."

"That's easy to do, when the menu only gives you one option." Loflin smiled, then broke off to chew.

"Maybe the owner believes in destiny." Devereaux caught a trickle of stray sauce with a napkin. "Like Hindus, or whoever. Or your mother."

"Maybe."

They ate in silence for the next few minutes.

"How did it go this morning?" Devereaux looked at Loflin out of the corner of his eye.

It had been her mother's funeral that morning. Loflin had come to the chicken truck directly from the service. She still had on her black dress, which was starting to cling in the afternoon sun, and she was self-conscious about the piece of hiking sock she'd used to disguise the electronic ankle bracelet she was forced to wear.

"As well as you'd expect." Loflin dropped a bone onto her plate. "No one came. It was just the minister and me. But look on the bright side. I've finally found a benefit to having a psychopath for a mother. I didn't have to spring for a giant wake."

"I'm sorry I couldn't be there."

"Don't be. It would have been weird. It's better for me to draw a line on my own. Now I can move on."

"What are you going to do?"

"I don't know. A lot depends on how the trial works out, I guess. My lawyer's optimistic, and he seems to know his stuff. Say thanks to Alexandra for hooking me up with him, by the way."

"Will do."

"If I'm not locked up, I was thinking about taking a trip. Around Europe, maybe. I need some distance. My mother's gone, but she's not *gone*. Do you know what I mean? She was a constant voice in my head, controlling what I thought and what I did for so, so long. For all my life, really. Manipulating me. Keeping me off balance with psychological tricks. Now I need to learn how to be myself. How to make my own decisions. To figure out what I like. What I want. Who I am. I think I need to stay well away from here until I don't feel like her hand's always on the wheel, you know?"

"Do you think that's possible? Can you escape something like that?"

"Cooper, are you testing me? Of course you can escape. Look at you. You're nothing like your father was. Ethan wouldn't be alive if you were. Nicole wouldn't be. And look at me. Last time we passed this place, I was ready to help get you killed. But I didn't. I left it late, admittedly, but I chose my own path in the end. Everyone does. Or can. Destiny's not set, like my mother said it is. We're all free to make up our own."

Chapter **One Hundred and Thirteen**

*Two Months Later*

ALEXANDRA CUNNINGHAM HAD TOLD NICOLE THAT Devereaux was her father when she thought he might die, following the explosion.

On reflection, Cunningham realized this made no sense, since she'd already told her daughter that her father was dead. Fortunately, Nicole took the apparent resurrection in stride. And once the truth was out there, Cunningham didn't feel she should take it back.

Without consciously planning to, she had asked Devereaux over for dinner one night after he got out of the hospital. The evening went well, and she asked him over again one night the next week. And the next. Twice, the week after that. And so on.

Nicole seemed to like the direction things were heading, too. Devereaux appeared to be happy. He started to bring little gifts. Flowers for Cunningham. Outfits for Nicole's Barbies. Increasingly nice bottles of wine. And while Cunningham would never have admitted it to anyone else, she was starting to wonder if she'd been wrong about Devereaux eight years earlier. Whether it could have worked out with him.

Whether it could still work out . . .

---

Cunningham had wrapped up lessons early on purpose that day and had sent Nicole outside to play. She was looking forward to the evening. She'd overspent on a new dress from Theodora—black, short, and clingier than anything she'd worn in ten years—and she was determined to make sure the meal was extra special, too. She was trying out a new recipe she'd found in *Bon Appétit*—steak and mushrooms in tequila sauce—and was scared she'd ruin it if she rushed.

Devereaux arrived bang on time. He sat on one of the stools at the breakfast bar and they chatted about everything and nothing while Cunningham put the finishing touches to the steak. He helped to roast the corn. He set the table, tactfully arranging the Sheffield silver flatware, which Cunningham had inherited from her mother, to cover the various scratches and dents that Nicole had made while playing with her dolls. And when it was time to eat, he went and called his daughter in from the yard.

Nicole was messing around in the far corner with a handful of her favorite Barbies. She turned and smiled when she heard Devereaux's voice. Her hair was hanging in perfect ringlets. Her blue eyes sparkled. Her rainbow-striped dress was still mostly pristine.

She watched until Devereaux had gone back inside. Then she went to check on the two naughty Barbies. The pair she'd caught talking to the girl next door's new Bratz dolls after she'd specifically told them not to.

She made sure that the twine securing their arms behind their backs was good and tight. She adjusted the manacles she'd made out of heavy-duty paper clips so they pinched a little harder around their ankles. Then she took a wooden cocktail stick and jabbed it into the first doll's eye. She pulled out a nail scissors she'd taken from the bathroom and chopped off one of the second Barbie's fingers. She was about to slice off its ear as well when she heard the squeak of the screen door opening,

behind her. Nicole froze, fearing it was her mother. Sh
wouldn't understand . . .

"Hey! Where's my little girl?" It was Devereaux
who'd appeared on the back porch. "Put those doll
down. I told you—it's time to eat."

"OK, Daddy!" Nicole relaxed. She slipped the scissors back into her pocket and turned around, beaming.
"I'm coming . . ."

# Acknowledgments

My deepest thanks go to the following for their help, support, and encouragement while I wrote this book. Without them, it would not have been possible.

Kate Miciak, editor extraordinaire; and the whole team at Random House.

Janet Reid.

Richard Pine.

My friends, who've stood by me through the years: Dan Boucher, Carlos Camacho, Joelle Charbonneau, John Dul, Jamie Freveletti, Keir Graff, Kristy Claiborne Graves, Tana Hall, Nick Hawkins, Dermot Hollingsworth, Amanda Hurford, Richard Hurford, Jon Jordan, Ruth Jordan, Martyn James Lewis, Rebecca Makkai, Dan Malmon, Kate Hackbarth Malmon, Carrie Medders, Philippa Morgan, Erica Ruth Neubauer, Gunther Neumann, Ayo Onatade, Denise Pascoe, Wray Pascoe, Dani Patarazzi, Javier Ramirez, David Reith, Sharon Reith, Beth Renaldi, Marc Rightley, Melissa Rightley, Renee Rosen, Kelli Stanley, and Brian Wilson.

Everyone at The Globe Pub, Chicago.

Jane and Jim Grant.

Ruth Grant.

Katharine Grant, Jess Grant, and Alexander Tyska.

Gary and Stacie Gutting.

And last on the list, but first in my heart—Tasha. *Everything, always . . .*

If you enjoyed *False Positive*,
read on for an exciting preview of

# *False Friend,*

the next thrilling Cooper Devereaux novel by

# **Andrew Grant**

Coming in hardcover and eBook from
Ballantine Books

Summer 2017

Chapter *One*

THE FLAMES WERE ALREADY TWENTY FEET TALL.

They were a fierce orange color, twisting and writhing above the gash they'd torn in the building's flat roof. Tyler Shaw thought they looked like the souls of sinners trying to escape the hell that must have somehow been unleashed inside. Clouds of dense, filthy smoke were spewing from a row of broken second-floor windows, staining the blue Alabama sky the kind of dirty black that hadn't been seen in Birmingham since the iron-works closed down. In his house across the street, lurking behind the faded bedroom drapes, Shaw could smell it. His eyes began to water. The fumes were bitter and sharp, not sweet and welcoming like the smoke from the barbeque pits and campfires he'd missed so much while he was away. And he could hear the sirens. The place would soon be swarming with fire trucks.

And with police.

*Why?* The word bounced frantically around inside Shaw's head. Why was this happening? And why now? Had he made a giant mistake, coming back? Was it all over for him? Was he finally finished?

COOPER DEVEREAUX SCANNED THE PACKED ROWS OF SEAT all around him for the hundredth time, and what he saw only confirmed his conclusion: Despite the name of the play—and the alarming number of people who'd come armed with family-sized boxes of Kleenex—*he* was the only one in the place who was truly *misérable*.

Devereaux had wanted to spend his Saturday afternoon at his cabin, working on its damaged roof. But Alexandra—his what? Girlfriend?—had other plans. She'd been desperate to see the show together, and was so delighted when another lawyer she'd done a favor for had bagged her tickets that Devereaux hadn't had it in him to disappoint her. And on balance, he figured that sacrificing one afternoon's satisfying labor was a small price to pay to make her happy. He'd been separated from Alexandra for eight years, and Devereaux was ready to do—almost—anything to strengthen his newly repaired relationship with her. And with Nicole, their seven-year-old daughter. He was still just getting to know the little girl. Devereaux glanced down at her, stretched out in the seat between him and Alexandra. She looked up and smiled, then went back to watching the play. Or pretending to. Devereaux could see that she was paying more attention to the banged-up doll she'd insisted on bringing than to the action on the stage. *Smart kid*, he thought.

Devereaux had mentioned his lack of enthusiasm for Alexandra's playgoing scheme to a couple of the other detectives in his squad the day before, but they'd told him not to worry. A trip to the Alabama Theater was worth it just to see the inside of the building, they'd said. Devereaux didn't agree. The contractors who'd handled the refurbishment certainly hadn't skimped on the gold leaf or the extravagant palette of colors, but the result made Devereaux feel giddy. The red and green octagons decorating the underneath of the long sweeping arches reminded him of the suckers on an octopus's tentacles, reaching around to grab him. And the broad illuminated dome set into the gilded ceiling made him feel like a flying saucer was hovering overhead, waiting to spirit him away. Or perhaps that was just wishful thinking . . .

Devereaux was aware that his attention was wandering. His head kept filling with images of the flawless monochrome interior of his apartment in the City Federal building. It was only a couple of blocks away. Could he sneak out, head over there, grab a beer, listen to some real music, and be back before the final curtain? There was time. But no. He couldn't take the chance. Alexandra would notice. She'd be upset, and that was the last thing he wanted. So he fixed a smile on his face, dragged his attention back to the stage, and realized he'd lost track of what was happening. This Valjean guy and his cronies wanted to go beyond some barricades? OK. But weren't they the ones who'd built the barricades? Why pick that spot, if they wanted to go past? Why not build the barricades farther away? And why stand around singing about their own lack of planning skills? What was the point in that?

Before he could torment himself any longer, Devereaux felt his phone begin to vibrate. He discreetly checked the number and saw it was his boss, Lieutenant Hale. An opportunity to escape? Devereaux felt a flood of relief wash over him. He turned to mime 9-1-1 to Alexandra

and felt a tiny part of that relief turn to guilt as she sho
him daggers in return. Then he pushed the feelings away
slipped into the aisle, and hurried to the foyer to answe
the call.

"Cooper? Apologies. I didn't want to pull you out o
the show." Hale's voice sounded distant and hollow, sc
Devereaux guessed she had him on speakerphone.

"Don't worry about it." Devereaux crossed to the ornate, circular four-person French-style lounge chair
below the chandelier in the center of the rectangular
space. No one else was sitting on it, but Devereaux decided he'd prefer to stand anyway.

"You're not enjoying it?" Hale sounded surprised.
"Actually, that can wait. We've got a situation. At a
school, out on 31st Street, Southwest. Near Jefferson
Avenue."

"Jones Valley?"

"Right. You know it?"

"I went to it. For a while, anyway. It was my first high
school."

"You must be mixing it up with somewhere else. This
one's a middle school."

"It's the same place. They changed it after I left. What
happened there?"

"A fire. A big one. Lots of damage, by the sound of
it."

"Anyone hurt?"

"No reports of any casualties. Shouldn't have been
any kids around as it's not a weekday, and there's no onsite janitor or maintenance guys anymore."

"Good. Want me to head over there?"

"No. No point. The uniforms are already canvassing
the area, and no one will be able to get into the school
itself for another couple of days, because it's not safe.
But listen. The fire chief just called. This isn't confirmed
yet—the science guys need more time to collect samples
and run tests—but his gut feel is that the blaze was
started deliberately."

"Lightning striking twice."

"What do you mean?" Papers rustled on Hale's desk. "There's no mention of previous fires in the report."

"It was a long time ago." Devereaux glared at an usher who'd appeared from an anteroom at the far end of the lobby, apparently ready to shush him. "November 11, 1961. The date was in the school crest. Some crazy student torched the place. Burned it to the ground. Maybe history's repeating itself."

"Maybe it is. But we'll get to that later. For now, step one is to interview the witnesses. The fire chief needs some very specific information, until the lab work comes back. I'll forward you his email. The uniforms have got the local residents covered, but we also have four passersby who called 911. I want you and Tommy to go talk to the first one. Right away, while his memory's still fresh. And before he reads anything about it in the press. I'll include his deets in the email."

Devereaux crossed the shiny black-and-white tiled floor, stepped outside, and paused beneath the illuminated canopy on Third Street as he felt the warm air engulf him. He imagined his old school in flames, and couldn't help but smile. Not because he'd particularly disliked the place. But because he was struck by the irony. Today, he was being sent to investigate the fire. Back when he was a student, he'd have been the first one the police would have blamed for it.

*Labor Omnia Vincit,* the school motto said. *Labor overcomes all difficulties.* Despite the creepy Nazi overtones, Devereaux had always found it to be true during his high school years. Especially as it didn't stipulate *honest* labor . . .